To Cat

with best wishes for
a pleasant read.

James D. Farrelson

THE DEADWOOD CONSPIRACY

THE
A Novel by James D. Garretson
DEADWOOD
CONSPIRACY

DeHart Publications, Co.

Library of Congress Catalog Card Number: 95-83065

Printed in the United States of America

Cover and book design by
Ogle Design
Carmel, Indiana

To Nancy and Tom without
whose encouragement and support this project
would never have reached fruition.

❧

Characters

The Administration

President of the United States, Seth Hansen
Chief of Staff of White House, Ed Collins
National Security Advisor, Dr. Tyler Tollefson
Vice-President of the United States
Secretary of State, Crawford P. Staton
Administrative Assistant to Secretary of State, James Lowenstein
Secretary of Defense, Nelson Thompson
Chairman, Joint Chiefs of Staff, Admiral Ogden Birchfield
Director of Secret Service, Donald Schroeder
Attorney General of the United States

The Congress

Speaker of the House, Clayton Harley
President Pro Tem of the Senate, Jordan Howard, of Alabama
Chief of Staff to Senator Howard, James Cavanaugh
House Majority Leader, Alan Brownell
House Majority Whip, Buddy Schumacher
House Majority Caucus Chairman
House Chairman of Ways and Means Committee
House Chairman of International Relations Committee
House Chairman of Judiciary Committee, Ed O'Bannon
United States Senator from Arizona, Jake Lewellan
Administrative Assistant to Senator Lewellan, Rollie Lampworth

The Federal Bureau of Investigation

Director, Alec Jameson
Special Agent, Bert Mattox
Agents: Peters, Akers, Sparks, Michaels, and Johnson
Director of Forensic Lab, Dr. Gradle

Central Intelligence Agency

Director, George Heffelfinger
Associate Director, Thomas Ashburn
Agents: William Manchester and John Martin

Others

Israeli journalist, Isaac Weissman
Weissman's secretary, Rosie
International assassin, Abdul
Travel agent, Margaret "Maggy" Mosele
Industrial executive, John Fairchild Chamberlain

THE DEADWOOD CONSPIRACY

DAY 1

CHAPTER 1

Washington, D.C.
April 12
2:00 P.M.

War! Military confrontation! Young American boys dying for flag and country! Terrible consequences for any failed foreign policy. The ominous consequences passed through the mind of President Seth Hansen like cascading ocean waves as he sat behind his impressive oak desk in the Oval Office. He was troubled by the turn of events in southern Russia and the discussion held within his National Security Council just minutes earlier. Seated across from him in a Queen Anne side chair was Secretary of Defense Nelson Thompson.

"Thank god the Secretary of State came through for us in that telephone hookup from San Francisco. He's one man the Joint Chiefs listen to. I thought you and Oggy Birchfield were going to slug it out in the Cabinet Room." The President smiled at his old friend who took the jibe with good humor.

"As a matter of fact, I would have relished the opportunity of punching that reactionary in his arrogant fat face. Maybe I could have knocked some sense into him," Thompson grimaced.

"Well, you have to give Oggy his determination and his skill. I picked him as chairman of the Joint Chiefs because by all accounts he had the best mind among the members of the service chiefs at the time." He paused, "Do you think I made a mistake, Nels?"

The Secretary glanced at his fingernails resting on the wooden arm of the chair. "No, I don't believe so, Mr. President. I get frustrated with the old curmudgeon, but he knows his business, and I can always depend upon his being prepared. I've never heard him say, 'I'll check on that and get back with you.' He's sharp, all right. I just wish he were more pliable in his thinking. He's just itching for a chance to unleash that massive military and naval machine he commands. He's so unlike General Powell a few years ago who seemed to have a better understanding of the limitations of power."

"I know, Nels, but we can control him, and his term as chairman ends in July. I'll entertain a recommendation from you on replacing him at that time, if you like."

"Let me sleep on it and see how we come out of this scrape with the Russians. If he doesn't push us into an all-out war, maybe we can keep him. Let's just wait and see." Thompson crossed his slender legs as he changed positions.

The President reached for a gold letter opener, a gift he had received from a Middle East potentate during the preceding two years, and leaned back in his chair twirling the dagger between his two index fingers. "This whole mess in Armenia is really troublesome. Somehow we have to contain this situation and not get pulled into a confrontation with the Russians. That's the stuff world wars are made of—silly mistakes and miscalculations."

The Secretary hesitated only momentarily. "Quite frankly, Mr. President, that's what scares the hell out of me when Birchfield begins blowing off. Sure, we could move three divisions of troops over to Turkey and Iran, but we'd have enough initial logistical support for only two weeks. The Russians have thirteen divisions stationed in the Trans Caucasus and seven divisions in Turkistan. Add to that another dozen divisions that could be moved from central Russia—the old East Germany divisions—and we're looking at an army of nearly a million men. And they'll be fighting near their own territory. We'd have to maintain a five-thousand-mile supply line."

There was a buzz on the President's white phone console. He pushed a button connecting him to his chief of staff. "What is it, Ed?"

"Sorry to bother you, Mr. President, but I thought you'd want to know that we just received a brief message over the hot line teletype. President Chenkov will send his reply to your earlier inquiry at 3:00 this afternoon, Washington time."

"That's just great, Ed. You know I have that damn wreath laying at Roosevelt's Memorial at 3:00. How long is that supposed to take, anyway?"

"Sir, we have you leaving the White House at 2:50, arriving at the memorial at 2:55. There will be several members of Congress, of course the Vice-President, and two of President Roosevelt's grandchildren present. Allowing you time to exchange greetings, we believe you could leave by 3:20 and be back in your office by 3:30. It will take that long to translate his message, anyway."

The President exhaled slowly. "Very well. But you be sure I don't get bogged down over at the memorial. Go ahead and ask the members of the National Security Council to plan for a 5:00 meeting."

"Yes, sir, Mr. President."

The President punched the off button on his speaker phone. "Well, Nels, by 3:30 we're going to find out one way or the other what that Russian bear is up to."

The Secretary had returned his papers to his briefcase and secured the locks. "Yes, sir. I had better get back to the office and be sure Oggy doesn't launch the troops too soon." He stood to leave.

"Go ahead. And, Nels..." The Secretary, who had started for the door, turned around. "Keep your good humor." The President smiled broadly, then turned very serious. "You know, Nels, I depend on you more than you can imagine. If anything would happen to me, I'd expect you to be the one to hold the new government together."

The Secretary paused briefly with a mixed feeling of concern and wonder to gaze at his old college roommate and friend of nearly thirty years. Strange that the President would make such a comment. "Yes, sir, I'd do my best. Goodbye, sir."

"Goodbye, Nels. See you at 5:00."

*****

The crowds cheered and waved at the President's black limousine as it rolled down Pennsylvania Avenue at 30 mph. The new Lincoln with its thick armor and bubble top could not be missed by the thousands of tourists who lined the streets. The President graciously responded with the same half wave gesture that John Kennedy had made famous.

Ed Collins, the President's chief-of-staff, sat in a jump seat facing the President and was reviewing the itinerary for the upcoming ceremony. "The Vice-President's car is right ahead of us, sir. He has the Speaker of the House and the House Majority Leader with him. Senator Howard—the President Pro Tem—the Senate Majority Leader and Senate Whip should already be at the memorial, sir. Senator Dixon, chairman of the Senate subcommittee on Natural Resources should also be present. As you know, he never misses a chance to attend anything involving the Interior Department. It's his meal ticket. I think New York's two senators are also to be present. They want to remind everybody of where FDR was from."

The President looked quickly at his aide. "Isn't Howard the last member of Congress to have served while Roosevelt was President?"

"Yes, sir. He was a congressman from Alabama from 1943 to 1951, before entering the Senate. To hear him tell it, Franklin Roosevelt was his political godfather. I don't think he believes we've had a real president since FDR died."

"I know. I know." The President continued to smile at the growing crowd along the sidewalks. "I still don't understand what's so special about today, outside of its being the anniversary of FDR's death."

Collins looked up from his notes. "We're doing it because Senator Jordan asked you to do it. He retires at the end of the year and won't be in office for the new memorial's dedication."

The President continued to wave as the limousine approached Ninth Street and was slowing down. "I sure wish Roosevelt's new memorial over at the Tidal Basin had been ready for this ceremony. Be sure I send a memo to Interior to get an update on its completion. I feel like I'm visiting a headstone in a cemetery at this place. I never have thought it was fitting for the man who served in this office longer than anybody else. After all, it's little more than a traffic island."

"Yes, sir, I'll prepare the memo when we get back. Here we are."

The President's limousine was now surrounded by a dozen Secret Service agents on foot as the car pulled to a stop next to the sidewalk in front of the small memorial. One of the agents, his eyes canvasing the crowd across the street and the windows in the Pennsylvania Center above, opened the President's door on the right side. As the President lifted himself out onto the sidewalk, a low roar erupted from the crowd, along with applause.

A slender, elderly gentleman, mahogany cane in hand, sporting a thinning mane of white hair, stood slightly stooped on the sidewalk facing the President as the chief executive straightened himself. "Good day, Mr. President. Good to see you." The Senator held out his slightly trembling hand.

The President exchanged a warm handshake with the Senate President Pro Tem. "Jordan, how the hell have you been? You look great, just great."

"Thank you, sir. I appreciate your flattery, but I'm afraid these eighty-eight years of mine are taking their toll, especially in these arthritic knees." He pointed with the cane toward his right leg.

The President decided to change the subject. "Well, one thing those years are worth, Jordan: you're the only man here today who served with FDR. I suppose you remember him quite well." As soon as the words left his lips, the President knew he had made a mistake. Senator Howard could droll on for hours with FDR anecdotes. But to his surprise the senior senator from Alabama appeared reticent.

"Yes, I do, Mr. President. And I'm sure you've heard every one of them more times than you would like to admit. You know, I was just looking at this bronze marker here in front of us before you arrived." The two men took two steps toward a metal marker which lay in the ground next to the sidewalk. The inscription explained how Roosevelt had called his friend, Associate Justice Felix Frankfurter, to say that if ever Congress decided to erect a memorial to him, to make it a small marble slab in front of the Archives Building.

"You know, Mr. President, I was here on this date in 1965 when President Johnson helped dedicate this memorial. Averell Harriman was the main speaker, and this was just a traffic island then."

The President smiled and squeezed the senior senator's shoulder. "You have a great memory, Jordan. When you retire, we're going to miss your link to the past. I hope you know that." The President's smile was genuine, and the senator seemed moved. "Now, let me see who else is here." He turned and began shaking hands with the row of congressional delegates. The younger Vice-President followed in line behind the President—a practice at which he had developed some skill in the preceding two years. At the end of the row of congressmen and senators, the President was introduced to two middle-aged men, identified as grandchildren of the thirty-second President.

*****

Bert Mattox continued to be absorbed in his reading. Addendum H of the thick report he had received from the CIA only an hour earlier detailed the assassination of both the foreign minister and trade minister of Kuwait. The two men had been attending a meeting of OPEC ministers in Cairo. Security had been quadrupled due to death threats. Nearly forty bodyguards surrounded the two men everyplace they traveled outside the Marriott Hotel. No one could see them, let alone get close enough for a shot. As they were traveling by Mercedes limousine from the hotel to an appointment with the President of Egypt, their car was blown up, killing both instantly. A crater in the street indicated that large amounts of plastic explosives had been placed under a heavy iron sewer manhole cover in the middle of the street. The explosion had to have been set off by remote control, since there were at least six automobiles in the caravan, and the explosion did not occur until the ministers' car was exactly over the heavy iron cover.

Mattox looked up from his legal pad. John Martin, the young courier from Langley who was instructed to return the file to the agency after Mattox was finished, was looking out the fifth floor window of the J. Edgar Hoover Building at street activity below. "What's going on, Martin? Some kind of parade?"

Martin did not turn from the window. "No, sir. It's the President, across the street. Quite a crowd has gathered. Looks like the Vice-President and several members of Congress are also there."

Mattox pushed his chair back and walked over to the window to join the young agent. Down below and across the street, the President was shaking hands with many of the dignitaries present. The Secret Service and the D.C. police appeared to have the crowd well back from the FDR Memorial site. Mattox ran his palm over his prematurely balding head. "Looks like the President is going to lay a wreath at FDR's Memorial, Martin. It must be some kind of anniversary." For even the veteran FBI agent, a glimpse of the President was always a treat. Despite his high rank within the bureau, Mattox's opportunities to see or meet the President were few. In fact, he had never met President Hansen, though he had voted for him. He decided to watch the festivities a while longer. He needed a break after an hour of reading at his desk.

*****

At precisely 3:03 an honor guard of two Marines stepped forward, carrying a large wreath of red and white carnations. The President and Vice-President stepped in front of the guard as the two soldiers lifted the wreath and moved slowly toward the six-foot-wide marble stone resting about twenty-five feet from the sidewalk. The rest of the congressional delegation, along with Collins moved in behind the President. Nearly four dozen members of the media, mostly photographers, were clamoring in a roped off area several yards to the side and slightly behind the marble stone. The view gave them ideal angle shots of the President bowing his head and touching the floral wreath as the soldiers placed the floral piece slightly to the far side of the marble stone, allowing Roosevelt's name still to be seen.

President Hansen bowed his head in meditation, and those around him followed his example. The solitude of the moment was punctuated by a slight gust of wind that blew the hat off the head of the House Majority Leader. Congressman Brownell leaned over behind his colleagues to retrieve the expensive felt hat, which he needed to protect his balding head from the sun.

As his hand barely touched the fleeing homburg, his ears popped from the impact of the explosion. There was a massive impact of the bodies of his colleagues piling upon him, and his last conscious sight was of the hat shooting away in a torrent gust; then all went black.

*****

Mattox and Martin stood paralyzed as they witnessed the mammoth fireball before them. In what would appear to them later to be only fractions of seconds, the window in front of them shattered, and the two men, using their arms to shield their faces, dove to the floor, the muted roar from below following.

The pain of the concussion ripped through Mattox's skull. He covered the back of his head and neck with his hands. The thought of death rushed through his brain as the eerie quiet following the explosion subsided. He opened his eyes to see the young CIA agent sprawled several feet away.

"You okay, kid?" Mattox reached over and put his hand on the agent's shoulder.

"Yeah. I think so. I don't feel any pain." The young man whose eyes were stretched wide open in terror, began feeling over his body.

Both men jumped up and patted themselves down. The breeze from the open window caught Mattox's attention. His eyes were moist from irritation, and the acrid taste of smoke reminded him of what just had happened.

"Come on, Martin. We've got to get down there."

Both men raced toward the door just as Mary Alice, Mattox's secretary, entered after having heard the crashing window. As Mattox passed her, he yelled, "Call 911 and get all the emergency vehicles you can across the street to the Archives Building. The President's been hurt."

Martin rushed ahead toward the elevator and frantically pushed the down button.

"Not the elevator, Martin. It's going to be clogged. Use the stairs. It'll be quicker." Mattox led the young agent toward the stairwell.

Within three minutes the two government agents were racing across Pennsylvania Avenue. The scene was one of horror and chaos. Moans from hundreds of people could be heard from the memorial area.

A crying mother cradled her young blond daughter in her lap in the middle of the street, caressing the child's cheeks. Babies and young children as far away as the Navy Memorial, a half block away, were howling. Many were fleeing in fear.

The area was still rancid with the smell of smoke and burning flesh. Partial bodies were strewn around the green memorial site, dark red blood soaking into the turf, in sharp contrast to the new spring grass. Mattox and Martin began inspecting charred and mutilated faces, turning over torsos. At one point Mattox could hear the younger Martin vomiting, as he continued tearing through the human debris looking for the President of the United States.

Behind them a uniformed police officer came running with his 9-mm weapon pulled and aimed at the FBI agent's head.

"Halt! Halt, I say."

Mattox looked over his shoulder. "I'm Mattox from the FBI. We have to find the President. Help me, goddamnit!" He turned back around and continued his search.

The perplexed officer decided to yield. "Anything you say, sir." He returned the weapon to his holster and began assisting Mattox as they carved through the legs and arms and torsos sprawled atop the ground.

After several minutes of fruitless effort, Mattox realized there were no recognizable faces. A crater at least fifteen feet in width and two feet deep had replaced the white marble Roosevelt memorial. The devastation of the scene began to settle over Mattox. He quickly concluded that no one could have survived such a violent explosion.

"I count twenty-two bodies, Mr. Mattox." It was Martin, who stood nearby as Mattox searched the pockets of one of the blue suited torsos lying near the memorial site for some kind of identification.

"I'll bet nearly all of the President's Secret Service detail are among them, Martin." He continued to turn over the mutilated and bloody remains, face up when possible, looking for some sign of life.

"Over here, Agent Mattox." It was the police officer.

Mattox jumped up and stepped over three partial corpses to where the officer was cradling a nearly bald, middle-aged man. The sight of a full body intact seemed astonishing. "Who is it, Officer?"

"Don't know him. He's been hurt pretty badly, though." The officer was using his own handkerchief to wipe away the blood from the comatose face. A flash of recognition enveloped Mattox. "I think that's Congressman Brownell. He's the House Majority Leader. Is he still alive?"

The black officer looked up. "He's breathing. That's all I know."

Sirens could be heard approaching the scene. Other uniformed officers were also arriving on their motorcycles. A sergeant approached the trio of men. "Who's in charge here?" he asked.

Mattox straightened his back. "I'm Bert Mattox of the FBI. I don't believe any of the Secret Service detail survived the blast. You'd better call the White House immediately. Unless I miss my guess, we have a hell of a crisis on our hands. More than the President died here, today."

A dark blue Buick screeched to a stop a few feet away from the island. Two men in tan summer suits jumped out and ran toward Mattox. The taller of the two spoke, "I'm Baker from Secret Service. What's the situation?"

Mattox identified himself, Martin, and the uniforms. "I'm afraid they are nearly all dead. I can't tell you which one is the President or the Vice-President, but Martin and I both saw the two of them from my office across the street . I assume some of these other men are members of Congress. Congressman Brownell appears to be the only survivor." He pointed to where one of the police officers was hovered over the Majority Leader.

"I'd suggest, Baker, that we get this entire area sealed off as soon as possible. Blockade at least a ten-block area." Mattox extended his arm in a circular fashion around him.

Baker looked puzzled. "Why so far?"

"Because, if I'm right, this explosion was remotely detonated, and the killer is probably within sight of this spot. Now, the longer we wait, the better his chances are of getting away." Mattox's voice sparked with irritation.

"Of course! You're right." Baker appeared momentarily flustered.

"Use one of these officers' radios, Baker. You'll need the D.C. police for this." Mattox pointed toward a cluster of uniforms near the curb. Baker responded quickly and ran toward the group.

By now paramedics in white coats were arriving and moving through the bodies. Mattox rubbed the top of his high forehead with his left hand. "Goddamn. If only I had been a little quicker. It was right in front of me, and I never put it together. Goddamnit!"

"What was that, sir?" Martin was still standing beside him.

"Come on, Martin; we have work to do."

*****

The lobby of the Firemen's Insurance Building, located two blocks to the east of the explosion at the intersection of Pennsylvania and Seventh Street, was filled with panic-eyed men and women rushing for telephones, restrooms, and other offices. Word of the catastrophe had already spread. Many of the tourists outside, who had seen or heard the explosion, had sought shelter in the building. Children and women were screaming. Strangers stopped to talk to one another, exchanging descriptions of what they had seen. Isaac Weissman, a reporter for a Tel Aviv newspaper, started to enter the lobby from the Seventh Street entrance. He had just returned from afternoon coffee with a friend when the explosion occurred. The impact had driven him to the ground.

He knew the President's published schedule; that was part of his job. The wreath laying ceremony had not seemed important enough to sacrifice his daily rendevoux with Maggy, so he had skipped it. As he picked himself up from the sidewalk, he could see the smoke and confusion over by the Archives Building. He guessed what had happened. Four years of service in the Israeli Army and eight years of journalistic experience covering terrorists' attacks in his native land had provided him enough experience to know that no one could have survived the blast. He was sure the President and Vice-President were both dead. His first thoughts were of the story and the need to rush a preliminary report to Tel Aviv.

He pulled his notebook from his inside pocket and scribbled his observations of the scene so that he could include added color in the report. Within three minutes he had enough to file an initial story. He started for the main door of the building just as a panicking mob was trying to both leave and enter at the same time. In the doorway he collided with another man and was nearly knocked to the ground.

"Shit!" he shouted. "Take it easy, man."

Weissman looked up at the dark-skinned man hovering above him. He was about his own height, but with a distinctive Arabic appearance. The man sported a thin mustache beneath a prominent nose and deep-set brown eyes. Weissman's eyes locked onto those of the stranger. They were eyes filled with anger, and for a brief second a hint of recognition crossed his mind. The stranger said nothing, but moved quickly around Weissman and was lost in the crowd.

Weissman had dropped his notebook. He leaned down to retrieve it when he spotted a brown wallet. The stranger must have dropped it. He picked it up with the same hand that held his notebook. Straightening, his eyes searched the crowd for the stranger, but he had disappeared, so he continued into the building. He knew the longer he waited, the more difficult it would be to gain a clear line overseas. Absent-mindedly, he stuffed the wallet into his coat pocket and moved toward the elevator.

*****

The assassin had preplanned his escape route. He would walk the four blocks north to G Street where he would enter the underground Metro center. He would take the Metro to Farragut Square, then transfer to another train going northwest to Dupont Circle. There he would take a cab to National Airport. His flight was scheduled to depart at 5:45. He would have less than a two-hour wait by the time he arrived. The authorities should still be in a state of chaos by then. As he entered the G Street Metro Center, he tried to appear as inconspicuous as possible. At 3:30 in the afternoon, the station was not crowded, but those standing around were talking excitedly to one another. He passed the turnstile, entered his ticket, and walked along the underground platform waiting for his train.

He spotted a concrete bench and sat down. A gray-haired black woman was seated on the opposite end. Leaning back, he stuck both hands in the pockets of his windbreaker.

"Damn!" the man muttered. Something was wrong. In the right pocket he could feel the transmitter and antenna, but in the left pocket his hand felt nothing. What had happened to the wallet? Had he left it in the office? He distinctly remembered stuffing it back into his pocket. He could not afford to let that wallet be found with his fingerprints all over it. If it were ever traced to the dead CIA agent in Florida, and a connection made with the assassination, the CIA would assume they finally had the fingerprints of the world's most notorious assassin, Abdul. He had to go back to check the deserted office from which he had detonated the bomb. Damn! He was sure he had stuffed Manchester's wallet in his pocket. How could this happen? He uttered an obscenity in his native Arabic language, which the elderly lady appeared to ignore. He began running back toward the entrance. The elderly lady slowly looked after him and muttered distastefully, "Foreigner!" then returned her attention to her magazine.

CHAPTER 2

San Francisco
12:10 P.M. (PST)

The ballroom of the Hyatt Regency on the lower level of the hotel was packed with the economic and political kingpins of central California. The Secretary of State's address had been given great coverage in the California press. To those most interested in trade with Pacific Rim nations, the address was of special interest. Twenty-five hundred men and women had given the Secretary a standing ovation following his introduction, but their enthusiasm had been restrained. This was a man whose interest in Pacific trade was known to be less than enthusiastic. On the other hand, like millions of other Americans, this crowd found the large, grandfatherly figure on the dais an engaging personality.

Crawford Staton had been introduced only five minutes earlier and had spent the early part of his speech softening up the crowd with his New England cornball humor. The audience was warming to the Secretary. However, in the far corners of the room, a buzz of voices began to be heard. A few members of the audience had radio plugs in their ears, and a couple even had miniature television sets. Already word of the Washington disaster was being broadcast throughout the world. The Secretary tried to ignore the interruption when a Secret Service agent walked up behind him and whispered in his ear. The Secretary's face turned ashen.

He bowed his head solemnly and then faced the audience. "Ladies and gentlemen, I have just received word that the President and the Vice-President of the United States were the victims of an explosion in Washington just minutes ago. Their condition is not known at this time. I ask everyone in this room not to panic, but to join me in prayer." The Secretary bowed his head as the audience rose in unison and turned absolutely quiet.

Staton paused, reaching for comforting words. "Dear Lord, we ask that you give our nation strength in this terrible hour, that you spare the lives of our beloved President and Vice-President, that you be with their families in this time of need, and that you give all of us in this room the strength to endure. God bless America. Amen."

Quickly, the Secret Service agent grabbed the Secretary by the arm, and the two disappeared behind the blue and white curtains that formed the backdrop for the dais.

*****

Two Secret Service agents held open the service elevator near the kitchen for the Secretary. Jim Lowenstein, the Secretary's administrative assistant, followed his boss into the elevator. They were surrounded by eight agents. The elevator moved to the top floor of the hotel where the Secretary and Lowenstein returned to the suite they had left less than twenty minutes earlier. Staton walked straight toward a man talking on a red phone in the far corner of the room. "What's the story, Mr. Sanders?" The head of his security detail was conversing with Donald Schroeder, the director of the Secret Service, on a direct line that had been specially installed for the Secretary's visit.

Sanders cupped the receiver with his hand. "It looks bad, Mr. Secretary. We believe the President, the Vice-President, and most of the Democratic congressional leadership were killed in the explosion." Sanders returned to his conversation with Washington.

"Oh, my god!" uttered Staton as he collapsed onto the white floral sofa in the middle of the room. "Get confirmation as soon as you can, Mr. Sanders." He then looked up at Lowenstein who was hovering over him. "Jim, try to get through to Ed Collins at the White House. See what he knows."

"Yes, sir." Lowenstein turned and walked into the Secretary's bedroom to use the telephone.

Sanders again cupped the receiver of the red phone. "Mr. Secretary, we now have confirmation from Washington. Director Schroeder reports that both Eagle and Echo are dead."

Staton looked up, puzzled. "Eagle and Echo?"

"Sorry, Mr. Secretary. Those are our code names for the President and Vice-President."

"Where did it happen, for God's sake? Surely not in the White House."

"No, sir, in front of the Archives Building."

Staton then remembered President Hansen's teasing of him earlier in the day about the ceremony commemorating the death of President Roosevelt and how the 64-year-old Secretary of State was about to be eligible for Roosevelt's great legacy—social security. He also remembered that the Speaker of the House and Senate President Pro Tempore were supposed to be present. Staton had been around Washington politics long enough to know the pecking order. A shudder passed over his body. "What about Speaker Harley and Senator Howard? Were they at the explosion."

"Yes, sir." It was Lowenstein standing at the door to the bedroom. " Mr. Secretary, I'm afraid that Ed Collins was killed in the explosion, also. I've got Dr. Tollefson on the line. He confirms that Speaker Harley and Senator Howard were also both killed in the explosion." Tyler Tollefson was the President's National Security Advisor. "He advises you to return to Washington immediately, Mr. Secretary."

Staton sat motionless, the impact of the news from Washington slowly settling in. He looked back at his young aide. "Get the Attorney General on the line, Jim." The Secretary heaved his 275 pounds out of the sofa and began pacing. Sanders continued to talk in low tones on the red phone.

"Mr. Secretary, Director Schroeder would like to speak with you." Sanders extended the red receiver toward the Secretary, who crossed the room to take the call.

"Yes, Mr. Schroeder, what in the hell happened?"

"A heavy explosive was apparently planted beneath the FDR Memorial and detonated electronically. The power of the explosion ripped the marble memorial into thousands of pieces turning them into shrapnel, much like a hand grenade. I'm afraid almost everybody standing within twenty-five feet of the front of the memorial was killed instantly."

"You said, 'almost everybody.' Did anyone survive?"

"Congressman Brownell is in critical condition, sir. He received a sharp blow to the head and is in a coma. He must have been standing behind all of the other people, who in turn provided a shield. It is the only explanation, sir." Schroeder hesitated only momentarily. "Mr. Secretary, if we are correct, and I will have absolute confirmation within the next ten minutes, then, sir, I believe you are next in line of succession. I have pulled in every agent we have in the Bay Area, and your hotel should be secured within the next thirty minutes, Mr. Secretary. I strongly urge you not to leave your suite until all our agents have arrived." After a pause, Schroeder continued. "We need to protect the continuity of the office, Mr. President."

The phrase, *Mr. President*, stunned the Secretary momentarily. He felt the dark realization of what was happening creep over his body. It was a cold feeling. He was speechless.

"Mr. President, are you still there, sir? Mr. President?"

"Yes, Mr. Schroeder, I'm still here. I've asked my assistant, Jim Lowenstein, to contact the Attorney General for specific instructions. I will not assume the Presidency without his direction. Do you understand?"

"Yes, sir. I think that wise. I'll be back to you shortly. Would you ask Agent Sanders to keep this line open, sir?" Staton handed the receiver back to Sanders. "He wants you to keep the line open."

Lowenstein reentered the room. " I have the Attorney General on the line, Mr. Secretary. He's in his limousine on the way to the White House."

"Good." Staton crossed the room and took the call in his bedroom, ignoring the bed and standing erect to his full six-feet, four-inches. "Jacob, are you there?"

After a short instant the Attorney General answered, "Yes, Crawford, I'm here. I'm sorry for the delay, but I had to turn on the scrambler to be sure our call was not being monitored."

"Jacob, I understand from Director Schroeder that the President, the Vice-President, Speaker Harley, and Senator Howard were all killed in the assassination today. Is that correct?"

"Crawford, as far as I know that's correct. You must understand, there is complete chaos back here. None of the bodies were recognizable, and identification has to come from fingerprints. I had a team from the FBI take prints before the bodies were removed to the hospital. The bureau has confirmed the identities of the four you mentioned, plus Senators Ackerson, Druding, Dixon, Goldstein, and McConkle. In addition, there are another dozen bodies we have not identified, but we believe most of them were Secret Service agents and Marines."

Staton paused, hoping not to sound anxious. "Jacob, does that mean I am next in line to become President?"

"Yes, Crawford, I believe so. I had my staff get out a copy of the 1947 Presidential Succession Act, and I believe it is very clear that you, as senior member of the Cabinet, are next in line."

"Does that mean I should take the oath of office, Jacob?"

There was no hesitation from the other end of the line. "Yes, sir, I believe you should. As you know, we have never had a situation where anyone below the rank of Vice-President has ever been called upon to take the oath. I would assume you should do so as soon as possible." There was a pause, "Crawford?"

Staton hesitated. The Attorney General was a brilliant lawyer, but he was obviously in distress. The Secretary needed confirmation. "Jacob, would you take offense if I called the Chief Justice?"

"Absolutely not, Crawford. I think it prudent on your part, but I feel sure he'll confirm my advice to you."

"Jacob. Are you at the White House, yet?"

"Yes, sir, we just pulled up, and from the look of the limos around here, I'd say almost all the Cabinet have arrived."

"Do me a favor and have the White House switchboard find the Chief Justice. I think he's still in Washington, but he may be on vacation this week. Those operators are better than this hotel phone system. The White House operators can patch through the call."

"Yes, sir, I'll do that immediately. What about the Cabinet? We shouldn't meet without your permission at this point. Even without the other four successors, you're the senior Cabinet member. Should I tell everybody to go back to work? What would you like us to do?"

Staton thought for a few seconds before responding. "Go on in there, Jacob, and convene the meeting. Have me hooked up so I can take part by phone, say, in ten minutes. I'll tell Sanders here, my security chief. If nothing else, maybe I can reassure the others."

"Good idea, Mr. President. I'll tend to it immediately. Is there anything else?"

"No, I can't think of anything. I'll be talking to you in about ten minutes."

"Yes, sir." Again there was a pause. "And, Crawford, God bless you."

"Thank you, Jacob, but before the day is out, we're going to need His blessing on a lot more people than just me. Talk to you later."

Staton replaced the receiver on the phone by the bed. He thought about calling his wife, but a glance at the small portable clock on the bedstand which he always carried with him on trips and which was always set on Washington time, told him it was now 3:45 in Washington. He knew she was taking her afternoon nap. No need to disturb her. She'd only begin drinking before he got home. God, how was she going to handle this pressure? He told Sanders to get the call to the Cabinet ready; then he again began pacing.

The phone ring startled the Secretary. "This is Secretary Staton."

An operator's voice was unusually nervous. "Just a second, Mr. Secretary, I have the Chief Justice on the line. Go ahead."

"Chief, I assume you have heard the news by now."

"Yes, Mr. Secretary, I have. I'm still in my office here in Washington. The whole building has been in a frenzy. The news reports indicate that the President and Vice-President may have been killed. Is that right?"

"Worse than that, Mr. Chief Justice. The Speaker of the House and President Pro Tem of the Senate were killed, too. That's why I am calling you. The Attorney General believes that based on the

1947 Succession Act I should take the oath of office as President as soon as possible. I would like your opinion, sir."

There was a long pause on the Chief Justice's end of the line. "Well, Mr. Secretary, you caught me off guard. Senator Howard is confirmed dead? Oh, my god! He was the godfather to my oldest son."

Staton waited for the Chief to regain his composure. He had not known that the two men were close friends, but that was the way in Washington. Live in the town long enough, and the friends pile up. Certainly both the Chief Justice and Howard had been around for a long time. Staton remembered that Howard served as chairman of the Senate Judiciary Committee—the oversight committee of the courts. It was probably natural that the two men had spent time together.

"I'm sorry, Mr. Secretary. Let me see. I believe the Attorney General is right. If memory serves me right, following the President Pro Tem, the Cabinet, in order of seniority, are to succeed to the office. Yes, that's right, I believe. I would advise you to take the oath as soon as possible." There was more hesitation. "My god, Mr. Secretary, just think of it—think of the chaos in the country. We need to assure the nation as soon as possible that somebody is in charge."

Staton realized that the Chief Justice had a point. Even though the deaths of the President and others had not yet been officially confirmed, the media would be speculating. The more they speculated, the more confusion there would be throughout the nation. He knew he had to act fast.

"Thank you, Mr. Chief Justice. Again, my sympathies over the loss of Senator Howard."

"Thank you. . . . Mr. President . . . Good luck."

Staton returned the receiver and shouted through the open door to the living room for Lowenstein. "Jim!"

The young aide appeared immediately. "Jim, we need a federal judge as soon as we can get one over here. Also, I imagine the media are going crazy downstairs. As soon as the judge arrives, I want you to allow a pool of no more than six from the media to come up to the suite. Then tell Sanders to arrange for our plane to take off within the hour. I want to get back to Washington."

Lowenstein answered quickly. "Yes, sir." He turned to walk
out, then returned. "Mr. Secretary, may I offer a suggestion?"

"Sure, go ahead, Jim."

"Sir, you'll recall the Russian situation in Armenia. I'm not
suggesting that today's events in Washington are connected, but,
on the other hand, they might be. At the very least, the Russians
are going to know we are in a mess over here. They may take
advantage of the situation. Perhaps you should take some action
to let them know you're watching them."

Staton had been reminded again that he was in charge, that the
world was still out there, and mischief was constantly afoot. He
now had to serve as President of the United States and protect his
nation's interests. "Good idea, Jim. I'll call Tollefson and suggest
that we implement Step I of *Operation Thunderburst.* Thanks for
the suggestion."

"I'm here to serve, Mr. President." Lowenstein left to converse
with Sanders.

Staton sat down on the edge of the bed and began
reflecting over the conversation held in the NSC meeting a few
hours earlier. He had been connected to the meeting through a
telephone hookup. The President had wanted him involved in the
meeting because of the volatility of the situation in southern
Armenia. His old friend, Admiral Ogden Birchfield, chairman of
the Joint Chiefs of Staff, had argued vehemently for the full
implementation of *Thunderburst,* a Defense Department plan to
deploy nearly 36,000 troops and support within a ninety-six-hour
period any place in the world.

The plan had been developed following the experience in
1990 and 1991 with Iraq. That deployment had taken far too long
in the minds of defense analysts. *Operation Thunderburst* was
designed to accelerate the deployment process.

The President and Secretary Nelson had been dead-set against
the earlier use of *Thunderburst.* They both had felt the action
would be provocative based on the fact that neither Iran nor
Turkey had been invaded. Staton had always favored improving
relations with the old Soviet Union, later the Commonwealth, and
most recently the Russian Federation, and even during his Senate

days as chairman of the Foreign Relations Committee, he had been considered a moderate on American-Soviet relations.

The decomposing of the great Russian Commonwealth led by Boris Yeltsin and the subsequent takeover by the old Ministry of Defense had set those relations back, but there had been no sign that the revitalized Russian military machine was ready for foreign adventure. Birchfield and others had been correct back in '91 after the attempted Communist coup against Gorbachev had failed, and the breakup of the Soviet Union and the death of communism had appeared a done deal. There were those who had argued that the demise of communism in the USSR had negated the need for a large defense establishment. Birchfield had argued that the United States could not depend on the situation's remaining constant in the changing Russian political unions.

The breakup of the republics had hurt Birchfield's arguments initially, but much of the public had forgotten that the mighty war machine created by the Communists still existed, and somebody over there had his finger on the nuclear trigger. The intelligence agencies of the United States knew of the potential for another coup and a return of the right wing hierarchy in the old Soviet empire. Not all those opposed to Gorbachev and Yeltsin had gone gently into the night, merely underground.

The inevitable failure of the Commonwealth leaders to bring about necessary economic changes fast enough had been assured with the resulting loose knit union, which had provided less cohesion than the American states during the Articles of Confederation. The animosity and rivalries that existed among the republics had manifested themselves into economic barriers between the various republics. The resulting chaos and poor harvests had generated labor strikes, empty stores, and a call for change.

The euphoria that had existed in the West at the time of the 1991 changes had not been based on a true understanding of the Soviet peoples. While many in Moscow and St. Petersburg had supported Yeltsin and the death of communism, well over half the people in the old USSR had felt comfortable under the old system. At least they had been able to eat, and if prices had been high, at least goods had been available.

The American military always had been sensitive to the situation. Attempts to replace senior Communist commanders had not removed from the officer ranks those who understood that order was preferable to disorder. They also had possessed a greater sensitivity to the national interest and world events. Many had not been able to come to grips with the decline of the Soviet Union as a world power.

The right wing politicians constantly reminded the Russian people of the impotence of the Yeltsin regime. The effort by nationalists in Chechnya in the mid '90s to break away and the terrible beating Russian soldiers took only reinforced the right wing's criticisms of Yeltsin as an ineffective leader. Old line Communist bosses in the provinces aided the chaos because they knew only through chaos could they regain power. Sooner or later the Russian people would tire of impotent leadership, of shortages of foods and consumer goods, and the terrible inflation brought on by an economy that was neither centrally controlled, nor consumer driven.

Old man Nixon had warned the nation's leaders back in '92 that if they did not provide economic aid to the Russians and other republics in CIS, totalitarian leaders would re-emerge and take over the government. However, because of a long recession and huge deficits, neither Congress, Bush, nor Clinton was willing to write any large checks for foreign aid. In the end, Nixon was proved right.

Yeltsin became increasingly bellicose as his drinking continued unabated. Eventually, he lost popular support. Mikhail Gorbachev, who had resigned in 1992 during the violent revolt of parliament against Yeltson, reemerged as the generals' candidate for President, but he declined to be controlled. The generals then turned to Viktor Chenkov, the old Communist party leader in Siberia. He had led the Communist party after it had changed its name to the Social Democratic Party. He was subsequently elected to the Russian presidency, but American intelligence agencies knew that the generals were calling the shots. While most of the republics that had broken away refused to rejoin a new federation, the Ukranians had all but become a suzerainty, and Russia had taken on the role of big brother to many of the others.

Now the long standing nationality and religious rivalries in Armenia and Azerbaijan were festering anew and causing a serious international rift between the West and the newer Russian leadership. Birchfield and his American right wing supporters had been quick to erupt and argue for the strongest possible response to the new Russian government.

Staton had argued against deployment of *Thunderburst* until the Russians responded to the President's inquiry made over the hotline earlier in the day. His view had prevailed, as it usually did within the councils of government. But Lowenstein was right. No one could tell at the present juncture if the assassinations in Washington were connected with the Russians or not. Step I would be a logical reaction for a nation to take following such a calamity. At least, it would show that there was someone in charge of the huge military machine controlled by the President of the United States.

Staton picked up the phone again. "Is the conference call ready to the White House?" In but a few short seconds, the operator connected the call. Staton could hear the low-level chatter in the Cabinet Room.

"Gentlemen and ladies, thank you for all assembling so fast. Is everyone present?"

The Attorney General responded. "Yes, Mr. President, all except the Secretary of the Treasury who is attending the NATO financial ministers conference in Brussels. I have already filled everyone in on our conversation earlier, Mr. President."

"Thank you, Jacob. By the way, if memory serves me, Treasury is next on the list of Cabinet seniority. Is that right, Jacob?"

"I believe you're right, Mr. President."

"Then we need to get the Secretary of Treasury back here immediately and make sure he has ample Secret Service protection. If anything happens to me, he's next."

A cold shiver ran through the veins of most of those in the room. The realization of the day's events was difficult to assimilate. The thought of more deaths and confusion was almost too much to absorb.

"Secretary Thompson, are you there?"

"Yes, sir." The Secretary's voice was weak. The death of his best friend had been a tremendous shock. Hansen's last words,

'*Nels, if anything would happen to me, you'd have to hold this government together*' still rang in his ears. He felt as if he were bogged down in the mire of a surrealistic nightmare.

"Nels, I feel terrible about President Hansen, and I know how close you were to him. Please accept my sympathies."

"Thank you, Mr. President, but we must focus on the future, now. What can we do for you?" The words were strong, reinforced by his commitment to his dead friend.

"Nels, until I get back, you are the ranking Cabinet member there. I'd appreciate your staying in the White House where I can communicate with you at any time."

"No problem, sir. I am at your disposal."

"Jacob, what do we know about the assassination?"

"The President's Secret Service detail was pretty much taken out by the explosion. As you know it is a violation of federal statutes to kill or to attempt to kill an officer of the federal government, including members of Congress. Accordingly, the FBI is responsible for handling the investigation. I have already talked to Alec Jameson, the director, and he has assigned his top special agent, Bert Mattox, to spearhead the investigation."

"Sounds like you're on top of it, Jacob. You will keep me informed, will you not?"

"Yes, sir. I've asked Director Jameson to give me reports every hour."

"Good. Now, Nels, I think we had better proceed with Step I of *Thunderburst*."

The Secretary of Defense started to interrupt, "But, Mr. President! "

"Now, hold on, Nels. I know your position, but let's just stop and think. Even if the Russians are not involved in these terrible assassinations, and I pray to God they aren't, common sense dictates that they're going to figure we're in a stew over here. We need to take some action that shows somebody is in charge. Step I is merely an alert status, as I recall. It cancels all leave and orders all pilots and military personnel designated for *Thunderburst* to report to their bases. Is that correct?"

"Yes, sir, that's correct." Secretary Thompson acquiesced to Staton's logic. Hopefully, Birchfield and the other Chiefs wouldn't take this move as a go ahead for a full-scale launching of *Thunderburst.*

"Good. I have sent for a federal judge to administer the oath of office in my suite here within the hour. I'll also have media representatives present. I should be in my plane and back there within five hours. I'll see you all then."

Secretary Thompson, as senior Cabinet officer present, took the lead. "God be with you, Mr. President."

"Thank you, Nels, and thank you, all." The click of the line going dead could be heard from the speaker phone. A silence pervaded the Cabinet Room until Secretary Thompson stood.

"Ladies and gentlemen, we have work to do. This government must give every appearance of functioning. I will alert Admiral Birchfield of the President's order regarding Step I of *Thunderburst.* I would suggest we all meet at Andrews Air Force Base to welcome President Staton when he returns. That should be near midnight. Do you all agree?" There was a general nodding of heads. Thompson took his leave to find a phone. The other Cabinet members slowly moved toward the door. Very few had anything to say.

*****

At 1:30 PST, Secretary Staton stood beside Judge Sue Yu-sung, the first Oriental female judge appointed to the bench in the northern federal district of California. Surrounding them were the mayor of San Francisco and the governor of California, both of whom had attended the luncheon and who Staton thought might add credibility to the ceremony, Lowenstein, six Secret Service agents, and six members of the media, four with cameras.

A news release issued from the White House just twenty minutes earlier confirmed the deaths of the President, the Vice-President, and the leaders of Congress. The same news release reported that, upon the recommendation of the Attorney General of the United States and the Chief Justice of the United States, Secretary of State Crawford P. Staton would be sworn in as President at 4:30 EST in San Francisco.

The television technicians had rigged a live feed from the living room of the Staton suite. Precisely on cue, Judge Yu-sung extended a *Bible* in her left hand and raised her right hand. Secretary Staton placed his right hand on the *Bible* and raised his left hand. "Please repeat after me, Mr. Secretary."

The Secretary of State, now standing as erect as possible, repeated the oath of office. "I, Crawford P. Staton, do solemnly swear that I will execute the office of President of the United States and that I will to the best of my ability preserve, protect, and defend the Constitution of the United States. So help me God."

Chapter 3

J. Edgar Hoover Building
3:45 P.M.

Bert Mattox was the senior investigative special agent within the Federal Bureau of Investigation, a fact well-known among Washington insiders. The director of the bureau made little secret of his admiration or backing of the forty-five-year-old career lawman. Attempts by a few powerful congressmen to stymie investigations of influential constituents back home could never touch Mattox. Director Jameson made sure of that. Nor would rivals within the bureau cross him, including the two deputy directors. But in fact, nearly everyone in the bureau liked and admired Mattox. He had made clear a few years earlier that he had little interest in administration, so those with aspirations of leadership within the bureau felt no threat.

Success in the bureau had not come cheaply to Mattox. He had paid with two failed marriages and two teenage sons from his first wife he now hardly knew. After Phyllis had remarried and moved to Los Angeles, Mattox had little opportunity to play the concerned father. The boys had seemed to bond well with Phyllis's second husband anyway. As far as he knew, they were straight kids. They sent the obligatory birthday, Father's Day, and Christmas cards. Photographs allowed him to keep pace with their changing physiques, faces, and hair styles. He had not actually seen the children for five years. It wasn't that he disliked the boys, or that he was indifferent toward them. In his line of work, concentration, intensity, and no loose baggage seemed to be most beneficial. But like many bachelors, loneliness had become an accepted roommate, and there were times he longed for a family.

Mattox did not look like the Hollywood version of a successful investigator. He lacked the rumpled appearance of a Colombo, the muscular, tall torso of a Mike Hammer, the suave air of a James Bond. With a height of just over five feet ten inches, he carried his 185 pounds well. His youthful blond hair was now light brown and laced with a few indistinguishable gray strands, but unfortunately there just wasn't enough hair. While full in the back and on the sides, only loose strands still rested horizontally on the top of his dome. His handsome face was set off with soft but large blue eyes. His mouth was wide enough to sport an infectious smile with a perfect set of gleaming teeth and a large dimple to the left of his lips. He wore suits well, preferring grays, blacks and blues—all two button—no vests or double breasted. All in all, Mattox rendered the appearance of a handsome, middle-aged man, whose upright posture and athletic ability allowed him to be attractive to women, without being threatening to their husbands.

Mattox and Agent Martin sat alone in the fifth floor conference room. His office was still being cleaned. The younger Martin sat quietly across from the senior agent as Mattox began to reread the report sent over to the bureau by the CIA's deputy director, Thomas Asburn, just hours earlier.

He opened the file folder. The title page merely read *Abdul*. On the second page was a photograph, obviously several years old. It showed six young men, all in their late teens or early twenties, standing on top of an Israeli tank. Each man was waving an Uzi automatic weapon in the air, as if in triumph. A red circle was drawn around the face of the young boy furthest to the left. A Palestinian, he had short dark hair, deep-set eyes, a prominent bent nose, and broad shoulders. The photograph was grainy, but the intense look of emotion on the face of the young man could not be lost.

```
Name: Abdul
Real Name: Unknown
Alias: Mosef Aman; Joseph Pittman, Josef
  Packman, Ari Mohammad Krosagi
Birthdate: Approximately 1950
Place of Birth: Jordan (assumed)
Parents: Unknown
Wife: Unknown
Children: Unknown
Profession: Paid assassin
```

Mattox made a few notes on his pad. Not much here except age and appearance. Even the name Abdul provided little information. He may as well have been named John. He turned the page. A copy of a computer printout presented a narrative on the assassin.

```
    The assassin, Abdul, was born in a
refugee camp in Jordan sometime near 1950.
There is no record of his parents or of
his birth. It is believed Abdul was raised
by the PLO and trained while in early
childhood in terrorist activities. Sources
close to the PLO report that he was one of
the organization's most outstanding
prospects--courageous, daring, immune to
pain, and full of religious zeal.
    Only one photograph exists of the man
suspected of being Abdul. The photograph
was taken by a PLO member following the
successful ambush of an Israeli tank in the
Gaza Strip in 1969. All other men shown in
the photograph have been identified and
confirmed dead by Israeli intelligence
sources. Abdul escaped Israeli soldiers,
who captured him briefly two months later.
```

In his escape, four Israeli soldiers were killed. It is believed he was involved in the capture, torture, and murder of the Agency's station chief in Beruit. He is also suspected of being involved in the terrorist bombings in both Italy and Greece in the early 1980's.

As relations between Israel and its Arab neighbors improved in the early 1990's, Abdul left the PLO out of bitterness. It is reported that no one within the PLO ever was close enough to Abdul to gain information on his correct name or his family. He is suspected of being a homosexual or at least asexual. Reports from Agency personnel in Zurich detail rumors of plastic surgery on an unknown Arab at an exclusive clinic on the outskirts of the city (see Addendum A). The clinic was destroyed by an explosion and fire in 1991, suggesting he may have completed his recovery by that time. All records and the medical staff in the clinic were destroyed and killed in the initial blast.

Since 1991, Abdul has been available for hire by international crime syndicates, drug cartels, and terrorist organizations. Contact is always made through an elaborate maze of intermediaries. Initial contact has been traced to Algiers, which is presumed to be his home base. Efforts to enlist the aid of Algerian military and police officials have proved to be nonproductive. Abdul has enough important government personnel on his payroll or is so elusive

that Algerian officials scoff at the notion
he resides in their country.

Abdul's first assassination appears to
have been the Foreign Minister of Columbia
in June, 1991. Mr. Alfonso Carvella and his
wife were killed as their armed car
exploded outside the American Embassy in
Mexico City. Eight other bystanders and
guards were killed in the explosion.

Since that time no less than 22 deaths
have been traced to Abdul through Interpol
and intelligence communities throughout the
world. His modus operandi normally favors
explosives, although in two instances he
employed rifle fire, and in two instances
overdoses of prescription drugs were admin-
istered intravenously.

Sources within the Mossad in Israel
claim his price ranges from no less than
$100,000 to $1,000,000, depending upon the
target. Payment is always in cash or by
electronic transfer to an unknown numbered
bank account believed to be in the Grand
Cayman Islands.

A complete list of suspected targets of
Abdul can be found in the Addenda with
dossiers on all incidents.

In 1994 the Agency launched a covert
operation to capture Abdul by attempting to
employ him for an assassination of a Middle
East trade minister opposed to American oil
interests. His fee of $500,000 was paid
according to Abdul's directions in Morroco.
The agent assigned to deliver the money was
later found with one 45-caliber bullet in
his head. An examination of the corpse
pointed to a brutal torture including
incisions made near the agent's genitals.

(See Addendum E.) The sanction on the trade
minister was never carried out, and the
Agency suspects Abdul had prior knowledge
of the Agency plan.

Mattox closed the file and raised his head slowly to face the
young CIA courier. "You know, Martin, if I had received this
report just twenty-four hours earlier, we might have prevented
today's tragedy." He leaned back and tapped the folder with his
fingers. "But we can't waste time moping about what might have
been. We have plenty of work to do. Director Jameson wants to
meet with us in ten minutes, and I've called a meeting of our top
agents for 4:30. Let's get upstairs."

Mattox grabbed the folder in front of him as well as his yellow
legal pad and darted for the door. Martin followed in close pursuit,
wondering about his own role in Mattox's investigation. After all,
he was a duck, a very young duck, out of water. An Agency man
in the bureau.

*****

The private mahogany paneled conference room of the
director of the Federal Bureau of Investigation was packed.
Fifteen men sat in chairs around the ornate mahogany table, while
another two dozen agents stood against the walls around the room.
One of the agents turned the television off and closed the cabinet
door that stored it just as the director entered and took a seat at the
end of the table. Mattox sat near the middle of the table. The
swearing in of the new President, covered on national television,
had taken less than a minute.

"Gentlemen, I appreciate your quick response to this meeting.
I know many of you are deeply involved in other cases, but at this
point in time nothing is more important to this bureau and to the
nation than trying to identify and capture the perpetrator or perpe-
trators of these assassinations." The director spoke firmly, and
Mattox noticed that the shaking in his right hand had subsided.
The man looked considerably better than he had seen him a few
minutes earlier.

"Now, as you all know, Special Agent Mattox will be in charge of this case. While there may be national security implications to this situation, the fact remains this is a criminal investigation. No less than fifteen federal statutes were violated today. I have been in contact with the Attorney General, and he has assured me of the entire department's cooperation. I expect to be kept fully informed on the progress of the investigation. The Attorney General has requested hourly reports. I received word just fifteen minutes ago that President Staton will be arriving at Andrews tonight at 11:50. I need not tell you how anxious he is for information on our progress." The director folded his hands and placed them in his lap. "Now, Bert, why don't you take it from here."

Mattox straightened the legal pad resting in front of him. He had spent about thirty minutes organizing the investigation prior to the conference meeting. He and the director had already agreed on their plan of attack. "All right, gentlemen, let me start by introducing to you Agent John Martin of the CIA. Director Heffelfinger of the Agency has asked if he could have a liaison with us during this investigation since one of the chief suspects is an international terrorist. I asked for Martin, and the director approved just before we arrived for this meeting." Mattox did not reveal how upset Heffelfinger had been with Mattox's suggestion. The director would have preferred a more seasoned agent, but Mattox did not want anyone from the Agency who would be second guessing him during the course of the investigation. He did not need more of Washington's famous interagency bickering. Heffelfinger had not been in a position to argue, and Martin's approval was not much more than a *fait accompli.*

The room contained the most senior staff members of the bureau stationed in Washington. The youthful appearance of the CIA liaison was not greeted with any outward display of enthusiasm, but those closest to Mattox through the years understood how he thought and correctly guessed why Martin had been chosen.

Mattox looked across the table at Dr. Gradle, head of the Forensics Laboratory in the bureau. "Doc, do you know what caused the explosion?"

The white-haired Gradle, just two years from mandatory retirement, leaned forward. "This is preliminary, mind you, but we believe a large amount of plastic explosive, specifically C-4, was planted beneath the marble stone that comprised the Roosevelt Memorial. We found residue on several fragments of the stone."

Mattox wrote on his pad, then looked up. "Do you know how it was detonated?"

"Yes, sir, we found several sections of a locust tree that stood behind the stone. A minute laser-generated channel had been burned through the trunk, and a small gauge wire inserted through the channel. We believe this wire ran from one of the branches through the trunk to the root system and was attached to the explosive. If we are correct, any small radio device could have provided the detonation by using the wire as a receptor for a radio signal."

Agent Sparks, one of the senior members of the bureau, asked, "What about the explosives, Doc? Were they planted beneath the stone?"

Gradle leaned back in his chair. "We believe they were buried beneath and to the rear of the stone, so that the impact would propel the fragments of the stone forward toward the President and his party, much like shrapnel." Dr. Gradle paused to remove his glasses and wipe them with a linen handkerchief. "Make no mistake, Mr. Sparks, this was a professional operation. The equipment used was very sophisticated. These explosives were planted in such a deliberate manner to inflict the harshest damage to those standing in front of the memorial. "

Director Jameson looked quizzical. "Wasn't the site checked by the Secret Service?"

Mattox answered. "I checked with Don Schroeder about half an hour ago. He says the entire grounds were searched yesterday evening and again this morning, including the use of dogs trained to smell out explosives. Apparently they were buried deep enough to avoid detection." Mattox turned back to his pad. "Which means they must have been planted some time ago."

The senior agent turned to his right. "Michaels, I want you to check with the National Park Service. Find out if any contracts were let on landscaping of the memorial site. If so, when and by whom? You know the routine."

Michaels nodded and scribbled notes in a small pad he carried.

Mattox then turned toward Sparks. "I want you to talk to the staff at the White House. Find out who planned today's ceremony. How long has it been planned? Who had advance notice of it? I've got to believe that our assassin, or assassins, had enough prior notice to plant those explosives several weeks ago. If I'm right, then we may be dealing with somebody on the inside of our own government."

The assembled men looked at each other as a low murmur floated throughout the room. The thought of a conspiracy involving officials of the government was both surprising and frightening.

Mattox was reviewing his several pages of notes. "By the way, Sparks, I also want you to assign several of your best people to finding any film or video tape taken at the site during the ceremony. Concentrate on areas across the street in sight of the trees Dr. Gradle mentioned. If this explosion was electronically set, the assassin must have been within eyesight of the memorial. Look for windows, especially in the buildings on the north side of Pennsylvania Avenue."

He paused again. "And though I hate the thought of it, you better check both Justice and our own building. There must be dozens of windows that had a view of the memorial from our two buildings."

Mattox turned the page of his pad. "Our number one suspect at this time is an international assassin known only as Abdul. We received word only today from Langley that they had information Abdul was in the country. Furthermore, they report that they believe he had made a prior entry into the country sometime since the first of the year. That meshes with our theory that the explosive was planted some time ago."

"We have only one photograph of Abdul, and I'm afraid it's twenty-five years old. I have asked our graphics specialists to take the photo and computer and age the young Abdul. We also understand that he may have undergone cosmetic surgery, so we have brought in a plastic surgeon from over at George Washington Hospital and had him help our graphics specialists. They have come up with a half dozen possible looks for this Abdul." Mattox nodded to Martin who began passing out the 11 x 14 inch composites containing all six faces.

"As you can all tell from these renderings, the sketch in the upper left is based on an enhancement of the original photograph. All the other renderings have attempted to add twenty-five years to the face. Three have mustaches of varying sizes. Two have altered noses and cheek bones, and each has a differing amount of hair, though we believe, based on the region and his background, Abdul still has a full head of hair."

Mattox allowed time for everyone in the room to get a copy and to examine the several faces. "Copies of the composites in your hands are to be distributed to every office within sight of the memorial. The D.C. police are already conducting a search, looking for suspicious persons, especially Middle Eastern types, and for evidence of the detonation device. I want these composites plastered all over the D.C. newspapers and on the television. Set up a bank of phones in the basement to receive calls from anybody who may have seen anyone resembling one of the renderings."

"I want the car rental agencies, Dulles, National, and the Baltimore airports covered. No one is to leave whose face hasn't been checked. The Metro is to stay closed for at least twenty-four hours. I want every taxi company contacted and the composites distributed to every cabby in the city. I want the bus station given the same scrutiny as the airports. That goes for the train station, too."

With his list completed, Mattox began handing out assignments to teams of agents around the room. He knew every one by his first and last name. He demanded reports from each team on the hour. A command center had been set up in the basement. Mattox would work out of the center.

"Tap every source you have, gentlemen. This is the most important case in which any of us most likely ever will be involved. Now get to it."

Everyone left except for the director, Mattox, and Martin. The director asked Martin to allow him time for a private conference with Mattox. The young agent dutifully made his exit.

Mattox and the director had met only three years earlier when Jameson, a former federal district court judge from Birmingham, Alabama, had been appointed to the position. Mattox's familiarity with the South after ten years of assignments in that region had given him an advantage in both understanding and dealing with the more mercurial judge. Mattox had also found that the judge liked his bullshit thin, not thick. The agent knew just how far to go, and that was an inborn instinct in judgment that separated the successful career bureau men from those who retired in Indianapolis after twenty unexciting years.

"Bert, I'm afraid I have one more request for you." Mattox noticed that the director's palsy had returned as he fumbled with his papers. "It's no secret to you that I have a health problem. Hopefully, I'll be able to control this damnable thing with medication. In the meantime, someone from the top echelons of the bureau has to face the media. In fact, we have a press conference scheduled in the auditorium at 5:15. I would like for you to handle the media."

Mattox started to protest, but the director raised his wobbly hand to stop him. "I know all the reasons why you don't want to do it, Bert, but look at me. How much confidence is the nation going to have in this investigation if they see a shaking old man giving them information? They would assume that I was weak, and the investigation was in trouble. You and I both know the work done by the bureau has very little to do with the competency of the director. We need to be conscious of our image, Bert. I think it is important to the nation at this point in time."

Mattox was still uneasy. "What about one of the deputy directors, Judge?"

The director shook his head. "Then people are going to ask, why I didn't make the announcements and the briefings. With you at the head of the investigation, it is only natural that you would be out front with the public."

Mattox took a long breath. He knew the director was right. "Okay, Judge, but when this is over, you owe me a big one." He smiled at his friend and mentor.

The director sighed with relief.

Chapter 4

Washington, D. C.
4:00 P.M.

The assassin walked as fast as he could without appearing conspicuous. As he approached the Seventh Street entrance to the Firemen's Insurance Building, he spied a police officer standing guard. Slowing down, he continued his walk as if he knew exactly where he was going. As he placed his hand on the brass handle of the glass door to push it open, the police officer stopped him. "I'm sorry, sir, but nobody is allowed in or out until our men have completed their search."

Employing his best American accent, he asked, "How long is that gonna take, man? I'm supposed to meet my ol' lady in there at 4:00?"

"Sorry, sir, but our men just started about five minutes ago on the bottom floor. They're working their way up. I'd say it will be at least an hour ."

"Shit, man. What about my ol' lady?"

"She can't leave either. She probably knows by now that you can't get in. You might try calling her."

Appearing disgruntled, Abdul turned, muttering to himself, and stalked back up Seventh Street. The police officer turned his back to speak to several other people. Abdul darted into an alley that ran on the north side of the building. About half way along the building, he found a solid, steel fire door. It was locked. He pulled from his trouser pocket a black leather pouch containing burglary tools. After just a few seconds of tinkering with the lock, the door opened. Abdul ducked in and found himself in a dark boiler room, lighted only by a single florescent fixture mounted on the far wall near a work bench.

A line of six lockers rested against the wall next to the work bench. He opened two before he found what he wanted, a set of dark work overalls. He took off his jacket and tied it around his waist, then climbed into the overalls. Fortunately, the uniform was an extra-large, providing him ample room. He turned up the trouser legs which were about three inches too long, then moved toward an interior door, which he opened slowly. The corridor was filled with people mingling together and conversing. The assassination was the obvious topic of conversation. He opened the door all the way and walked out in a deliberate gait toward the stairwell. With luck the police had not yet gotten to the fifth floor.

As he passed each floor, he opened the hallway door enough to observe the activity in the corridor. On the third floor he saw a police uniform entering an office. He closed the door gently and continued his climb. At the fifth floor he opened the hallway door and walked to the office at the end of the corridor. Strangely, the hallway was vacant.

He unlocked the door and rushed into the vacant office area from where he had detonated the bomb. The carpeted floor was bare. "Damn!" he muttered in English. He checked the other room and its closets. The wallet was nowhere to be seen. He stopped to think. Where else could he have lost it? The face of the bearded Jew in the doorway flashed through his mind. They had bumped with quite a jolt, as he recalled. Could the wallet have dropped out of his pocket? Must have been there. He knew the man was a Jew from his appearance and his fixation on Abdul's eyes. Over the years he had become quite adept in identifying his most hated enemies.

The Jew had been entering as he was leaving, which meant there was a good chance he was still in the building. But where? He knew he was standing on the top floor of offices. Only storage space occupied the sixth floor, which was more like an attic. He would have to check each floor for a Jewish or Israeli organization. That would be his best bet. Washington was full of Jewish leagues and societies and information clubs. This building probably housed such an organization. He left his office and walked down the hallway, glancing at the name on the brass plate beside each office door. Nothing on the fifth floor.

A search of the fourth floor also found nothing. He did run into more people in the corridors as he descended the building, but all ignored him, including two police officers. On the third floor he stopped at an office with a nameplate of a Tel Aviv newspaper which he recognized. That could be it. He tried not to look conspicuous as about a dozen people mingled in the hallway talking. He knew the Jew would recognize him if he entered the office. He could not afford a scene. He needed to find out if this was the office of the Jew.

He reached into his overalls pocket and felt a large cloth. He pulled out a slightly soiled aqua cloth towel, probably used by workmen to wipe their hands. He wadded the towel in his palm and began rubbing the narrow window next to the door as if he were cleaning it. He also strained to see through the half-pulled venetian blinds to the interior. Over to the right he spotted the Jew. A woman, probably a secretary, occupied a desk to the far left. The Jew was talking on the telephone. There were too many policemen in the building to attempt anything that could cause suspicion. He decided to wait. He retreated to the stairwell. Few people used the stairs, preferring the two elevators servicing the building. He would wait inside, pretending he was loafing from his work if anybody inquired as to what he was doing.

He thought about his appearance, but Washington was filled with an array of nationalities. No one would take notice of his dark complexion. He would wait and listen carefully for a door to open and shut. He looked at his watch. It was 4:40. He would miss his plane, but he could catch another flight. If necessary he could steal a car and drive to the Baltimore airport. He sat down on the second step of the stairs and leaned his head against the wall adjoining the door. Years of practicing his profession had made patience his friend.

*****

Inside Weissman's office, the Israeli correspondent had just finished filing his story. It was near midnight in Tel Aviv, and his paper published an afternoon edition. He had plenty of time to file follow-ups. He leaned back in his chair and stretched. He began retracing the events of the past couple of hours since the death of the President. A call to the White House press office had confirmed the deaths of the President, Vice-President, and twenty others. He had watched on a small television on his secretary's desk as Crawford P. Staton had been sworn into office. He needed to find out more about Staton. His readers, not to mention his editors, would be most interested in Staton's past actions regarding Israel.

A slight pain in his left hip reminded him of his collision downstairs a couple hours earlier. Why had that man looked so familiar? He then remembered the wallet and walked over to the coat rack where he had hung his suit jacket and found the wallet in the pocket. He returned to his desk and opened the conventional brown leather wallet. A wad of currency in denominations of $50 first caught his eye. A quick count found twenty bills. Not many people walked around with $1,000 in their pockets. He then spotted an official looking CIA identification card belonging to a William J. Manchester. Something was wrong. The picture on the ID did not match in any way the face of the man he had bumped downstairs. What was more startling, he recognized the name on the card. It was Bill Manchester, Maggy's old boyfriend.

He had first learned of Manchester from Maggy on the cruise he had taken a year earlier. He had been talked into the cruise by Rosie, his secretary, in part to get out of the emotional funk that was plaguing him since the death of his wife and daughter in a terrorist attack on a bus in Jerusalem two years earlier. Maggy had been alone, also. A travel agent, herself, she was trying to forget Manchester after a three-year relationship. They had met at a midnight buffet and spent most of the remainder of the cruise talking, and for the first time in two years, he found himself laughing. Since then while he had entertained secret thoughts of romance, Maggy had never given any indication that the relationship would be anything other than one of friendship. He had concluded that was enough. He needed a friend, a confidant. They had discussed Manchester a number of times, though Maggy had been careful not to discuss his professional involvement

Why would that Arab have Manchester's wallet? Surely, it must be stolen. He began fanning his Rolodex, looking for a number at Langley. He found the press office and dialed the number. After three rings a recording answered, giving him four options to execute. He chose to dial for the operator.

"Good afternoon, may I help you?" No identification of the agency. This was typical of the spooks over at Langley.

"Yes, I'm trying to get ahold of Mr. William Manchester. I believe he has an office there."

"Just a second, sir, I'll transfer you." After two rings, the pleasant voice of a youthful sounding secretary answered the phone.

"This is Mr. Manchester's office. May I help you?"

"Yes. This is Isaac Weissman. I'm a journalist from Tel Aviv. Is Bill in, please?

"I'm sorry, sir. Mr. Manchester is out of the city. He isn't expected back until tomorrow."

"Could you tell me when he left, ma'am?

"I'm sorry, sir. We are not allowed to give out that information. Can I take your name and have him call you when he returns?"

Weissman hesitated before answering. "Yes, do that. The name is Isaac Weissman." He spelled the name slowly. "Tell Bill I'm a friend of Margaret Mosele. He can reach me at 202-555-3535."

"Yes, sir, Mr. Weissman. I'll give him the message. Have a good day."

Weissman hung up. Out of town? Surely he would not have left without his wallet. On the other hand, this Arab could have taken it days ago, giving Manchester time to replace his credit cards and identification. Credit cards?

Weissman began checking all the pockets inside the wallet for credit cards. Instead, he found a small yellow Post-it containing a scribbled telephone number. He recognized the area code as Virginia. He knew from Maggy that Manchester lived in a townhouse in Alexandria. But why would he be carrying his own phone number? He decided to dial the number.

The phone rang only once when a deep voice with a British accent answered. "The Chamberlain residence. May I help you?" Chamberlain? Must be someone important to employ such a polished domestic.

"Yes, is Mr. Chamberlain in?"

"No, sir, I'm afraid he's at his office in Washington. You can reach him there, sir."

"Thank you." Weissman pondered what to do. "Excuse me, but I have misplaced his office number. Do you have it?"

"I'm sorry, sir. We are not allowed to give out Mr. Chamberlain's private numbers. I would have assumed that if you had this number, you would have his office number."

"Yes. Yes, I do. But I'm in a telephone booth in Washington, and I don't have my Rolodex in front of me."

"I'm sorry, sir, but I cannot give you his number. You might try the switchboard at JFC Industries, sir."

"Thank you. I'll do that. Goodbye."

Weissman hung up the phone and leaned back in his chair. John Fairchild Chamberlain, chairman of the board and founder of JFC Industries, the second largest manufacturer of armaments in the United States. Why would Manchester have his home number? He continued examining the wallet. Deep in one slot normally used for credit cards, he fished out a Bicycle playing card—the ace of spades. How peculiar! Just one card. Manchester was out of town. Weissman scratched his cheek, pondering what to do. The journalist knew he couldn't get through to Chamberlain. Perhaps, just perhaps, Maggy would know something. He reached down and dialed her office number, but the line was busy. "Shit!" he muttered. The line was always busy.

*****

A knock on the office door was followed by a police officer sticking his head inside. "It's okay to leave anytime. We've completed our search of the building."

"Any luck, Officer?" asked the secretary on the far side of the office.

"Afraid not, but we thank you for your cooperation."

"Cooperation?" shrugged Weissman, after the officer had left. "Where the hell are we going to go anyway? We still have a 10:00 deadline to meet, Rosie."

"Yeah, I know. By the way, Isaac, the FBI is scheduled for a news conference about now. Do you want to watch it?" Rosie pointed to her desktop six-inch color Sony.

Weissman pushed his chair over next to Rosie's so he could watch the conference. This would save him a trip up the street. He also grabbed his notebook in case he needed it.

Bert Mattox, looking as fresh as if he were starting the day, approached the cluster of microphones engulfing the podium on the stage of the auditorium in the J. Edgar Hoover Building. He read from a written statement in which he recited many of the same observations that he had made minutes earlier in the director's conference room. At the close of his statement, he peered directly at the camera.

"We believe that the most likely suspect in today's multiple assassinations is an internationally known professional assassin. This man's identity is so secret that he is known only as Abdul. We have reliable intelligence that Abdul entered the country within the past week. We have only one photograph of the man, and it is several years old, but with the help of our computers and specialists from George Washington Hospital here in Washington, we have been able to develop a half dozen possible appearances of Abdul today."

Mattox then held up the page with the six composites for the cameras to see. An aide distributed copies of the composites to the reporters present.

Weissman stared at the little screen. None of the six faces looked quite right. All of the mustaches were wrong, but the eyes—there was something familiar and threatening in the eyes. They were the eyes of a fanatic. Weissman immediately thought of the Arab he had bumped into at the entrance to the building following the explosion. They were the same eyes. The Israeli correspondent could not take his eyes off the screen until the camera returned to Mattox's face. A phone number flashed on the screen, and Mattox continued talking, but Weissman had closed him out. His mind was trying to assemble the facts in front of him.

If the man downstairs was the assassin? If he did drop the wallet? If the CIA was involved with the assassination? If the assassin realized he had lost the wallet? Too many loose ends. But one thing was for sure. There must be a connection between the CIA and the Arab. And if the Arab was the assassin, he would undoubtedly return for the wallet, and if so, Weissman's life was in jeopardy.

If Manchester were involved, then maybe Maggy could be in danger. He had to act quickly. He jumped from his chair and rushed over to his Rolodex. He found the number of the Criminal Investigations Office of the FBI. He punched the numbers hurriedly. "This is Isaac Weissman. I am a journalist from Israel, and I believe I have important information about today's assassination. I must speak to Mr. Mattox immediately."

The secretary tried to pawn the call off on another agent, but Weissman was persistent. He would not talk to anybody but Mattox. Finally, out of frustration, she called the special agent's secretary. "Mary Alice, there is an Israeli journalist on the line who says he has important information on today's assassination. He insists on talking to Mattox. Is he in?"

"He just finished the press conference and is on his way to the basement command center. You can reach him on extension 5441."

"Thanks." The receptionist then dialed the four digit extension. Mattox answered.

"Mr. Mattox, I have an Israeli journalist named Weissman on the line who says he has information about today, and he will only talk to you. Would you like me to transfer the call, sir?"

Mattox had just arrived at the basement command center, and thoughts of hundreds of crank calls running through the evening gave him pause, but he had to start somewhere. Most of the calls would come to the phone banks, anyway. "Yeah, go ahead. I'll take it."

He signaled Martin to take a seat while the secretary transferred the call. The two men were the only two occupants of what would have been called the "Situation Room" at the Pentagon or the White House. Within hours there would be a beehive of activity in the room. Weissman's voice came over the receiver.

"Special Agent Mattox, is that you?"

"Yes, this is Mattox. Is this Weissman?

"Yes, it is. Listen. My office is located in the Firemen's Insurance Building over at Seventh and G Streets, not far from you. This afternoon, minutes after the assassination, I was trying to get into my building when I ran into a man who looked a great deal like your composite."

"What time was that, Mr. Weissman?" Mattox was writing down a note on another legal pad.

"Couldn't have been much more than three or four minutes after the explosion. I was in a hurry to file a story, so I can't say I was paying too much attention to the people around the place, except I bumped into this guy, and, well, I think he dropped a wallet." Weissman hesitated.

"Go on, Weissman," Mattox was listening more intently.

"Well, I stuck the wallet in my pocket, thinking the guy might come back for it later. I just opened it a few minutes ago, and the name and photo ID on the inside don't match the man I hit downstairs."

"So maybe the guy is a thief?" Mattox was beginning to dismiss the call.

"No, sir. The identification card inside is of a CIA agent."

Again Mattox's attention became riveted on the call. "Who is the agent?"

"I'd rather not say, Mr. Mattox, at least not over the phone. This particular agent is a former boyfriend of someone very close to me, and I need to talk to her first."

"Don't play games with me, Weissman. We're talking about the assassination of the President of the United States and half a dozen of the nation's top leaders. Now, what the hell is the agent's name?" Mattox's irritation was more pronounced by the pressure of the situation. Normally, he could have been more under-standing and coaxing in his approach.

Weissman was not intimidated by the agent's anger. "No way, Mattox. I have to talk to my friend, first. Tell you what, however; you meet me in one hour at my apartment building, and I'll give you the wallet. No one else, Mr. Mattox. Just you. I will not deal with anybody else. I live at the old Best Western Center City Hotel at Thirteenth and M Streets. See you in one hour." A quick click indicated to Mattox that Weissman had slammed down the phone.

"Shit! Why me, Martin? Why me?" It was a rhetorical question, and the CIA agent had no idea what was needling the special agent.

*****

Weissman looked down at the open wallet on his desk. His brain was amesh with conflicting thoughts. He pulled the ID, the telephone number and playing card out of the wallet and walked over to the Cannon copier next to the side wall and placed the items on the glass plate. He ran one copy. He then returned to his desk and replaced the card and ID in the wallet. He opened his desk and pulled out a large 11 x 13-inch manilla mailing envelope and sealed the copy paper inside. He failed to notice that the Post-it was sticking to the back side of one sheet of the copy paper. The reporter printed Bert Mattox's name on the cover. He then walked over to his secretary and laid the envelope on her desk.

"Listen, Rosie. I want you to keep this for me. Now don't think anything is wrong, but if anything should happen to me, I want you to be sure that Bert Mattox over at the FBI gets this information. You got that?"

Rosie looked up with a puzzled expression. She enjoyed her rapport with Weissman. They often could joke about their sex lives, and each enjoyed trying to top the other with raw sex oriented jokes. They could be serious when it came to business, but she had never known him to act in such a cloak and dagger manner before. She hesitated and looked down at the envelope and then back up at Weissman. "I'll take care of it." She hesitated again. "Are you all right, Isaac?" There was real concern in her face.

Weissman turned to cross the room and grab his suit coat. "Yeah, yeah, I'm fine. Don't make more out of this than there is. I'll probably ask for that envelope back tomorrow. Don't worry." He reached down and picked up the wallet and placed it in his jacket pocket and then started for the door. As he turned the door knob, he turned to Rosie. "Tell Maggy if she calls that I'm on my way over to see her and for her to stay put. I'll explain when I get there."

Rosie waved her hand. "You got it, Isaac. I can't believe on the biggest news day of the century, you're going to go get laid." The secretary mocked seriousness and shook her head. Weissman did not respond with his normal laugh. He closed the door and walked straight for the elevator. Three other people were waiting for the doors to open. The eye peeping through the stairwell door took note of the crowd, and the door quietly closed. He would find the Jew outside.

Chapter 5

Washington, D.C.
5:30 P.M.

The elevator doors opened on the first floor, and the half dozen occupants lightly jostled one another in getting out. Weissman walked directly to a bank of telephones in the lobby, only a few feet from the stairwell. He had not wanted to talk to Maggy in front of Rosie. He fumbled for a quarter in his pocket and then dialed his girlfriend's number at the travel agency. This time the line was open. After just two rings the soft voice of Maggy Mosele answered. "Capitol Travel. Maggy speaking. May I help you?"

The sweet, low-pitched voice of Maggy Mosele, laced with a sexy Southern drawl, was reassuring to Weissman. "Maggy, listen up. I'm on my way over to see you right now. Something has come up."

"Are you telling me, Isaac! Isn't it terrible about the President and the others? The boss thought about closing, but figured there's going to be a lot of calls from out of town agencies seeking connections with hotels in Washington. Whenever the funerals are held, this town will be packed."

"Maggy, I'm short on time. Let me ask you. Have you seen Manchester lately?" There was a long pause on the other end of the line. "Maggy, are you still there?"

"Well, yes. He dropped by a couple of days ago to pick up a ticket to Orlando. Said he was going to take a vacation. I knew better, Isaac. He had a return flight for last night. But one thing I learned in dating a spook, you don't ask too many questions."

Weissman was more puzzled. Manchester was due back the previous night. Why did his secretary say he wouldn't be back until tomorrow? He had more questions but was feeling uneasy talking in the lobby. "Maggy, you stay put. I should be there in about ten minutes." He hung up before she could reply.

The stairwell door, which had been opened a tiny crack, closed. Abdul had heard enough. The Jew had identified Manchester. He needed to retrieve the wallet and eliminate the Jew. He also knew now that someone named Maggy knew Manchester. She would have to be eliminated, also. He took off his overalls and threw them down the stairwell to the basement. He hurriedly put on his windbreaker and opened the door again. The Jew was already at the entrance. He could not let Weissman get into a taxi alone. He pushed open the glass door and followed Weissman. The journalist was standing at the edge of the curb waiting for a cab to come near enough to signal. Abdul approached him quietly from the back. Looking both ways, he noticed that the sidewalk was nearly barren of pedestrians.

The assassin had already removed the knife he kept strapped to a leg holster beneath his trousers. Now concealed in his jacket sleeve, he allowed the knife to fall forward into his palm, a skilled action learned from repeated practice. He pressed up against Weissman as the journalist raised his arm to signal a taxi.

"Go ahead, Jew. Get the taxi, but we're both taking a ride." Weissman flinched from the pressure of the knife point against his back. He knew resistance would be fatal. If this was the infamous Abdul, his skills in killing far outdistanced Weissman's knowledge of self-defense. He continued to wave at the taxi turning the corner. The black African cabby pulled up in front of the two men.

"Tell him to take us to your home." Abdul pushed the knife slightly forward for emphasis. Weissman dutifully obeyed. The two men climbed into the back seat, and Weissman gave the cabby the address of his apartment.

*****

Thirty minutes later Weissman lay naked in his living room, sprawled out in his blood-drenched velour recliner. His face was a mash of bloody pulp. Abdul's torture methods were excruciatingly brutal and always effective. The razor sharp knife had performed its work well along sensitive areas of the face and genitals. The head of the Jew's penis and one of his testicles lay on the table next to the chair, where Abdul had made Weissman look at them. Only the white bathroom towel stuffed deep into Weissman's mouth had prevented his screams from being heard outside the walls of the former hotel suite.

Weissman had tried to be brave. He had ignored his tormentor's questions and had spit in his face, but no man could withstand the kind of professional skill a demon like Abdul had perfected. In the end, he had identified Maggy and explained her prior relationship with Manchester. He could not explain why the telephone number was not in the wallet, and that had infuriated the assassin. The deep cuts expanding Weissman's mouth from one molar to the opposite was the price he had paid for not having provided the answer to the assassin's question.

The Israeli journalist was unconscious now. He would die from loss of blood and trauma within minutes. The assassin had gone into the bathroom to clean himself. He had carefully stripped to his own shorts to avoid splashing blood on his only set of clothes. However, as his mind churned, he realized that it was imperative that he alter his appearance. He had seen the FBI composites on Weissman's television, which he had turned on to cover the muffled screams of the Jew.

He looked in the bathroom mirror and mentally tried to compare the reflection with the sketches he had seen. All of them had depicted a man with a full head of hair. He jerked out each of the drawers of the bathroom vanity and finally found a pair of scissors. He began cutting out large sections of his hair, letting them fall into the sink. Then he covered his head with shaving cream. Within minutes Abdul had shaved his head clean. He also shaved the mustache. He remembered that one of the constants of the composites had been the eyes. He needed to hide his eyes. Glasses? Sun glasses would not do. It was too near evening. He needed tinted lenses, just enough to keep any passerby from focusing on his eyes. He would have to find a pair at an optical shop.

Who had Weissman told about the assassin? Had he described him to anybody? If so, he would also need to change his clothes. He walked into Weissman's small bedroom. The closet was on the far wall. Inside he selected a pair of charcoal colored wool slacks. They felt snug around the waist, but the length was nearly perfect. Several shirts in a clear plastic bag were hanging to the left. He ripped open the bag and picked out a light blue oxford cloth. He then tried on a black blazer. The jacket felt tight, but so long as he didn't button the jacket, it would be fine. He would keep his own boots. Comfortable foot apparel was absolutely necessary when moving rapidly. His experience had taught him the value of his feet.

He returned to the bathroom to observe himself in the mirror. The glasses would be the crowning touch. Satisfied that he no longer closely resembled the television sketches, he grabbed his own clothes and scooped them into a large wad and tucked them under his arm. He would dispose of them someplace else. He took another towel and wiped at the places he remembered he had touched. He had been careful about what he had handled, conscious of the fact that the American authorities might take prints once the body was found.

Finally, he leaned over and lifted one of Weissman's eyelids. The pupil was dilated. He felt under the nose for breath. The Jew was dead. No loss. Now he had to find the Jew's whore. He remembered the secretary in Weissman's office. A quick glance at his watch told him it was nearly 6:15. Surely the girl would have left the office by now, but just in case he would try calling her. He found the Washington directory resting under the beige phone on the small wood desk in the living room. He remembered the name of the newspaper etched on the brass plate by the office. He found the number and dialed. After five rings he was about to hang up when a female voice finally answered.

"Excuse me, Miss, but I am trying to locate Mr. Isaac Weissman." He had learned the Jew's name from the credit cards in Weissman's own wallet.

"Well, sir, Mr. Weissman is out right now, but I expect to hear from him later. Our office is open until 10:00 this evening. Could I take your name and number? I'll have him call you as soon as he returns." Rosie spoke in her most professional, but relaxed voice.

"Thank you, Miss, but I'm calling from Kennedy Airport in New York. I had Isaac's number from Maggy. My plane leaves in just a few minutes for Tel Aviv. I do need to talk to Isaac before I leave. I won't be near a telephone for about another six hours." Abdul was playing it by ear. All he needed was a number or an address for the whore.

Rosie pondered the inquiry. "May I ask who's calling, please?"

"My name is Jacobson. I know Isaac through Maggy. I work for the government, and Isaac asked me to get some information for him. It's pretty sensitive, and I thought, in light of today's events, he might want it before I leave."

The name Jacobson did not ring a bell, but Isaac knew many people in the government whom she did not know. "Well, Mr. Jacobson, you might try Isaac at Maggy's office. I believe that was where he was going when he left here nearly an hour ago."

"Thank you, Ma'am, but I don't have my address book with me. I packed it in one of my bags. I only have Isaac's number because I wrote it down on a napkin earlier today when he called. Do you have her number, please?"

Rosie hesitated, but quickly decided that if this Jacobson was for real, Isaac might not forgive her if he had some really good information that could go in before the 10:00 deadline. "Just a minute, Mr. Jacobson." Rosie put the caller on hold, then crossed over to Weissman's desk and found Maggy's office number in her boss's Rolodex. She picked up his receiver. "Mr. Jacobson, the number is 555-5332, and that's also in the 202 area code."

"Thank you, Ma'am. I very much appreciate your help." Abdul depressed the phone's switch, then dialed the number the secretary had just given him. The phone rang twice.

Maggy Mosele answered. "Capitol Travel. This is Maggy. May I help you?"

"Yes, how late are you open tonight?"

"We normally close at 6:00, sir, but we'll probably be open for another hour or so tonight. Did you need reservations, sir?"

"Possibly. I need to check with my wife first. We're in a downtown hotel. Could you tell me where you're located? Possibly we can drop by."

"Sir, we're located in the lobby of the Capitol Hilton on Fifteenth Street."

"Thank you so much. We may see you shortly." He replaced the receiver.

No sooner had he returned to the bathroom to clean up the sink, than the phone rang. Abdul, startled by the ring, walked back and stared at the phone across the room. Perhaps it was the secretary. Perhaps it was Maggy. What if the whore was leaving the office? He decided to take a chance. He lifted the receiver and murmured an unrecognizable grunt, as if he were sleepy.

"Mr. Weissman, there is a Special Agent Mattox down here in the lobby. He says you were expecting him." The voice of the young desk attendant waited for a reply, but none came. The assassin slammed down the receiver and fled the apartment. At the end of the hallway, next to the elevator, he found the door leading to the stairwell and stepped inside. He listened carefully for steps from below, but there were none. Mattox, or whoever was downstairs, probably would take the elevator. He slowly descended the steps, listening carefully for a door below to open. Weissman's apartment was located on the eighth floor. The descent took several minutes, and on each landing Abdul stopped to listen carefully. On the ground floor he took a deep breath and walked out into the small foyer. No one would know from what floor he had come. He glanced around the lobby. He saw a thin-haired man of medium height, arguing with the young black man behind the counter to his right.

"Goddamnit, kid, did you read that ID? I'm with the FBI. Now you get a key, and we're going up there."

Abdul stepped toward the glass doors located not more than fifteen feet from the elevators and stairwell. The sooner he left, the better. As he let the glass door close behind him, he turned to see Mattox and the clerk entering one of the elevators. Nothing was going right on this assignment. Time for him to take out the Jew's bitch and get out of the city. He turned south on Thirteenth Street. He knew the Capitol Hilton was within walking distance.

*****

After repeated knocks with no response, Mattox ordered the young clerk to unlock the door. The man fumbled through his key ring before finding the master key he needed. He opened the door and stepped inside. Staring across the living room, he could see Weissman's mutilated body sprawled out in the chair facing the front door. "Oh, my god!" he screamed. His stomach muscles tightened instantly. Using both hands to cover his mouth, he ran for the bathroom, the vomit already springing up from his stomach, preventing him from uttering any other sound.

Mattox, who was only two steps behind the clerk, squinted. His stomach muscles also tightened, but the veteran agent had seen too much horror in his twenty years to throw up. The nude body was drenched in blood. The eyes were both closed. Mattox reached down to feel for a pulse, but there was none. The dead man's face did not look familiar. His thick black beard was soaked with dark red blood, little of it dried. Much of the man's skin had a gray coloration, undoubtedly due to the massive loss of blood. A glance between the man's legs forced Mattox to turn his head in revulsion. This had been a most senseless and cruel torture. Was this Weissman?

He listened to the clerk retch in the toilet. He needed an identification quickly. Darting into the bathroom, he grabbed the clerk by the back of his shirt collar and shoved him into the living room. He knew the man was traumatized, and he hoped the rough treatment might help bring him back to some degree of coherence. "Look at this man, kid. Is this Weissman?"

The young man began retching again, this time unable to cough up any more from his empty stomach. He nodded in the affirmative as he fell to his knees in agony. Mattox let go of the young man's collar and looked around for a phone before spotting one on the desk. He took out his handkerchief and lifted the receiver, then called his basement command center. Martin answered.

"Listen, Martin, this guy Weissman, who was supposed to have a lead on Abdul—I've found him. He's been butchered. There can't be any coincidence. Abdul must be our man. Weissman's body is still warm, and the blood hasn't begun caking, yet. My guess is our man is still somewhere in the downtown area. Be sure you keep the area sealed. Concentrate around the Center City area. I'm going to look around some more for the evidence Weissman said he had for me. He said something about the CIA. I'll keep you informed. In the meantime, have Sparks send a team over here to check out Weissman's room. I want everything dusted for prints, the whole shabang. I'll call back in a few minutes." He replaced the receiver gently. The clerk was still retching on the floor, bent over in a fetal position.

Mattox reached down and began pulling the distraught clerk to his feet, reciting words of comfort as if he were a priest. "That's okay. Let it out. It isn't pretty, kid. I want you to get ahold of yourself and go downstairs and call the D.C. police. Tell them we have a homicide here; that the FBI is on the scene, but that they had better come. Go on, now." He gently nudged the man toward the door. Once in the hallway, the young man straightened his back partially and sprinted to the elevator.

Mattox returned to the small apartment. It took him about five minutes to search the bedroom, the bath, and the living room. In the bath, which reeked from the clerk's vomit, he found batches of black hair in the sink. Abdul had left in a hurry, or he would not have been so careless to leave the hair where it was visible. There was no brown wallet to be found, only Weissman's own black wallet lying on the floor. The half dozen credit cards he owned were spread on the floor as if they had been dropped together. The journalist's press credentials listed his office address in the Firemen's Insurance Building on Seventh Street.

Mattox stared at the wallet. What was it that Weissman had said he was going to do? He was going to talk to a girl first. That was it. Who was the girl? Surely, she could not have done this to him. This was a professional job. Someone very strong had worked on Weissman. Neither his feet nor his hands were bound. No woman could have inflicted this. Still, the girl must be the key. She supposedly knew the CIA agent. Who was the girl? He walked around the room. There were no pictures, no letters, nothing indicating a girl. He needed to find her. If she wasn't involved, then her life was in danger now. Abdul was trying to get information out of Weissman. The girl had to be the key. Where would he start to find her? If there was nothing here, then perhaps Weissman's office held the key.

He picked up the phone and called Martin, again. "Listen, Martin, I want you to meet me in five minutes at Weissman's office. It's located in the Firemen's Insurance Building on Seventh Street, within sight of the Archives Building."

"Yes, sir, right away."

Mattox started to hang up when he remembered. "Oh, Martin, pass the word. Our Arab killer has gotten a haircut. My guess is that he's bald." Then he hung up, turned, and walked out the door, closing it neatly behind him.

*****

On L Street a black panhandler with one leg missing, sporting a beard stubble and wearing a cheap green flannel shirt and dirt-stained bluejeans, approached the assassin. "How 'bout a dolla', Mista? How 'bout a dolla' for some food?" Abdul started to shove the panhandler aside, when the man's eye patch caught his eye.

"How would you like fifty dollars?" Abdul smiled at the wino.

"Hey, man, I ain't no pervert. All I need is a buck, just a lousy buck." The panhandler started to back up, using a beat-up hospital-issue wood crutch to assist him.

The clean-shaven Arab slowly followed after him, reaching into his pocket and pulling out one of Manchester's $50 bills. He began waving it. "Relax. All I want is your eye patch. That's all I need. Fifty dollars for your eye patch."

The drunk stopped his retreat. "That's all you want—this fuckin' eye patch?" He ripped it off his head, exposing what appeared to be an excellent second brown eye. "You got it, man." He handed the patch to Abdul, who took it, then thrust the fifty dollar bill into the shaky hand of the bearded indigent. The man squashed the bill in his palm and turned and began walking at break neck speed for a man with one leg. He was headed for the tavern on the corner.

Abdul placed the foul smelling patch over his head and eye. He found a nearby store window to view his reflection. He looked too much like the old Jew warrior—Dayan. But at least he didn't resemble in any way the old Abdul, whose sketch was becoming memorized by people all over the world.

The front entrance to the Capitol Hilton was located around the corner of the next block. He picked up his pace as he spotted the Trader Vic's sign on the lower corner of the building. He stepped briskly around to the main entrance and into the lobby.

Scanning the interior, he tried to adjust to one good eye. Several store fronts were located to the right. He turned and casually walked toward them. The second window advertised Capitol Travel Agency. Through the glass front he could see one woman behind a desk, two men sitting at other desks, and a middle-aged couple examining brochures. He would wait. Too many people in the lobby and in the agency to move now. The girl had to be Maggy. He passed on by to the small drugstore in the corner of the large lobby and purchased a newspaper. As he returned past the travel agency, he noticed the girl was talking to the young couple, pointing to one of the brochures. He returned to the lobby where he found a comfortable oversized chair and sat down. He would pretend to read the paper as he watched for the girl to leave.

Chapter 6

Martin was waiting for Mattox in the lobby as the special agent pulled his car up in front of the main entrance to the Firemen's Insurance Building. He ignored the *No Parking* signs and rushed inside.

"Have you located his office, Martin?"

"Yes, sir. It's on the third floor."

Martin pushed the elevator button, and the doors opened immediately. The building was nearly vacant. Only the security guard at the desk in the lobby paid any attention to the two lawmen.

After leaving the elevator on the third floor, both men saw the light coming from an office halfway down the hall. They assumed it was Weissman's. The men approached slowly, Mattox with his revolver drawn and raised above his head. Martin passed the office door and then threw himself against the wall next to the narrow window adjoining the door. Carefully, he peered inside. A middle-aged, red-haired woman was applying lipstick at her desk to the left. He signaled Mattox with one finger and visibly relaxed. Mattox lowered his weapon to his side. He then reached for the handle of the door and shoved it open. The woman jumped, smudging her lipstick past her mouth onto her cheek.

"What in the world?" She dropped her compact on her desk at the sight of Special Agent Mattox's gun and raised her arms as if in surrender.

Both men hurriedly searched the large room. Martin checked a closet door to the right, behind an empty desk. He signaled Mattox that it was clear.

Rosie recovered her composure quickly. "And who in the hell are you two to be busting in here like the Gestapo?" She had dropped her arms, but Mattox could tell she was one angry woman.

"I apologize, Miss . . .?"

"Who wants to know?" the defiant secretary answered.

Mattox pulled out his identification as he introduced himself. "My name is Mattox, Bert Mattox. This is John Martin, one of my colleagues. As I was saying, I apologize for our rather brusque entrance."

Rosie was only slightly mollified. "Well, did you ever hear of knocking?" Mattox's name rang a bell. Isaac had written his name on the envelope in her desk, but he said to give it to Mattox only if something happened to him.

Mattox gave another try. "Again, I'm sorry. You still didn't give me your name."

"Rosie. Just call me Rosie. What can I do for you gentlemen?" She folded her hands on the desk in an over exaggerated fashion.

Mattox got right to the point. "This is Isaac Weissman's office, is it not?"

"Yes, it is, but he's not here, as you undoubtedly know. He left about an hour ago."

"Rosie, I have some very bad news for you." Mattox dropped his tone. "I'm afraid Mr. Weissman is dead."

Rosie's face turned pale. Her eyes began to moisten, but she steeled herself from crying.

"Dead. Are you sure it was Isaac?"

"Yes, Rosie, we are. I just found him in his apartment on M Street. He had been brutally tortured and then killed." There was no way to lessen the blow. Mattox had to move fast.

Rosie lowered her head as she struggled to maintain her composure. "Oh, my god. I was afraid something was wrong.

When he left, he wasn't himself." She then remembered the envelope. She reached inside her top drawer and pulled it out. "I suspect you are the Mattox this was intended for. Isaac gave it to me before he left and told me to see that you got it if anything happened to him." She handed the envelope over, then reached for a tissue in her purse.

Mattox examined the cover. His name was spelled out in capital letters. He reached down on the secretary's desk and picked up a plastic letter opener and neatly sliced open the end of the envelope, then returned the opener to the exact place he had found it. Inside was a single white page. He pulled it out to examine. He immediately recognized the CIA identification, but not the face. "Martin, come over here. Do you know this guy?" He showed the young agent the copy paper.

"Manchester? Yeah, I've heard of him. He supposedly operates on the covert side of the shop, but it seems to me someone said he had been called back last year. I believe he's got an office on the third floor out at Langley, at least I think I saw his name in our directory."

"You know anything else, like why some maniac like Abdul would have his ID?"

"No, sir, I don't. Like I said, Manchester is known for the spook stuff. I've never heard many people talk about him. I do know he is highly respected by the brass."

Mattox looked back at the paper. "I assume Weissman made a copy of the contents of the wallet. There isn't much here." He looked at the now lightly sobbing secretary. "I'm sorry, Rosie, but I'm afraid I have to ask you some questions. Are you up to it?"

The secretary waved at the special agent indicating she was fine. "I know. I know. What do you need?"

"Did you see the wallet that Mr. Weissman had?"

"No, sir, I didn't. I noticed that he was working on something over at his desk. He was pretty agitated, as I think back; I saw him make that copy which you have, but that's all."

"Do you know anything about this card—the ace of spades—or this telephone number?"

"No, sir. I didn't see any of that stuff." Just then she noticed the yellow Post-it stuck to the back of the paper the special agent was holding. "Excuse me, Mr. Mattox, but there is something on the back of that paper."

Mattox turned the paper over and peeled off the small note. He matched it with the copy on the front side. They were the same. Weissman had not returned the number to the wallet. If Abdul now had his wallet, which Mattox was betting on, the assassin would surely miss that phone number.

"Look, Rosie. Weissman called me a little over an hour ago and told me he had seen the man we believe killed the President today. He also said there was a connection between this Abdul and a CIA man. Well, apparently, we now know the CIA agent. His name was Manchester. Did he mention that name to you?"

"No, sir, he did not."

"Weissman wouldn't tell me over the phone who it was. He said he had to talk to a girl first. Said that she knew this agent. Did he say anything about that?"

"No, sir," the secretary paused as she reflected, "but he did tell me that if Maggy—that's who he was probably talking about, Maggy Mosele—if Maggy called, to tell her that he was on his way over to her office and that she should not leave."

Mattox pondered the information. Had Weissman seen this girl before Abdul butchered him? Was the girl a key? What was her connection to Manchester?

"Rosie, do you have this girl's telephone number?"

"No, but it should be in Isaac's Rolodex over on his desk." She pointed to the desk opposite hers on the other side of the office.

Mattox and Martin darted for the desk and began thumbing through the index. They found *Mosele, Margaret*, with two numbers listed. Mattox recognized the downtown Washington exchange and decided to try it first. He dialed the number, but it was busy. That meant someone was still there. The girl was now the link. He had to talk to her as quickly as possible. He tore Mosele's card from the Rolodex, put it in his pocket, and moved toward the door. As a second thought, he turned around to the secretary who was now staring aimlessly at her desk.

"Rosie, are you going to be all right?" Both the tone of his voice and his manner expressed compassion.

"Yeah, I'm okay. You just find the bastard who killed Isaac."

Mattox glanced at his watch. It was 6:55. With a parting smile of understanding at the grieving secretary, he softly swore, "That's a promise, Rosie." Then he opened the door, and he and Martin were gone.

*****

Maggy Mosele was worried. Isaac was due well over an hour ago. Where could he be? And what was all this stuff about Manchester? Her affair with the CIA agent had lasted nearly three years, off and on, depending on when he was in town and not racing around the world on some assignment. But that had been over for nearly a year. She saw Manchester on occasion. He still purchased most of his commercial airline tickets through her agency. They had developed a friendship in recent months that seemed to transcend the active sex life they had enjoyed for so long. He seemed always to be concerned about her welfare, even had Weissman checked out after Maggy had mentioned him several times. At first she had resented his interference, but later realized her old lover was merely looking out for her best interests. Anyway, Bill had never seemed to be lonely. He always had a relationship going with an attractive companion somewhere. She had suspected that even during their time together there had been other women, probably spread from Jerusalem to Melbourne.

It was nearly 7:00. Her manager, a small, diminutive man in his mid-fifties who found time to travel a great deal on the freebies provided by the airlines and resorts, had left two hours earlier. He had been visibly shaken by the news of the assassinations. One of the senators from New York, McConkle, had been a steady customer of the agency, and the manager seemed quite shaken over the news of his death. He had left instructions for her, Ted, and Jake, two of the other agents, to stay open to at least 7:00. The phone had rung continuously, mostly inquiries from out-of-town agencies that Capitol Travel used often when planning clients' trips.

Ted and Jake were already clearing off their desks and shutting down their computer terminals. Ted noticed Maggy's worried expression and walked over to her desk. He was only twenty-eight, and Maggie was in her mid-thirties, but the young agent had adopted the role of the little brother over the past eighteen months they had worked together. Isaac had liked Ted, mainly because he had the best Yiddish accent for telling jokes he had ever heard. Tonight, however, with the assassinations and the late hours, he was all seriousness.

"Maggy, is something wrong?" He was hovering in front of her desk. She looked at her watch again. "It's only that Isaac called a little after five and said he was going to come right over." She turned to look out the plate glass front of the agency. There were several people, probably hotel guests, mingling and talking. "I suppose he might have gotten derailed on covering the assassination. You know he has a 10:00 deadline?"

"That's probably it, Kitten. Hell, this is probably the biggest news day this town has ever witnessed, and that includes the Kennedy killing. How about letting me give you a ride home? The Metro is down, according to the TV, and I imagine most of the cabs are taken, also."

She looked at her watch again, then outside in the lobby. "Okay, Ted. I'd appreciate the company and the lift. Where's your car?"

"It's over at the garage on K Street. Why don't I go get it while you lock up. I'll pick you up at the south entrance." Ted was smiling, trying to act cheerful for the sake of his adopted big sister.

"You got a deal. You go ahead. I'll meet you in five minutes. I'll be on the curb."

"Great. See you in five." With that Ted turned on his heel and left by way of the glass door leading to the hotel lobby. Jake was close behind, waving to Maggy as he left.

Maggy began cleaning off her desk, piling the reservation requests and itineraries in two different piles. A travel agent's desk was always a mess. The paperwork was sometimes unbearable. She reached behind her desk to grab her purse which she kept in the bottom drawer of a file cabinet next to the wall. When she turned back around, she nearly jumped out of her seat from fright.

A dark-skinned, bald man with an eye patch and wearing a black blazer was standing erect in front of her desk. She had not heard him enter the agency.

"Excuse me, Miss. I must have startled you. I apologize. I hope you haven't closed yet. I need to confirm some reservations I have to Mexico City. Would it be an inconvenience to check them for me?" The man smiled pleasantly though the one good eye seemed to penetrate her soul. There was something strange about the man's appearance, something that looked familiar.

"Well, sir, we are closed, but I guess I could check your reservations. Why don't you have a seat, and I'll turn on my terminal. It will take just a minute to come up." She leaned over her terminal which sat on an arm of her desk and flipped a switch at the back . The man pulled up a chair and sat, though he never took his eye off the girl. Just as she was about to ask the man's name, the phone rang. Her immediate thought was that it might be Isaac. She reached over to the edge of her desk and hurriedly grasped the receiver. Unlike her normal rehearsed routine she blurted out, "Hello, hello!"

"Maggy, is that you?" It was Rosie, Isaac's secretary, on the line.

"Yes, Rosie, it's me. Have you seen Isaac? He was due here nearly two hours ago. I was beginning to get worried." Maggy stared at her guest as she talked, though her mind was elsewhere. She didn't notice the man place his hand inside his coat pocket.

"Listen, Maggy, I'm afraid Isaac isn't going to make it." There was a long pause on the line as Rosie chose her words carefully. "We think Isaac had a lead on the man the FBI believes killed the President. He's very dangerous, Maggy. The FBI just left here to talk to you at the agency. I was hoping to catch you in time before you got away."

Maggy's eyes narrowed as Rosie was talking. She was facing the man not more than a few feet away. She focused on his coat lapel. A small round gold pin, about the size of a dime, commemorating the 175th anniversary of Thomas Jefferson's founding of the University of Virginia, her alma mater, glistened in the fluorescent light. It was exactly like the pin she had given Isaac as a momento two weeks earlier. The pin had been a gift from her father, and Isaac had liked it, so she had pinned it on his coat following a quiet dinner at their favorite Jewish deli. She had not seen any others in Washington. The dark man's wool blazer also had the top button missing, as did Isaac's. She repressed an instinct to scream, realizing how dangerous that might be. As fear gradually gripped her, she fought to remain calm.

"Thank you, Rosie. I'll look out for them. Goodbye." She hung up the phone without allowing Rosie to continue. She could hear Rosie's voice pleading "Maggy, Maggy," as she replaced the receiver. She turned to face her computer screen.

"Excuse me, sir, I'll have to get a form from my colleague's desk. She rose quickly and walked around her desk, past the assassin. The man watched her every step. She reached down on Ted's desk and picked up a completed itinerary of another client, then turned. The killer was ten feet away on her left; the door was less than that straight ahead. Her instincts won over her logic. She ran for the door, pushing it forward with both hands. The assassin was unable to stop her in time, but was fast upon her heels. She turned to her right, hoping Ted was in his car at the curb. She ran as fast as she could toward the south entrance to the lobby. Several people in the hall turned to stare at the fleeing woman and the bald man pursuing her. The man knocked an elderly couple to the lobby floor when he came charging out of the travel agency.

Maggy pushed at the big glass doors at the south end of the building. Ted had not arrived yet. She didn't know what to do. Her only thought was to shout, so she began screaming at the top of her voice. A dark blue Oldsmobile pulled up to the curb just in front of her. John Martin was on the passenger side and was the first to shove open his door next to the hysterical, screaming woman. "What's the matter, Miss? " He had his hand gently on the woman's elbow. She turned and pointed toward the hotel lobby doors.

"Help! Help! There's a killer in there." She kept pointing toward the hotel entrance.

Abdul had stopped just short of pushing the doors open when the girl started screaming, and the dark car pulled up to the curb. As the driver got out on the far side of the car, he recognized the face of the FBI pig whose news conference was played and replayed on the television set in Weissman's apartment. Mattox's eyes locked on the face of a bald man in the blazer behind the glass door. Abdul knew he had been recognized and was conscious of the dozen or so people in the lobby staring at him. He had to get away. He turned and began running toward the main lobby, taking a turn at the large grand staircase, and running up the carpeted steps two at a time. On the mezzanine he spotted an open elevator and ran for it as the doors were closing. A man in a dark blue business suit saw him coming and held the doors open.

"Thanks," the winded Abdul answered as he fought to gain his breath.

"No problem. You must be in quite a hurry?" asked the businessman.

"Been late all day." The doors closed.

Fortunately, the elevator was going up. The assassin stood back from the man to examine him. He was about six feet tall, in his mid-fifties or early sixties, and was wearing an expensive toupee. Only a trained eye would have noticed the fake hairpiece. Abdul looked down toward his shoes, then over to the man's hands. He was holding a folder with his hotel card latch. The envelope read Room 731. The man in the dark suit got out on the seventh floor. Abdul punched the eighth floor button. At the next stop he rushed out and down the hall toward the small sign marked *Stairs*, with an arrow pointing to the right. He quickly ran down to the floor below. He opened the door and looked at the two rooms across the hall—710 and 712. The businessman's room was to the right and on his side of the hall.

The businessman, a jeweler from New York, in town for a business meeting, heard a knock on his door. He squinted through the small peephole in the door and recognized the man he had just left on the elevator. He shrugged and opened the door only enough to see out. "May I help you?" he asked.

"Yes, sir, I believe you dropped something in the elevator." The man at the door held out his hand.

The inquisitive businessman opened the door nearly all of the way, his attention drawn to the empty palm of the stranger. In a second the man at the door closed his hand and then opened it again quickly. A six-inch blade shimmered in the light. The hand moved quickly toward the businessman's mid-section. The jeweler doubled over in pain. His loss of wind made screaming impossible. Abdul pushed him toward the inside of the room and quietly closed the door behind him.

*****

Downstairs in the Capitol Travel Agency, Mattox was talking on the telephone while Martin was consoling the shaken Maggy Mosele.

"That's right. I want this hotel sealed off immediately. No one gets in or out. Is that clear? I want every room, every closet, and every air vent checked from roof to basement before anybody leaves." He continued for another five minutes, giving instructions to the command center. He had already alerted the hotel security who were guarding all exits. He knew from talking to witnesses that Abdul had gone up the stairs and into an elevator. There was no way out. They had the assassin trapped.

After Mattox had finished, he walked over to Weissman's girlfriend and sat down in a chair opposite her. He nodded to Martin to move away, then placed his hands gently on the woman's knees. "Miss Mosele, I know you've been through a terrible ordeal, but it is very important that I ask you some questions."

The woman lifted her head to look at Mattox's face. His soft blue eyes expressed understanding and kindness. She needed comfort. She sniffled a couple of times, and the tears stopped. She was embarrassed at her show of hysteria. Maggy Mosele had prided herself on her self-control, ever since she had been a freshman in college in Charlottesville. She almost had been raped by a drunk senior at a fraternity party. Only a kick to the man's groin and her own quick reaction allowed her to escape the man's room. From that day forward, she promised herself never to be taken advantage of again and never to display any feminine outbursts. If she were to survive in the world of men, she would have to be as strong as the men with whom she was dealing.

"What about Isaac? Is he dead?" She already knew the answer. The coat and lapel pin had told her that the man who chased her through the lobby had been in Isaac's apartment. Rosie's cautious choice of words told her, also, that Isaac was gone.

"Yes. I'm afraid he is." Quickly Mattox added, "And I'm very sorry, but I'm sure you want to help us catch his killer as soon as possible."

Again, she stared into the agent's comforting eyes. "Yes. That's right. I do. What can I tell you?"

Mattox took his hands off the woman's knees and straightened himself in his chair. "For starters, we know there is a connection between this madman, Abdul, and a CIA agent named William Manchester."

Maggy looked stunned. She started to protest, but Mattox held up his hands.

"Let me finish. Isaac bumped into this Abdul as he was entering his office building following the explosion at the FDR Memorial. The man apparently dropped a wallet, which Isaac found. Sometime later Isaac began going through the wallet. In it he discovered an official CIA identification card for William J. Manchester. So we believe that Abdul had Manchester's wallet."

"But that doesn't make any sense. . .what did you say your name was?" She realized for the first time she did not know the names of the two men who had saved her.

"My name is Mattox, Bert Mattox; I'm with the Federal Bureau of Investigation. This is Agent John Martin from the CIA." He nodded toward Martin, who was sitting on top of Ted's desk, legs dangling to the side, listening to their conversation.

"Well, Mr. Mattox, that just doesn't make any sense. Bill wouldn't give away his wallet. That ID card was one of his most sacred possessions. He would never let that out of his sight." The realization that Manchester might also be dead rolled through her mind slowly. "Oh, my god! Do you think Bill is dead, too? Did that man kill Bill, too?" Maggy was on the edge of losing control again. Mattox reached over and squeezed her arms to calm her.

"Now settle down. We don't know that. We haven't been able to locate Manchester, but we understand from his office that he's out of town. As soon as he returns, we'll have an explanation."

"But he should be back by now. I booked his flight two days ago. He was due back last night." Mattox's gentle pressure on her arms was all that was keeping the young woman from falling apart.

"Take it easy, Maggy. That's what your friends call you, isn't it? Maggy?" Mattox continued to hold her arms. Maggy nodded affirmatively.

"You say Manchester was due back last night. Where had he gone?"

"Orlando. Said he was going on a vacation, but nobody goes to Orlando for just two days of vacation. But I didn't ask any questions. Bill doesn't like questions."

Mattox turned his head toward his CIA assistant. "John, call your people over at the Agency and find out if they know why Manchester was in Orlando. Also have them check his home to see if he's back."

Martin noted with some satisfaction that the special agent had used his first name for the first time.

Mattox turned back to the travel agent. "Now, Maggy, listen to me." He waited for the girl to look him in the eyes again, to be sure she was alert. "Isaac told me on the phone that he was going to talk to you about this before he gave me the wallet. Did he talk to you?"

"Yes, he called me and asked about Bill, but he said he would be right over and for me to wait. He never made it here." She began to wilt again, but Mattox continued to exert pressure on her arms.

"He talked to you, then. Did he mention a telephone number or anything else except Manchester?"

"No. That's it. We couldn't have talked for more than a minute or two. He said he'd be right over, and we'd talk about it then." She leaned backwards, struggling to regain her composure. Mattox released his hold.

"So Isaac never made it here. That means Abdul must have gotten to him between the time he left his office and before he got here. Since you don't have that wallet, and it isn't in Isaac's apartment, then Abdul must have it. But why is he after you? It could be he found out about you and Manchester. We don't know what his connection to Manchester is, yet. Or it could be the phone number. Maybe that's the key. Maybe he thinks you have the telephone number."

Maggy looked puzzled. "What phone number?"

"One that was in the wallet. Isaac intended to return it to the wallet, but it got stuck on the back of a photo copy he made of the contents, which he left for me at his office. If that was the original number, then it wasn't in the wallet that Abdul found."

"Abdul. Abdul. Who is Abdul? Doesn't he have a last name?" Maggy was more angry now than scared.

"Maggy, we're not even sure if Abdul is his name. We know hardly anything about him except he is probably the most thorough, cold-blooded and successful assassin in the world today." Mattox turned his head slowly toward the door. "And he's in this hotel this very minute, and I'm going to find the son-of-a-bitch."

Chapter 7

Abdul had just finished wiping up the small spot of blood from the carpet. Fortunately, most of the blood from the stomach wound had been absorbed in the businessman's clothing, which Abdul had since removed from the corpse and tossed into the corner of the small closet. He had accelerated the man's death by choking his windpipe with his strong right hand. He did not need a messy corpse.

The assassin reached under the nude businessman's arms and dragged him into the bathroom where he placed him on the toilet stool. The man was still limp. Abdul took the man's elbows and placed them on his naked knees, opened the palms of his hands and placed the face in the hands. Hopefully, he would stay in place until after the expectant room check. He returned to the closet where he found the jeweler's garment bag containing a navy blue, pin-striped suit, and three white shirts. He checked the collar—seventeen inches. That would do nicely. His own neck size was just a half inch smaller. He knew from looking at the man in the elevator that his coat and trouser size would work.

The assassin returned to the bathroom and removed the jeweler's hairpiece, which had been held in place by a small piece of adhesive tape under the dome of the toupee. Looking down, the dead man gave every appearance of being hung over and sick, rather than dead. The sides of his head disclosed the shadow of freshly shaved hair. Apparently the jeweler had preferred a full toupee to a partial hairpiece that would have blended into his own hair.

The assassin placed the hairpiece on his own barren scalp and gazed into the large wall mirror. With a little adjustment and combing, it would work. The eyes were still a problem. He returned to the bedroom where he made a visual search from one piece of furniture to another. Nothing. He then remembered the jeweler's suit coat which was lying neatly on one of the two double beds in the room. He picked up the coat and began patting the pockets. A sense of satisfaction passed over him as his hand felt the impression of a large pair of glasses in the inside pocket.

He pulled them out and laid the coat back on the bed. The black plastic frames contained oversized lenses and bifocals, which would be perfect for his needs. Abdul returned to the bathroom mirror and tried on the glasses. The dead man had been either farsighted or wore contact lenses, but he had needed considerable magnification for his reading. The blurry bottoms did not bother the assassin.

Satisfied with his facial change, he returned to the bedroom and stripped off Weissman's clothes. He reached in the closet and took out one of the heavily starched white shirts and the blue suit. The shirt and the suit fit well, if not perfectly. He gently placed his new suit coat on the back of the straight chair by the narrow walnut-veneer desk on the side wall. He would have to be convincing for the police when they arrived. It took him little time to prepare his scenario.

He glanced down at his right leg. The knife could not be detected beneath the new trousers. However, the blade was not going to be enough. He would need firepower once he left the hotel. Again, he began searching the room. Leaning down on all fours he felt under the bed nearest the wall. To his delight he discovered an attache case. He pulled the burgundy case toward him. The expensive leather case was locked tight. There were no combinations, only two key locks. He returned to the closet to retrieve the jeweler's trousers. There he found a set of keys in a small brown leather holder. He returned to the bed, sorting the keys as he walked. He first tried to insert the smallest of the keys into one of the locks, but to no avail. He then used the next smallest key. Each lock snapped open.

Inside were an assortment of documents, most appearing to be contracts. But more importantly, resting on top of the documents was a snubbed nose 38-caliber revolver. That was a start. All six chambers were loaded. Besides the documents and two felt tip pens nestled in the lid flap, the case was empty. However, something did not appear quite right. The compartment was not deep enough for the size of the case. His fingers followed along the edges of the interior until he felt an impression of a very small button, which he pushed. The bottom of the case sprang open, revealing two small cloth bags. He lifted out the dark purple pouches, then closed the lid to the case.

The two bags were both small and very light. He took them over to the desk and turned on the large ceramic lamp. Sitting down, he carefully opened one of the bags and emptied the contents onto the desktop. Nearly two dozen bright diamonds rolled out. The corners of Abdul's lips turned upward, which was as close as he ever came to a natural smile. Now he understood why the man carried the gun. He quickly opened the other bag and another two dozen gems rolled onto the desktop. He was no expert on the value of precious gems, but the contents on the desk had to be worth thousands of dollars. He would keep them as a bonus for all his additional trouble. He replaced the diamonds in the two bags and slipped them into the outside pocket of the suit coat hanging on the back of his chair.

More important now was planning his escape. How was he going to get out of the hotel and eliminate the girl? The FBI man, Mattox, was also a problem. He had seen Abdul and had recognized him. One or both had the telephone number and the girl knew about Manchester. He had to protect his client. That was part of his professional responsibility. He had already deduced that the client and Manchester knew each other and it would be far better if that association were never made known. On the other hand, the client might be helpful. He lay down on the bed next to the window and began reflecting on how this assignment had started.

A meeting had been held in Algiers with the courier, Lampworth. He had acted so confident, but Abdul had detected an amateur. The amateur could never have found him through the maze of contacts necessary, involving over six stops at clubs and bars in a forty-eight hour period. The effeminate Lampworth had made it through the maze, and that would have taken professional help. Initially, that thought had been worrisome for Abdul.

Lampworth's sealed pouch had carried his instructions and the money transfer. In reading the instructions, which had been produced by a laser printer, Abdul had made the connection. Not only was Lampworth, the courier, to be eliminated but so was a CIA operative named Manchester. Now he knew who had guided Lampworth. Manchester had been the agent who had tipped him off about the CIA sting operation aimed at capturing him. He had always wondered if the $100,000 he had paid Manchester had satisfied the agent.

The two had originally crossed paths a year earlier in Tunis at the time he had accepted a contract on the country's interior minister. Manchester was working his own operation with the minister at the time. Abdul had attached a bomb beneath the official's limo. He had waited deliberately until the minister had deposited Manchester at his hotel before detonating the explosive. Manchester knew his life had been spared and that a payback was expected.

The inclusion of Manchester's name in his present client's instructions had not been a problem for Abdul. He owed the American nothing. All debts between them had been paid, and, afterall, business was business. Removing him would eliminate one more dangerous operative who knew how to get to the infamous Abdul. He knew, too, that he would have to change the maze.

The instructions had included the date and place of the primary assignment, as well as the names and positions of the four major targets. He also was instructed not to remove Lampworth and Manchester until after April 5, one week before the main hit. Included in the packet of information accompanying the instructions was the address of the Lampworth family's Florida home and Manchester's office and home telephone numbers. Neither was to be killed in the Washington area. The lengthy instructions promised that Lampworth would be at the Florida site between April 6 and April 12. Catching him in the boat on the fog-draped lake had been an added bonus. However, trying to straddle two fishing boats while tying the man's legs to a twenty-pound can of cement used as Lampworth's boat anchor and then sending him to the bottom of the murky lake had taken strenuous effort. Lampworth's Starcraft had been returned to its slip, and no one in his trailer camp had appeared to notice that he had arrived or left.

Given his knowledge and experience, Manchester was going to be much more of a problem. Abdul had to first lure him to Florida. That would take enticing bait. After the work on Tarpon Lake in west Florida had been completed, he returned to his inexpensive motel room just off International Drive on the west side of Orlando. He waited two days, then called Manchester's office to leave a message with his secretary.

He had told the girl to tell Manchester that the man from Algiers had called to say he had met with an accident in Orlando and that his itinerary had to be altered. He could be reached at the Hilton Hotel in Buena Vista. Manchester should ask the desk clerk for messages in his own name. He indicated he would wait only forty-eight hours. Abdul knew that if Manchester were a part of the conspiracy, he would come to Orlando. If he were not, the agent's own curiosity also would attract him.

As expected, Manchester had flown to the central Florida tourist empire. At precisely 5:00 p.m., as per his instructions, Manchester had dialed the telephone number Abdul had left in his message at the Hilton desk. The number was to one of the bank of telephones located inside the entrance to the EPCOT Center west of Orlando. Both men had spoken cryptically, but Abdul had specified their meeting place for four hours later at one of the several lakes bordering the long entrance into the grounds of Disney World.

He had expected Manchester to be more cautious. The fact that the veteran agent appeared unduly casual about the meeting reinforced Abdul's belief that he was a part of the conspiracy. Manchester had not heard Abdul approach him from the covey of trees bordering the lake. At 9:00 the sky was pitch black with very little moonlight and only the distant vapor lights spread intermittently along the sides of the nearby road providing limited illumination. A quick karate chop to the base of Manchester's skull had rendered him unconscious. He had then dragged the CIA agent's body down to the lake and held his head under water for several minutes.

After feeling no pulse, he entered the shallow lake himself and guided the floating corpse about fifty feet to an area filled with tall reeds and water lilies. Hopefully, several days would pass before the body was discovered. Taking Manchester's wallet had been an afterthought, designed to slow down identification of the dead man. He had thrown the agent's credit cards into the lake. He should have thrown the entire wallet, but the large amount of cash and the telephone number were too enticing.

A knock on the hotel door startled him. Quickly, he placed the gun well under the mattress of his bed and walked over to the door, quietly closing the bathroom door in the process. He peered through the peephole. Two uniformed police officers were waiting. There was another knock. Abdul felt his toupee to reassure himself, then took the glasses from his shirt pocket and put them on before reaching for the latch. "I'm sorry, gentlemen. I was taking a nap. What can I do for you?" Abdul mimicked an effeminate dialect.

The older of the two officers spoke. "Sir, I don't want to alarm you, but we believe there is a very dangerous killer hiding somewhere in this building. We are making a room-to-room check. I'm afraid I'm going to have to ask you to allow us to check out your room."

Abdul stepped back. "Why, come on in. I don't think you'll find him here, however."

The officers started to enter the room when the older policeman saw the bathroom door closed. "Sir, I'll need to check the bathroom."

Abdul, who had planned this scene minutes earlier. "Well, officer, I just wish you wouldn't. What can I say? A friend, a very close friend, is visiting me, and he just doesn't feel well."

The two officers tried not to show their discomfort with the seemingly gay guest. Again, the older officer responded. "I'm sorry, sir, but we have our orders." He then knocked on the door. There was no response. He knocked again.

Abdul, continuing his charade, finally offered, "Officer, I don't believe he is going to answer you. He's very embarrassed. You'll have to open the door. Go ahead. The lock doesn't work."

The officer looked hard at the assassin, then at the door. After pausing momentarily he reached down to turn the handle and pushed the door open enough to insert his head. The sight of the older closet homo hiding his face nauseated the officer. He jerked the door shut. "We'll just check the rest of the room if you don't mind, SIR." The officer had overemphasized the word "sir" purposely to let Abdul know he did not approve. A quick walk-through, a check under the beds, and a peek in the closet were enough. Both officers were anxious to leave. "Sorry to have bothered you."

After the two officers left, Abdul pressed an eye against the peephole. The two men were shaking their heads as they moved down the hall to the next room where the older officer knocked on the door. Satisfied, Abdul returned to the bed. He had to get out of the hotel, and Chamberlain was his only key. He remembered the telephone number from when he had called from the airport earlier in the day. He did not like making contact, but he had few options left. He reached over to the phone on the small night stand separating the two beds and punched "9" for an outside line. He then remembered he had no credit card, and Virginia was long distance. He would have to go through the hotel switchboard. A pay phone would have been better, but he did not dare leave the room. Abdul knew using the switchboard was risky. Under normal circumstances he would never have done so, but he was trapped. No doubt the FBI would trace his call from the hotel's telephone records, and the man in Virginia would have a great deal of explaining to do. But if he could escape the hotel and the country, his job would be finished. Others could fend for themselves. He depressed the toggle switch on the phone and punched zero. After two rings the hotel operator answered. Abdul gave her the number he wanted.

The same polished voice he had heard earlier answered. "The Chamberlain residence. May I help you?"

"Yes, I would like to talk to Mr. Chamberlain, please."

"Who shall I say is calling, sir?"

"Tell him it is his friend from Algiers."

There was a wait of about three or four minutes when a different voice, but one accented with cultivated diction, answered. "This is John Chamberlain. Who is this, may I ask?"

"Listen, Mr. Chamberlain, you know who this is or you would never have taken the call. I would have preferred that we not have this conversation, but I've got a problem. Unless I eliminate a certain woman, you are about to be linked to William J. Manchester."

There was a long pause before Chamberlain answered. "Why would anyone think I know this Manchester fellow, anyway?"

"Look, Chamberlain, I don't have time to play games. I eliminated Manchester in Florida, as instructed. I took his wallet so he wouldn't be identified. For some reason his wallet had your telephone number in it. A few hours ago I lost the wallet in a crowd downtown. I found the man who had recovered it, but unfortunately he knew this Manchester, and so did his girlfriend. Now, if I am to protect you, I need to get rid of the girl and the FBI man who has stuck his nose into all of this."

Again, after a long pause, "I don't see how I can be of assistance to you." It was obvious that the capitalist barron was being as noncommittal as possible.

"I don't think you completely understand, Chamberlain. I can leave this town tonight and leave you to the mercy of the FBI. My guess is you would have an army of government agents all over your home by tomorrow morning. Now if you can help me tonight, I believe I can spare you that embarrassment."

"How can you do that?"

"I need for you or someone you trust to call the switchboard of the Capitol Hilton Hotel and leave a brief message. Indicate that your name is Abdul and that you have already escaped from the hotel. You want to make a deal with Mattox. You will give him the names of the people who hired him in return for a guarantee of safety. Tell them that you will meet Mattox and the girl named Maggy at the Vietnam Memorial in two hours. Tell him that you will know if there are any other police or FBI people around, and if you see any, the deal is off, and he and the girl are open targets. Tell him to stand on top, near the V of the memorial." The assassin had memorized the geography of nearly all downtown Washington as preparation for the assignment.

"Is there anything else?" Chamberlain was being both brief and cryptic.

"No, that's all. But don't talk to Mattox, personally. Give the message as quickly as possible and hang up. I would suggest you find a pay phone away from your house to make the call, but I need the call made in the next fifteen minutes."

"Yes, I see. Goodbye." Chamberlain had cut him off.

The assassin was angered by Chamberlain's abruptness, but on the other hand, the man was obviously intelligent and realized the less said on his part the better. He would give the capitalist pig twenty minutes. He would then take the elevator to the lobby. If the hotel exits were unguarded, he would know the message had been delivered. If not, Chamberlain would be next on his list.

*****

John Fairchild Chamberlain held down the toggle switch on top of his phone for nearly a minute while he contemplated what to do. He finally replaced the receiver and opened his center desk drawer to find his personal address and phone book. He checked for a number, then placed his call. After three rings, he recognized the answering voice.

"This is the eight of spades. We have a problem." Chamberlain repeated Abdul's story and instructions.

The voice on the other end of the line paused to digest what he had heard. "Leave it to me. In the meantime, you had better review our alternative plan in case you were contacted."

"I don't believe that's necessary. I have all our contingencies memorized. I feel confident I can derail any problems at this end. You just handle the man from Algiers."

"I will. He's given us two hours. This is almost too good to be true."

*****

A police officer knocked on the travel agency door. Mattox and Weissman's girlfriend were both examining the composites the bureau had prepared earlier; both looked up from her desk. The officer was holding the arm of Ted Sizemore, one of the travel agents.

Maggy smiled faintly. "It's okay, Mr. Mattox. That man works here. He's a friend of mine. I was to ride home with him." The sight of the confused looking friend was a comforting sight. As soon as Mattox signaled the officer to let the man enter, Maggy rushed over to his arms and hugged her bewildered colleague.

"What's with all the police and sealing off the hotel? I thought I would never get in. I hope they don't tow my car. I left it outside in front of the hotel entrance."

Maggy leaned back to look at the face of her young friend, then with reserved anger asked, "Where in the world were you, anyway? I thought you said you'd be at the south entrance in five minutes."

"I'm sorry, Maggie. I couldn't find my ticket at the garage. I finally had to pay $25.00 for the full 24 hours, since I couldn't produce the damn ticket. But what's going on?"

Maggy looked to the FBI agent for help. Mattox walked over to introduce himself. "Your friend, here, Miss Mosele, was almost killed by the same man who we believe killed the President and murdered Mr. Weissman earlier today."

The face of the young travel agent blanched, and his mouth dropped open. "Oh, my god!" He looked at Maggy, then at

Mattox. "He was here, here in the hotel?" He looked back at Maggy. "Are you all right? Did he hurt you?"

Maggy smiled softly. "I'm fine, thanks to Mr. Mattox and Mr. Martin over there." She pointed to Agent Martin who was talking quietly to the command center on a phone at the far desk.

Just then a second line rang. Mattox walked over and punched line two of the phone on Maggy's desk. "This is Special Agent Mattox."

After several seconds, Maggy and Ted could see the agent's face tighten. They sensed something was wrong.

"He said all that? You're sure you got the whole message?" Again there was a pause. "Are you sure the call originated from outside the hotel?"

Maggy crept slowly toward her desk. She was worried.

"Thank you, operator. I appreciate your efficiency. Would you connect me with Agent Sparks? He should be in the hotel manager's office. Thank you." Mattox cupped his hand over the receiver. "Abdul just called from outside the hotel. Shit!"

He removed his hand as soon as he heard Sparks' voice. "Listen, Sparks. We just received a call from outside the hotel. From the wording of the message, I'm sure it's our man. Call off the room search. Meet me back here in the travel agency as soon as you can." He slammed the phone down and stared pensively at Maggy Mosele, who was waiting for an explanation.

"Maggy, sit down, would you?" He offered her a chair, then took a seat facing her. "Maggy, I'm sure this call was authentic because he mentioned both you and me in his message."

Maggy's face tightened, and her eyes narrowed.

"He wants to meet the two of us in two hours. He says he has information on who hired him to kill the President and that he will trade that information for a guarantee of safety. He was specific, however. He wants to meet the two of us by the Vietnam Memorial in two hours."

Maggy sat expressionless. Mattox felt uneasy. He could not read what the young woman was thinking.

"Maggy, I can't order you to come with me. I can't even ask you. I'm just telling you what he said to the hotel operator."

Ted rushed over and put his arm around Maggy. "No way, Mr. Mattox. No way. She's been through enough. You can't risk the lives of private citizens like this. She has her rights, by god."

Maggy seemed to relax. Her lean body slowly wilted as tension from the last hour began finding a release. The tough resolve that she had developed in college was returning. She looked up at her young colleague. "Ted, Mr. Mattox already said he was not going to force me." Then, turning to face the special agent, she added "But I want to go. I want this beast captured, and I want him to pay. He will pay, won't he, Mr. Mattox?" She peered deep into Mattox's eyes for a positive response.

"Yes, he'll pay. We'll guarantee him safety, but not immunity. This nation would never allow a man who killed the President, the Vice-President, and half a dozen of the nation's other top leaders to plea bargain. He'll pay, all right."

"Then I'm going with you. I owe it to Isaac and to Bill."

Mattox looked intently at the beautiful woman sitting within inches of him. Now that she was composed, her eyes clear, her skin relaxed, he noticed the real face, a beautiful face—high cheekbones, a small straight nose, just the right amount of eye makeup, not enough to smear her face from tears swelling up in her eyes. Her dark brown hair was fastened in a bun on the back of her head—a businesswoman's professional look. He guessed that once undone, her hair would roll down below her shoulders. Her lips were large, but not oversized. They had only a trace of lipstick on them, and that a cross between peach and pink. She was, indeed, a striking woman.

"Maggy. . . may I call you Maggy?" He smiled pleasantly.

She liked his smile with the gleaming white teeth and the large dimple that set off his face. "I'd like that, Mr. Mattox."

"No, you don't. If I call you Maggy, you call me Bert. I'd like that."

"Okay, Bert. Do we have a deal?" She stuck our her hand. Ted looked down, shaking his head in disbelief.

Mattox paused, then took her hand. "We have a deal, Maggy." His expression turned serious. "But understand, this is risky and very serious business. You must do everything I tell you. I'll protect you, but you must follow my instructions. Agreed?"

They were still holding hands. "Agreed," she said.

Agent Sparks entered the office, along with two other men in suits. Mattox looked up at them. "Okay, men, we have work to do. Sparks, John," he pointed toward Martin who was still manning the open line to the command center and relaying the conversation he had overheard from Mattox and Mosele, "We need to think this out." The other agents remained silent. They had no idea what Mattox had in mind.

Chapter 8

The man from Algiers had no trouble leaving the hotel. By the time he had exited the elevator, the lobby was full of hotel guests anxious to talk to one another about the day's events and to find a restaurant that might still be open. He joined a group that was leaving through the main Fifteenth Street entrance. There were still D.C. police officers present, but they did not appear to be restricting pedestrian flow. Once out on the sidewalk, he had turned left toward Lafayette Park, located just north of the White House, some two blocks away.

The park was full of families, some praying, others standing silent, gazing at the north view of the nation's presidential mansion. A solemn mood pervaded the throng of mourners. Several television crews had set up for live reports to their networks and stations. Abdul continued his walk on west to Twenty-first Street when he cut south, passing George Washington University and the State Department along the way. The evening was balmy, temperature in the sixties, a clear night with a slight string of clouds in the west, casting a hue of purple and orange from the setting sun. Soon it would be dark, and he would need to be in his place.

He had worked out the details of his plan while resting in the hotel room. The Vietnam Memorial was one the most popular tourist attractions in the nation's capital, eventhough the war had been over for nearly three decades. Veterans, children of those killed, MIA's, and now their grandchildren, still visited the site in great numbers almost every day of the year. At 9:30 the mall area separating the Washington Monument and the Lincoln Memorial should have fewer tourists. The FBI man and the whore would be easy targets.

He had not tested the businessman's weapon, but a cursory examination convinced Abdul the revolver was in prime condition. He would need only about twenty feet to be accurate. He would wait near the Albert Einstein Memorial, located on the Constitution Avenue side of the National Academy of Science Building. The dense garden surrounding the memorial would provide good cover while he waited. Few of the thousands of tourists in the area knew of the Einstein Memorial, which was hidden from view by a small, thick patch of trees. He glanced at his watch. He still had almost an hour before the two targets were due across the street. Again, his patience would be a valuable asset this night.

*****

Mattox, Martin, and Mosele sat in the special agent's Oldsmobile at the F Street corner of Constitution Avenue. Across the street they could view the panorama of Constitution Gardens surrounding the reflecting pool. The Vietnam Memorial was off to the right, not far from Daniel Chester French's monument to the great emancipator. The two government agents sat in the front seat keeping their trained eyes on the open fields in front of them. Maggy sat in the back seat, smoking a long, thin Virginia Slim, one supposedly low in nicotine. She had asked permission, and both men in front had encouraged her, knowing that the cigarette might help her relax.

Sparks and twenty other agents were parked in eight cars, stretching from the south side of the Lincoln Memorial to

Seventeenth Street. They had instructions to remain inconspicuous and not to leave their cars until they received a signal that Mattox would transmit over the tiny microphone dangling down from a cord on his left arm inside his suit coat.

Mattox attempted to lighten the tense atmosphere within the car. "John, how did a nice looking fella like you end up in this dirty business?"

"I suppose the bureau is clean business in comparison, Mr. Mattox?" Agent Martin kept a straight face.

"Call me Bert. That agent shit gets old after a while." He caught himself after the profanity left his mouth. He turned around to face his passenger in back. "I'm sorry, Maggy. I should watch my mouth."

"Forget it. A good *shit* or *fuck* once in a while is good for the soul."

The two men in front burst out in laughter. The comment was not so funny as surprising, and the tension of the moment eased.

Mattox took a handkerchief from his lapel pocket and wiped his eyes. "You know how to take the starch out of a man, don't you, Maggy?"

She took the comment as a compliment. "I try."

Mattox replaced the handkerchief, folded as neatly as before he had removed it from his pocket. "I think swearing is my greatest vice, too many years of living alone and too many hours spent with only masculine company. I'd like to break the habit one of these days." Then he remembered his original question. "Back to you, John. You asked about the bureau. No, I wouldn't say it's any cleaner work. We get the dregs of society, but we don't get involved in all that covert action you boys at the Agency thrive on."

"Thrive on? You gotta be kidding, Agent. . . I mean, Bert. I was recruited right out of the University of Iowa three years ago. I spent two years in training, first in cryptography." He remembered the civilian in the back seat and turned to face Maggy. "That is learning how to encipher and decipher codes—I was a math major at Iowa—then six months in Ranger training, and for the past six months I've been nothing but a glorified errand boy in the deputy director's office. I wouldn't call that covert, dirty, or even exciting, for that matter. I've seen more action today than I've seen since a group of us in the fraternity sneaked into Iowa State's stadium and burned *Hawkeye* into their beautiful green turf."

Maggy and Mattox both chuckled. After flipping her cigarette out the window, Maggy leaned forward and placed her chin on the backs of her two hands which she rested on the front back rest. "Why do you stay with the CIA if you don't like it, John?" The agent turned sideways and smiled. "Who said I didn't like it? I know one of these days after I get my fair amount of seasoning, they'll put me in the field. That's what I'm looking forward to, the international travel, visiting all those places around the world I only read about in Cedar Rapids and Iowa City. Hell, I was nineteen before I ever saw a body of water that you couldn't see across to the other side. A bunch of us in the frat house drove to South Padre Island in Texas on the gulf during spring vacation of my freshman year. Ever been there?"

Mattox shook his head. Maggy gazed ahead across the street but answered the young agent. "No, but I've seen the gulf from the Florida side. It is beautiful, especially after a tough winter up north."

"You can say that again. That's what I really want to do—travel. I want to see the Mediterranean, the Pacific, the South Sea Islands, the Indian Ocean."

Mattox interrupted. "Hold on there, boy. What in the world would the CIA be doing in the South Sea Islands of the Pacific?"

Martin smiled broadly, "I just may have to be the first to establish a station there, won't I?"

All three enjoyed a small laugh.

Mattox glanced at the digital clock on his dash. It was 9:25. Turning serious, he looked directly at his two passengers. "Okay, it's time for Maggy and me to go. John, you stay here. You have your earpiece so you can hear me over this radio. This is a matter for the bureau. I don't want you getting your ass in a sling. Remember, you're liaison. Got it?"

Martin was not happy, but he acknowledged his assignment. "Just as you say, Bert."

Mattox turned his attention to Maggy. He did not like risking a civilian in this venture, but risks were required if Abdul could be captured. Capturing him was far more important than killing him, as much as the thought of shooting the bastard between his two deep brown eyes appealed to the agent. If there were others involved, they needed to be found. This wasn't going to be another Dallas, not if he had anything to do with it. The agents selected for stakeout were the bureau's finest. They all had their instructions.

"Maggy, when we get out, I want you to stay right next to me. I'm going to hold your hand, like we were sweethearts. Whatever you do, don't let go of my hand. I may swing you to one side or throw you to the ground at a moment's notice, but don't let go. Do you understand?"

Maggy took a deep breath. "I understand. Let's go and get this bastard."

*****

The assassin had checked his revolver one more time. The safety was off. He slipped the gun up the sleeve of his blue coat. He knew how to cup the barrel in his right hand and let the weapon fall into his palm the moment it was needed. In the meantime, no casual observer would notice anything unusual this late at night. He gazed up from the bench facing the large copper figure of Einstein sitting on a concrete bench with a benign smile creasing his lips. Softly he uttered, "Don't look so smug, Jew. I have years left to kill hundreds more of your kind." He spat at the sidewalk. Time to begin his casual stroll.

He left the garden by way of the south entrance and walked east along the sidewalk. There was a crosswalk ahead, about half a block. Traffic was still heavy for the time of night, no doubt due to the season and the assassination. There were also more tourists than he had anticipated still roaming through the mall area. He could not understand what these Americans saw in so much stone and masonry. However, the more people, the better. He might need someone for a hostage or a shield. He knew he would recognize Mattox and the girl long before they could detect him. He had the advantage.

If the FBI man followed his instructions, he and the girl would be above the break in the V of the memorial in less than five minutes. He crossed the street leisurely, his hands swinging at his sides. On the south side of Constitution Avenue, he joined in with two older couples as they moved toward the east entrance to the stone walkway in front of the memorial. Descending the inclined cobblestone walk slowly, Abdul kept his head aimed at the brilliant black slabs of marble with nearly 55,000 names individually chiseled into them. The names were a blur and made no impact upon the Arab. His eyes were trained above them. He had carefully observed the people roaming around the area. He prided himself on recognizing police types, and he saw none. Nearly everyone was in a small or large group including women and a few children. No police agency in America would risk women and children. That was one of their chief weaknesses.

He kept shuffling along the stone path, his eyes aimed above. To the right he could see a man and woman strolling together, holding hands, emerging from the shadows. The powerful lights of the park service behind him, aimed at the black marble, would soon expose the couple. The man and woman continued to walk on the grass above him, moving to his left. The man was wearing a dark suit, and the woman—yes, it was the Jew's whore. It was them. This was going to be too easy. He increased his pace as he neared the center of the memorial. The couple had stopped just above him, not more than twenty feet away. They were looking north, toward the State Department. Their backs were to the assassin.

He allowed the gun to fall into his hand. His finger felt its way to the trigger. He glanced around and still saw no one suspicious, except for two unarmed National Park Rangers. He began to lift his right arm. There was no way these two would escape.

To his right he had not seen the little boy approaching him. "Hey, mister, is that a real gun?" The excited boy pointed at the Arab.

From above the memorial Mattox turned to see the revolver pointed at his head. He lunged to his left and fell on top of Maggy just as the weapon discharged, the bullet passing over his head. Abdul's view was now blocked by the top side of the memorial. The two rangers were running in his direction. He fired once, hitting the first officer in the chest at point blank range. The uniformed officer lurched backward onto the cobblestone walk, blood gushing from his severed aorta and washing his shirt in vivid red.

Screams rang out from the crowd, and people began fleeing. The other ranger joined them. The little boy was still standing next to Abdul's right leg. Abdul gazed down on the boy, his eyes teaming with hatred, but quickly he switched the gun to his left hand and reached down and scooped the boy up with his right arm. He turned and began jogging toward the Lincoln Memorial, turning around constantly, using the crying child as a shield.

Mattox and the girl continued to lie on the ground. Mattox raised his head slowly to peer over the edge of the memorial. He saw the man in the blue suit holding the boy with one arm and brandishing the revolver with his other hand. He spoke excitedly into his radio microphone dangling from the sleeve of his suit coat, "Bravo! Bravo! We're both okay. The subject has a hostage. Approach with care. I repeat approach with care. He is moving toward the Lincoln Memorial. Remember, we want him alive."

Maggy's face was buried in the grass. Mattox gently placed his hand on the back of her soft hair. "Maggy, are you all right?"

She turned so she could see Mattox. "I'd better be. You just told all your buddies we were fine." She was too frightened to smile. Mattox patted her gently.

"Good girl, Maggy; you stay here. Martin, if you can hear me, come over to the memorial and look after our girl. I'm going after Abdul."

He reached under his coat and pulled out his service revolver and held it to his side. He squeezed Maggy's shoulder one more time and then began crawling along the grass above the memorial like an army recruit. He was not going to let the assassin out of his sight.

The small boy continued to kick and scream, crying for his mother. Mattox glanced to his left. A young man, seemingly no older than Martin, was restraining a woman who fought to reach her frightened son. The man was lying on top of the hysterical mother. Mattox looked back toward the assassin. The man was now running full tilt toward the Potomac side of the Lincoln Memorial. Mattox knew Sparks was located on the south side. He raised his left hand to his mouth hurriedly to speak into his radio. "He's coming your way, Sparks. Remember, he has a hostage, a little boy, and we must take him alive. He's headed toward the river, maybe the Lincoln dock. Keep an eye out."

Mattox was now back into the shadows, away from the glaring memorial lights. He sprang to his feet and ran parallel to the assassin and the boy. The lights around the Lincoln Memorial were much softer. He would have to keep his distance. The assassin crossed the circular drive around Lincoln's monument as he headed for the south side. Just as Mattox reached the front of the Lincoln shrine, he heard a cursing scream from the killer as he released his hold on the little boy. Abdul jerked his right hand to his mouth. The boy who must have had strong teeth, was running back across the curved street toward his parents. The assassin started to raise his gun, when Mattox yelled, "Stop right there! FBI! You are surrounded." He pointed his gun with both hands directly at the assassin, but he was more than two hundred feet away. Mattox knew his weapon's accuracy was no good at that distance.

So did the assassin. He turned and kept running toward the river, entering the shadows. Mattox continued his pursuit. He heard the sharp crack of two gun shots, then a third. He rounded the corner. Sparks and another man were sprawled out on the grass about fifty feet from the street. Mattox stopped as he approached his old friend, Sparks. He reached down to touch his colleague's neck, feeling for a pulse. There was a throbbing. He saw blood oozing out of the downed agent's shirt, near his stomach. Mattox screamed into his hand held microphone, "Two agents down on south side of the

Lincoln Memorial. Send help. Everyone else move toward the dock. I think we have our man trapped."

He then rose and rushed over to the other agent. He recognized the man as Ken Johnson, one of the bureau's senior agents. Johnson's picture had appeared in the bureau's internal newsletter only the previous week. He was retiring at the end of the month. Mattox felt for a pulse. There was none. Anger swelled up inside the veteran agent.

He glanced in the direction of the river. There was an incline on the grass as it approached the Potomac nearby. Mattox moved forward in a crouching position. He heard noise behind him. Several other agents had caught up. He signaled them with his left hand to stay down. Slowly, he continued to move toward the river. A clump to his left seemed out of place, not like natural landscaping. He took both hands and pointed his revolver toward the indistinguishable object. There was no movement. As he inched closer, the form of another downed body took shape. "Oh, god! Not another one." He straightened slightly, but still with his gun aimed at the form in front of him.

He was within a few feet of the body. Mattox squinted at the sight of the familiar blue suit. It couldn't be. He reached down and touched the shoulder, but there was no movement. As he rolled the body over, the dark hairpiece slid off the head of the corpse. Two deep brown eyes stared aimlessly in the moonlight. The right hand still held a gun. Mattox reached down and threw the weapon aside. He felt for a pulse, but there was none. He again reached down toward the face and moved the chin. A bullet had entered the Arab's head from the left side, just above the temple.

"Shit!" he shouted. Mattox stood and stared at the dead man, who he knew was the President's killer. What a tragedy they could not capture him alive. It was going to be Dallas all over again. Either Sparks or Johnson must have gotten him before they went down. He shook his head. "Goddamn rotten luck!" He then remembered that he was wired. "Subject is down. I repeat subject is down."

Mattox returned his own revolver to its holster. It had never been fired. He walked back to his two fellow agents. He saw

Johnson's weapon lying next to the body and picked it up. He sniffed the barrel. It had not been fired. He now assumed Sparks had shot the assassin. Several other agents were hovering over the still breathing Sparks. One was loosening his collar and tie, while another placed a folded suit coat gently under his head.

"Where's his weapon.? Has anybody seen his weapon?" An agent kneeling down near Sparks raised a gun in the air. "Here it is. He had it in his hand when he went down." Mattox walked over and took the revolver from the agent. He turned the cylinder in the pale light. All six bullets were still in their chambers. If neither of these agents had shot the assassin, then who had?

"All you men—did any of you fire at the subject? Goddamnit, let me know right now!" Mattox was clearly angry. All the other agents responded quickly in the negative.

"Well, somebody besides Sparks and Johnson fired a shot that killed Abdul. If it wasn't any of us, then there must be somebody else around here. Spread out and conduct a search. Let's find whoever it was before he gets away. Now move!"

All but the two agents caring for Sparks began scrambling in different directions. All had been through this routine before and knew how to spread themselves out.

Mattox's eyes darted around the area. Whoever had shot Abdul was probably gone by now. Mattox handed the two weapons to one of the agents tending Sparks. "Keep these and don't let them out of your sight. They're important evidence." He turned to walk back to join Maggy and Martin at his car.

The special agent was perplexed. There must have been another gunman who wanted Abdul dead. Why? Because he could expose those who had hired him. If that were the case, and those who killed the Algerian wanted to stop the investigation at Abdul's doorstep, then Maggy might be in trouble, too. An uneasy thought that all his agents were concentrated in one place, several blocks from Maggy and John, began to sink in. Mattox accelerated his pace toward his car, parked nearly five blocks away. As he broke into a full run, he remembered his microphone and shouted, "John, keep Maggy covered. You may be a target. Keep her covered. I'll be right there."

As Mattox reached the Vietnam Memorial, where just minutes earlier he nearly had been killed, he heard another two distinct, staccato shots, more like a rifle than a hand gun. Fear gripped him. He pulled his own weapon from its holster and held it tightly as he continued to scream, "John, John, I'm on my way."

As he neared Constitution Avenue, across from his car, he could see no sign of life. The front and back passenger doors were open. The dome light inside the Oldsmobile cast an eerie haze on the sidewalk. He approached the automobile carefully, both hands gripping his weapon, which he held close in front of his chest. He crossed the street. The screaming sirens of ambulances and police cars could be heard in the distance. He glanced around him on all sides, but there was no sign of another living soul. He inched forward. Suddenly, the sight of a man's pant leg twisted beneath the front door caught his eye. He dropped his gun to his side and rushed forward. Martin was lying on the seat, face down, his right arm hanging limp and touching the floorboard.

"Oh, shit! Shit! Shit!" Each expletive exploded from Mattox's lips with increased emphasis. He quickly checked the back seat. Maggy was lying on her back, face up, her eyes closed. Mattox could see no blood. He holstered his weapon and leaned down on top of the girl with the beautiful face and felt for a pulse. There was a strong beat. He took her chin with his right hand and moved her head gently back and forth. On the left temple was a red crease. Maggy had been grazed by a bullet as she was getting into the car.

Again, Mattox remembered his microphone. "We have a Code One emergency. That's a Code One emergency at my car. Two people down. Send for paramedics immediately." He then leaned over the front seat and placed his hand on Martin's neck. There was no pulse. Hurriedly, he backed out of the car and came around to the front seat. He grabbed Martin's waist and pulled him to the sidewalk. In the process he could feel a moistness on the agent's back, where Mattox's hand rested. Martin had been shot in the back. He placed his ear on the agent's chest. There was no sound.

Mattox reached down and straightened Martin's head and tilted it slightly backward. He began to administer mouth to mouth resuscitation. There was no response. He continued the procedure as an ambulance, siren wailing, pulled up next to his car. Two white-coated paramedics jumped from the cab and ran around the car. "We'll handle that now, sir. Please stand back."

Mattox at first did not hear them. His only thought was of saving the life of the young agent. "Come on, Johnny boy. You still have that office to open in Tahiti. You can make it, John." Mattox stared at the relaxed young face. His eyelids were closed, and he had no expression. There was no response. One of the paramedics, a large black man, placed his hand on Mattox's shoulder. "Please, sir, we know what we're doing."

Mattox turned around, confusion in his eyes, and stared at the paramedic. He let go of Martin's face and slowly stood. The two men from the ambulance kneeled and began their work. Mattox watched for a few seconds, then remembered Maggy. He turned back to the car and lifted from the seat the limp body of the woman he had sworn to protect and placed her gently on the sidewalk. She began to stir. Mattox's heartbeat increased in excitement.

"Maggy, Maggy, it's me, Bert. Can you hear me?"

Slowly, the eyelids lifted, exposing two glossy brown irises. "John, is that you?" she murmured. "John? John?"

"No, Maggy, it's Bert. Can you hear me?" He placed his arm under her back and lifted her forward until her face was no more than inches from his own. Her breathing was labored but steady. She tried to focus her eyes.

"Bert?"

"Yes, Maggy, it's Bert. How do you feel?"

"Bert. What happened? John and I were getting into the car, when everything went black. She lifted her right hand to her temple where she had been hit. Removing it, she tried to focus her eyes on the dry flakes of blood smeared on her fingers. "Did someone hit me?"

"No, Maggy, a bullet grazed your head, but you're going to be fine. You hang on, you hear?" He continued to cradle her in his arms, rocking gently.

He turned to watch the work of the paramedics. One had brought a gurney and oxygen tank from the emergency vehicle. The black paramedic was attaching a mask to Martin's face. He overheard the other attendant say, "It doesn't look good, Harvey, doesn't look good at all."

Mattox kept rocking. Though he was not a religious man, he found himself uttering a quiet prayer. "Please, Lord, let him live. He's too young. Let him live."

Maggy peered at Bert's face. She started to reach up and touch it, but her hand dropped, and she lapsed into unconsciousness. Mattox continued to rock her as he watched Martin loaded into the ambulance. Another emergency vehicle was pulling up as Martin was being loaded. A woman and man jumped out and ran over to Mattox. "Are you all right, Mister?" asked the female paramedic.

Mattox looked up, his eyes moist, "Yes. I'm fine. This is Miss Mosele. She's received a grazing bullet wound to her temple. Please look after her."

A half dozen of Mattox's agents led by Carl Peters finally arrived, all of them panting from the long run from the Lincoln Memorial. Mattox stood as the two paramedics attended to Maggy. Mattox turned to his men. "I'm going to ride to the hospital with Miss Mosele. Agent Martin is in the other wagon. It doesn't look good. I want twenty-four-hour protection for both of them. You hear? Twenty-four-hour protection—not from the D.C. police, but from the bureau. Someone is still out there. He tried to kill them once. As soon as he finds he was unsuccessful, he'll try again."

Peters, a young agent who had assisted Mattox in an earlier investigation of city government corruption in Philadelphia, responded. "You got it, Agent Mattox. You sure you're okay?"

"Yeah, yeah, I'm fine." Mattox turned back to see Maggy being loaded into the ambulance. The woman in the white coat looked at the special agent. "She's going to be all right, sir."

Mattox's entire body relaxed. He replied, "Thanks, but I'm going with you." He walked to the back of the ambulance and climbed in. The high pitched squeal of the siren was muted inside the vehicle. He sat next to the medic on a cot across from Maggy.

The medic had hooked up a heart monitor to Maggy's chest. Mattox leaned back and stared at the serene face.

Who would want her dead? And why Martin? It would be morning before he realized that the killer might have mistaken Martin for the FBI special agent. It had been an exhausting day. He closed his eyes. Sleep would be a comfort, but little rest would befriend him this night. There were too many questions stirring in his mind to allow him to sleep. Too many questions.

Chapter 9

President Staton sat at the desk in the forward compartment of the Boeing 747, the late Vice-President's plane; however, any plane that carries the President of the United States is designated *Air Force One*. The aircraft's massive communications systems allowed the President to spend most of the trip on the phone. He had expressed his condolences to the widows of all the officials killed earlier in the day. It had already been decided by President Hansen's family that the official funeral would be on Sunday, the 16th.

At the urging of the State Department, Mrs. Hansen also had agreed to a joint funeral with the Vice-President to be held at the National Cathedral. Four days would allow the State Department to make preparations for all the foreign dignitaries who would want to attend. If John Kennedy's funeral were any indication, security, protocol, and traffic problems would bring horrendous headaches during the next several days. Mrs. Hansen had insisted that, following the lying in state in the Rotunda of the Capitol on the 15th and the funeral on the 16th, her husband's remains would be returned to their hometown in Michigan for burial in their local cemetery.

The Vice-President's family had expressed a desire that he be buried in Arlington Cemetery. His internment would be on the 16th, following the funeral. Staton knew he would have to attend all the various ceremonies, including the trip to Michigan. Like a death in the family, the millions of people of the United States needed to vent their grief. It was part of the mourning process, and the new President was the head of their national family. Wherever he could be present, a gentle reassurance would pervade the nation.

Finding those responsible for the assassinations was high on Staton's agenda. He had known and liked Seth Hansen. They had been colleagues for seven years in the Senate, and for nearly twenty-seven months they had teamed together to forge a lessening of tension in the Middle East and the construction of a more coherent foreign policy regarding China and Europe. The death of President Hansen had been as devastating to Staton as if it had been a member of his own family. He was angry, and he wanted to know who was responsible. He hoped it had not been the Russians.

The Secretary of State shifted his weight in his lounge chair and reached for the hot cup of coffee the flight attendant had brought moments earlier. The petite white porcelain cup appeared awkward in the large New Englander's hand. Staton's height and 275 pounds suddenly felt uncomfortable in the narrow seat designed for the late Vice-President.

Staton was well aware of his size and had taken ample advantage of it through the years to intimidate less secure politicians and colleagues, first in the state legislature, then in the governor's mansion, and finally in the Senate of the United States. Now nearing his 65th birthday, the large bear of a man resembled very little the tight-bodied, clear, brash young governor of thirty years earlier. Four terms in the Senate, a safe seat with only token opposition, had allowed him to set a more relaxed pace during the past decade. Becoming chairman of the Foreign Relations Committee had led Staton and his wife, Gwendolyn, down the Washington party circuit and embassy row. That was fifty pounds ago. The new weight, garnered from the talents of the finest chefs in the nation's capital, now manifested itself in more awkward movements and heavy breathing. One of his chief problems on television interview programs was his labored breathing into the tiny microphone attached to his lapel.

But if Staton's body had become pudgy and soft, if his rugged face, now lined heavily with aged creases and a constantly crimson nose, betrayed too soft a lifestyle and a decaying physical presence, his mind was still alert, fortified with forty years of public experiences and anecdotes. Indeed, Crawford Staton was one of the most well-liked and admired men in the nation. His ready use of a ribald story, his slow delivery, and his disarming demeanor had captivated many an audience, large and small. No one truly disliked "Crawfish" Staton, as the insiders called him— not to his face, of course.

Gallop had found Crawford Staton the President's most popular appointment. In fact, the Democratic National Committee had been disturbed by the latest private polls which showed Staton the most popular man in the administration, eclipsing even the President by a half dozen points. In an age of sleekness, of technological stereotypes, of the ominous presence of nuclear annihilation, the old craggy face of Crawfish Staton was as reassuring and comfortable as grandpa's rocker. A man of obvious pleasant countenance, of intellect, of honey rhetoric, Staton was a Rockwellian portrait of what America wanted in a leader.

Staton momentarily longed for those more carefree days in the Senate. A smile creased his lips as he reflected over the nickname given him by his colleagues during his early years— Crawfish. The name stuck not long after one of the annual National Press

Club Gridiron galas, in which the larger members of the Senate were spoofed in a skit focusing on their appetites. Several newsmen portraying members of the Congress devoured plate after plate of crawfish and shrimp, all the time singing a parody to *Shrimp Boat's Are A'Comin'*.

His plane was now well over Pennsylvania. The pilot had just announced that they would be landing in twenty minutes, right on schedule. Lowenstein had already prepared the short address Staton would deliver when he arrived. He knew all the Cabinet would be present and that security would be no problem at Andrews Air Force Base.

He already had been informed of the capture and death of the assassin from the Middle East. Initially, Staton had breathed a sigh of relief, knowing the Russians were probably not involved, but when the Attorney General had given him the FBI director's more detailed report, suggesting the conspiracy ran much deeper, the President's concerns increased. It was still possible the unraveling of a conspiracy could involve foreign governments or even people within the American government. In times of crisis one's mind could run rampant with speculation.

Staton worried about his wife. Gwen had been the perfect congressional wife. She had joined all the right clubs, entertained influential men and women as her husband's hostess, but in the past half dozen years, she had found it necessary to fortify herself with more and more gin in order to face her chores. Staton had tried to make her realize she had a problem, but she only scoffed at his pleadings. She would not seek counseling because in her own mind she had no problem. So what if she liked a drink once in a while, she could control it.

Staton had dispatched his oldest daughter, Natalie, who lived in suburban Chevy Chase with her stockbroker husband, to be with her mother and hopefully to keep her sober. For the next several days, the world's media would be dissecting and analyzing every move and gesture she would make and every word she would utter, either in private or public. The nation needed a strong First Lady in times of crisis nearly as badly as they needed a strong President. He had talked to Gwen after Natalie had arrived at the house and filled her in on the day's events. He tried to warn her of the microscope they all would be under. He had subtly mentioned the need to be strong and to resist temptation. He knew she understood. Despite her refusal to admit to dependency, she and Staton had always really understood each other.

Fortunately for the new President, the plane was not carrying a great number of passengers who might have proved to be a distraction. Besides about forty media representatives who had signed on for the original trip, a Secret Service detail of about ten men and one woman, only Staton and his aide, Lowenstein, were flying back to the nation's Capitol. He had taken about ten minutes to walk back to the seats occupied by the media. He had exchanged pleasantries, asked for their understanding and help, and before he left, shaken the hand of every journalist. For the most part, these were men and women who had followed him for the previous two years. This would be the end of the line. An enlarged and different press corps would be covering the White House.

Back in his compartment, he had handwritten an order declaring a national month of mourning, and he had signed an executive order prepared by Lowenstein, giving all federal civilian workers paid leave on Monday, April 17, the day of President Hansen's burial. Lowenstein had kept in touch with the White House office staff, attending to details. So much of the Presidency was associated with detail.

He had taken a call from Admiral Birchfield, his old friend, who felt it imperative that he give the President an update on events along the Iranian and Turkish borders when he arrived. Birchfield had suggested that the two could discuss the matter in the Marine helicopter between Andrews and the White House.

Staton had not given thought to going to the White House when he returned. It was still the home of Mrs. Hansen and her family. He was tired and had only thoughts of driving to his own home in northwest Washington, but Lowenstein had reminded him that the West Wing of the White House was still the nerve center of the government. He had reluctantly agreed to Oggy's request, though he made it plain he wanted to be home at a decent hour.

Staton, sitting in the high back leather chair riveted to the floor, looked out the window at the increasing number of lights below. He raised his arms and stretched. Oggy was a good friend. They had shared many a laugh and romp together back in the 50's when they both had been young lieutenants, junior grade—Oggy out of the Naval Academy and Staton fresh from an ROTC program at Boston College. He respected his friend's intellect, but not his view of the Russian menace. He knew Birchfield better than anybody else in the government, and he felt confident he could control his old friend.

He had discussed the present Russian situation several times during the flight home with Secretary Thompson, who had remained at the White House. Chenkov's message had been translated. It had been vague and had made references to the intolerable situation in Armenia and the transgression of that ally's sovereign borders by Muslim terrorists from Turkey and Iran. All Russian troop movements, he claimed, had been defensive in nature. It was exactly the kind of message Staton himself would have composed had he been Chenkov. He knew this was just the first round.

Staton respected Nelson Thompson's calm demeanor and his intellect. The two men had not been intimate, but his years on Capitol Hill had trained him to separate those with substance from those with bluster. Seth Hansen had been fortunate to have had such a loyal and brilliant friend. Staton would have to use all his persuasive powers to keep Thompson.

The seat belt light blinked on. Staton reached to his sides. He had to adjust the one strap to its full length in order to connect the buckle. Staton's mind began to drift. Down deep he had no reservations about his ability to handle the job. He just hoped the country would give him support. He closed his eyes and rested. It would be his last few precious moments of solitude for some time.

*****

Mattox looked at the clock on the far wall in the nurse's station. It was 11:30. He had been at the hospital for nearly forty-five minutes, sitting outside the emergency room where several doctors were trying to save young Martin's life. Maggy was in the ER, also, but the nurses and orderlies had insisted that he wait outside, that he would only be in the way. FBI agents were already stationed at the entrance and exits to the wing of the hospital. No one entered or left without authorization or an official hospital badge.

Behind the large glass partitions, a youngish doctor, dressed in hospital greens and well-worn tennis shoes, opened the curtain to the cubical into which Martin had been wheeled. Mattox had met him briefly. The doctor walked slowly through the trauma center and opened the door to the waiting area. An expression of disappointment was frozen on his face. "Mr. Mattox, I'm sorry. We tried everything, but he was gone before he ever got here. Should we contact his family?"

Mattox stared through the windows at the curtain, then back at the doctor, not quite focusing on what the trauma surgeon had just said. "Oh, yeah, his family. Frankly, Doctor, I don't know anything about his family. I know he's from Iowa. We'll have someone from the Central Intelligence Agency contact you. They'll have all the details you need." He then remembered Maggy. "What about Miss Mosele? How is she?"

The doctor stretched his arms behind him. "Oh, she'll be fine. She suffered a contusion on her right temple and a concussion from the impact, but she'll be okay. We're going to keep her overnight, but she should be released by noon tomorrow. Right now she's resting, and I think that's best. One of the nurses is with her. It will be necessary to wake her every hour. That's routine in concussion cases. If you don't mind, I'd rather you wait until tomorrow to talk to her."

"That's fine, Doctor, but once it is known she survived, I believe there is a good chance another attempt might be made on her life. I want these agents to stay here, and I'm afraid I must insist that strict adherence to their instructions regarding personnel near her bed be followed."

"I see no problem with that, Mr. Mattox, but you really need to take that up with the administrator. I just work here." The doctor tried to muster a smile, but he was too weary. He was near the end of his shift, and, like most weeknights in a city hospital, there had been no shortage of knifings, shootings, and drug overdoses.

Mattox started to thank the doctor when he remembered his friend, Sparks. "What about Agent Sparks. Is he going to make it?"

"We sent him up to surgery just after he arrived. It was a gunshot wound in the stomach, but I've seen lots of those in here. I feel sure he'll be all right, though he may have to change his eating habits for a while. He should be out. . ." the doctor glanced at the wall clock, "in about another hour. He'll be in recovery up on the fourth floor."

"Thank you, Doctor." Mattox extended his arm and shook the young resident's hand. It was nearly 11:30, and his forty-five minutes in the lounge had given him a chance to rest. He decided to go home and shower, change clothes, and then go back to the office. Both the director and the Attorney General would have plenty of questions at sunrise. He started to walk toward the parking lot exit when he remembered he had no car.

Mattox took aside one of the two agents guarding the main entrance and asked him if he would mind giving him a lift home. The younger agent, who knew the stature of the senior special agent, was anxious to comply. He offered to bring his car from the main parking lot to the emergence room entrance. Mattox thanked him and started to go back to his chair, but paused, then returned to the trauma center and asked the nurse in which bay Miss Mosele was located. The nurse pointed through the glass partitions to Number Four, toward the center of the emergency room.

Mattox opened the door to the trauma center and walked directly over to Number Four, where a curtain was pulled all the way around the bay. He pulled the curtain back just enough to see Maggy sleeping peacefully. Her relaxed face contained a serene countenance. Mattox could not understand why this girl was so special to him. He had known dozens of women, been in love at least half a dozen times, but as he gazed down at the peaceful face of Maggy Mosele, there was a special feeling swelling inside him — one of guardianship and responsibility, as well as concern. She had been through so much during this day. He swore to himself that she would have to endure no more. He let loose of the curtain, turned, and walked briskly toward the ER entrance.

*****

In the study of his country home, John Chamberlain flipped off the television with his remote control. He had just watched the latest network updates on the reported FBI killing of the man who was suspected of the mass assassinations earlier in the day. The report also made reference to several FBI agents having been shot, but there had been no confirmation from the FBI on any deaths within their bureau. He walked over to his desk chair and sat down. He again reached inside his top drawer to find the number he had called several hours earlier. He could never remember telephone numbers. Most of the time he had secretaries place his calls.

As he listened to the phone ring at the other end, he picked up a pencil and began doodling on a small white pad he kept on the top of the desk. After four rings there was an answer.

"This is the eight of spades. I understand the Algerian problem has been solved?"

"That's what I understand. My man tells me our other two concerns were also taken care of. I think everything is going according to plan."

"Yes, I believe so. Good night."

DAY 2

Chapter 10

The command center in the basement of the Hoover Building was quiet. The phone bank down the hall was now manned by only two agents. Since the announcement of the death of the assassin, calls had dropped off sharply. Mattox had returned to the center at 1:00 in the morning. At 3:00 he had been able to grab a couple hours of sleep on the cot he had ordered for the corner of the room. He was now fully dressed in a button down white shirt, burgundy club tie, and dark blue slacks. A matching suit coat was hanging neatly on a nearby rack.

Most of his agents had reported back during the course of the evening, but he had sent them all home by 2:00 to get some rest. Now he was holding a briefing with six of his key team leaders. In front of him on the long conference table lay several pages of scribbled notes. He had torn the pages into pieces and arranged them in front of him in a sequence that only he understood. He was due for a press briefing at 8:30, which he wanted to keep short. He had already decided on his morning agenda. Picking up Maggy Mosele from the hospital at noon was paramount in his mind.

"Now, gentlemen, let's go over what we have. Michaels, what about the National Park Service?"

Michaels responded without referring to his notes. "We know that in late February all the landscaping behind the FDR stone mysteriously died. Park officials blamed it on a bad winter. In a routine bid procedure, they let a contract out to a Virginia outfit called Sundown Nursery. It turns out Sundown Nursery was only in business for two weeks. It operated out of a post office box in Alexandria. Records from a nursery wholesaler in Alexandria show Sundown purchased nearly $3,000 in materials within that two weeks and paid cash—no paperwork or signed receipts."

Mattox looked around the table at his team. "I think we can assume that Abdul, or whatever the son-of-a-bitch's name was, created Sundown Nursery, and it was probably he who replaced the plantings over at the FDR Memorial." There was a bobbing of heads in agreement. "Anything more from the lab?"

Peters responded. "The lab confirms that C-4 plastic explosive was used at the site. Dr. Gradle believes, based on the crater size and impact of the explosion, at least four pounds were used. We know the power of the explosion took out the President and Vice-President, the Speaker of the House and six senators, two Marines, two of President Roosevelt's grandsons, and nine of the Secret Service detail. In addition. . ." Peters flipped through his notes, "we had five other Secret Service men seriously injured. Congressman Brownell was critically wounded. Eight of the media suffered cuts and contusions from flying debris, and no less than 200 spectators from as far away as across the street suffered injuries from the flying debris."

The young agent hesitated as he turned more pages in his notebook. "We know from tree fragments that the explosion was set off by remote control. We found the antenna in the tree fragments, and the detonator was found in a dumpster near Weissman's apartment. A fingerprint on the device matches that of the assassin. We believe the assassin detonated the bomb from the Firemen's Insurance Building two blocks away, but we haven't determined from what room. CNN, however, has some footage they are sending over that might be helpful."

Mattox pointed his finger at Akers, one of his most thorough agents. "I want you to take a team back over to that building and search every goddamn office that fronts the memorial. I want fingerprints of all window sills. I want everyone in those offices questioned to see if they remember seeing this nut." Akers was writing his instructions in a small notebook.

Mattox returned to his notes. "Who has Sparks's report?"

Akers spoke up. "I have, sir. We know from interrogating President Hansen's staff that the suggestion for the ceremony yesterday came from Senator Howard's office nearly three months ago."

Mattox wrote a note to himself. "I'm going to follow up on this one. As far as I'm concerned this is the key to our conspiracy. If we can find who set up yesterday's party, we'll be on the way to identifying who hired Abdul."

Mattox paused to review his notes. "We're getting stonewalled from the Agency on Manchester. I have an appointment with Heffelfinger this afternoon. Not even the Agency is going to block this investigation. I have Director Jameson's full support on this. I'll go public if that cocksucker Heffelfinger tries to cover up anything." The men at the table had never seen the normally controlled Mattox so agitated.

Mattox turned to his secretary sitting off to the side with her steno pad. "Mary Alice, omit the reference to the CIA director, will you?" For the first time he smiled, and the tension around the table lessened noticeably. Mary Alice winked.

"Now, where was I? Oh, yes, Manchester. We need to concentrate on his wallet—the phone number and the playing card." Mattox reached toward the top of his assembled papers and picked up the original Post-it housed in a celephane bag. "This number has been identified as the private residence of John Fairchild Chamberlain, CEO of JFC Industries. Now, I caution everybody here that this information is to be kept in this room. Chamberlain is a very important man in this city, in this nation, for that matter. We don't know why Manchester would have the number. We do not know if Chamberlain himself knew Manchester. It could be someone else who lives or works at the house." Mattox paused. "The fact that Abdul went after Weissman's girlfriend, however, suggests to me that the telephone number is important. We'll have to handle this one carefully. I'll talk to Chamberlain." Mattox carefully placed the pouch in his shirt pocket, also.

"Next, Peters reports that during the course of the evening, our assassin killed a businessman in the Capitol Hilton Hotel named. . ." he stretched to read one of his notes, "Bernard Casterline, from New York City. From Abdul's body we recovered forty karats in diamonds, which we assume were stolen from Casterline, and a wig which a clerk at the hotel identified as looking like Casterline's hair. She had not known he wore a wig, but apparently this guy Casterline was a frequent guest at the hotel. Casterline's body was discovered late last night by a maid."

Mattox leaned back in his chair. "Now here I have a problem. How did he get out of that sealed hotel? Why did he want to meet both Miss Mosele and me alone? It certainly wasn't about his own safety as he said in his message. The fact that he tried to shoot us disproves that notion. No! He wanted us out for some other reason. Perhaps it was our knowledge of the wallet or our ability to identify him. Or, it could still be Miss Mosele's relationship with Manchester."

Mattox continued speculating as he stared at the far end of the room. "We know from the CIA dossier that Abdul worked alone, yet he knew someone in this area, or at least they knew him. Someone killed him last night, other than one of our agents. That person also killed Agent Martin and tried to kill Miss Mosele. We can assume that Abdul may have made contact with someone outside the hotel who in turn called in the hotel operator. Damn it! Why didn't I think of that at the time? Anyway, we need to find out if there is any record of calls going out from Casterline's room during the time the hotel was sealed yesterday." Mattox pointed to Carl Peters. "Peters, you go back to the Hilton and check their telephone records." Peters nodded.

Mattox again leaned forward. "Now to last night. The lab has made a ballistics check on the slugs recovered from Sparks's stomach, Ken Johnson's body, the car where the two bullets aimed at Mosele and Martin were found, and the one taken from the assassin. The bullets found in Sparks and Johnson match those fired by Abdul's gun, which we found at the scene. We also know he shot that National Park Ranger. I saw that, myself. But the bullets taken from Abdul and the car also were fired from a different weapon. They did not come from Abdul's gun."

"One of our agents found a casing on the landing of the Lincoln Memorial. We assume it came from the weapon used to kill Abdul and probably used to kill Martin. Mattox reached over to pick up the report from Dr. Gradle. "The bullets taken from the ranger, Sparks, and Johnson were all fired from Abdul's 38-Special, made by Charter Arms. The bullets taken from the car and from Abdul were 6-mm PPC cartridges." He looked up at his men. "As you all know, the PPC cartridge is designed for accuracy, not to explode upon impact. All three of the shots at Abdul and Martin and Mosele were fired from considerable distance. The killer must have used a telescopic sight and possibly a laser finder."

Mattox laid down the report. He rose, stretched his arms, and began pacing around the table as he thought aloud. "Gentlemen, the fact that Abdul was killed by another party and that another attempt was made on Miss Mosele's life suggests that yesterday's assassination was the product of a conspiracy and that the others involved want the trail to stop with the assassin. It is possible Martin was killed because the killer mistook him for me. It was dark, and the shot came from some distance away."

Mattox walked all the way around the table, his eyes fixed on nothing in particular. "That means that both Miss Mosele and I might still be targets once it is generally known that we're both still alive. I don't want any mention of John Martin's death made public at this time. I'll clear that with Heffelfinger this afternoon. The killer will wonder who the man with Maggy was. When they see me on television this morning, they are going to know that I'm still around. I can't avoid that. Finally, I want no mention made of Manchester until we nail down his whereabouts. We know he picked up his ticket to Orlando, so we'll start there. I want our Orlando office to check every hotel in the area."

Mattox returned to his chair and glanced at his watch. "It's 8:25. I'm due at the auditorium in five minutes." He waited, but there were no questions. "Now, as soon as I announce that Abdul was killed by someone other than the FBI, conspiracy theorists all over the country are going to begin inundating us with calls and idle speculation. We'll have to restaff the phone bank. I know nearly all of what we receive will be bullshit, but we can't miss a chance that someone might have a legitimate lead for us." He looked around the table. "Let's get at it, gentlemen." With that he stacked his notes in a neat pile and handed them to Mary Alice. He reached for his suit coat and started for the door with his legal pad in tow. "Time to meet the press."

*****

In his ornate office on the first floor of the Sam Rayburn Building on Capitol Hill, Congressman Buddy Schumacher sat at his large oak desk. As House Majority Whip he was the senior member of the majority party still able to function in the House of Representatives. He had suffered through a sleepless night. The Congress was facing the most serious crisis in over 200 years. At sixty-five, Schumacher had held a seat in the safest district of Michigan for nearly twenty years. His confinement to a wheelchair from a traffic accident suffered the previous year had caused him to give serious thought to retirement. He had kept his job as Majority Whip after the Democratic caucus had voted unanimously not to accept his resignation; but, after all, he had been an effective whip. He knew every member of the caucus by first name and could recall their voting records instantly upon request.

Along with Speaker Harley and Alan Brownell, the three leaders had made an effective team in harnessing votes in support of the President's programs. Brownell had been one of his strongest supporters during his convalescence at Walter Reed Hospital. He had not missed a day of either visiting personally or calling Mrs. Schumacher, offering to do whatever he could to help. Brownell had been the one to make the motion at the caucus to refuse his resignation. Now Brownell was still listed as critical in George Washington Hospital, and other House members were looking to Schumacher for leadership. He had not been prepared for such an undertaking.

Sitting in front of his desk were the House Democratic caucus chairman and the chairmen of the Judiciary, International Relations, Ways and Means, and Rules committees. These were the power brokers of the House of Representatives. Once they closed a deal, it stayed closed. They represented varying constituencies, and seldom could all five agree on every measure. It had been Brownell who had molded them into a team and made individuals swallow their pride from time to time and support the *team*, as he always called the clique. Now here they all were, waiting for word from the hospital and speculating about the future leadership of the House.

"Buddy, you have to stand for Speaker. We need a leader, now. I love Alan as much as the rest of the men in this room, but we do not have the luxury of waiting. This nation is in a crisis. Why I have it on good authority that the Russians are mounting an offensive against the Turks and Iranians this very minute. The President is going to need the support of a united Congress." The plea came from the chairman of the International Relations Committee, a veteran legislator with a thick Bronx inflection in his diction and a raspy voice. Some said he sounded very much like the legendary Al Smith.

"I appreciate your point of view, Blanton, but I will not be stampeded. Alan Brownell is the best friend I have in this town. I will not call for an election until we know his condition and his prognosis. You all know that he is the logical man to become Speaker of the House. And, Blanton, the House is in spring recess until next week. With the Speaker gone, only the President can call us back into session."

"Buddy," it was Ed O'Bannon, chairman of the Judiciary Committee, "we might have a more serious problem than anyone in this room has contemplated." Everyone turned his attention to the white-haired congressman from New Jersey. Congressman O'Bannon was holding a cup of coffee. He had been unusually silent since the meeting had started.

"Last night about 9:00, I received a call from my grandson back in Tom's River. He's a bright kid, a senior in high school there. He asked me a question that I had not considered. Seems young Eddy is taking a civics course, and he read to me a footnote in his textbook. I had him repeat it several times, and I wrote it down." O'Bannon leaned forward and placed his cup on the Majority Whip's desk. He reached in his pocket and pulled out a piece of note paper. "Now, mind you, Eddy had gotten his book out to read about Presidential succession. He's a bright kid, Eddy. Anyway, his textbook had this footnote to a statement about the 25th Amendment and the 1947 Presidential Succession Act. I quote, *A Cabinet member is to serve only until a Speaker or President pro tem is available and qualified.*"

The other men in the room looked quizzical. The Ways and Means chairman, not an attorney, spoke first. "I never heard of that before. I've just always assumed that the Secretary of State followed the President Pro Tem in the order of succession."

O'Bannon had folded the note and returned it to his pocket. "So did I. I had a copy of the 1947 Act at home, so I looked it over." This time he picked up a law book resting on the front of the Majority Whip's desk, which he had brought with him to the meeting. He opened to page 380. "Chapter 264, passed July 18, 1947, Be it enacted, et cetera, et cetera. Here it is in section (d), and I quote:

If, by reason of death, resignation, removal from office, inability, or failure to qualify, there is no President pro tempore to act as President under subsection (b) then the officer of the United States who is highest on the following list, and who is not under disability to discharge the powers and duties of the office of President shall act as President: Secretary of State, Secretary of the Treasury, Secretary of War, Attorney General, Postmaster General, Secretary of the Navy, Secretary of the Interior, Secretary of Agriculture, Secretary of Commerce, Secretary of Labor.

The International Relations chairman interrupted. "That sounds clear to me. Crawfish Staton was the senior cabinet member on the list to succeed to the office."

O'Bannon held up his hand. "Now, wait a minute. Note, it says ACT as President. Let me read on. I quote paragraph two of this same section.

An individual acting as President under this subsection shall continue so to do until the expiration of the then current Presidential term, but not after a qualified and prior-entitled individual is able to act, except that the removal of the disability of an individual higher on the list contained in paragraph (l) or the ability to qualify on the part of an individual higher on such list shall not terminate his service.

Again the Ways and Means chairman spoke up. "Well, I'm no lawyer, but it seems to me that the language is clear. If there ain't no higher qualified person, he serves until the end of the term. Ain't that right, Ed?"

"Well, maybe not. The problem deals with the definition of the phrase *prior-entitled individual*. It's true the Speaker and Senator Howard are deceased, therefore not qualified, but it is possible that if the House elects a new Speaker, or if prior to that the Senate selects a new Pro Tem, then that person meets the intent of the language."

The Whip asked, "How in the hell can we determine what *prior-entitled* means? You lawyers could have a field day with that. Every judge in the nation might have a different interpretation."

"Hold on, Buddy. As you know, all laws are passed with an accompanying legislative history which often spells out in detail any ambiguous language that might be found in a bill. I called my staff director last night and asked him to check this out. I met with him this morning before I came over to this meeting. He claims that my grandson was right, that the intent of the law is to be sure there is always an "elected" official in the office, not an appointed official."

"How important is this legislative history thing, Ed? It seems to me we could be stirring up a hornet's nest. I remind you this nation ain't never seen a crisis as big as the one we have right now, and ole Crawfish is pretty well respected out there in the country. If we go chargin' over to the White House and tell him he's gonna have to give up his office, he might just tell us to go to hell." The chairman of Ways and Means was clearly uncomfortable.

"Let me get this right, Ed." The caucus chairman was about to ask his first question. "If we do nothing here as long as Alan is in the hospital, and the Senate selects a new Pro Tem, then that man can become President of the United States, is that right?"

"If you accept my interpretation, yes, that's correct," answered the Judiciary chairman.

"Well, Holy Mother of God, do we have a problem!" The caucus chairman was sitting on the edge of his chair. "You men realize of course that all six of the senators killed yesterday were Democrats. Right now the Republicans hold a two-vote majority in the Senate. If they push for a Pro Tem, and they believe Ed's interpretation of the Succession Act, hell, they might demand that the Presidency be turned over to them. Shit! We can't have that."

The Whip leaned forward in his wheelchair, "Wait a minute, those six senators are going to be replaced by the governors of their states, aren't they?"

"Sure, Buddy, but have you thought about who those governors are? New York now has a Republican governor. He has two appointments. That would give the Republicans fifty seats, minimum. That means a deadlock, fifty to fifty. But what worries me is those Republicans in the Senate. If they get wind of this, they'll move before all the Democrats can be replaced, while they still have a majority."

There was a noticeable uneasiness in the room, and for several seconds no one said anything. Finally, the Whip asked the obvious question. "Well, what are we going to do?"

"Seems to me we have to elect a Speaker before those guys across the way elect a Pro Tem." The caucus chairman leaned back in his chair.

"Okay, assume we can get called into session and hold an election, and Alan is still incapacitated, who are we going to elect?" The Whip stared across his desk at the eyes of each man, and to a man they all looked away.

"Well, come on, fellas, who we gonna elect? Surely, you have a suggestion?"

Ed O'Bannon finally broke the ice. "Well, Buddy, do you think you could handle the job?"

"Hell, no! I might be able to preside over the House, but with the possibility of the Presidency hanging over me, no way. Who else do we have?"

The caucus chairman, the youngest and most ambitious of those in the room, and a Midwesterner with twelve years of service under his belt, hesitantly spoke. "I suppose I might be considered a possibility. I am third in rank behind the Speaker, given my position as caucus chairman."

The older committee chairmen squirmed in their chairs. The suggestion was not well received. O'Bannon, the oldest of those present finally responded. "Look, Charlie, I like you. I voted for you. We all did; but, I'm not sure you are the best man at this point in time to lead the United States of America, and, after all, that's what we may be talking about, running this big nation of ours. Quite frankly, I think the caucus would have trouble with your selection."

The caucus chairman looked more defensive than hurt. "Well, who's it going to be? One of you fellas?" He looked at each one. No one responded.

After another long period of silence, the Whip intervened. "It looks to me like we can't reach a consensus right now. Besides, we still have several questions unanswered. Is Ed's interpretation correct, for one thing. We need to check that out, but I think you'd all agree that we need to be very discreet at this point. Ed, why don't you have Steve Burnstein over at the Library of Congress check into the succession question. He's a presidential scholar. I'll call my friend who runs the Center for the Study of the Presidency up in New York. I've attended several of his conferences and know him well enough that I think he'll maintain our confidentiality after we talk." The others nodded in agreement.

"This will give us time to check on Alan and to give some thought to alternatives to Alan. I hope you all realize that part of the success of this House during the last two sessions has been the effectiveness of this team. If we break up now, there will be chaos within the caucus. We lost too many leaders in the last two or three elections." The other men remembered nearly eighty senior members of the House choosing retirement so that they could keep their fat campaign funds. A few walked off with over a million dollars. After 1994 no member of Congress could retain such funds after retirement. They also remember the Republican landslide in 1994.

Ed O'Bannon rose from his seat, lawbook stuffed beneath his arm. "Well, boys, it looks like we have a hell of a lot to think about. I move we adjourn."

The others stood and left the office, leaving Buddy Schumacher to muse over his options. He was deeply fearful of the Presidency. Sure, Roosevelt had served over twelve years in a wheelchair, but he had been a much younger man when he started. No! Alan Brownell was the best man in the House of Representatives to be President, if only God would spare him.

*****

There were very few people roaming the halls of the Philip Hart Senate Office Building when Bert Mattox checked through the security scanner at its southwest entrance. He had called to make an appointment with Senator Howard's chief of staff. The senator's office was on the fourth floor. In spite of having an ornate office in the Capitol Building, the senator maintained another office in the Hart Building, mostly for his personal staff that tended to the business of his home constituency. Jim Cavanaugh had been the Senator's chief of staff for nearly twenty years.

Mattox found Senator Howard's office off the west hall, overlooking Capitol Hill. As long time chairman of the Senate Judiciary Committee, he undoubtedly had enjoyed his view of the Supreme Court building on his left. Cavanaugh had a smaller, but impressive office next to the senator's. Mattox was shown in by the only secretary working that day. Her smeared mascara was testament to her struggle with her tears all morning.

Cavanaugh rose from his desk as Mattox entered. The two men exchanged a half-hearted handshake, and each found a chair. Mattox knew that the executive assistant was still suffering from the loss of his long-time mentor. The executive assistant was a short man, about five feet, six inches in height. His hair was a salt and pepper mix, but the creases in his face and the veins in his hand convinced Mattox the man was in his sixties.

"I suppose you served Senator Howard for many years, Mr. Cavanaugh?"

"Thirty-five, to be exact, the last twenty as his chief-of-staff. He was a wonderful man, a gentleman from the old South. You just don't see his kind around here anymore. This place will miss him. I can tell you that."

"Mr. Cavanaugh, the reason I asked for this meeting deals with yesterday's tragedy. We received word from the White House that Senator Howard was the one who had requested the President's attendance, yesterday, and that he had organized the memorial service. Is that your understanding?"

"Well, it was no secret that the senator was a great admirer of Roosevelt. He was the last member of the present Congress to have served while FDR was still President. I'm not surprised that he would have wanted to honor Mr. Roosevelt."

"Then it was his idea for yesterday's ceremony?"

"Now, wait a minute, Mr. Mattox. I don't think that's quite correct. Senator Howard had been more interested in the new monument being constructed over at the Tidal Basin. He had been quite agitated that construction was going so slowly. I think he really had his mind set for some kind of grand ceremony for its opening. On the other hand, you know he announced his retirement at the end of his present term. I suppose he was beginning to believe he'd be gone before the new memorial was finished."

"Mr. Cavanaugh, that may well be, but the people with whom we spoke at the White House were quite clear that it was Senator Howard who had prevailed upon President Hansen, requesting his participation yesterday. We have a copy of the letter he sent the President."

"That may be. Let me get the file." Cavanaugh rose from his chair and disappeared into the outer office. In less than two minutes he returned, holding a light blue legal size file folder. "Here it is. We keep files on everything in this office. Never can tell when you may need them." The assistant began thumbing through the file. "Yes, here's a copy of the letter to the President. You were right about that, but let's see what else we have."

Mattox tried to read some of the papers as Cavanaugh stacked them to his left after scanning them. He thought about asking for the entire file, but his experience dictated he show deference to members of Congress, even dead ones.

"Interesting!" Cavanaugh leaned back to read a memorandum he had picked up from the file. "This is a memo from Senator Jake Lewellan of New Mexico. It's dated January 20. He's the one who suggested to Senator Howard that there be a tribute to Roosevelt prior to Senator Jordan's retirement. He suggests that the senator might try to persuade the President, Vice-President, and congressional leaders to pay their respects at some brief ceremony on April 12, the anniversary of his death in 1945. Here, you can read it for yourself." The short man stretched across the wide desk to hand the memo to Mattox.

Mattox read the one-page memorandum. "Could I get a copy of this to take with me, Mr. Cavanaugh?"

"That's easy. I'll have our secretary make a copy when you leave. Only take a second. What else can I do for you?"

Mattox crossed his legs. "Tell me about Senator Lewellan. All I know is that he's from some western state and that he's big on defense."

Cavanaugh leaned back in his oversized leather chair, clasping his small hands behind his neck. "Lewellan? Let me see. He's into his second term from New Mexico—a Vietnam veteran. Received the Congressional Medal of Honor as an enlisted man. Graduated from the University of New Mexico and got his law degree at Stanford, I believe. He serves on the Armed Services Committee and the Judiciary Committee. Currently, he is chairman of the Senate Intelligence Oversight Committee. Basically, that means they oversee the CIA and NSA. Takes less seniority for that committee, but you need to be clean as a whistle. I believe he's well liked by the conservative side of the house. Senator Howard thought he was a bit too rigid that way, but, of course, Senator Howard never could get the New Deal out of his system."

Mattox was writing down notes in a small pad he carried with him at all times. "Pretty good summary. Anything else?"

Cavanaugh leaned forward and dropped both his arms onto his desk. Mattox could not shed the uneasy sense that the man looked far too small for the large desk. "Off the record, and I'll deny that I ever told you, Agent Mattox, the man has no sense of humor. That's not generally well-known. He employs a pretty good speech writer to lace his talks with one liners, but I saw a copy of one of his speeches once, which he had inadvertently left on a podium. The word 'smile' had been written in red ink in those places where his ghost writer had intended the senator to be humorous. Hell, the man doesn't even know when he's being funny. I guess if that's his greatest vice, he's heads above many of the other yoyos I've seen walk these halls." Cavanaugh was not smiling. "Remember, that's between you and me. I don't need the senator as an enemy, yet. I still have a couple years left before retirement."

Mattox folded his notebook and slipped it casually into his inside coat pocket. "Thank you, Mr. Cavanaugh. You have been a big help. If you'll give me a copy of the senator's memo, I'll be on my way." Mattox stood.

Cavanaugh picked up the single sheet of paper and led the agent toward the copier. Mattox would have to find Lewellan's office before he left Capitol Hill.

Chapter 11

The White House
9:00 A.M.

The members of the National Security Council were all in their seats examining the text of President Chenkov's message of the previous day. As President Staton entered the room, followed by Lowenstein, everyone stood. Staton walked around to the center of the table where he seemed surprised to see Deputy Secretary of State Engledow standing at his own normal position. The Secretary of State always sits to the President's right. The chair next to Engledow was vacant. Staton stopped and placed his hand on the top of the back of the dark leather chair. He paused to read a small brass plate attached there.

President Seth J. Hansen
The Cabinet Room
White House

Staton caressed the chair for several seconds, then remembering where he was, took his seat. He was conscious of the importance of appearing in control.

"Gentlemen, I called this meeting for this morning to explore possible courses of action we might take in light of the Russian threat in Turkey. You've all read Chenkov's message. As far as I'm concerned there isn't much there in terms of explanation, but I didn't expect much. Director Heffelfinger has some new information for us. George, would you?" The President deferred to the CIA director, who was sitting at an end chair. The director rose and moved to a podium located near the corner of the room. Beside him was an easel. An aide placed on the easel an enlarged satellite photograph mounted on half-inch poster board.

"Mr. President, gentlemen: this photograph was taken eight hours ago. As you know, these were daylight hours in the Black Sea area." He took a laser pointer` and directed it toward a portion of the photo. "This first shot, taken by one of our satellites, shows the location of the Russian fleet in the Black Sea. If you look carefully, you can see the new nuclear carrier, *Lenin*, four battle cruisers, twenty destroyers and frigates, and we presume about a dozen support submarines beneath the water. I might add that these cruisers all have missile launching capabilities—some nuclear, some not. This ship," the director's pointer projected a red dot to a small blur near the *Lenin*, "carries approximately twenty-four helicopters."

The aide replaced the photograph with another. The director again projected his pointer. "Here we see the same fleet, only it has moved fifty miles closer to the Straits of Bosporus. This photo is four hours old."

The aide again exchanged photographs. "This last photo was taken one hour ago. You will note that there is no question, the entire fleet is headed toward the Straits. It has advanced another forty miles. We estimate that at its present speed it will be entering the Straits at midnight tonight their time, or about 4:00 P.M. our time." The director nodded at the aide, who took down the photograph. Heffelfinger dropped the small metallic pointer into his suit side pocket, then resumed his seat at the table.

President Staton scanned around the table. "Are there any questions or comments?"

Secretary Thompson had not seen the photographs prior to the meeting. Under President Hansen all intelligence data from the Agency had been sent to him prior to NSC meetings. Apparently,

Dr. Tollefson had new instructions about their dissemination. He would talk to Tollefson later. "Mr. President, I believe there is little question about the direction of the Black Seat fleet, but we have no new intelligence suggesting an offensive buildup on the Turkish border."

Admiral Birchfield, sitting across from the President, next to the empty chair of the Vice-President, interjected, "Secretary Thompson, I can't believe you don't view this move by the Russians as a planned offensive against the Turks. They know we watch those Straits like a hawk. We have for most of this century. The Russians have always looked upon the Straits as a lifeline for their empire. On the European side of their vast nation, it is their only link to the Atlantic from their warm water ports on the Black Sea. Surely, Mr. Secretary, you can understand that before they would take any offensive action against Turkey by land, they would first move to secure those Straits. They cannot afford to have the Turks and what's left of NATO cut off their channel to the Atlantic."

Thompson faced the volatile chairman of the Joint Chiefs of Staff. "You believe, Admiral Birchfield, that the movement of the fleet is a prelude to an offensive move along the border, is that correct?"

"Yes, I do, sir, and I might add I speak for all the Chiefs."

Thompson knew immediately that Birchfield and the Joint Chiefs had seen the satellite photographs before the meeting and had discussed the situation. For the first time since he had taken office, the Defense Secretary felt at a disadvantage in sparring with the admiral. Thompson surmised that the President had directed the pictures be sent to his old Navy buddy. He had probably discussed the matter with Tollefson, and Tollefson had mentioned Hansen's order to send them to Thompson. It troubled him that the new President had more confidence in the saber rattling admiral than in him. "What do you propose, Admiral?"

"Go to the next step of *Thunderburst,* of course—Step II, and in a hurry. We need to let the Russians know we're on to their game."

"And if you are right, Admiral, and the Russians proceed with their plan, your logical next move would be to Step III— deployment. Is that correct?"

"Yes, sir, that would be only prudent."

"Then we move 36,000 American soldiers to within twenty miles of the Armenian border. We will have over fifteen divisions posed against us at that point, six thousand miles from our shores. Do you really think we can hold our own against such massive opposition, Admiral Birchfield?"

"I don't believe it will come to that. As I said yesterday, Mr. Secretary, the Russians have never had to face us straight up. They have always used surrogates. When they face the prospect of having to send their own troops against the finest trained army in the world, they will pause. I guarantee it. They really don't know how far they can push us before we would launch our missiles. If they were to completely overwhelm our men, they would have to worry that domestic pressure and public opinion might force President Staton into a retaliatory act by using our missiles. Don't you see, we can't lose? They cannot afford a confrontation, not as long as we have the edge in nuclear delivery systems, and thanks to Gorbachev's efforts to cut back on hardware, and Yeltsin's decision to disarm over 2,000 of their missiles, we still have that advantage."

"But what if you are wrong, Admiral? What if the Russians feel their own sovereignty is so important they will risk war with the United States to protect it? What if they believe that President Staton, in the middle of the worst domestic crisis this nation has ever faced, never would launch the missiles? You may be sending this nation into World War III and into a nuclear exchange that could spell Armagedon."

"Secretary Thompson, I believe you aren't being realistic. The Russians do have tactical and strategic advantages over us in a one-on-one confrontation in this locality. No question about that. The point is that they know we can see everything they do through our satellites. They have a history of taking an inch at a time. They'll take an inch, and if they see no resistance, they take another inch, then another. As long as we do nothing, they will keep moving forward until they have taken all of Turkey and Iran and then threaten the oil fields of the Middle East. No, sir, the only way to deal with the Russians is to stop them from moving too far. I think we can do that with a cattle prod. We don't need a shotgun."

"With all due respect, Admiral, I think you're playing with dangerous dice. Surely, there is something we can do of a diplomatic nature. Surely, we can make known to Chenkov that any attempt by his forces to cross the border would only cause the most grievous consequences. We still have substantial economic pressures we can apply. In the past five years, American businesses have poured nearly $50 billion into their economy. Our trade has risen by over 300 percent. They can't afford to jeopardize that investment. In the long run, their economy is still their Achilles' heel. That's where we should be placing the pressure."

A weary Secretary of the Treasury, whose plane had arrived from Europe only two hours before the 9:00 meeting, interjected. "I think Secretary Thompson has a point here. At my meetings in Brussels, the other finance ministers reported that combined European trade with Russia and its special allies is now more than twice that of the United States. That amounts to tremendous leverage, gentlemen."

Birchfield was not finished. "Mr. Secretary, what assurance do you have that our NATO allies will jeopardize that trade over the defense of Turkey? When the Italians invaded Ethiopia in the 30's, and the League of Nations condemned them, not one damn European nation cut off trade with Mussolini. Not one. And when Hitler walked into the Rhineland, what did the Europeans do? Not one damn thing. I tell you when push comes to shove, the Europeans are thick as thieves. They will not sacrifice their new found Common Market prosperity to protect the Turks. No, sir. They will not."

President Staton, who had been listening to the debate intently, interrupted. "Gentlemen, it seems to me that in all this discussion we can glean some good. First, I think Admiral Birchfield makes a decent point about the Russians taking an inch at a time. Going to Step II of *Thunderburst* does not necessarily commit us to Step III.

As I understand Step II, our soldiers are airlifted to deployment points in Crete, Italy, and Saudi Arabia. Is that right, Admiral?"

"Yes, sir, that is correct. We estimate forty-eight hours will be necessary to accomplish that phase."

"Then I think we should proceed."

Thompson started to protest, but realized Staton had made up his mind.

"Secondly, I think we should begin discussions immediately with our NATO allies. How far are they willing to go? Will they back us with economic sanctions? We need to have these answers as soon as possible." He turned to Engledow on his right "Bill, I want you to personally call the foreign ministers of every one of our NATO allies. Start with Britain, then France, then Germany. Use the new fiber optic cable that we installed last year in the Atlantic. That way we'll be able to detect any eavesdropping. I never trusted those satellite transmissions."

Thompson felt better. At least Staton was going to try diplomatic channels. Maybe he was just playing with Birchfield, or placating him, while he pursued a less provocative course of action. The Defense Secretary had confidence in the robust new President. Staton could control Birchfield. Of that Thompson had little doubt.

"Finally, gentlemen. I think our greatest vulnerability right now is that the Russians may think that due to our current leadership crisis, we might be too confused and too disoriented to act. I believe it is absolutely essential that we give every outward indication that this government has not missed a beat. President Hansen may be gone, but the government continues unabated. That's why I intend to announce my selection for Vice-President this afternoon."

There was a collective effort on the parts of most of those in the room to catch a breath. No one expected the President to move so quickly. The Secretary of the Treasury asked, "Mr. President, do you really think that's prudent at this time? We haven't had the President's and Vice-President's funerals, yet. I mean, won't a large segment of our population believe you're moving too fast?"

The Treasury Secretary fumbled for words. "I guess I mean, Mr. President, don't you think many people will think you are acting in bad taste?"

Though not a delicate way to phrase the question, everyone in the room had the same thought.

"Yes, Mr. Secretary, I think I run that risk. However, historically, the people of this nation have rallied behind new Presidents in times of crisis. I am counting on that kind of good will. Frankly, I'm not concerned about what's best for me, politically, right now. I'm thinking of what is best for this country. I think one of the best signals I can send to the Russians is to show them that this government continues, strong and in control."

No one in the room took issue with the President. There was enough logic in his reasoning. The announcement had caught them all off guard, and each man in the room needed more time to digest the impact of his decision. None really had stopped to speculate on who the President might select. That would come later.

The President turned to his Attorney General. "Jacob, would you give us an update on the investigation into the assassination?" Most of those present had watched Bert Mattox's press conference earlier in the day. The Attorney General's announcement that another assassin was loose in Washington and that Mattox and a woman named Mosele were on his or her hit list would be news to the entire Security Council and its staff.

*****

The new President asked Secretary Thompson to stay after the NSC meeting for a few minutes. They had adjourned to the Oval Office where they found seats opposite each other on the sofas near the fireplace.

"Nels, what do you make of this situation? I thought the Russian army was in a mess from the cutbacks initiated by Gorbachev, the separation by the dozen or so republics, and the large influx of minorities within the military over there."

"Well, yes and no, Mr. President. It's true that they did suffer cutbacks under Gorbachev, but remember they had over two million men in Europe which he had to pull out after the East European nations separated and withdrew from the Warsaw Pact. He couldn't just turn them loose. There were no jobs for them in the civilian sector. So he allowed attrition to reduce the size of the army and the navy. He cut back on sophisticated new missile and other hardware systems and began the cutbacks he and Bush had agreed to in 1991 in the START treaty. But after regaining power, the military commanders who control Chenkov were able to get manning tables back to, let's say, 1985 standards. That's 4.2 million men, Mr. President, as compared to our 2.2 million."

"Yes, Nels, but he has a hell of a long border to protect from some hostile neighbors. What is it, something like 60,000 kilometers?"

"Yes, sir, it is. However, the largest concentration of Russian forces has been in the Trans Caucasus and in nearby Turkistan, on the other side of the Caspian Sea. Despite their independence in 1991, these former Soviet provinces share a common fear of China, and that fear has led them into an alliance with Moscow. And remember, the Russians still have two nearby fleets, one in the Mediterranean, the other in the Black Sea. It's the latter that Heffelfinger sees moving toward the Straits. Between the two fleets, they could be a potent force, especially with their air power. Birchfield is right about the Straits, Mr. President."

A small smile crossed Staton's lips, but he made no reference to the Birchfield—Thompson debate. "What about the ethnic problem. This whole mess is due to Muslims versus Christians— another goddamn religious war. I am so sick of these goddamn religious conflicts. If it isn't here, it's the Shiites versus the Sunnis in the Middle East, or the Moslems versus the Jews, or the Catholics versus the Protestants in Northern Ireland, or the Sikhs versus the Hindus in India, or the Moslems versus the Hindus in India and Pakistan. I tell you, Nels, if we didn't have religion to deal with, this world would be a lot more peaceful."

Thompson responded, "I agree, Mr. President, but as far as the Russian military situation is concerned, their military high command does a good job in separating Muslim from Christian troops in their assignments. About a third are Muslim, but in this situation in the south, they will use their Border Troops, which are Russian.

"What about their quality, Nels?"

"Let me give you a comparison, Mr. President. In 1976, 69 percent of American enlistments had a high school diploma. By comparison 72 percent of Soviet conscripts had a high school diploma. The figures in the 1990's are comparable, despite President Hansen's best efforts at educational reform. We've been able to get our figures up to over 88 percent, but the Soviets are now pushing 90 percent. No, sir, in terms of education, anyway, the Soviet soldier is every bit as competent as an American. However, there is one problem they have that we don't."

"And what might that be, Mr. Secretary."

"Language. We have a common language in spite of the large Spanish speaking population that has entered the country during the past three decades. The younger Hispanic kids, those who enlist, speak perfect English. But in the old Soviet Union, while Russian is taught in all schools, we estimate that nearly 40 percent of Chenkov's troops use Russian as a second language, and a large percentage of that number are not comfortable in the language."

"Does that pose a problem for them in this situation?"

Thompson paused as he thought. "I doubt it, sir. I can't believe that Moscow would attempt any major military move with less than their best trained units. The Border Troops and the Internal Security Troops, along with the Strategic Rocket Forces, are their best trained personnel."

The Secretary hesitated only momentarily. "Quite frankly, Mr. President, that's what scares the hell out of me when Birchfield begins blowing off. Sure, we could move three divisions over there, but we'd only be able to provide enough logistical support for two weeks. This isn't like the '91 Iraqi conflict, when we took over six months to stockpile all the munitions and food and other support material before we began our land assault."

Thompson stopped referring to his papers and looked directly at the President. "The Russian alliance has thirteen divisions stationed in the Trans Caucasus and seven divisions in Turkistan. Add to that another dozen divisions that could be moved from central Russia—the old East Germany divisions—and we're looking at an army of over a million men. And they'll be fighting near their own territory. We would have to maintain a six-thousand-mile supply line."

The President dropped his chin onto his chest as he digested the report. "And you believe *Thunderburst* won't work. Is that the bottom line?"

Thompson paused, studying the arms of his chair while he prepared an answer. "Mr. President, I think *Thunderburst* might work in our own hemisphere if we have limited objectives—such as the capture of Noriega a few years back, but in all honesty, sir, I don't think we have a snowball's chance in hell of winning a direct confrontation with Russia six thousand miles from our own shores."

The President lifted his eyes toward Thompson, but not his chin. "What about Admiral Birchfield's contention that the Russians would never risk a direct confrontation with us because of our superior nuclear capabilities?"

Thompson had already prepared his response. "And what if he's wrong, Mr. President? As your Secretary of Defense, I cannot make a recommendation to you that could cost thousands of American casualties without an excellent chance at success on the basis of a guess of intentions. Birchfield is too much a gambler for me, Mr. President."

The President leaned forward in preparation to stand. "Well, Nels, we'll just have to see. We'll just have to see." The President's words drifted off as his eyes focused on the fireplace. The reality of being President of the United States and its accompanying burden was sinking in.

*****

Senator Jake Lewellan's office was located in the Richard Russell Senate Office Building, next to the Hart Building. Mattox flashed his identification to the receptionist in the senator's office. "I'm Bert Mattox, Miss. I wonder if the senator is in?"

The attractive young blond with a dark tan smiled broadly. "Why, Mr. Mattox? I saw you on television. You're in charge of the assassination investigation, aren't you? I can't believe I'm talking to you."

Mattox was surprised at the spontaneity of the young woman—not at all like most of the professional Senate staff members. "Thank you, Miss. Are you new here?"

The bubbly receptionist smiled sheepishly. "Kinda. Most of the senator's staff is off for the Senate break, and I'm a temporary. My sister is Senator Lewellan's chief research assistant. I'm their old standby, I guess. I've done this for nearly two years."

Mattox thought the lack of inhibition in the young blond was refreshing in Washington.

"Well, you're a credit to the senator, Miss," Mattox turned on his charm and smiled broadly, " but the senator, is he in?"

"Just a minute. I'll check with his personal secretary." The pretty blond picked up the receiver from her console and spoke to Lewellan's secretary in an adjoining office. Mattox glanced at his watch—10:15. He needed to be at the hospital by noon. The blond replaced the receiver of her phone. "Mr. Mattox, the senator is in his office. He's tied up just now, but if you'd like to have a seat, his secretary said the senator could see you in about fifteen minutes."

Mattox glanced at his watch. He had enough time. "Excuse me, Miss. I hate to be a pest, but is there a place in private I could use a phone? I need to call my office." His broad smile had its effect on the young receptionist.

"Yes, sir. Mr. Lampworth, the senator's chief-of-staff, is out of town. Why don't you use his office. It's over to the right, there." She pointed with her pencil.

"Thank you, Miss. And you will let me know as soon as Senator Lewellan can see me?"

"Oh, yes, sir. I'll come right in and get you."

Mattox spent about ten minutes on the phone with Mary Alice who had heard from Peters at the Capitol Hilton. There had been only three long distance calls made from Casterline's room, two to New York and one to the now familiar number in Virginia. There was still no word from Akers in the Firemen's Insurance Building. The hospital had called. The administrator of the hospital was fit to be tied. He had been denied access to the trauma center because he had forgotten his badge. Maggy Mosele had called. She was feeling better and looked forward to seeing Mattox at noon. Mattox noted a tone of mischievousness in Mary Alice's voice when she mentioned Maggy. Sparks had regained consciousness. His condition had been upgraded from critical to serious. His family was with him. The director had called twice. He wanted Mattox to contact him at his first chance.

Mattox had his secretary transfer his call to the director's office. As he waited, his eyes wandered to the credenza behind the desk, and an 8x10 framed color photograph of a man in his thirties standing next to an older man, each holding up two tiny fish and laughing. Mrs. Cooper, Director Jameson's secretary, answered the phone. Mattox wheeled around in his chair to pick up a pen on the desk in case he needed to make notes. "This is Bert Mattox, Mrs. Cooper, is the director in?"

"Yes, sir. He's expecting your call. Please hold." Mrs. Cooper rang the call through to the director.

Alec Jameson came on the line. "Bert. I saw you on television this morning. You looked great. You must have had a restful night." The director knew that Matttox had spent most of the evening in the basement command center. The director's needle still worked. That was somehow reassuring to the special agent.

"What's new? The Attorney General just called. He gave a briefing to the National Security Council about an hour ago. The President is very anxious for progress reports. That's why I've been trying to reach you."

Mattox brought the director up to speed, including his present wait for Senator Lewellan to see him. The director asked Mattox if he thought it wise to be running around without body guards. Mattox had scoffed at the suggestion of protection. "How am I going to do my job if I have to tug a half dozen armed guards around? I know how to take care of myself. Don't worry." But the director would worry. Mattox was too important to the bureau and to the investigation at this point, not to mention that he had developed a fatherly affection for his chief agent.

No sooner had Mattox hung up the phone and started to return to the reception area, than the blond secretary opened the door. "The senator will see you now, Mr. Mattox."

As Mattox left the chief-of-staff's office, two men were walking out the main door toward the hall. He recognized the one man as Baker, the Secret Service agent, whom he had seen at the FDR Memorial after the explosion. What was the Secret Service doing in Lewellan's office?

Lewellan's suite of offices was not as large as Senator Howard's, but that was the way in Congress. Move up in seniority and get a bigger office. The senator's personal office was handsomely decorated with Indian blankets, stacked on the sofa, and reproductions of Remington paintings adorning the walls. The room possessed a distinctive Western flavor.

Lewellan stood when Mattox entered and offered his hand. There was no smile. He offered Mattox a chair to the side of his desk. "What can I do for you, Agent Mattox? I saw you on television yesterday and this morning. I might add, you handle yourself very well. Ever think about politics?"

Mattox thought the senator was making a joke, but there was no smile. "No, sir, I'll leave that to people like yourself, who have more patience with the media than I do."

"You do need patience. But again, what can I do for you?"

Mattox pulled out the copy of the memo that Lewellan had dictated to Howard several months earlier. "Senator, I understand from Senator Howard's staff that the suggestion for yesterday's ceremony had come from you." He handed the memo to Lewellan to read.

"This came from me, all right, but I don't remember sending it." He read through the memo carefully. His legal training would not allow him to speed read. He finally came to the closing. "This memo was prepared by Rollie Lampworth, my chief of staff. His initials are right next to mine at the bottom, under my signature." Lewellan handed the memo back to Mattox who noted the slug of initials at the bottom—*JEL/rl/ms*.

Mattox realized the 'JEL' was Lewellan, the 'rl' was Lampworth, and the 'ms' was one of the secretaries in the office. "Then you didn't prepare this, Senator?"

"No. I don't believe I did. But I don't prepare or read most of the material that goes out of this office. I depend on good staff people to protect me and my signature." Lewellan's attention drifted over to a glass bookcase next to the wall. A reproduction of Fredrick Remington's sculpture *Rattlesnake* was resting on top of the four drawer case. "That must be what Senator Howard meant the other day when we were leaving a hearing of the Judiciary Committee. He squeezed my elbow as we were getting out of the elevator and said, 'Good idea about FDR, Jake.' I never knew what he meant until right now. He thought the ceremony yesterday was my idea."

"Senator, your receptionist said Mr. Lampworth was out of town. Do you know where I can reach him?"

"He's not back, yet? I thought surely after yesterday, he'd be back here as soon as he could catch a plane. I only know that he asked me about a week ago for some vacation time. He said his father was ill in Florida and that he needed to visit him. The Senate was in recess, so I told him to go ahead."

"Do you know where in Florida, Senator."

"Tarpon Springs—I believe that's near Clearwater. My secretary can get you the address if you like."

The phone rang, and the senator picked it up immediately. "Yes. Could you give me a minute, please?" He cupped the receiver with his left hand and turned toward the agent. "Mr. Mattox, I'm afraid I have an important call here. Is there anything else?"

Mattox stood and returned the memo and his notebook to his inside pocket. He did not offer his hand. "No, that should do it. I'll let myself out and get Mr. Lampworth's address from your secretary. Thank you, sir."

"No problem. Good luck, Agent Mattox." Lewellan watched Mattox close the door, then leaned back in his chair and took his cupped hand away from the mouth of the receiver. "I must say, I'm surprised to hear from you, Mr. President."

*****

Outside in the reception area, the receptionist had just handed Mattox the address and telephone number that Lampworth had given the senator's secretary. "Here it is, Mr. Mattox. We haven't heard from Rollie for nearly a week. That isn't like him. Normally, when he's on vacation, he checks in almost every day." The phone rang, and she reached down to pick up the receiver. "Yes, he's right here. Hold on." She handed the receiver to Mattox. "It's your office, Mr. Mattox."

"This is Mattox."

Mary Alice's voice was tense. "Mr. Mattox, you had better get to the hospital as fast as possible. Someone just tried to kill Miss Mosele."

Chapter 12

Mattox drove like a maniac across the downtown area, his portable red light set high on his hardtop and his siren blaring. In route he called the command center on his car phone and ordered a search for Lampworth, reciting the address provided by Lewellan's secretary. In less than ten minutes, his new Buick came to a screeching halt directly in front of the emergency entrance to George Washington Hospital. Throwing open the door, he dashed past three of his agents guarding the outside doors and did not stop until he came to the windows of the trauma center. Two of his agents were standing on either side of the bed in bay four. Both were attempting to console Maggy Mosele, who appeared in complete control of herself.

Seeing Maggy sitting upright on the edge of her bed, fully dressed with her eyes alert and sparkling, sent feelings of both relief and excitement rushing through the special agent. He took a second to compose himself and then opened the glass door and made his way to Maggy's bed. "What happened here?" He looked sternly at his agents.

Maggy interrupted. "It wasn't their fault, Bert. A man whom I thought was an orderly—he was dressed in greens and had a

badge stuck to his coat pocket—came up to my bed and said he
had to give me a shot before I left. I don't like shots anyway, so I
asked what it was for. He said it was to make me rest. I told him I
didn't want to rest and that I didn't want the shot. He kept insisting
and pulled out a syringe and was going to force the shot on me. I
knocked the syringe out of his hand and started screaming at him.
He must have sensed everyone in the ward was staring at him, so
he took off running."

Mattox noticed that Maggy had combed her soft brown hair to
hide the wound on her temple. He had been right about her hair
length; it dropped just below her shoulders and softened her
overall appearance. He turned to the senior of the two agents.
"And why didn't you men stop him?"

"We didn't know what he was doing. We couldn't hear Miss
Mosele yelling through those damn windows. This guy in surgical
greens comes whipping by us, saying he had an emergency in
surgery. He looked official enough and had a badge."

"Did you get a description of the man?"

"Yes, sir. He was about six feet tall, had a blond flat top and
blue eyes, was athletic looking and fair complected, and had no
facial scars that were noticeable and no mustache. Looked like a
military type. He used the word "sir" two or three times."

"Have you phoned in his description?"

"Yes, sir. Both the bureau and D.C. police have his description.
We've put out an APB."

"Good work." Mattox turned back to Maggy. "Where's the
syringe? We might be able to lift some prints."

Maggy pointed to a doctor a few feet away. "Ask Dr. Reuben.
He's the one who picked it up, but I don't think you'll get prints.
The orderly was wearing plastic gloves."

Mattox crossed the small corridor and tapped the resident
surgeon on the shoulder. "Excuse me, Dr. Reuben, Miss Mosele
said you picked up the syringe that an orderly tried to administer
to her. Do you know what was in it?"

The doctor took the agent by the arm to move away from his
patient. He spoke in a whisper. "Sir, I didn't want to alarm Miss

Mosele or any of our other patients, but my guess is that it's cyanide. It smells like cyanide, but we'll have to run a lab test to be sure."

"Do that, Doctor, and thank you." Mattox returned to Maggy's bed. She was now standing next to the two agents.

"And where do you think you're going, young lady?" Mattox smiled, hopefully to lessen any tension Maggy might be feeling.

"Home, Mr. Mattox. I need a shower, and I have to call my boss." She looked around the bed and bed stand. "Where's my purse, anyway?"

One of the agents pointed toward the nurse's station. "One of our agents found it on the floorboard of Agent Mattox's car, Miss Mosele, and brought it in this morning and left it at the nurse's station for you."

Maggy nodded her head. "Good. Let's go."

As she started toward the nurse's station, Mattox reached out and gently grasped her elbow. "Not so fast. For a woman, or a man for that matter, who has had three attempts made on her life in the past eighteen hours, you're acting awfully cavalier."

Maggy turned and smiled. "And what would you have me do, Agent Mattox, crawl up into a little hole somewhere and hide my face for the rest of my life? I figure you professionals will find the man who tried to kill me."

Mattox's expression turned serious and concerned. "Look, Maggy, it's not as simple as all that. We're dealing with a well-financed, highly organized conspiracy. The man who tried to kill you last night also killed John Martin and Abdul. He's a professional. The fact that this orderly knew you were alive, that he knew what hospital you were in, that he wore an authentic picture ID all suggest that we aren't dealing with a simple nut here. He undoubtedly knows where you live and where you work. This man and the people he works for want you out of the way."

Mattox reached down and took Maggy's hand in his own. "Look, Maggy, there's no way you'll be safe at your place. I promised yesterday that nothing would happen to you, and I keep my promises; but I need your cooperation. I want you to stay at my condo in Alexandria for now. I'm going to be busy and won't be using it much. I'll have agents protecting you. I live in a complex that will be easy to secure."

"How long do you expect me to live this convent-type life, Bert? One day? Two days? Two weeks?"

"Give me a couple of days. We're really pretty good when we put our minds to it." He smiled broadly, and Maggy responded reluctantly with her own faint smile.

"Okay, two days. But could we stop by my apartment and pick up some things?"

"Why not tell the agents here what you need, and they'll pick them up. Your place may be booby trapped by now. My men will know what to look out for."

"You're always thinking, aren't you? Okay, but two days, that's all."

"You got it." Mattox squeezed her hand. Maggy's face was occupying more of his conscious thoughts. He knew he couldn't afford such a luxury. He needed to concentrate on the investigation. "Now you go with these men, and I'll drop by to see you later." He glanced at the clock on the wall. "I've got an appointment over at Langley in half an hour. Promise me you'll follow the agents' instructions."

Maggy pursed her lips in a pouting expression. "I will." Then as Mattox started to turn to give instructions to his men, she added, "But, Bert, you be careful, too. They may want you."

Mattox winked at Maggy, then turned toward his two agents to issue instructions.

*****

Mattox had visited the CIA headquarters in Langley on several occasions, mostly for seminars and briefings, but he had never met the well-known director of the agency, George Heffelfinger. He knew from a brief biography he had read in *Time* that the Minnesota native was a former congressman, that he had served in

Army intelligence while in the service, and that he had a reputation as a thorough and tough taskmaster. He was known to be wealthy, having inherited his fortune from the family railroad interests that dated back into the nineteenth century. One of the long held premises in Washington was that people who had inherited their wealth were less likely to be corrupted than those who had earned it themselves. People born into wealth take money for granted. Those who claw their way to the top never lose the temptation to acquire more.

At precisely 1:00, the director's secretary announced to Mattox that Mr. Heffelfinger would see him. She showed him into a large office decorated in a modern Scandinavian motif. Heffelfinger was seated behind his wood and fiberglass desk with a bank of large windows behind him. Mattox assumed that the large man, sitting in front of the director's desk, was Thomas Ashburn, the deputy director. Both agency men stood and offered their hands as the special agent entered.

"Good to see you, Mr. Mattox." Heffelfinger was attired in a dark gray herringbone sportcoat that appeared several years old. "You're becoming quite a celebrity. My daughter even asked about you last night after your press conference. How goes the hunt?"

All three men found their seats. "Well, Director, I understand you received a briefing from the Attorney General this morning, so you have a pretty good background on what we've found. What you probably don't know is that another attempt was made on Margaret Mosele's life about one hour ago, while she was still in the hospital."

Heffelfinger looked curious. Ashburn showed no expression. The director asked, "You said an attempt. I assume she is all right?"

"Yes, sir. The assailant was going to inject her with a lethal dose of cyanide, but he panicked when Miss Mosele protested. He had the presence of mind, however, to skip by our agents who were standing guard in the corridor, I regret to say. Now, Director Heffelfinger, it's about Miss Mosele that I need to talk to you."

"I don't know that we can help you, Mr. Mattox. I have never met the woman." Heffelfinger was doing all the talking.

Mattox hesitated as he looked back and forth at both men. He then explained the relationship between Mosele, Weissman, and Manchester.

Both agency directors sat impassively, listening to Mattox's explanation. Heffelfinger leaned forward in his chair. "I don't see where any of this involves our agency, Agent Mattox."

Mattox restrained his growing anger. Years of service had trained him to conceal his inclination toward displaying deep emotions. "I find that difficult to understand. My people have tried to get information from your agency on Manchester. We have received no cooperation, none at all. We can't even tell you where the man was born. Now it is obvious that Manchester had some connection to the assassin."

Heffelfinger interjected. "Isn't that speculation on your part, Mr. Mattox. Agreed, the assassin had his wallet. He could have found it. He could have stolen it. There might be several plausible explanations."

"I'll give you that, Director, but surely Manchester would be the best person to answer those questions. We can't find him. Your agency will not even admit he works here. Why won't you cooperate, Director?"

"Now, wait a minute, Mr. Mattox. Don't accuse the Central Intelligence Agency of not cooperating. According to Mr. Ashburn, one of your agents called his office this morning, attempting to solicit information on one of our best operatives. We don't just hand out that kind of information over the phone. We had no way of knowing that the call might not be fake. It could have been a reporter. We have a policy of protecting our agents, Mr. Mattox. I hope you can appreciate that." Heffelfinger again leaned back in his chair. Ashburn repositioned his large torso. Mattox thought him nervous.

"Okay. I'll accept that, but I don't think you would challenge my credentials. Perhaps you can fill me in on this Manchester and allow me to talk to him."

The two agency heads glanced at each other briefly before Heffelfinger spoke. "Mr. Mattox, let me give you some background. Bill Manchester has worked for this agency for nineteen years. For the past ten years, he has been one of our most effective operatives overseas. He has fluent command of a half dozen languages, including several Arabic dialects. His specialty has been North Africa. Two years ago our agency attempted to capture this Abdul fellow. We had a lead on how to contact him in Algeria. In the course of the operation, another one of our agents who was to make contact with Abdul was brutally killed. The agency lost a half million dollars on that effort."

Heffelfinger rose and walked around to Mattox and leaned against the front of his desk. "Manchester was not involved in this particular operation, but he was stationed in Morocco at the time. Somebody tipped off Abdul about our plan. That's the only explanation of why our other agent was so brutally killed. I'll spare you the details of his death."

Mattox interrupted. "I've seen his handiwork, Mr. Heffelfinger."

"So you know how cruel this devil could be. At the time we saw no connection between Manchester and our efforts to capture Abdul. Then last year Manchester was recalled to Langley in a purely routine rotation. We try to make sure all our undercover agents don't lose contact with their home base and roots."

Heffelfinger reached behind him on the desk and picked up a thick manilla folder and began fumbling through it. "About six months ago, it came to our attention from one of Manchester's colleagues that the agent was driving a new Mercedes 450 SL, a convertible, I believe. That car costs over $50,000 today. Very few of our agents make that kind of money. The report gave cause for our internal affairs people to check out Manchester's bank accounts." Heffelfinger was still thumbing through the folder when he stopped and pulled out a ledger sheet. "It seems our Mr. Manchester had deposited in his account over at the Arlington National Savings Bank nearly $90,000 over a period of three months. Each deposit was for exactly $9,000. As you know banks are required to report to the Treasury Department any deposits of over $10,000—part of the government's effort to find tax evaders and drug dealers. Manchester knew that and was very careful."

Heffelfinger replaced the folder. "As you might guess, our people became suspicious. For the past four months we have had Manchester under observation. I don't think he knew, but he might have. He was awfully good. One of our best."

Mattox leaned forward. "So you think it might be possible that Manchester tipped off Abdul about your operation and that in return he received a bundle of money for his efforts. Is that it?"

Heffelfinger returned to his seat. "In a nutshell, yes. I think you can see why we were reluctant to let out that kind of information. We haven't confronted Manchester as of yet with any accusations because, quite frankly, all we have is circumstantial evidence. We surely don't want you fellows at the bureau spooking him so he flees the country on us."

"But none of this explains why Abdul would have Manchester's wallet. Has Manchester notified the agency that he's missing his ID? I would think that standard operating procedure."

Heffelfinger picked up a pencil from his desk and began rubbing his temple with its eraser. "As a matter of fact, he hasn't. In fact he has not been here for three days. We know that he booked a flight to Orlando for personal business. There's no reason for him to be there on official business."

Mattox pursued his questioning. "Since you knew he was going to Florida, I assume you had him followed?"

Heffelfinger hesitated. "No. We didn't find out about his trip until after he left. You see Capitol Travel is owned by the agency, through a blind subsidiary, of course. We run a lot of our commercial travel through there, and it allows us to keep better records of our people's travel expenses."

Mattox was surprised. "You mean Margaret Mosele works for the CIA?"

"In a manner of speaking, yes, but she would never know it. We keep the travel agency activity separate from official operations. The manager doesn't even know of our connection, but one of the agents, a fellow named Ted Sizemore, works for us. He's the one whom we depend on for any unusual transportation requirements by our people. Actually, the Capitol Travel Agency has proved quite profitable. It's provided us with a surplus every year it's been open. Saved the taxpayers a considerable amount of money." Heffelfinger was still playing with the pencil.

Mattox flipped a page in the small spiral notebook he had taken from his suit pocket. "Back to Manchester. You know he went to Orlando, but you don't know why or where he is staying."

Heffelfinger did not respond. Finally, Ashburn spoke for the first time. "As a matter of fact, we do have an idea of why he went to Orlando. Manchester's phone has been tapped for the past four months. His secretary took a call four days ago from a man who said he was from Algiers. He wanted to meet Manchester in Florida. Said he had sustained an injury and that his itinerary had to be changed."

"And you didn't ask Manchester about the message?" Mattox was having trouble believing the ineptness of the agency.

"If we had questioned him, he would have known we had tapped his phone and would have figured out he was under suspicion. As for the cryptic message from Orlando, there was nothing incriminating. We could never have made a case with just that message. We needed more. In the meantime, we assumed there was a possibility that Abdul was in the country, and that's what I communicated to your Director Jameson the day before yesterday and why he asked us to share Abdul's file with you. Please believe me, Mr. Mattox, we had no idea that Abdul was headed for Washington or that he had any intention of assassinating the President, Vice-President, and the rest of them. We had no idea."

Ashburn's explanation was plausible. "What about Manchester? Do you think he's skipped the country?"

Heffelfinger rejoined the conversation. "Quite frankly, I doubt it. We still have the problem with the missing wallet. Manchester would never have left without his wallet. You reported to us that it had contained nearly a thousand dollars. And we know from checking with his bank that he has not withdrawn much of what he has saved there. His expensive car is still parked at National Airport; we checked on that. If he were going to leave the country, I have to believe he would need his financial resources."

Mattox paused as he finished writing in his notebook. His mind was rife with more questions than answers. "So you think Abdul may have eliminated Manchester, is that correct?"

"We think it is a viable possibility. We have people looking all over Orlando at this very minute," Ashburn responded.

"That makes two of us. Our people in Florida are doing the same thing. Let me ask you something else. Does either of you know John Fairchild Chamberlain?"

Heffelfinger leaned forward with a surprised expression. "John Chamberlain? Of course, I know him, known him for years. He contributed to my campaigns back in the early 80's. What's he got to do with this?"

Mattox was hesitant, but it was necessary to pursue all his leads before he left Langley. He might not have both Ashburn and Heffelfinger together again. "We have not released this information, even to the Attorney General, but Manchester's wallet contained the Virginia home telephone number of John Chamberlain. We're assuming Manchester had the number."

Heffelfinger looked puzzled. "Why would Manchester have John's number? I don't even have his number, and I consider John a close friend."

Mattox continued. "More than that, sir. We know that Abdul called this same number from the Capitol Hilton Hotel yesterday afternoon during the time period we were conducting a room to room search of the hotel."

Heffelfinger looked perplexed. "You say Abdul called John's home number. Are you positive?"

"Yes, sir, I am."

Heffelfinger stood and began pacing behind his desk in front of a set of large bulletproof windows. "I have always considered John Chamberlain an honest man and a patriot. Most people think he's a Republican because of his money, but I know for a fact he contributes to as many Democrats' campaigns as Republicans'. He's on a dozen corporate boards, countless charities. He personally contributed two million dollars for the construction of the new FDR Memorial going up over at the Tidal Basin. In fact, one of his subsidiaries, a masonry supplier and contractor, is supplying all the limestone and labor at cost. President Hansen told me that himself. John and his wife must have been guests of the Hansens for a half dozen state dinners over the past two years. There's just no way I can believe John Chamberlain could be involved with this Abdul or with the murder of the President. It just makes no sense."

Mattox waited for the director to finish his pacing and return to his seat. "Sir, I have no reason to believe that Mr. Chamberlain is involved in any way. All we know is that we have his phone number. We don't know if Chamberlain was at home to take the call. We don't know how many people work or live at Chamberlain's residence. There are a great number of questions that need answering, but I think you would agree, we need to pursue them."

Heffelfinger turned to look out his windows at the new green foliage of the Virginia countryside. "Of course, of course. You should do that. But what I can't understand is why Manchester would have that number. Why? Why?" Heffelfinger was deep in thought.

Mattox turned his attention to the deputy director. "Mr. Ashburn, is there any reason that one of your agents would be carrying around a playing card, specifically the ace of spades?"

Ashburn mused for a few seconds. "No, I can't think of any. Why, was there an ace of spades in Manchester's wallet?"

"Yes, sir."

"No official reason, I can tell you that."

Mattox made a note in his book, then returned to Ashburn. "One final point, sir. John Martin. He was killed last night. His body is being held at the hospital's morgue. They have inquired about notifying the family. I know he was from Iowa, but that's all. Would your agency take care of the notification, sir?"

"Of course. I didn't know Martin well. I met him when he picked up the packet I sent to you yesterday, but I regret I can't even remember what he looked like."

"He was a fine young man, Mr. Ashburn. He was a credit to your agency. He was in many ways representative of the best in this country. I'm going to miss him." Mattox was putting away his pad as he stood.

"Then you knew Martin well?" Ashburn asked as he and Heffelfinger also rose.

"Yes, sir, I'd like to think I did. In one sense, he saved my life, and I intend to make sure that whoever killed him is found. If it's the last thing I do, I will find his killer. Thank you both."

The two agency leaders watched Mattox leave. Ashburn turned to the director. "George, I didn't want to say anything in front of Mattox, but wasn't Manchester at that cocktail party Chamberlain threw for Senator Lewellan a few months back, over at *Dominique's*. I thought you were there?"

Heffelfinger scratched his chin. "I guess I don't remember." He paused to think. "Wait a minute; that was a fund raiser, wasn't it, the one with the actors and singers? I missed that one because of my daughter's piano recital at the National Gallery. I remember your telling me it was an expensive affair."

Ashburn resumed his seat. "It sure was. Come to think of it, I don't remember your being there. That's right, you asked me to go for you. Well, anyway, I'm almost positive Manchester was there. That was before we suspected him of anything."

Heffelfinger, who was still standing, turned again to gaze out his window. "God! John Chamberlain. I just hope to hell he was in St. Croix yesterday."

Ashburn sat silently.

Chapter 13

J. Edgar Hoover Building
3:00 P.M.

The track lighting above the conference table in the basement command center glared down upon the small torn yellow fragments of paper that Mattox had arranged in front of him. These were the various components to his investigation. Some were facts; some were speculation, and some were questions. Many veterans in the bureau preferred an old fashioned chalkboard, others a bulletin board. Mattox preferred his method because it was easier for him to move the papers around, like pieces of a puzzle.

The special agent was standing, bent over the long, walnut, formica table, arranging the fragments of paper. Carl Peters, an agent with only six years of experience in investigation, but a man who had impressed Mattox on two previous projects, sat in a chair across the table. In front of him on the table lay his open notebook and a pen. Mattox had not spoken for nearly twenty minutes. Peters knew better than to interrupt with questions.

Finally, Mattox began thinking out loud. "There was something that Heffelfinger said about Chamberlain that has been bothering me. One of Chamberlain's subsidiaries was donating the stone and labor for the new FDR Memorial. But Senator Howard's man, Cavanaugh, told me that the old man was angry about the delays in finishing that new memorial. It stands to reason that had the new monument been finished by yesterday, the ceremony involving the President would have been moved to the new site." Peters noted Mattox's main points in his pad.

"Carl, I want you to find out what the delay was on the new FDR Memorial. Call the park service again; they were coordinating the effort." Mattox issued the instruction without looking up.

"Yes, sir. I'll use the phone in our office next door." He stood and left through the only door into the room.

Mattox already had received a report from the bureau's Tampa office that Lampworth was not at his father's address, which it turned out was located in a trailer park. The father wasn't there, either. A call to the elder Lampworth's Illinois home found the father feeling fine. He had returned to Rockford for business nearly three weeks earlier. He indicated his son had called on April 5th and asked permission to spend a few days at the trailer. The park office had a record of the younger Lampworth checking in, but not checking out. The interior of the trailer appeared normal and clean, except for a suitcase and garment bag with Roland Lampworth's airline tags attached.

The elder Lampworth was known to keep a bass boat at the park's dock on Tarpon Lake. An examination of the boat had disclosed a small pool of dried blood on the back seat. The Tampa office had called in the Pinnellas County Sheriff's Department to begin dragging the large lake.

Chamberlain was emerging as the key to the puzzle. Chamberlain knew the President. He had some connection with Manchester. Abdui had called his home. He was a heavy contributor to political campaigns. One of his companies worked on the new FDR Memorial. Outside of the telephone number, however, there was nothing to connect Manchester to Chamberlain. They certainly didn't run around in the same social circles. And where did Lampworth fit in? His memo, at least according to Senator Lewellan, had set in motion the events that had led to the FDR anniversary ceremony. There was no direct link between Lampworth, Lewellan, Chamberlain, or Manchester. Too many loose ends.

Peters returned moments later. "Mr. Mattox, I just spoke to the deputy director of the park service, and he says the stone masons have been out on strike for four months. He also said Senator Howard's office was all over his ass to expedite the completion. They were under so much pressure that the park service offered to adjust the original agreement with the contractor and pay the wages the union was demanding, but the contractor refused. The contractor was the Tideland Construction Company of Richmond, Virginia."

Mattox added quickly, "Which, my good friend, I'll bet a year's salary, is owned by JFC Industries, or John Chamberlain. We now have one link. Chamberlain's subsidiary refused to settle a strike with its most crucial union, the masons, which in turn delayed the completion of the new Roosevelt memorial and forced yesterday's ceremony to be held at the old memorial. Great! Now if I could only find a link between Chamberlain, Manchester, and Lampworth."

The telephone at the end of the conference table rang. Mattox waved Peters off as he reached for the receiver. "This is Special Agent Mattox." The agent's face showed no emotion for the two minutes he listened. "You have a positive ID? His wallet was missing? Were any other papers found on the body that would be helpful to us? How did your people discover him?" After another lengthy explanation from the other end, Mattox closed. "You've been a big help, Mr. Ashburn. Thank you very much."

Mattox returned to his puzzle. "Manchester is dead. His body was found in a lake at Disney World. The Orange County coroner is going to conduct an autopsy this evening at the Agency's request."

Mattox went silent for another few minutes while he pondered the new information. Peters could not restrain his curiosity. "Mr.

Mattox, excuse me for interrupting, but how did they find him and identify him?"

Mattox looked up as if brought back to reality. "In checking the hotels in the area, one of their men ran across a desk clerk at the Hilton in Buena Vista who remembered holding a message for a man named Manchester. The message was left by a man who fits our description of Abdul. Manchester made a call from the hotel lobby, then returned to the clerk and asked for directions to the entrance to Disney World. The maintenance staff at Disney found a John Doe's body yesterday and sent the corpse to the Orange County morgue. The Agency checked the fingerprints of the John Doe against those of Manchester, and, of course, they matched."

"Did they find anything else on the body?" Peters felt more at ease.

"Nothing to identify him." Mattox continued to stare at his table. "Manchester's dead. Probably killed by Abdul? Why? Revenge? Revenge for what? The agency believed Manchester tipped off Abdul about one of their operations to capture the bastard. They also believe Abdul paid him off. Revenge makes no sense. Why would he kill Manchester just prior to the biggest hit in his life? He was too smart to jeopardize his primary assignment. Why pick Florida? Manchester knew Abdul was in Florida. He received a message from him. The fact that Abdul knew how to contact Manchester and that Manchester responded by flying down there suggests to me a meeting was being arranged."

"Maybe they had a disagreement and Abdul lost his temper," Peters offered.

"Possible. But Ashburn said . . ." Mattox looked for one of the pages from his small notebook which he had placed on the table, "that the man from Algiers had been injured, and his itinerary had been changed."

"We all saw Abdul running across the Mall last night. He didn't look hurt to me, Mr. Mattox," Peters observed.

"That's right, which means he lied about his injury. That must have been meant as bait. But what about the part about his itinerary being changed? What was his itinerary? We know now that he planned to kill the President and that he had been planning it for weeks. He was here several weeks ago to plant those goddamn explosives. Abdul would only have left a message like that for Manchester if he knew that Manchester would know what his itinerary was."

"So Manchester knew about the assassination plan!"

"He must have. Why else would he have rushed to Florida? Why didn't he tell his superiors? The only answer is that he didn't want them to know." Mattox looked across the table at Peters and smiled slightly. "You know, Peters, I believe we know now that CIA Agent Manchester was a part of the conspiracy to kill the President. Now if we can only link Manchester to Chamberlain or Lampworth." Mattox stood straight up and stretched. "Miss Mosele may have some of the answers. She practically lived with the guy for three years. God, she doesn't know about Manchester's death, yet. I better get home and tell her."

Mattox took his coat off the rack near the door. "Peters, you stay here. You can reach me in my car or at home if you hear anything on Lampworth. Also, have Akers begin a check on Chamberlain. Before long I'm going to have to talk to Mr. Big."

*****

The President looked up from his desk as Lowenstein ushered Admiral Birchfield, Secretary Thompson, and Secretary Engledow into the Oval Office. He waved all four men to chairs in front of his desk.

"Gentlemen, a few minutes ago I had a call from George Heffelfinger. He reports that the Russian fleet has taken positions in the Straits of Bosporus near Istanbul. The fleet is now stationary. He also reports a build up of Russian divisions near Yerevan, the Armenian capital city, located north of Mt. Ararat.

From that point Heffelfinger says they could launch an invasion of both Turkey and Iran."

Thompson asked quickly, "How many divisions are there in Yerevan, Mr. President?"

"At least four, though it's nighttime over there now, and George is relying on forward observers he has in the area rather than the satellites."

Admiral Birchfield, hearing the news with a smug expression glued to his face, hammered the arm of his chair with his left fist. "I knew they would do this, Mr. President. I knew it! We must move forward with Step III of *Thunderburst*, sir. Our efforts so far haven't had any effect on them; that's apparent."

"I'd like to hear from Bill on his talks with our allies." Thompson turned toward the Acting Secretary of State.

"I'm afraid I don't have much encouraging news, Mr. President." The Deputy Secretary placed his half-lens reading glasses on the bridge of his nose and read from the notes he had brought with him. "Canada will back any demands we make economically, but urges us to use caution militarily. They are not prepared to send troops. Germany has the biggest economic investment in Russia and its allies right now. As you gentlemen know, Germany's economy is now the third largest in the world, behind the United States and Japan. The recession they suffered in '91 after unification has been followed by continued prosperity. The foreign minister indicated it would be very difficult for his government to suspend trade at this time, and there was no way they would freeze assets. They have more money invested in Russia today than vice versa. They think such action would be more devastating for them than for the Russians."

"Doesn't surprise me one bit. I knew after Kohl and Gorbachev put that deal together back in '90, that those two would get in bed together. Mr. President, you can forget the Germans. They're just going to look out for themselves." Birchfield spit out each bitter syllable.

Thompson was undeterred. "What about the rest, Bill?"

"France is equivocating as usual. Britain's Labor government doesn't know at this time. Quite frankly, Mr. President, I'm not surprised. Since Labor won the last election, the new government has made a shambles of the British economy. Their graduated renationalization policies are playing havoc with their balance of trade. I don't think they have any leverage that would be helpful to us."

The President shook his head. "That's a real disappointment to me, Bill, but I agree with you. I wasn't able to make any headway with their new government regarding graduated reductions in NATO forces. They wanted large cutbacks as fast as they could get them. They were blinded by Yeltsin. That government must have tunnel vision. I'll be glad when they're forced into elections again."

Engledow removed his reading glasses and twirled them with his fingers over the arm of his chair. "The Benelux countries are scared as hell that we're going to bait the Russians into a war. They don't feel prepared, militarily. As you know there is a strong anti-military sentiment in their respective parliaments. Italy, Portugal, and Greece are all willing to support economic sanctions, but no military action. Unfortunately, their investments in the Russian republics amount to less than $5 billion."

Engledow dropped his papers on his knees. "I'm afraid, Mr. President, we can forget Britain, France, and Germany regarding economic sanctions. The Canadians are the only significant player left in terms of economic power. None of our allies wants a military confrontation. At this point, Mr. President, I have to advise you that any military action taken by the United States will probably have to be taken unilaterally."

The Chairman of the Joint Chiefs was leaning forward on the edge of his chair. "Mr. President, we knew from the beginning that our allies would fold. *Thunderburst* was designed as a unilateral action. All I see in the Secretary's report is confirmation of what the Chiefs have believed for several years and which, I might add, we have factored into our strategic planning. I say again, if we don't stop the Russians now, we will sacrifice both Turkey and Iran and who knows what else in the months ahead."

Thompson interrupted. "Mr. President, I have to disagree with Ogden. I agree that our allies aren't providing the support we need for effective economic pressure, though I remind you that if you combine Canada, Italy, and the United States, we're probably talking about a third of the Russia's foreign trade at this point. We don't know what their reaction would be to sanctions. We haven't proposed them, yet. In fact, Mr. President, except for President Hansen's query and Chenkov's response yesterday, we have had no dialogue with them on this matter. Mr. President, it is still too early to commit troops."

Staton reached down on his desk and picked up the gold letter opener that Thompson remembered Seth Hansen rolling around in his hands only twenty-four hours earlier. Staton used the opener as an extension of his hand, like a baton. "Nels, I appreciate your point of view. I'm going to send Bill to Moscow this evening to begin those negotiations you recommend. Hopefully, he can talk some sense into those militarists now in control. I had hoped Chenkov might indicate he was coming to President Hansen's funeral, but I received a call from the Russian ambassador saying his President would be unable to attend. He's sending a delegation headed by the speaker of their lower house of parliament. Can you believe that? They're not even sending their foreign minister or any representative of their federal government."

Staton pointed toward Engledow. "Bill, I want you to call their foreign minister and tell him you're on your way over there with a very important personal message for Chenkov from me. Tell him you're departing this evening. You draft a letter for me and I'll sign it before you leave. Indicate that any attempt by the Soviet Union to violate the sovereignty of Turkey or Iran will be considered by this government to be an unfriendly act. Tell him, explicitly, the United States will defend its allies militarily and that we will use every effort at our disposal at the United Nations and with our

allies to impose the most severe economic sanctions available."
Staton waved his gold opener at Engledow. "Now don't use a lot
of that nice diplomatic language. I want a direct and assertive
letter. Invoke the old Truman Doctrine, the NATO pact, and the
UN charter if you have to. Do you have that?"

Engledow nodded. "Yes, Mr. President."

Thompson breathed a sigh of relief. Birchfield, however,
glared at the President with slightly disguised contempt.

Staton then turned toward Thompson. "Nels, I do see your point
of view, but I think I have to make Chenkov realize that I mean
business. I don't want him taking my letter and throwing it in the
trash, shrugging his shoulders and saying that ole Crawfish Staton
ain't got the guts for a fight. No! I am going to order both you and
Admiral Birchfield to proceed to Step III of *Thunderburst*."

Before Thompson could protest, the President turned to
Birchfield. "Now, Admiral Birchfield, this means our troops will
be sent to points in Turkey and Iran. Where are those points?"

Birchfield, feeling his second wind, lighted up as he reached
over to his briefcase, pulling out a folded map, which he opened
and spread on the President's desk. "The best landing strip in the
area is at Malatya. It's the only city in the eastern section of Turkey
with much population, about 110,000. We'll land there and deploy
to within twenty miles of the Armenian border. We'll send about a
third of our troops to Tabriz, here in northern Iran." The admiral
pointed to a spot southeast of Malatya."

"How long will it take?" Staton leaned back in his chair.

"Step II is now in progress, and our troops should be at their
points of debarkation by twenty-four hundred hours this evening,
Washington time. I would say that, if all goes according to plan,
the first contingent of our troops should be deployed in Turkey and
Iran by twelve hundred hours tomorrow, noon."

Thompson's frustration boiled over. "Mr. President, I ask you
to reconsider this action. The Russians haven't had time to react to
Step II as of yet. Our troops won't reach their bases in Crete and
Italy until midnight. You're backing Chenkov against a wall. The

Russians are a proud people, Mr. President. Bill will be in Moscow by morning. Surely, that's soon enough, sir, before we move to Step III?"

"No, Nels, it's not. My reading of Chenkov and the generals is that they perceive the United States to be weaker now than at any time in the past two or three decades. Admiral Birchfield may be right in his analysis of their resolve in the face of strong American action. As commander-in-chief I have a responsibility of preserving our security, and that includes honoring our commitments to our allies. If I tiptoe now, even our allies are going to think I haven't got the guts for decisive action. No, I believe I must move now. When Chenkov gets my letter, I want him to know I am not afraid to act."

Staton hesitated momentarily. "And he has to be made to believe that this policy goes beyond me. He needs to see that our government, in spite of yesterday's tragedy, continues unabated as the Constitution and our laws provide. That's why I have asked Lowenstein to call a press conference for 4:30." Staton looked at his watch. "That's in about half an hour." I intend to tell the American people about this Russian threat and what I am doing about it." There was a pause as Staton looked each man in the eye, "and then I'm going to announce my choice for Vice-President. There will be no question in Chenkov's mind or in the American people's mind that there is continuity in our government."

Thompson began to speak, but Staton held up his hand. "No, Nels, I've made up my mind. I'm proceeding on a three-prong approach—diplomatic, military and political. Now, I expect you gentlemen to give me your full support."

"Without question, Mr. President." Birchfield snapped to attention.

"Of course, Mr. President. I shall have the draft of your letter to Chenkov ready in an hour." Engledow also rose to leave.

Thompson wanted to stay and attempt to persuade the President to rescind his order to deploy Step III, but he realized that if Staton had already called a press conference, he had made up his mind on his course of action prior to their meeting. Any effort on his part now would be fruitless. "Yes, Mr. President, you have my support."

Lowenstein showed the three men out. As the door closed behind them, Staton slammed the gold opener down on the desk. "Damn!" he muttered.

Chapter 14

Mattox quietly unlocked the door to his first floor condominium. No need to frighten Maggy. He had checked both the patio and main entrance to his building. Two agents were stationed at both locations. In addition, six agents were spread around the periphery of the complex to watch for intruders, in spite of the one entrance to the small development.

Mattox took off his suit coat and wrapped it around a dining room chair. His home was neither large nor plush, but the three main rooms were tastefully decorated and neat. If Mattox had a fetish it was neatness. His bedroom door, located to the far left, down a small hallway, was slightly ajar, so he stepped silently across the salmon-colored carpet and pushed lightly on the door. A sleeping Margaret Mosele was lying in a semi-fetal position on his bed, clad only in a satin slip. The sight of the slender figure with the milky complexion, tight body, and long silky hair sent a shiver through Mattox. He closed the door without latching it.

Returning to his living room, he loosened his tie and kicked off his shoes and removed his dark socks, then collapsed into his favorite recliner and pushed back. Fatigue was overpowering him. In reflecting over the previous two days, he realized that he had been able to sleep for only two hours. In a matter of seconds, he was snoring softly.

Moments later a shrill scream aroused Mattox from his deep slumber. He shot forward in his chair, his eyes glossy, and his mind in a state of confusion. There was a second scream coming from his bedroom. He darted for the door and shoved it open. Maggy was now in a full fetal position, her fists smashed tightly against her eyes. She was sobbing.

Mattox rushed to the bed, sat next to her backside, and placed his hand on her shoulder. "That's all right, Maggy. I'm here. Take it easy. Nobody is going to hurt you. Just relax." He caressed her arm gently. The feel of her soft skin was both comforting and stimulating.

Maggy jerked around and threw her arms around Mattox's neck. "Oh, god, Bert. I saw him. I saw that terrible face."

Mattox embraced the slim body pressed tightly against his chest. He felt her breasts pushing against him, and a comforting sense of intimacy engulfed him He tried to calm her. "That's okay, Maggy. Who did you see?"

"It was awful, Bert. It was the man at the hotel with the eye patch, the man who tried to kill me. That horrible brown eye of his, it kept staring at me. I saw it again just now. I was running, but that eye was still chasing me. I couldn't get away. He kept getting closer. It was horrible."

Mattox continued to hold the trembling body clinging to him. He could feel the wetness of her tears seeping through the shirt on his shoulder. "It was a nightmare, Maggy, that's all, a nightmare. He's dead. I saw the body. He isn't going to hurt you. I promise." He continued to hold her as the sobbing abated. Soon the crying stopped altogether, but Maggy kept her head buried between Mattox's neck and shoulder.

Finally, after sensing that she was under control, Mattox released his hold and gently pushed her sensual body backward. "Maggy, we have to talk. Are you up to it?" He looked hard into her eyes. The tears were gone, but redness remained. She nodded her head as she regained her composure.

"Are you sure?"

"Yes, I'm better, now. Thank you."

"Maggy, I have some bad news." He held her shoulders firmly, expecting the worst. "Bill Manchester's body was recovered this morning in Florida. He was found in a lake, drowned."

For several seconds Maggy did not react. In her own mind Bill had died earlier, once she had heard that Abdul had his wallet. The news was a confirmation, not a revelation, but the finality of Mattox's words was slow in sinking in. She did not cry, but lifted her arms around Mattox again and held him firmly. She needed support, and Mattox was pleased that he could provide it. Again, she buried her head on his shoulder. "I expected it," she whispered softly. She neither wimpered nor cried, but continued to embrace Mattox for support.

"Maggy, I need to ask you some more questions." Mattox spoke softly to the back of her head. He had not held a woman like this in years. There was a comforting feeling to the situation. The loneliness that had followed him since his last divorce had made him vulnerable . There was an intimacy he now felt that aroused memories of his first two wives, of companionship, and, of course, of sexuality.

"Go ahead and ask, Bert." She would not release her hold on the FBI agent.

"Maggy, did Manchester ever mention the names of either John Chamberlain or Roland Lampworth to you?"

She remained silent for several seconds as she thought. "Chamberlain? Isn't he the wealthy industrialist who's involved in all the charities around the city?"

"Yes, he's the one. Did Manchester ever mention him?"

She pushed herself back until her face was only inches from that of Mattox. "As a matter of fact, back in November Bill asked if I would go with him to a reception at *Dominique's*. The reception was hosted by Mr. Chamberlain and was a fund raiser for Senator Lewellan. Bill said the tickets were $1,000 each. I asked him how he could afford it, but he said Chamberlain had given him a comp. It was an unbelievably lush affair. Charlton

Heston, Bruce Willis, Chuck Norris were all there, as well as famous singers and comedians. I met Mr. Chamberlain—really distinguished looking and very polite. I was very impressed with him. Why do you ask?"

Mattox shrugged. "His name came up in our investigation, that's all. What about Lampworth? Does that name ring a bell?"

Maggy placed her right index finger against her lower lip as she searched her memory. Mattox focused on her lips. They were larger than those of most women, but not too large; very kissable, he thought. He was having difficulty with his concentration.

"Lampworth? Lampworth? That name rings a bell. Let me think. Last January Bill called and asked me to book two first class seats for him and another man to Cairo, Tunis, Algiers and Marakech. That wasn't unusual for Bill. He travelled that area often, though normally in business class. What was more unusual was he insisted I put the two tickets on his personal American Express card, not his company account. He told me who the other man accompanying him was. It might have been Lampworth, Lamberdini, Lampshade, I don't know." She shook her head. "But there would be a record of the purchase at the travel agency. I could call Ted and have him check for you, if you like?"

Mattox considered her request. "How about your manager; could you check with him, rather than Ted?" Mattox realized that any query made to Ted Sizemore would find its way back to Ashburn and Heffelfinger, and he didn't need any interference at this point.

"Sure, I can do that. But is there a reason you don't want me to ask Ted?"

"No, no. It's just that the manager might be more appropriate. I don't want your buddy getting involved anymore than he has to."

"Anything you say. I'll need to use the phone." She reached across the bed to dial the number of her agency. Mattox watched her body stretch, the soft pink satin slip drawing up on her sleek thighs. She possessed a tight, athletic torso—no fat, no rolls. She could have easily passed for a woman ten years younger. Mattox knew from a report on Maggy prepared overnight at the bureau, that she was 34-years old, but age seemed meaningless now. His fingertips lightly caressed Maggy's hip as she talked. She made no attempt to pull away.

Maggy spoke to her manager and asked him to check the records for the reservations she had made during the first fifteen days of January. As the manager put her on hold, she turned her head toward Mattox and smiled, but said nothing. Mattox's hand slid down her back side, caressing as it found its way along her buttock. The manager came back on the line and gave Maggy her information. She replaced the receiver then leaned back toward Mattox. Self-consciously, he jerked his hand away and felt embarrassed.

"R. Lampworth was his name. Left on the eighth. They were due back on the sixteenth."

Mattox had his linkage. Manchester knew Chamberlain. He received complimentary tickets to a $1,000 reception. He traveled to North Africa with Lampworth. The reception was for Lewellan. It was all coming together. A smile creased his lips.

He was about to call Peters when Maggy put her hand on his cheek. "Bert, please don't think of me as uncaring. I mean for not crying over Bill. Our romance ended months ago. And Isaac— well, he was very dear to me, but we were just friends, nothing more. There are things about you that remind me of him—your sensitivity, your caring, your resolve to get things done." She hesitated and dropped her hand. " Bert, you've been wonderful to me. I appreciate that." She hesitated, then slipped both her arms around his neck and leaned forward to kiss him. Her lips were moist and full. Mattox could not resist her advance.

He took her in his arms and kissed back hard. Their mouths opened, and their tongues began exploring each other as they collapsed on the bed. Mattox's hands returned to Maggy's back, then lower. She began rhythmically pushing her hips into his groin. They could not stop kissing as they rolled over until she straddled him on top.

Mattox found the hem of Maggy's slip as he moved his hands under the satin and up her side and back. The soft skin passing his fingers and palms stirred him. He could feel himself fully aroused.

Maggy's rhythm was intensifying. She leaned away and broke off their passionate kiss. Without saying a word, she reached down to pull at his tie and his shirt. He found himself helping her, ripping his shirt as he fought with the buttons. She found his belt buckle and loosened his trousers. She could feel his passion beneath her. After winning the struggle with his shirt, Mattox reached down with both hands to assist her in removing his pants and shorts.

Mattox was on his back, oblivious to his nakedness. Maggy sat on his lap, hunched over and staring longingly at his soft blue eyes. He reached down below her waist and lifted the slip over her head. Her ample breasts weaved above him, the nipples protruding, hard and firm. He leaned forward and cupped one of the breasts in his mouth and massaged it with his tongue. She threw her head backward and closed her eyes as guttural sounds murmured from deep in her throat.

Mattox pulled Maggy toward him. As her body gradually reclined, his tongue explored more of her upper body, then in a serpentine motion worked its way back to her lips. They embraced passionately and rolled over. The rhythm of their bodies increased as did the sounds in Maggy's throat. Mattox was reaching a climax early. Maggy whispered loudly, "Yes, yes, yes!" In an instant they both spent themselves and collapsed into each other's arms.

The combination of lack of sleep and lovemaking had its effect on Mattox. He rested his head next to Maggy's on the pillow. In all his years with women, he could not remember ever being aroused to such a point of exhilaration. A feeling of contentment rolled through his weary body as his eyes closed, and he drifted into a wonderful slumber.

The sharp ring of the bedside phone awoke Mattox within minutes. He glanced at his clock radio on the bedstand. It was 5:30. The phone continued to ring at his side of the bed. He reached over for the receiver and knocked it to the floor. As he rolled over to pick it up, Maggy's naked body followed him and nestled next to his as he lay on the far edge of the mattress. Her warm skin was comforting.

"This is Bert Mattox." He stumbled with his words.

"Is everything all right, Mr. Mattox? This is Carl Peters."

"Yes, yes, everything's fine here. I dropped the phone. That's all. What do you have?"

"Sir, we just had a call from our Tampa office. The Pinnellas County Sheriff's Department pulled Roland Lampworth's body from Tarpon Lake twenty minutes ago. He had been shot. The killer had tied Senator Lewellan's aide to a bucket of concrete, probably used as a small boat anchor. No question that he was murdered."

Mattox's eyes opened wide. Lampworth dead; Manchester dead—the only two men who could link Abdul with Chamberlain or Lewellan. "Any indication how long Lampworth has been dead?" Mattox felt a stir in Maggy's body.

"The sheriff's deputy who pulled him out estimated maybe a week."

"A week! That means the CIA man didn't do it. It had to be Abdul or somebody else." Mattox did not want to use Manchester's name and disturb Maggy. "We're getting closer, Peters. Have the Tampa and Orlando offices check car rental agencies. Fax them our artist's new sketch of Abdul. See if he was in the area a week ago." Mattox's concentration was broken by a moist tongue exploring his neck and his ear. He could feel Maggy's nipples as they pressed against his back.

Peters' voice brought the special agent back to reality. "Yes, sir. By the way Director Jameson called. He left a message for you."

"What is it?"

"You are to meet him at 7:50 this evening at the west entrance to the White House, the one separating the West Wing from the EOB."

"What's that about?"

"You have an 8:00 appointment with the President of the United States."

Mattox tried to roll over, but his path was blocked. "Oh, shit!" he muttered.

"Yes, sir, is that what you'd like me to report to the director?"

Mattox coughed. Peters had a sense of humor. He continued to cough and laugh as he sat up on the edge of the bed. "No, no. Don't tell him that, Peters. Call and tell him I'll be there." Mattox felt Maggy's hand on his back. He turned around to see her smiling, gentle face gazing up at him from her pillow. The President or Maggy? There was time for both. "I'll talk to you later, Peters." He started to hang up when he heard the agent's pleading voice again. "What is it, Peters?"

"Did you watch the President's press conference last hour?"

"No, I did not," Mattox answered irritably.

"President Staton announced who he was recommending for Vice-President."

"And who would that be?" Mattox wanted to end the conversation as quickly as possible.

"Senator Jake Lewellan of New Mexico."

Chapter 15

The caucus chairman was the last of the team to arrive in Majority Whip Schumacher's office in the Rayburn Building. Buddy Schumacher had asked his friends to take seats on the sofa and side chairs away from his desk. He sat in his wheelchair. His long-time secretary served drinks for everybody as they entered. After handing the caucus chairman his Chevis Regal and water, she closed the door behind her.

"I don't believe Crawfish. I just don't believe him. Of all the people to pick, why Lewellan? If it ain't red, then it's dead as far as that man is concerned. He's the last of the cold war fanatics. He's had a hard on for the Commies ever since he got back from Vietnam. I don't think the man has much interest in Congress except it allows him a forum to give hell to the Commies. I thought ole Crawfish was smarter than that." The chairman of Ways and Means sipped at his bourbon after his outburst.

The chairman of International Relations placed his gin and tonic on the table in front of him. "Well, you heard him on television, earlier. He has a crisis on his hands with the Russians. I suppose he feels that if he wants to put the fear of God into them, they'll back off. Maybe he believes that if the Russians know that Lewellan is helping to mold American foreign policy, they'll back off."

Ed O'Bannon scratched his temple. "Nevertheless, it's not like the Crawford Staton I've known for nearly thirty years. Gentlemen, he's got a first rate mind. He was the stabilizing influence in the Hansen administration. He's the one man that all those saber-rattlers over in the Pentagon can't buffalo. He's been around too long. No, what bothers me is that it's out of character for Crawford. It's so out of character, it gives me pause to think he may be cracking under the pressure over there. Just think of it. He's sailing along with two and a half years of success in his foreign policy. All of a sudden, he's thrown into the middle of a terrible domestic and foreign policy crisis. Crawford's nearly sixty-five years old; he's overweight. Perhaps the pressure, his health, and his age are catching up with him. It may be too much."

Buddy Schumacher interrupted. "I had a call from Secretary Thompson an hour ago. Some of you know we're both from Michigan and that we've been friends for several years. Anyway, he's concerned, very concerned. He thinks the President is moving too fast militarily. Do any of you know what *Thunderburst* is?"

The International Relations chairman answered. "It's the Pentagon's plan for instant deployment of up to three divisions of combat troops to any place on the planet within ninety-six hours."

Schumacher continued, "That's right. Thompson has never been sold on *Thunderburst* in terms of responding to the Chinese or the Russians. He has always thought there were logistical problems in successfully deploying so many troops that fast, and he has concerns about maintaining supply routes over great distances during a prolonged period of time. He approved the plan two years ago, right after he came aboard as Secretary, thinking that it would be useful in our own hemisphere. When he found out sometime later that the Chiefs wanted to use it against China or Russia if necessary, he began quietly to bury the program. The Chiefs out-maneuvered him, however."

Schumacher took a long drink of his bourbon. "Nels believes that, at best, *Thunderburst* is a bluff, that the Pentagon cannot maintain its position in Turkey or Iran over a prolonged time frame. Birchfield and the Chiefs are counting on the Russians to back down. Thompson doesn't believe they will, and he sees the President being backed into a corner to the point he might have to consider using nuclear missiles."

"Jesus H. Christ!" The Ways and Means chairman sprang to the front edge of his seat. "Is he serious? Nuclear war over some godforsaken scrap of land in western Turkey and northern Iran. Shit, I can remember when most Americans would have stood up and applauded if the Russians had slapped those Iranian assholes in the teeth a few years back. Now, we're supposedly buddy-buddy with the sons-of-bitches. If you ask me, we ain't got no business in that part of the world."

The International Relations Chairman objected. "Now, wait a minute. We do have treaty commitments. I can see the President's rationale for standing by our allies." He paused and turned to Schumacher. "However, I am concerned about Thompson's assessment. Crawford has always been a man who preached diplomatic channels before military. This isn't like him."

Ed O'Bannon, the Judiciary Chairman, interrupted. "Excuse me for changing the subject, gentlemen, but my concerns go much deeper than naming Lewellan Vice-President or some temporary foreign crisis. We have a Constitutional crisis on our hands. I talked to Burnstein from over at the Library of Congress this afternoon. I think he might have been prepared for my call. He said that back in 1981 he had been requested by several members of Congress to research the same question when Reagan was shot. Remember when Axexander Haig got the whole succession line screwed up? That triggered the inquiry. He says there is no doubt in his mind of the intent of the law based on its legislative history. Congress intended that a Cabinet member serve as Acting President only until Congress could select new leaders."

"That seems pretty clear cut, Ed." The caucus chairman was almost finished with his scotch.

"Not too fast, my friend. Burnstein went on to say that the law has enough ambiguity in it, however, that if Crawford wanted, he could refuse to relinquish the office. The mistake came, Burnstein says, when the Attorney General advised Crawford to take the oath of office. He should never have taken the oath. He should have merely assumed the position as an acting chief-of-state until Congress could reorganize. But the cat's out of the bag, so to speak, since Crawford did take the oath. Millions of people saw him do it. We saw him do it. And from watching the television a few minutes ago, I'd say Crawford Staton is not about to give up the Presidency without a fight."

The caucus chairman, who was beginning to slur his words, slammed his empty glass on the table. "Well, goddamnit, the man shouldn't be President. And he sure as hell shouldn't foist that ass-hole, Lewellan, on us. We have to tell him he's got to step down. By god, it's the law!" He slapped the table again for emphasis, this time with his hand.

"Easy, Charlie. With whom are we going to replace him?" O'Bannon posed the question. He looked at Schumacher. "What's the latest on Brownell? Have you heard?"

"I talked to Alan's wife just before you gentlemen arrived. He's come around, but he slips back into unconsciousness period- ically. He's been in and out, in and out. The doctors are optimistic. The fact that he's regained consciousness, even for a short period, is encouraging. At this point, however, they can't predict when he'll come completely out of it. It could be next hour, tomorrow, next week. They say there's no way to predict."

The Ways and Means chairman slapped his knees. "So that's it. We have an aging, overweight, distraught man sittin' in the White House, not more than a mile from here, ready to push the button and send this country into a nuclear war with the Russians. We know he shouldn't be President, anyway, but we ain't got nobody to replace him with immediately. What the hell are we gonna do?"

Schumacher finished another sip of his bourbon. "Perhaps somebody should talk to Crawford and at least explain to him our position on the Succession Act. We might at least have a better reading of his mental state and his disposition toward relinquishing control at some future date."

"And who's going to talk to him? Not me!" The caucus chairman crossed his arms in a gesture of finality.

The Ways and Means chairman looked at O'Bannon. "Ed, you're the senior member here. You've known Crawfish longer than the rest of us. You two have been friends through the years. I think he might be more receptive if you spoke to him."

O'Bannon looked around the room. Everyone was nodding agreement. "I suppose I could. I don't feel uncomfortable talking to Crawford. We've had a pretty good rapport through the years, but I won't go alone. This is too important. Besides, as a mere committee chairman, I don't have standing to bring this to his attention." He turned toward the Whip. "Buddy, I think you need to go with me. You're the ranking officer of the House right now. You are the obvious person to make the appointment. Will you?"

Each of the other men around the table recited after one another, "Good idea."

Schumacher put down his glass. "Okay, Ed, I'll call over there and see if we can get in to see him in the morning. Is that acceptable?"

The rest of the team nodded their heads. The Whip turned the toggle switch on the arm of his electric chair and rolled over to his desk. He reached for the phone and pushed a button. "Mary get me the White House, please."

*****

At precisely 8:00 P.M. Bert Mattox, the director of the FBI, and the Attorney General were ushered into the Oval Office by Jim Lowenstein. The President was sitting in a deep cushioned floral chair across the room from his desk, staring at a fire blazing in front of him. Upon seeing his guests, Staton heaved his heavy frame from his chair and invited the four men to find seats on the two matching sofas facing each other near him.

"Well, Jacob, you brought the big hitters with you, I see." The President seemed to collapse rather than sit in his chair. Mattox detected a degree of exhaustion in the new chief executive.

The Attorney General introduced Mattox to the President. Staton had already met the FBI director on several previous occasions. "I asked for Mr. Mattox to join us this evening, Mr. President, because he is in charge of the investigation and can give you our most up-to-date information."

Staton turned his attention to the special agent. "Fire away, Mr. Mattox."

Mattox, who prided himself on his self-confidence, felt uneasy. He had never been in the Presidential office. The Presidential seal, the battle flags behind the President's desk, and the sight of the famous Crawford Staton reclining in the chair next to him could not help but generate an intimidating atmosphere.

"Mr. President, the Attorney General gave you a briefing this morning, so I won't recover that ground." Mattox then recited from his notes, including Manchester's involvement and Abdul's killing of Weissman and his attempt on Mosele's life. He ended by reporting on the killing of Abdul the previous night.

The President leaned his head back. "So we have a second killer on the loose, and you believe he was the man who hired this Abdul character?"

"Yes and no, sir. We do have a killer on the loose. This morning he made another attempt to kill Miss Mosele at George Washington Hospital by trying to inject her with cyanide. Again, he was able to get away. There's no question that whoever this person is, he wants Miss Mosele dead."

The Attorney General appeared confused. "I don't understand the woman's connection. Why is she so important? Why do they want to kill her?"

Mattox discarded his notes. "Because she is the hinge pin in this whole conspiracy. She and Manchester had an affair for over three years. Manchester booked all his commercial flights through her travel agency."

"So maybe Manchester is our killer?" The President was speculating.

"No, sir, Manchester is dead. His body was identified a few hours ago in Orlando, Florida."

"So Manchester is not your killer?" The Attorney General appeared puzzled.

"No, sir. We believe Manchester was involved in the conspiracy. He and a congressional aide to Senator Lewellan flew to Algeria last January. It is possible that they were there to contact and hire Abdul."

The President jerked forward as if he had been stung. "Senator Lewellan's aide? Where did he come from?"

"Mr. President, according to Senator Lewellan, his chief-of-staff, Roland Lampworth, is the man who initiated a memorandum to Senator Howard suggesting yesterday's ceremony at the FDR Memorial. The memo was sent to Senator Howard over Senator Lewellan's signature. The fact that Lampworth initiated the chain of events that led to yesterday's ceremony and that he accompanied Manchester to Algiers, suggests to us his involvement."

"Why not question this Lampworth fellow?" the President asked.

"Unfortunately, he too is dead. His body was pulled out of a lake near Tampa, Florida, this afternoon. He's been dead about a week—shot and tied to an bucket of concrete. Right now we are assuming he was another victim of Abdul."

As the President scratched his chin, Mattox noticed a heavy five o'clock shadow on Staton's face. "So two co-conspirators are found dead today, and yet, we still have someone running around trying to kill this woman, Mosele. That can only mean there are others involved. Is that correct?"

"Yes, sir." Mattox looked directly at the President. "Sir, do you know a man named John F. Chamberlain?"

The President's face again registered surprise. "John Chamberlain, the founder of JFC Industries, sure I know John.

Everyone in this town knows John. Surely, you don't suspect him. Hell, he was a big contributor to Seth's campaign."

Mattox kept his eyes riveted on Staton. "Mr. President, Mr. Chamberlain's home telephone number in Virginia was found in Manchester's wallet." He went on to explain Chamberlain's connection to Manchester and Lampworth as well as Abdul's call from the hotel.

"Jesus, Mattox, do you realize that you are accusing one of the most respected men in this town, in this nation, of being involved in this conspiracy? You're going to need more proof than you've shown me, here." The President appeared defensive.

"I realize that, sir, but right now Mr. Chamberlain is one of the keys to this investigation."

The President leaned back in his chair. "I hope you have this Mosele woman under protective custody, Mr. Mattox."

"Yes, sir, she is staying at my condominium in Alexandria. I'm spending most of my time at the bureau, anyway. I have agents guarding both the front and the back to the condo. Plus, we have a half dozen agents watching the periphery of the complex."

"What about Chamberlain? What do you plan to do about him?" the President asked.

"I have no choice but to consider him a potential co-conspirator and to place him under surveillance. I intend to ask the Attorney General to seek a court order allowing us to tap his telephones at home and at work. We're checking out his financial contributions to candidates, any past association with extremists, his telephone records, and his travel for the past six months. We'll also give him a thorough national security check. There is a chance that he is being blackmailed. We cannot overlook that possibility."

"Well, Mr. Mattox, you're the expert, but I would counsel you to move cautiously and to use discretion with John Chamberlain. He's a powerful man. Hell, once he gets wind of the national security check, he'll probably call me."

"Yes, sir, I imagine he will. I would appreciate your telling him that you are considering him for an appointment of some kind and that the check is routine. Would you, sir?"

"I suppose I could, but I don't like lying, especially to my friends."

"I know, sir, but it is important. One more thing. . ." Mattox hesitated. He knew how sensitive the next topic would be.

"Well, what is it, Mattox? I need to get home." The President was clearly tired and edgy.

"Mr. President, I have to tell you that Senator Lewellan must be considered under suspicion, also."

The President jumped from his chair, flinging his long arms in the air. "Jake Lewellan under suspicion? Mattox, you have to be absolutely crazy. Hell, that man is this nation's most super patriot. I just named him Vice-President, for god's sake. What the hell are you talking about? Jesus! I can't believe this."

The FBI director and the Attorney General exchanged glances. They had never seen Crawford Staton throw such a tantrum.

Mattox remained seated, but did not yield to the towering figure looming above him. "Mr. President, I remind you that it was a memorandum from Senator Lewellan which initiated yesterday's events. We only have his word that Lampworth authored the memo. He admits his signature is on the document. We also know that he has the support of John Chamberlain. I cannot ignore those facts, Mr. President."

Staton continued to stare down at the agent sitting on the sofa beneath him. "Mr. Mattox, let me tell you, Jake Lewellan is going to be the next Vice-President of the United States. I have invited him to sit with the National Security Council and the Cabinet. There is absolutely no doubt in my mind of his loyalty. Do you understand that, Mr. Mattox?"

"Yes, sir, I do, and I respect your opinion and what you feel you must do. But, Mr. President, I also have my duty." Mattox returned the President's hard stare.

Staton had a sense when he had failed to cajole an adversary into submission. Finally, he sat down. "You do that, Mr. Mattox. Is there anything else?"

Mattox indicated he was finished. The Attorney General stood, signaling the others that it was time to leave. The President remained in his seat, brooding. The Attorney General felt uncomfortable with the atmosphere in the President's Oval Office. "Thank you, Mr. President. We'll keep you informed."

Staton waved his hand, but said nothing. The three members of the Justice Department left as they had entered, being ushered by Lowenstein.

*****

The phone rang only once when a voice answered. "Yes?"

"This is the ace of clubs. We have a problem. The FBI knows of Chamberlain's connection to Lampworth and Manchester. Manchester had Chamberlain's telephone number. The Mosele woman has linked Manchester to a reception Chamberlain had for Lewellan last year. It's possible she might remember more of Manchester's activities. We don't know what Manchester told her."

"Do you know where she is being kept?"

"In Alexandria, at the home of Bert Mattox. There are two guards at the front and two stationed at the back, also a half dozen on patrol within his complex."

"Leave everything to me."

"What about Chamberlain?"

"If the woman is eliminated, I believe he will be able to take care of himself."

"And if she isn't?"

"We'll deal with that later. Goodbye."

Chapter 16

The three men stood in the lighted parking lot which formerly served as a street, separating the Executive Office Building from the White House. The Attorney General was disturbed. "I'll direct the Criminal Division to seek a court order for the phone tap yet tonight, but I want you to know all three of us are sticking our necks out on this one. Chamberlain is a powerful man with powerful friends. I need not warn you how important it is to use discretion in your investigation of his past."

"No, sir, I realize the sensitivity of this situation, but I believe he's one of the keys to this conspiracy. Better men have succumbed to power. But, like I told the President, it's also possible he was an unwilling conspirator. Almost all of us have something in our past we want to keep buried. The higher people go in life, and the more important they become, the more important it is to them to keep those skeletons hidden." Mattox was leaning against his new Buick.

Director Jameson turned toward the Attorney General. "Jacob, what did you make of the President's behavior in there? I thought he was going to pick Bert up and toss him across the room when he suggested Lewellan needed to be watched." Mattox noticed that the director's right arm was shaking badly. Perhaps it was the lateness of the day which was causing the tremor.

The Attorney General was reticent in his reply. Loyalty ran deep within the former dean of the University of Pennsylvania Law School. "Quite frankly, like you, I was surprised. It was completely out of character for Crawford. I've worked with the man for over two years, and I have never seen him get that riled. It could be this Russian business. It may be getting to him."

"Perhaps, but it bothers me, and I'm sure it bothers Bert that, when the President of the United States sees circumstantial evidence involving a man in a conspiracy to kill his predecessor, and he knows that man might become next in line to succeed him, he would have been more concerned about that man than protecting his own political hide."

The Attorney General shook his head. He already had his concerns, ever since the morning NSC meeting. Staton's reliance on military action ahead of diplomatic negotiations ran counter to his previous mode of behavior. He had agreed with Nelson Thompson that the President was backing Chenkov into a corner, but now wasn't the time to discuss his concerns, especially with the two outsiders. "Let's just give him some time. Crawford didn't get where he is by being stupid. He'll come around."

The director shook his head. "I hope so, Jacob. I hope so." He looked up at the moonless, starlit sky. "I think I'll go home. I feel very tired." He turned and slowly crept toward his Lincoln Town Car where his chauffeur was standing next to the back door. The Attorney General and Mattox waited behind, watching their friend move slowly away.

"Bert, I'm afraid our friend is failing. You know, when I taught law a few years back, I used several of his judicial decisions as cases in my classes. He was one of the best judges ever to sit on the federal bench. It makes me sick to see him afflicted with this Parkinson's thing."

Mattox nodded his agreement. "I had heard rumors, but I have never discussed it with him, sir."

"He's too much the old Southern gentleman to discuss his health. It wouldn't be proper. He'll just keep spending longer hours at his job until one day he'll trip or spill something that will embarrass him, and then he'll quit."

"That will be a sad day for the bureau, sir." Mattox hesitated. "Sir, what about the treatment I read about, where they inject tissue from dead fetuses into the brain of Parkinson patients? I thought that was supposed to arrest the problem."

"I suggested that to him. I even gave him the name of a specialist at the hospital at Penn, but he's reluctant on religious grounds. Using the tissue of a dead fetus bothers him very much. You know, despite his support for years of *Roe v.Wade* from the bench, he has always personally opposed abortion. The thought of using an aborted fetus to prolong his own life is abhorrent to him. But, I'm going to keep at him. Hell, he's only sixty. He's got a lot of good years left in him."

The Attorney General excused himself. He had to return to his office and call in his staff from the Criminal Division. Mattox unlocked his car. He glanced at the dashboard clock. It was 9:00. At least he might get one good night's sleep.

*****

As he sat in the back seat of his Lincoln, the Attorney General pondered the day's events. First, his concern about the heath of Alec Jameson had increased. He had tried to persuade his good friend to take advantage of the University of Pennsylvania Medical Center. All the AG could do is keep trying.

He also was concerned about the behavior of the President. Crawford Staton was his friend, and more importantly he was President of the United States. The Attorney General knew better than anybody that Staton was President primarily because he had instructed the Secretary of State to take the oath of office. Earlier in the day, his own deputy had brought to his attention the problems with the Succession Act. He had wrestled with the idea of discussing the matter with Staton, but realized after watching him this evening, it would have been a fruitless effort. Surely, members of Congress would raise questions.

He had weighed the pros and cons of warning the President of the possible challenge or waiting to let the Congress address the problem. In his own mind he could justify his action based upon what was needed for the good of the country at the time. Someone had to take charge. That was paramount. Even if he had not done his homework on the succession, an Acting President in the midst of a national crisis would never have worked.

But watching Staton tonight raised more questions in his mind about the fitness of his old friend for the office. He reached over in his briefcase and pulled out his small phone directory. Picking up his car phone, he punched in an unlisted office number. After several rings, the voice of the Secretary of Defense answered.

"Nelson, this is Jacob. I hope I didn't catch you too late?"

"It's never too late for you, Jacob. I'm always at your disposal. What can I do for you?"

"Nelson, would you hold for one second while I turn on the scrambler?" He reached down on the phone console and flipped a toggle switch. "Are you still there?"

"I'm here, Jacob. What's this all about?"

The Attorney General vented his doubts and frustrations. He reported on the night's briefing from Mattox and the President's violent reaction to the news about Lewellan. He explained his new concerns about the Succession Act and his rationale for having advised the President to take the oath of office. He needed some advice and someone with whom he could share his concerns.

"Jacob, I appreciate your sharing this information with me. I would advise, however, that you take no action at this time regarding the succession. Let Congress push that one. As a matter of fact, I talked to Buddy Schumacher earlier today. He already knows about the succession problem. The House leadership has been discussing it among themselves. Right now we have to help the President through this Russian situation. With Lewellan now involved in the NSC, it's going to be even more difficult to hold Birchfield in check."

"Perhaps you're right, Nelson. I appreciate your letting me lean on you. This whole assassination conspiracy and the President's behavior have me deeply troubled, and if John Chamberlain is involved, it's going to get very messy."

"I can't believe John is involved, Jacob. I've known the man for years. We both belong to Burning Tree. I've played golf with him and George Heffelfinger several times. I'm sure it's all just a bizarre set of coincidences. But, I agree with your agent. I think you have to proceed with the phone tap and national security check. You'll have hell to pay later if you try to block it."

"I agree. Nelson, again, thank you for your advice. You've been a big help."

"That's what we're here for, Jacob. We belong to a rather small club. We have to stick together."

The two men exchanged a few more pleasantries before they cut off. The Attorney General sank deeper into his leather seat, feeling a sense of relief that he was not alone in his concerns.

*****

At 9:30 Mattox turned left into the main entrance to his complex. A man he recognized as one of his agents waved to him from the shadows. The driveway seemed darker than usual. He stopped his car and rolled down the window. The agent, assuming the special agent wanted to talk to him, came running over to the Buick. "Yes, sir?"

"What happened to the lights? The security vapor lights are all off."

"They went out about fifteen minutes ago, Mr. Mattox. We called the electric company. They're sending a truck out, but they said it could be another hour or two before they could get here."

"Is everyone in place?"

"Yes, sir. We made a radio check at 9:00, as we do each hour. Everyone responded. We're due to be relieved at midnight, sir."

"Good. Thanks for your help. Keep your eyes open." Mattox smiled at the agent who was dressed in a windbreaker and jeans, attempting as much as possible to be inconspicuous.

As he pulled into his carport in front of the entrance to his condominium, he noticed the lights in the entire building of six units were out. He turned to look behind him. The lights to the units across the drive were still working, including the security lights in the entrance halls. Something wasn't right. He reached into the glove compartment for his 9-mm Luger. He had placed it there earlier in the evening when Director Jameson reminded him that he could not enter the White House with the weapon. He opened the door to the car and closed it as quietly as he could. Bending forward, he crept toward the entrance.

Thirty feet from the hallway door, he saw two men leaning against the outside wall. At the same time they saw him. They both reacted immediately by falling to the ground with their pistols raised and aimed at Mattox's head.

"Whoever is there, drop your weapon! This is the FBI." The unmistakable voice of Carl Peters was a welcomed sound.

"Peters, it's Mattox." He straightened up and placed his gun on the ground and raised his arms. He knew that in the shadows from such a distance they could not recognize him. The two agents sprang to their feet and walked slowly toward him.

As they came within a few feet, Peters dropped his weapon to his side. "It's okay, Abe. It's Agent Mattox." The other agent straightened and returned his weapon to its holster inside his suit coat.

"Sorry, Mr. Mattox. We couldn't recognize you. I thought it looked like you when you got out of the car, but I didn't recognize the car. And then, when I saw the gun, we thought it better to be safe than sorry."

"No need to apologize, Carl. I appreciate your quick reaction." He leaned over and picked up his own gun and replaced it in his holster. "How come you're working here? I thought you'd be in the command center. "

"Akers took over, sir. I was about to go home when we got a call about an hour or so ago that Agent Quillen was sick, so I volunteered to work the rest of his shift. It's only another couple of hours, and I live not far from here."

"Good man, Carl. I appreciate it. I really do. Everything okay? All these lights being out bothers me."

"As far as we know, sir. "

"I assume the patio is covered?"

"I'll check." All the agents on the security detail had earpieces hooked to a radio they wore on their belts. The microphones were on the end of a wire running down their sleeves to their hands. Peters lifted his left hand to his mouth. "Brewer, everything all right back there? Brewer? Brewer, this is Peters. Are you two all right back there?"

Mattox's anxiety returned as he could tell Peters was getting no response.

"Brewer! Goddamnit, answer!"

Mattox again pulled his gun and ran past the two agents toward the front hallway. Peters pulled his weapon and ran to his right, around the building. Abe, the other agent, with his weapon raised, followed Mattox. Inside the front door was a ten-foot wide hallway. A staircase hugged the wall on the right. Mattox's front door was on the under side of the staircase about fifteen feet into the entrance. The entrance hall was pitch black. Mattox felt his way along the far wall until he knew he was standing opposite his front door. He reached inside his pocket with his left hand and retrieved his key ring, then ran the various keys through his fingers. The condo key was a large Sargent make, which he knew he'd recognize by touch.

Satisfied he had the right key, he crossed the corridor and inserted the key into the lock. The latch turned, and he pushed the door open slightly. Just as he was about to enter, the agent behind him touched his shoulder and whispered, "Mr. Mattox, Peters says both agents in back are dead. He says the sliding glass door on your patio is open about six inches."

"Shit! Tell Peters to stay in place. You stay out here. I don't want this son-of-a-bitch getting away, if he's in here." But Mattox was more concerned about Maggy. He had promised to protect her. God! Let her be alive.

Mattox pushed the door open further, while at the same time diving to the floor and crawling through the entry. The interior of the living room was so dark he could see no more than a few inches in front of him. He knew a breakfast counter was to his right about four feet from the door. He turned toward the counter. As he raised his head slightly, he spotted the red dot in front of him. He ducked just as the muted sound of a pistol with a silencer broke the quiet. He also heard the bullet penetrate the wood cabinet beneath the counter.

Mattox lay flat, his heart pounding so fast he could feel the pressure in his chest. This was too much like the movies. Fortunately, he was a good shot and had kept in decent physical shape. An hour a day in the gym and thirty minutes a week at the shooting range had kept his skills well-honed. He rolled his body to the left until he was well away from the kitchen area. His foot was near enough to the front door to allow him to kick the door shut, just as he heard another shot and saw the red dot pass by the molding near in the door.

From the sound of the silencer and trajectory of the laser light, he guessed the intruder was crouched near or behind the sofa at the far end of the living room. The intruder had a laser finder attached to his gun. Mattox knew it was important that he not be visible from the sofa. An oversized clay jar holding a six-foot tall corn plant a few feet to his left was enough to provide him cover.

He again rolled on his back and came up behind the jar. The sofa was now between him and the patio door. There was just enough outside distant illumination to put the sofa in a silhouette. He needed to get the intruder to rise just enough so he would have a shot. He reached inside his trouser pocket for his key ring. Slowly and silently, he pulled the ring from his pocket.

A large brass platter, which he had purchased in San Francisco's China Town, was hanging on the middle of the wall to his right. He took the ring with his left hand and heaved the keys toward the brass plate. With the loud crash a figure lifted his head above the edge of the sofa. Mattox had the silhouetted head in his sights. He pulled the trigger, but heard nothing but a click. He pulled again. Another click. "Shit!" he whispered.

The gunman behind the sofa rose slowly. Mattox saw a dark arm rise. A small red light moved along the floor toward him, gradually making its way to the clay jar. Mattox knew the jar would never hide all of his head and torso. The red dot continued to move to the right of the jar, then to the left. Mattox tried to roll away from the light, but it kept following him. He rolled as hard as he could to his right, but his knee hit the corner of one of his end tables, and he uttered a quiet but intense profanity. The red dot followed him. He watched in horror as the dot hit his shoulder, then moved up his neck toward his forehead. He steeled himself, preparing to die when the sharp, loud crack of a hand gun broke his concentration. The light tumbled down from Mattox's head to the floor. He heard a thud in the direction of the sofa.

From the patio door he heard a friendly voice. "Mr. Mattox, are you okay? It's Peters."

Never had a man's voice sounded so sweet to Mattox. He looked up to see a shadow framed in the patio archway. There was no glare from the man. For the first time during the day, it dawned on Mattox that Peters was black. "Thank God!" he murmured.

"Mr. Mattox, are you all right?"

"Yeah, yeah. I'm over here. I banged my knee. Did you get him?"

"I think so." Just then an intense beam of light shot across the room from Peters's left hand. He was holding a hunter's lantern that one of the agents on the patio had kept. The light found Mattox who had both hands wrapped around his injured knee. Peters crossed the room to help him stand.

Mattox straightened himself, the pain already subsiding. "Let's see who the son-of-a-bitch was." Mattox unknowingly continued to whisper in the dark room. The two agents walked over to the back of the sofa and looked down. Peters's strong light beam started at the prone gunman's combat boots, up his black trousers to his black turtleneck sweater. The light continued up to a head hidden in a black ski mask. The man was lying face up, a small amount of blood dripping from a whole in his left temple.

"Let's see who we have here?" Mattox leaned down and removed the killer's mask. Neither agent recognized the handsome face in front of them. With blond hair cut in a flattop and dark blue eyes staring aimlessly toward the ceiling, his mouth was opened, exposing a perfect set of white teeth. He matched the description of the orderly at the hospital.

Mattox suddenly remembered Maggy. He snatched the lantern from Peters's hand. "Maggy. I've got to find Maggy." He crossed the room with the beam of light guiding him to his bedroom door which was slightly ajar. Slowly he pushed the door forward. He shined the light on the bed. A rumpled figure buried beneath a comforter was bent into a fetal position. A closer look showed bullet holes in the comforter about half way up the body. Mattox felt a sinking sensation in his stomach as panic gripped him. Not Maggy. No, not Maggy. He pushed the door open further and started for the bed. Then all went black.

*****

Mattox's next conscious thoughts were of light, bright, fluorescent light without any form. As he blinked repeatedly to focus his eyes, he realized he was staring at a ceiling. A sharp pain on top of his head felt like lightning had struck him. He reached for the pain with his left hand and touched a bandage. A soft hand then caressed his cheek, and he turned to see the welcomed face of Maggy Mosele smiling down at him. Draped in his white cotton bathrobe, she was sitting on the edge of the bed.

"Maggy, what happened? I thought you were dead."

"Take it easy, Mr. Mattox, there are other people in the room." Her smile broadened, and she continued to caress his face.

Mattox looked down toward the foot of his kingsize bed. Standing in a row were Peters, Akers, and Director Jameson. "Judge, what the hell are you doing here?" He started to lift himself, but the pain in his head forced him back down.

"Easy, Bert. When my best man is taken out by a 110-pound woman, I have to meet this lady." The director was smiling mischievously.

Mattox was confused. "What are you talking about? What hit me?"

Maggy put her hand over Mattox's mouth. "Let me explain, Bert. I'm afraid I'm the one who 'took you out' as the director puts it."

Mattox appeared even more confused.

"I was in the kitchen starting to make an omelet, until I opened your refrigerator and discovered you don't have any eggs, or milk, or butter. About that time the lights went out, and a couple of minutes later I heard someone playing with the patio door. I remembered your telling me to stay inside no matter what. So I picked up the iron skillet I had sitting on the stove and brought it back into the bedroom. A few minutes later I heard the patio door being pried open. I thought all the security men were gone. I took some pillows and put them under the bedspread to make it appear I was sleeping."

Mattox closed his eyes. He knew what was coming.

"I hid behind the door with my skillet. I was scared to death. The door started to open. It was so dark I could hardly see, except for the small amount of light coming through the bedroom window from the building across the courtyard. The door opened some more, and then I saw this small red light beam directed at the bed. Then I heard three muted gunshots, and I heard the bullets hit the bed. I was all set to crown the guy with the skillet when he came through the door, but he didn't come. Instead, he must have heard you because I heard him walk away."

Maggy caressed his cheeks again. "I listened hard, but all I could make out were noises, some whispering, a couple more muted shots, then finally a loud gunshot. I can't tell you how frightened I was. Then the door opened again, and a beam of light hit the bed. I didn't know it was you, Bert. I am sorry. Please forgive me." Her eyes were moist, on the verge of tears.

Mattox reached up with his right hand and held her face. "That's okay, Maggy. At least the director is getting some field time." The men at the end of the bed chuckled.

Mattox then remembered the intruder and the downed agents. "What happened to our agents on the patio?"

The men at the end of the bed stopped their laughing instantly. Peters answered. "They were shot with a rifle fired from the hill behind your place, about one hundred yards from here. I'm afraid both men are dead. We found the gunman's weapon on the patio. It was a SAKO Deluxe Lightweight, Finnbear Long Action rifle. He had three unspent 6-mm PPC bullets left in the chamber. I'll bet a month's salary the bullets match the ones we took out of Abdul and your car."

"What did he use inside? It wasn't a rifle."

"No, he had a Colt MKIV Series 80. It was one of those 38-super automatic 9-mm Lugers. Both weapons had scopes, laser finders, and silencers. Very sophisticated equipment and very expensive. This man was definitely a professional."

"Any ID?"

"None on him. We're running a fingerprint and a DNA check now. Should have the results back by morning."

The director walked around to the side of the bed. Mattox followed him with his eyes and then noticed on his radio clock that it was nearly 11:00. He must have been out for over an hour. Again, he started to raise himself from the bed.

"No, you don't, Special Agent Mattox." It was the director with his shaky hand on Mattox's chest, gently pushing him back. "You're going to get one good night's rest. You can thank Miss Mosele here for your first aid. I've seen worse injuries. I think you'll be fine in the morning." The judge was smiling down gently at him. "And, by the way, the next time you pull your weapon, make sure it's loaded."

Mattox knew any protest would be useless, and besides he was exhausted. "Anything you say, Judge, but it was you who said I couldn't take a loaded weapon into the White House." In a matter of seconds Mattox was fast asleep. The men left the room, leaving Maggy on the edge of the bed, continuing to caress the face of the man who had saved her life a third time.

Chapter 17

Virginia countryside
April 14
1:00 A.M.

Chamberlain fidgeted with his gold pocket watch as he paced his book-lined study. The call had come about thirty minutes earlier, asking him to make sure his butler and any other servants were sent away. Fortunately, only Edward, his long-time major domo, was sleeping in during the evening. He had awakened Edward and asked him to drive to his Washington office and retrieve some important papers he had left on his desk. Actually, the papers contained nothing but background material on a merger he was considering with two of his subsidiaries, but Edward had not argued. It was seldom that Chamberlain asked him to run such an errand, so the servant assumed it was important. Edward would be gone at least two hours. That should be plenty of time to discuss whatever his associate had in mind.

The wealthy industrialist sat down in an elegant French provincial chair and gracefully crossed his legs. An expensive Scottish briar pipe was gripped tightly between his teeth. A fire in the large marble fireplace cast a flickering light over his body. This was his favorite room with its walnut bookcases climbing a full twelve feet to the ceiling. Three walls of shelves housed volumes of leather and hard bound books, some obviously very old, others still containing their dust jackets.

Chamberlain's gray temples, ruby red velvet smoking jacket, and pipe served as support props for the image he had tried to portray to his colleagues and employees for several years—a man in charge of events. A man in control of every situation; a man of high intellect and courtly manners. If America harbored an aristocracy, the owner of this Georgian mansion had labored long and hard to project himself as part of that elite corps.

As he continued to stare at the fire, mesmerized by its flickering, his mind retreated to several weeks earlier in the same room, when he and his colleagues had finished their final group discussion of the momentous plans designed to change the nation and its direction. Manchester had been concerned about how the four would be able to communicate with one another to assure the others they were not being overheard by listening devices. The idea of the playing cards had seemed both superfluous and juvenile to Chamberlain, but the others seemed to be more comfortable, so he went along. He was always willing to compromise on the unimportant matters to achieve larger goals. That's how he had become wealthy.

The doorbell chimes startled him. The study was located on the back side of the mansion, and he had not heard an automobile pull up. The lights in the large entryway to the house were lit brightly as he crossed the black and white marble foyer to the entrance. When he opened the door, his friend was facing the drive."

"Looking for anything in particular?"

"I thought I heard someone. Probably just one of your gray squirrels." He turned and entered the house. The guest was wearing the same blue blazer and khaki trousers he had worn the last time they had met just nine days earlier.

Chamberlain closed the door, then led the way toward the study. "I was rather surprised you wanted to meet in person. I assume it is something we couldn't talk about over the phone." The man in the dark blue blazer closed the study door after he entered. "Aren't you forgetting something, John?"

"What?" Chamberlain paused. "Oh, the card, the eight of clubs. I left it upstairs in my wallet." He waved his hand in a manner of dismissal. "Don't worry, this house is checked each week for bugs. I can assure you we can't be overheard." Chamberlain took a seat behind his large, antique desk. "Actually, I never had much enthusiasm for your use of those cards as a code for communicating. I went along to placate our other two friends."

The man in the blazer took a seat opposite Chamberlain. "John, you've never had an appreciation for metaphor. While our code may not be sophisticated by your corporate standards, its simplicity works. That is, it should work. However, you've been careless, very careless."

Chamberlain looked offended. "What do you mean?"

"Did you know your telephone is probably tapped this instant."

The chairman of JFC Industries appeared both surprised and indignant. "By whom?"

"By the FBI. The Attorney General secured a court order approving the tap this evening."

"I don't believe it."

"You can believe it. Our friend, the ace of clubs, confirmed it to me earlier this evening." The guest unbuttoned his jacket.

"Oh, my god! Well, it won't do them any good. They won't learn anything listening in."

"I believe you, John, but there are other problems. You let Manchester get too close. Not only did he have your home phone number, but also his old girlfriend, Margaret Mosele, remembers attending that bash you threw for Lewellan last year. They also know about Lampworth, and since he worked for Lewellan, that is another connection to you. Who knows what Manchester told the girl during the past several months?" The guest showed no expression of anger or concern. He was merely reciting facts.

"But I thought she was to be eliminated." Chamberlain's demeanor betrayed his growing anxiety.

"Unfortunately, our man failed tonight. This time he was killed. That's another problem. They're bound to identify Stewart and trace him to your employment."

"He was on the payroll of one of my subsidiaries, not JFC Industries. There is no direct link between him and me. Anyway, he used to work for you."

"No, actually he did not. No one will find any record of his having been assigned to me personally. I was very careful about that, John. He worked for someone else. I merely employed him for, shall we say, special assignments. Stewart understood there could never be a direct connection to me. Unfortunately, since you are already under suspicion, when the FBI traces his current employment to you, it will be just one more connection. Messy, John, very messy."

Beads of perspiration dotted Chamberlain's forehead. He patted at them with a monogrammed handkerchief he kept in his silk robe. "Still, there's not enough evidence to directly link me with Abdul. Both Manchester and Lampworth are dead, as you and I agreed. I made that a part of Abdul's contract. There can be no direct connection to either of us."

"But John, it was your five million dollars that was used to pay him."

"Yes, but I used a bank draft on one of my accounts in Switzerland. That can't be traced."

"John, I would like to think you are right, but I discovered tonight that Manchester has been under CIA surveillance for the past four months. The Agency thinks Manchester was involved with Abdul and that Abdul paid him off. Manchester was careless, too, John. He failed to tell us that Abdul had given him a hundred thousand dollars and that he had deposited most of it in a bank in Arlington. The CIA is very good at chasing money, John. They may well find Abdul's secret bank accounts. When they do, they'll know how to trace the five million dollar draft you gave him. Another problem, I'm afraid."

"But that's an awfully big if." Chamberlain subconsciously began fidgeting with his watch. "Surely, some of this investigation can be derailed by the White House when the time comes?"

"And what excuse would they use, John? National Security? That won't fly; rather it would just create more questions. No, John, we have to give the FBI and CIA reason to believe that their investigation is at an end, that the conspiracy to kill the President has been solved."

"Well, how do we do that?" Chamberlain patted his forehead again with his handkerchief.

The man in the blazer straightened up in his chair and smiled gently at Chamberlain. The industrial giant noticed for the first time that his guest had not taken off his black gloves.

"John, we need to remember why we all became involved in this operation. Didn't we agree that the future of the nation was at stake, that Hansen's policies were going to lead the nation into economic ruin and put us at risk against the Russians? Wasn't that our initial motivation?"

"Of course, it was."

"And haven't we moved a great deal closer to accomplishing our goals?"

"No question."

"And did we not agree that if necessary we were all expendable in order to accomplish the greater good?"

Anxiety was giving way to fear as the corporate chairman squirmed in his leather chair. "I agree. We all agreed, but surely you don't believe that I am in any danger. There still is no direct link to me. The bank draft was on a numbered account created by one of my European attorneys. It can't be traced to me."

"Possibly true, John, but the FBI is relentless. They keep on a case until they believe they have their man. They believe this has been a conspiracy. They need to believe they have solved the conspiracy. Surely, you can see that, John?"

Chamberlain noticed that the hands of his guest had dropped from his view. He remembered he kept a revolver in the second drawer down on the right of his desk. Leaning forward, he reached slowly with his right hand toward the drawer. "But let's reason this out. What makes you think they'll stop with me?" He assumed his guest could not see him pull out the drawer. "I could leave the country, fake an accident on a boat. . ."

The silencer prevented Chamberlain from hearing his own death. The bullet entered his head just under the left eye. The man in the blazer winced when he saw dust particles fall from a book on a shelf behind the desk chair. He walked around the desk and felt Chamberlain's neck for a pulse. There was none. He removed the silencer from the military luger and placed both in his jacket pockets. He then examined the shelf of books behind Chamberlain's chair. A leather bound 1836 volume of the *English Book of Common Prayer* had a small hole in its binding. The man removed the book and found the bullet that had passed through Chamberlain's skull buried inside the thick pages. He removed the bullet and replaced the book.

Returning to the desk, the killer forced a large ruby ring from the small finger on Chamberlain's right hand and took the gold watch he had been clutching with his left hand. He felt the pockets of Chamberlain's robe and trousers, but there was no wallet. He remembered that Chamberlain's bedroom was on the second floor above the study. He ran out of the study, up the grand staircase to the landing on the second floor, and found the door to his former friend's bedroom open. The lights were still on. He spent nearly fifteen minutes searching the room for the wallet, in the process deliberately pulling out dresser drawers, tearing the covers, sheets, and mattress from the bed, and knocking over two lamps. He found Chamberlain's keys, his appointment book, about eighty-five cents in change, but no wallet. The eight of clubs—he needed the card.

Finally, he searched behind each of the wall hangings. Behind a Picasso pencil sketch of a ballerina he discovered a wall safe. "Damn!" he muttered. Chamberlain must have placed his valuables in the safe before he had retired earlier in the evening. He tried to turn the safe's handle, but it would not budge. No sooner did he touch the combination lock, than the screeching sound of a siren startled him.

The killer ran out of the room and down the stairs. He pulled open the front door and ran for his car. Fortunately, the estate was several miles from the nearest town. It would take any authorities several minutes to arrive. He had time to make his escape. The card would have to be left. Just as well, he rationalized. It would be one more link to Manchester. Without the third or fourth card no one would ever be able to determine the significance of their code. The wheels on his dark blue Chrysler Imperial sprayed gravel behind him as he shoved the accelerator to the floor. In what seemed like an eternity, he finally found the paved road outside the black wrought iron entrance to the estate. He turned right, heading back to the capital. He checked his speedometer. Fighting temptation, he set the cruise control for 50 MPH. No sense risking a speeding ticket near Chamberlain's house.

The further he removed himself from the scene of the murder, the more relaxed he became. The authorities would assume Chamberlain had been killed by a burglar. His bedroom had been ransacked, his ring and watch taken, his front door left open as if the burglar had been frightened away. There was no connection between Chamberlain and himself that could be traced outside normal social channels. He was safe. The plan could proceed. All roads would come to an end for the FBI in the study of John Fairchild Chamberlain.

*****

At 4:30 A.M. the phone rang next to the bed. He had been asleep for a little more than an hour. "Yes?"

"This is the ace of clubs. Did you hear the news?"

"What news?"

"The eight of clubs has been killed."

"How?"

"The local authorities believe it was a burglary. His butler was not home at the time. A team from the FBI is supposed to investigate later this morning."

"That's too bad, but perhaps it is just as well."

"What are you talking about? My god, he's dead!"

"Get ahold of yourself. Sure it's unfortunate, but stop and think. The FBI had him under suspicion, anyway. Perhaps now they will believe their case is closed. I'm afraid our friend wasn't as careful as he might have been. Had he lived, he might have eventually implicated the two of us. Now, there is nothing. I agree, it is sad, but maybe it is for the best."

There was a long silence on the other end. "My god, you killed him, didn't you?"

"Don't talk like that. Let it pass. We still have important work to do. I can't afford to have you fold on me now."

There was more silence on the line. "You're right. Don't worry about me. Perhaps it is for the best."

"That's better. Now, get some sleep. Tomorrow is a big day for us."

"Yes, it is. Good night."

DAY 3

Chapter 18

Alexandria, Virginia
April 14
8:00 A.M.

The sweet scent of brewing coffee stimulated Bert Mattox's senses as he stirred in his bed. He turned over on his side and opened his eyes. The clock on the bed stand blinked 8:00 A.M. The surroundings were comfortably familiar. He was covered with a sheet, blanket, and comforter. Within seconds he realized also that he was completely nude. The events of the previous evening began swimming through his brain. The panic of believing Maggy had been killed was followed by the comforting realization that she had survived.

The faint sound of a woman's singing voice filtered through the opened bedroom door. The sound was coming closer. Mattox recognized the old melody, ". . .to dream the impossible dream, to fight the unbeatable foe, to fight with the last ounce of courage, to reach the unreachable star. . ." It was Maggy's unmusical deep-pitched voice. He looked up as she came through his door carrying a tray.

"Well, Special Agent Bert Mattox, I see you finally feel like waking up and joining the world." She placed the tray down on the bed. "Today for your majesty, we have two slices of English muffin, buttered; two eggs, poached; peach preserves; three slices of bacon, and a pot of Folgers' best." Maggy was smiling broadly, obviously proud of her culinary accomplishment.

Mattox straightened himself and sat up, propping two pillows behind his back. With his hairless chest exposed, Maggy ran her index finger up from his navel to his lips, then leaned over and kissed him gently.

"And where did this feast come from, certainly not my refrigerator?"

"One of the agents outside was good enough to make a run to the grocery for me. Don't worry. I paid him with my own money. I am not a kept woman, I'll have you know." She sat back away from him on the edge of the bed. "Now, eat up."

Mattox was famished. His only nourishment the previous twenty-four hours had been a cold sandwich Mary Alice had brought him in the command center. He began devouring his morning fare as Maggy sat back and observed.

"Do you mind if I ask you something, Bert?"

Mattox fought to clear his throat. "Sure, go ahead."

"Why the FBI? I mean, I saw your law degree hanging in the hallway. Why not practice law?"

"I don't know. Too tame, I guess. I graduated from Indiana University in 1975, then got my law degree from Notre Dame in '78. My godfather lived in Indianapolis back then, and he was an FBI agent. He said a few years in the bureau would be excellent training for me to use later in private practice. At the time I was burnt out on studying, and a job with the bureau meant I didn't have to sit for the bar exam right away. Later, I got married and had a couple of kids. The bills kept mounting, and I guess I felt comfortable with a steady income. Anyway, the marriage didn't last, but the bills did." He took another long gulp of coffee.

Mattox dropped a forkful of egg down his chest. As he quickly wiped at it with a napkin from the tray, he paused, then glanced at Maggy with a twinkle in his eye. "I don't remember taking my clothes off last night."

Maggy responded sheepishly. "After you fell asleep and your friends left, I thought that you might rest better without those bulky clothes sticking to your body, so I removed them. I hope I didn't embarrass you, Agent Mattox."

Mattox chomped at his bacon. "What else did you do while I was asleep?"

Maggy stood. "That's for me to know and for you to find out." She turned toward the bathroom. "Now, I'm going to take a shower. I'm going to work today."

A piece of the English muffin caught in Mattox's throat as Maggy turned. He started to protest, but could only cough.

Maggy glanced over her shoulder, smiled, and winked. "Drink your coffee, Mr. Special Agent." She dropped the cotton robe from her shoulders, revealing the creamy texture of her slim body, then slowly walked into the bathroom. She deliberately left the door opened.

Mattox reached for his coffee and finished quickly what was left. The coughing stopped. He had finished his eggs and bacon and moved the tray to his side. He started to spring out of bed, but as soon as he stood, a sharp ache in his head slowed him. He momentarily caught his balance, straightened, and then proceeded to the bathroom.

Maggy was already in the single shower stall. The glass door was closed, but the fuzzy frame of her body was visible through the steam filling the shower stall. To his right Mattox could see the gauze patch on the crown of his head reflected in the full-sized mirror on the wall above the vanity. For one of the few times in his adult life, he was happy he had little hair in that area. The patch would come off painlessly.

As he pondered the view of his naked body, the reflection filled him with disappointment. As much as he had tried through the years to avoid a midline bulge, his chest kept sinking into his waistline. The roll around his midsection was unattractive. He took in his breath, hoping to flatten his stomach, but in a few seconds he had to exhale, and the roll returned. He turned his attention back toward the running shower. Maggy's humming resumed; this time it was a melody from an old Rodgers and Hammerstein musical. He couldn't remember which one. He crossed to the shower and opened the door. Maggy was bent over, facing the door as she washed her legs with one bare hand and a bar of soap in the other hand. She continued humming without looking up.

Mattox closed the door behind him and nestled up to his house guest. "I'm afraid this shower wasn't designed for couples." The hot water smashed against his face. Maggy, still bent down, reached over with her hand and soap and began massaging the special agent's calves. Her hand moved up to the thigh, then higher. Mattox could feel himself hardening. He reached down with his hands and with a gentle effort ran them over Maggy's smooth back. He could feel her tongue exploring him, generating a heightened sense of exhilaration. Within moments he was nearing a climax when the tongue suddenly stopped, and Maggy straightened. She thrust her hips toward him, and Mattox quickly responded by throwing his arms around her body. Mattox's hand slipped down until he had a grip on each cheek of her buttocks. She raised both legs, and he found himself thrust inside her and heaving.

She threw her head back. The guttural sounds in her throat were returning. Mattox had pinned her back to the polished tiled shower wall as his rhythmic thrusts increased in intensity, and the stream of water from the shower head bounced off his back. Within seconds he had exploded as again she screamed, "Yes! Yes! Yes!" She leaned forward and buried her head on his shoulder, biting hard into his flesh. Soon, she too felt the satisfaction of completion. The two lovers collapsed into each other's arms. They began kissing, gently at first, but soon their tongues were searching each other's mouths.

The loud ring of the telephone that Mattox had installed near the bathroom vanity exploded in their ears. The tile floors and walls of the bathroom seemed to amplify the sound to the point of being uncomfortably shrill. "Sorry, honey, but business calls." He released his hold on the wet, slick body of the woman he was trying with difficulty not to love. He opened the shower door and stepped out, closing the door behind him to allow Maggy to finish. He reached over to the wall and picked up the receiver.

"Sorry to bother you so early, Mr. Mattox; this is Peters."

"That's okay, Carl. I was taking a shower anyway. What do you have?"

"John Chamberlain was murdered last night."

Mattox did not notice his own stunned expression in the large mirror. "Murdered? By whom?"

"The Fairfax County Sheriff's Department is inclined to believe it was a burglary. According to his butler, a ring and watch that Chamberlain kept with him are missing. His bedroom was torn apart by someone searching for something. Whoever it was set off the automatic alarm when he tried to open a wall safe in the bedroom."

"Was anybody home when it happened?"

"Apparently not, sir. The butler claims he was sent by Chamberlain to his office in Washington to get some papers he had forgotten. The security guard at the JFC Building confirms that he was there at the time the sheriff's office believes Chamberlain was murdered. Mrs. Chamberlain maintains a condominium in Manhattan. I gather she and Chamberlain cohabitated only on social occasions."

"Do we have a team out there?"

"Yes, sir; they've been there since 5:00 this morning. They should be about finished."

"Could you pick me up in half an hour, and we'll drive out there?"

"Yes, sir, I'm on my way."

"See you then." He returned the receiver to the wall. The sound of running water had stopped. In the mirror he saw Maggy standing behind him drying her hair with a towel.

He turned around. "Maggy, John Chamberlain was killed last night. The police think it was a burglary."

Maggy straightened up and jerked her head backward so her long wet hair would drop to her back. "Chamberlain? He was that millionaire I met last year, wasn't he?"

"Yes. Maggy, I don't want you going back to work, yet. We don't know for sure who killed Chamberlain or why. There could be someone else out there stalking you. I want you to stay here."

"No way, Bert Mattox. I've had enough of this comfortable life of the rich and famous. The two men who tried to kill me are dead. I'm not going to live the rest of my life hiding and running away from shadows. Bert, I have to work. I am a working woman. I'm not one of those homebodies who lives by the television. I'd go nuts."

"But, Maggy, I can't guarantee your protection back at the travel agency. I can station guards there, but. . ."

"Oh, no, you don't. We don't need the agency becoming an armed camp. It wouldn't be good for business."

"Well, I can't allow you to go back there unprotected."

Maggy wrapped the towel around her hair. "Then I'm sticking with you, Mr. Special Agent. Wherever you go, I go. Take it or leave it."

Mattox glared down at the woman who had firmly set her chin and was standing completely naked, her hands on her hips and a towel wrapped around her head. The sight for some reason struck him as funny, and he began laughing. The more he tried to stop, the harder he laughed. Maggy stared at Mattox with a look of puzzlement. "What's so goddamn funny, may I ask? Are you laughing at my body?"

"No, no, no, Maggy. It's a beautiful body. It may even be a perfect body. He stepped out of her way so she could see their reflection in the mirror—the two of them standing totally nude—a pornographic rendition of Winslow Homer's *American Gothic*. There was something about the naked body in non-romantic settings that could be devastatingly humorous. Maggy tried not to laugh, but within seconds she, too, was bent over trying to catch her breath.

After several moments Mattox regained control. He took Maggy by the shoulders and turned her toward him. "Okay, Miss Mosele, you can tag along, but don't get in the way, don't open your mouth to strangers, and be as inconspicuous as possible. Agreed?"

Maggy hesitated, then raised her right hand as if to take an oath. "Scout's honor, Mr. Mattox."

Mattox thought about the time. Peters was due in less than thirty minutes. "How long will it take you to make yourself presentable?"

"Thirty minutes, but I've been known to finish in ten." She winked at him and smiled.

"Good enough for me." He reached down and picked her up in his arms and started to carry her toward his bedroom. "This will only take a few minutes." He walked toward his bed, kicking the bathroom door closed behind him.

*****

Lowenstein opened the door wide so that Congressman Schumacher could negotiate his wheelchair through the opening into the Oval Office. Ed O'Bannon followed close behind. No one else was in the room, but a small circular table had been set with Irish linen in the middle of the room and Presidential china invited four people to sit. One position was absent a chair; Schumacher assumed it was left open for him.

"The President will join us shortly, gentlemen. He's in the men's room, freshening up." Lowenstein directed the men to the table.

In a matter of minutes, President Crawford Staton bounded into the room from his nearby private office off to the left of the desk he had inherited from Seth Hansen. He entered, rubbing his hands together. "I'm starved. Ed, Buddy, I hope you brought your appetites with you." The President shook hands with each congressman and found his seat opposite Buddy Schumacher. "I hope you don't mind if Jim sits with us. Quite frankly, with all I've had on my mind lately, I've grown to depend on him to keep track of everything."

"Glad to have Jim stay, Mr. President." O'Bannon smiled at the aide, who in turn offered to pour coffee for the two congressmen.

Two porters, attired in well-pressed white jackets, entered the room, one carrying a large silver tray. The senior of the Hispanic servants placed a plate of ham, scrambled eggs, and fried potatoes in front of each man. Small bowls of fruit and Danish were already on the table. The President nodded at the two men, and they withdrew.

"You know, fellas, this place has the Capitol beat all to hell in terms of service. The food isn't quite as good, but I imagine we can improve upon that."

The congressmen chuckled. The President appeared to them to be in good form, and for certain he had not lost his appetite. The large breakfast was more than either member of the House was accustomed to consuming. Both had been warned by their doctors to cut back on fried foods and fats.

The foursome exchanged small talk as they ate. Lowenstein gave the guests an update on the funeral arrangements and the problems the President would be facing in terms of meeting with all the world leaders who were scheduled to begin arriving the following day.

The President was the first to clear his plate. "By the way, Buddy, what's the latest on Alan?"

"Mr. President, I'm very happy to report that he is completely out of his coma. Mrs. Brownell called my wife at six o'clock this morning to give us the good news. The doctors are still cautiously optimistic. Alan appears to be aware of his surroundings and has recognized his family, but his longer range memory appears not to have returned, yet. The doctors say it will be a matter of time."

"That's great news. I suppose you fellas will be reconvening next week, after the recess. Is Alan going to be able to stand for Speaker?"

O'Bannon decided to respond as Schumacher was trying to finish his coffee. "We hope so, Mr. President. In part, that's why we asked for this meeting."

The President pushed his chair back from the table a few inches. "I must admit, I did wonder what brought my two old friends here. I know I've been negligent in not keeping the Congress better informed the last couple of days, but quite frankly, I didn't know who to call. The Senate has no leadership, and I was waiting for Buddy, here, to let me know who was going to speak for the House."

"Understandable, Mr. President." O'Bannon pushed his chair back from the table so he could face Staton. "Mr. President, we have a very serious problem involving the succession that we feel we must discuss with you."

The President folded his arms together, a gesture that was becoming increasingly difficult for him as his girth increased. "Go ahead, Ed. We've been friends for nearly thirty years. You can speak freely here."

"Thank you, Mr. President. To be quite direct about this, we have been asked by several other members of the House to have experts examine the 1947 Succession Act. We have opinions from our own House counsel, from the Center for the Study of the Presidency in New York and from Stephen Burnstein over at the Library of Congress. Mr. President, all agree, based upon the legislative history of the act, that in the event that neither the Speaker of the House or the President Pro Tem are qualified to serve as President, then the office should devolve to the senior qualified Cabinet member; but only, and I must emphasize the word, only, until a newly qualified Speaker or Pro Tem is selected. It was the intention of the framers of the act that the Presidency would then pass from the Cabinet member to the Speaker or Pro Tem, depending on who became qualified first."

As O'Bannon explained his interpretation of the Succession Act to the President, Staton's eyes narrowed, and his lips tightened. The Whip noticed the same reaction from Lowenstein.

The President dropped his arms to his lap and leaned forward toward O'Bannon. "Ed, are you trying to tell me that I have no right to retain this office, that as soon as you boys elect your Speaker or the Senate selects its Pro Tem, that I have to pack my bags and head back to New England? Is that what you're trying to tell me?"

O'Bannon could not help but feel intimidated by the penetrating eyes of the President. They reminded him of Lyndon Johnson back in the mid-sixties when he had been called into the Oval Office and been brow beaten and cajoled to support the

President's position on Vietnam. He had been a greenhorn then, but even with his prestigious position today, Staton's stare had the same effect on him.

"Mr. President, please do not take this personally. Quite frankly, I believe you are the best man we have to lead the country right now, but the facts are that we are a nation of laws, and our duty is to uphold those laws."

"Look, Ed. I've taken the oath of office as President of the United States. I've sworn an oath to preserve, protect, and defend the Constitution. I know what my responsibility is. I didn't take an oath as an Acting President. I was advised by the Attorney General of the United States and the Chief Justice of the United States. Are you telling me your young hotshot lawyers over there in the House and this Burnstein, whoever the hell he is, know more about interpreting the law than the Chief Justice of the United States? Why, that's ludicrous!" The President slammed his hand down on the table, rattling all the china and crystal in the process.

Schumacher tried to rescue his colleague. "Mr. President, we're not questioning the advice of either the Attorney General or the Chief Justice at the time they gave it to you. We had just suffered a terrible shock—all of us. I feel sure they were giving you their best advice without the benefit of deep research. However, since that time, we've had an opportunity to re-evaluate the situation and to do the research. I agree with Ed that you are the best qualified man in the government to serve as President, but your permanent elevation to the Presidency is not the law. I feel badly about that, but it is not the law."

The President rose from his chair. O'Bannon and Lowenstein started to rise also, but he waved them back. He stood towering above the other three men below him. "Let me get this straight. You want me to relinquish the office as soon as there is a qualified replacement from Congress. My god, do you men have any idea what you're talking about? One of the reasons I haven't tried to talk to the Senate is that it's controlled by the Republicans right now. What happens if they try to elect a Pro Tem next week before the replacements of those killed two days ago have a chance to take their seats? Do you expect me to turn this entire government over to the opposition?"

O'Bannon started to answer, but he could tell the President was not finished.

"And then look at your own house. Hell, who are you going to elect? Alan Brownell is lying in a hospital delirious. Buddy, do you want to be President?" Staton's eyes stared directly down at the man seated across from him.

"No, sir. I've already made that perfectly clear to my colleagues."

"Then who do you have? Surely not that bozo caucus chairman of yours. Hell, you couldn't keep him sober long enough to memorize his way to the head around here. So who do you have?"

Both congressmen looked at each other. Neither had a response.

The President walked around the table, glaring down at his two guests. "Let me tell you two old friends what it's like around here. I've got a bunch of generals and admirals over in the Pentagon who want me to launch an attack against the largest army in the world. I have a bunch of reactionary maniacs in the Kremlin who couldn't find their ass with both hands. I've got an Acting Secretary of State in Moscow who can't get in to see the bastards. They won't talk to him or to me. In the meantime, the governments of Iran and Turkey are pleading with me for help. I have the leaders of the world coming to Washington tomorrow and every damn one of them wants a private visit with the new President of the United States. Now, I have a bunch of backstabbing congressmen who want to tell me that I am not legally qualified to keep the office of President."

O'Bannon again tried to protest. "Mr. President, we are not backstabbers. We're only trying to . . . "

The President waved him off. "Let me finish, Mr. Chairman. How successful do you think I'm going to be in trying to pull us out of this quagmire in the Middle East if our allies and those bastards in Moscow find out that I am an interim President? I'll tell you. Zilch. That's it, zilch. You can either kiss the Middle East goodbye or place me in an intolerable position where I may have to use our missiles if the Russians push me into a corner."

The two congressmen sat speechless. The threat to launch nuclear missiles was a shock to them both. They knew that a nuclear confrontation with the Russians would lead to unbelievable devastation in the United States. With Russian submarines roaming the Atlantic and Pacific, there was no way that the military could interdict all the missiles the subs could launch even with the first generation of SDI killer satellites in place. The two men were horrified.

The President walked around to his chair at the table and sat down. "Now, if you boys over on the Hill want to take the responsibility for launching World War III, go ahead. Make your case to the media. At the same time Chenkov and his generals will be watching CNN and making their calculations. Any chance I might have to negotiate our way out of this will be blown to smithereens. If you men want to take that responsibility, you go right ahead." Staton leaned back in his chair awaiting a response.

Neither congressman spoke for several moments. Finally, O'Bannon lifted his head and faced the President. "Crawford, I don't know what to say. I know the burdens of this office are awesome, but I had no idea we were that close to a nuclear confrontation. Perhaps Buddy and I should return to our colleagues and share your problems with them."

"No, Ed, I can't allow you to do that. I've probably told you too much already. If word leaks out about what I'm thinking, it could ruin all our efforts to negotiate with these nuts. I must ask you and Buddy both to respect the confidence I've shared with you today."

"But, Mr. President, that places us in a terrible position. You're asking us to take sides without being able to explain why to the leadership of the Congress." Buddy Schumacher was incredulous.

"I'm sorry, Buddy. I know you have a dilemma, but think of the dilemma and pressures I have. Why not let this pass? Begin the process of confirming Lewellan and let the country feel like things are returning to normal."

O'Bannon was uneasy. "Mr. President, getting Jake Lewellan confirmed by both houses isn't going to be easy. He's viewed as a one dimensional senator by most of our members. Placing him one heart beat away from the Presidency will be anathema to many Democrats as well as to the Republicans. Hell, he might get more Republican votes than Democrat."

The President leaned forward, placing his arm on the table. "Look, Ed, I need Lewellan. Those boys in the Kremlin are scared to death of him. Why do you think I picked him? If they know he's in place and that Crawford Staton is their best hope for avoiding a nuclear exchange, I think they'll back down. Without Lewellan, my chances are diminished substantially."

Both Schumacher and O'Bannon felt sick. The meeting had not gone the way they had envisioned. Both men sat in their seats, depressed with both a sense of defeat and bewilderment. Swallowing their pride, ignoring the law, and accepting Lewellan appeared to be the only options to avoiding a nuclear war.

Chapter 19

Carl Peters had been surprised when Mattox emerged from his home with Maggy Mosele beside him. He was even more surprised when she took a seat in the back of the car. Mattox explained his compromise with the defiant Miss Mosele. She could tag along with him so long as she kept out of the way.

Peters began his report as he slowly accelerated to leave the parking lot. "We received a report back this morning on the man we found in your home last night. Name is Stewart, John Stewart—age 35, unmarried, thirteen years in the Marines, reached rank of lieutenant colonel, and resigned his commission six months ago. He took a security job with Castleton Steel and Tubing, Inc., of Dover, Delaware. Turns out that Castleton is a subsidiary of JFC Industries."

Mattox turned his head toward Peters. "JFC Industries? That means another link to our friend, Chamberlain."

"Yes, sir. We made the ID from Stewart's fingerprints. Seems the man had top security clearance from the National Security Agency. He was a Naval Academy graduate back in the eighties and was on the fast track in terms of promotions. He had combat command on his record—both Kuwait and Panama. One of my sources at the NSA told me that had Stewart stayed in the service, the betting was he would have made general before he was forty."

"How come he quit?"

"Don't know, sir. Both his parents are dead, killed in that Korean passenger jet the Russians shot down back in the eighties. He has no living brothers or sisters."

"What was his last assignment in the service?"

"He was on the staff of the Secretary of Defense."

"Nelson Thompson?"

"Yes, sir."

Peters pulled into the entrance of the Chamberlain estate. The stone drive wound its way through a manicured lawn and tall cottonwood trees which were sprouting young spring leaves. Several dark cars were parked near the main entrance, including two clearly marked Fairfax County Sheriff's Department vehicles.

Peters found a parking space near the four-door garage to the side of the house. The three walked around to the main entrance where a uniformed sheriff's officer started to stop them. Peters flashed his identification before the young man could say anything. "Peters, FBI. This is Special Agent Mattox and Miss Mosele. Has our team finished, yet?"

"No, sir, but one of your men came out for a cigarette a few minutes ago and said they were almost finished."

Peters and Mattox exchanged knowing smiles. Akers was an addicted smoker, one of the few left in the Washington office. They walked through the open door and saw Akers standing at the rear of the large entry hall. Mattox led the other two in his direction.

"Good morning, Agent Mattox, how are you feeling?"

"Fine, Akers, and wipe that smirk off your face. You'll get hit with a frying pan one of these days."

"Probably right, sir, especially as much as I complain about my wife's cooking." He pointed through the open six-paneled walnut door. "He was shot in there, sir."

Mattox and the others entered the richly paneled study. Akers pointed to the desk chair. "They found the body in that chair." The corpse had been removed by the sheriff's office.

Maggy grasped Mattox's arm as she stared at the high back leather chair. Mattox turned to Akers. "You think it was burglary?"

"No, sir, I don't."

Mattox looked puzzled. "How come?"

"Come over here." Akers led them toward the desk and asked them to stand on the opposite side as he took a seat where Chamberlain had been sitting. "From the position of the body," Akers positioned himself in the chair as if he were working at the desk, "we know that the bullet entered just below his left eye and exited above his right ear. That means the gun that shot him must have been quite low. Go ahead, Mr. Mattox, try to line it up."

Mattox bent down in front of the desk trying to get a line on the trajectory of the bullet. "The gun must have been fired from below desktop level."

Akers straightened. "That's right, sir. In fact, we believe whoever killed Chamberlain was sitting in the chair behind you when he fired the shot. Does it make sense that Chamberlain would have casually sat behind his desk and carried on a conversation with a burglar? Doesn't to me."

Mattox pondered Akers's hypothesis. "If the bullet exited above the ear, then it must have ended up in one of those books behind him."

"That's right. We found the book." Akers stood up and removed the *English Book of Common Prayer*. "Here it is, sir. You can see the bullet hole in the binding, just below the title."

Mattox examined the collector's edition. He flipped through the pages. "I see where it entered, but where's the bullet?"

"Good question, Mr. Mattox. We've checked behind the books, and it never made its way out of that volume. The killer must have taken the bullet with him. Does that sound like your everyday burglar?"

"No, Akers, it doesn't." Mattox paused while he digested Akers's observations. "What else do you have? He handed the book back to Akers who replaced it on the shelf.

"We've talked to the butler. He's worked for Chamberlain for nearly fifteen years, and he has an ironclad alibi. It was unusual for Chamberlain to request Edward, that's the butler's name, to run such a long errand late at night. We checked with Chamberlain's secretary a couple of hours ago, and the papers Chamberlain wanted Edward to pick up were routine. Chamberlain had already reviewed them and had given her a memo to act upon them. It doesn't make sense that Chamberlain would have sent Edward on a wild goose chase unless . . . "

Maggy interrupted, "He wanted to get rid of him."

Mattox grimaced at Maggy. She shrank into a contrite, faint smile. "Sorry."

Akers nodded toward Maggy. "You're right, Miss Mosele. At least, that's how I see it. I think Chamberlain got rid of Edward so he could meet with somebody alone. If I'm right, Chamberlain knew the person who killed him."

"Any fingerprints?"

"No, sir. Chamberlain had a maid who cleaned this room every day, and I'm afraid she's pretty efficient. The only prints we've lifted are Chamberlain's. Whoever did this was very careful not to touch anything, or else he wore gloves."

Peters interjected, "He must have worn gloves. If the bullet is missing from the book, he surely handled the book, and you didn't find any prints on it, did you?"

"That's right, Carl." Akers was nodding his head as he spoke.

Mattox walked around the room, observing the walls and furniture. "What about the phone tap? Do we have anything on it?"

Akers pulled out his notebook to review. "Sorry, we received the court order at 11:30 last night, but the tap wasn't completed until about 1:00. In fact, the first thing we have is the alarm from the safe in Chamberlain's bedroom which was being transmitted to the local sheriff's office by phone lines at 1:20. We believe the killer tried to open Chamberlain's safe when the alarm went off. A deputy sheriff arrived here at 1:30 a.m. The front door was open; the lights were on, but the house was empty except for Chamberlain."

Mattox turned around. "So whoever killed Chamberlain wanted something in that safe. Where did you say it was?"

Akers pointed above his head. "Upstairs in Chamberlain's bedroom. The killer tore the hell out of the room looking for something."

"Let's go see for ourselves." Mattox walked past the small group near him and led them up the marble steps to the second floor. Akers pointed to the bedroom door which was closed. Mattox opened the door. The room was still in disarray. A man with a flash camera was finishing his work.

"Jesus, this room is as big as my entire condo." Mattox looked around the bedroom and spotted the opened safe on the wall next to the Chippendale chest placed opposite the bed. "Who opened the safe?"

"We did, sir, about an hour ago. We got the combination from Chamberlain's secretary."

"What was in it that was so important?"

"Actually, not very much—about $2,000 in cash stacked in the back, some diamond jewelry he kept in a small case, and his wallet. That's it."

"Where are they?"

"We have them in a bag over by the Chippendale. We've already dusted them for prints."

"Let's see what we have." Mattox walked over to the chest of drawers and found the plastic ziplock bag resting on the thick carpeted floor beneath the safe. He reached for the bag, then walked over to an antique circular lamp table near one of the windows. "Who's got gloves?"

Akers pulled a set of plastic medical gloves from his suit pocket and handed them over.

Mattox stretched them over his hands and picked up the bag. He pulled out the box and the wallet. He checked the small pine box first. The contents included a stick pin, four sets of gold cufflinks, and a lapel pin, all studded with large diamonds and rubies. He then opened a large, handcrafted leather wallet, folded once to fit a coat's inside pocket. He carefully pulled out the contents and laid them on the table.

"Let's see. We have a gold card American Express, a Visa card issued by Citicorp, a Virginia driver's license, about a dozen membership cards to clubs, a calendar book, six twenty dollar bills. That must be it." He held the wallet out and shook it. An eight of clubs floated to the table top.

"What do we have here?" Mattox picked up the card to examine it. "Unless I miss my guess, this card came from the same deck as the one we found in Manchester's wallet." He handed the card to Akers. "Check this out with Manchester's card."

He fumbled through the membership cards, but found nothing out of the usual. He handed them to Peters. "Better check with each of these clubs. See if either Lampworth or Manchester belonged to them."

He turned back toward Akers. "Did Chamberlain leave any note of any kind, anything that might indicate whom he was going to meet?"

"No, sir. We found nothing in his study, in this room, or anyplace else. He has a small private phone directory in his desk downstairs."

"Let's go have a look." Mattox led the three back down to the study. Maggy tried to keep a hand on Mattox's arm, but she could tell he was all business.

Downstairs, Mattox opened the top drawer of the desk and pulled out the small, brown leatherbound directory. He flipped through the pages. There were about fifty entries, some by full name, some by initials. He handed the book to Peters. "Check out all these numbers. I want a list of who was important enough to be in Mr. Chamberlain's private directory."

Mattox sat down in Chamberlain's chair and studied the desk. It was a magnificent French Provincial Louis XIV antique with an inlaid leather top. Except for a gold and ivory telephone on the corner of the desk and a blank pad of monogrammed paper next to it, the desk was clear. He looked up at Akers. "Did you check all the drawers?"

"Yes, sir. The second drawer down on the right was slightly opened when we arrived. There was a small 22-caliber silver plated pistol in it, but as best we can tell, it has never been fired."

Mattox shook his head. He pulled the white note pad over in front of him. There were indentations of writing on the pad. "Is there a pencil around here?"

Akers pointed to the top left drawer. "I believe there are several in there, sir."

Mattox opened the drawer and pulled out a freshly sharpened #2 lead pencil with the initials "JFC" imprinted in gold on the side. He grasped the pencil near the end and rubbed the side of the lead over the blank pad. In a matter of seconds he finished and held his head back to examine the pad. "There's nothing here but doodles. There's a clover leaf, three spades, and one word— DEADWOOD—all in capital letters."

No one said anything. Mattox leaned back in the comfortable chair and continued to stare at the pad. "Deadwood? Does that ring a bell with any of you?"

They all shook their heads. Finally, Maggy cautiously spoke. "The only Deadwood I've ever heard of is Deadwood, South Dakota. It was the setting for the musical *Calamity Jane.*"

"Calamity Jane?" Mattox repeated the name several times. "Wait a minute. Seems like I saw an old Doris Day movie on cable a few months back. She played Calamity Jane. Who was her boyfriend in that movie?"

"Howard Keel," answered Maggy.

"No, no. I mean who was Calamity Jane's boyfriend?"

"Wild Bill Hickok," Maggy answered again.

"That's right. Wild Bill Hickok. If history serves me right, wasn't he actually killed in Deadwood?"

Maggy shook her head. "Not in the movie."

Mattox smiled broadly at Maggy. "I imagine you're right, but I believe in real life he was shot in the back while playing poker in a saloon in Deadwood. I've played my share of poker over the years on long stakeouts. How about you boys?" Both Peters and Akers nodded.

"Ever hear of deadman's hand?" Mattox continued to smile.

A look of revelation crossed Peters's face. "Two aces and two eights, all black."

"That's right, Carl. Two aces and two eights. Manchester had the ace of spades. Chamberlain had the eight of clubs. Unless I miss my guess, the man who killed Chamberlain wasn't after money. He was after that eight of clubs. And, if I'm on target, we have two more people to find. One of them has an eight of spades, the other an ace of clubs."

Akers shook his head. "How juvenile! Four cards. Why would they need those cards?"

Mattox dropped the pad on the desk and stood, ripping the plastic gloves from his hands and handing them back to Akers. "I don't know that yet, but I'll bet my pension those cards are the connection." He looked at Peters. "Carl, get me the complete membership lists of all those clubs in the Washington area that Chamberlain belonged to. Then run a computer cross reference of all those names with the names you find in Chamberlain's directory." He grabbed Maggy by the elbow and started for the door, talking to the men behind him as he left. "Carl, catch a ride with Akers, will you? I'm going to the Pentagon."

Chapter 20

On his way to Arlington, Mattox placed a call to the Attorney General, asking him to clear the way for a meeting with the Secretary of Defense.

"Sure, Bert, but why do you want to see Nelson?" the AG asked.

"John Stewart, the man who killed Abdul, Martin, and two of my agents and who tried to kill Margaret Mosele, was assigned to Thompson's staff for nearly a year. I have to chase this down."

The AG's voice was strained. "Surely, you don't suspect Thompson was involved, Bert? Seth Hansen was his best friend. There's just no way he could have taken part in a conspiracy to kill the President."

"How confident were you that John Chamberlain had not been involved?"

There was a long pause on the line before the AG responded. "The two are not similar, Bert. Let me tell you a little about the Secretary of Defense. First of all, he is not a career politician. He was a close friend to President Hansen, dating back to their days as roommates in law school at Michigan. While Seth pursued a political career, Nelson worked his way up from counsel in a small electronics company, which his father-in-law started, to become

CEO of the third largest manufacturer of electronic testing equipment in the world."

Mattox continued to drive as he spoke into his car phone. "So he and Chamberlain were fellow industrialists. Right?"

"Yes, but let me go on. Nelson and his wife emerged into the upper crust of Midwestern society as patrons of the arts, as symphony trustees, and as Seth's largest campaign contributors. After his election, Hansen literally had to beg Nelson to accept an appointment to the Cabinet. As you may recall, there was a flap during his Senate confirmation hearings over his refusal to sell his stock in the family business, but that had been part of his agreement with Seth. That's where he got that dubious nickname Lord Horatio Nelson, a reference to the famous British naval heroes, Lord Nelson and Horatio Hornblower, the latter being based on Horatron Electronics, his family business."

"So far, I haven't heard anything that makes him any less suspect than Chamberlain, sir." Mattox continued to focus on his driving while Maggy dutifully kept to herself next to him.

"During the past two and a half years, Nelson has earned his spurs, Bert. At first, he felt his way carefully with the Joint Chiefs. I know because we had several discussions about his role. Later, after he realized all those ribbons and braid were nothing short of window dressing, he found it much easier to say no to them. The longtime friends of the Pentagon brass who sit on the Senate and House Armed Service committees gradually and quietly began questioning Nelson's judgment, especially his vetoes of the Chiefs' funding requests."

"So your point is, sir, that Secretary Thompson and President Hansen were in sync in terms of how they saw defense policy, and Thompson's personal and ideological ties to the President were too strong for him to be a part of any conspiracy to replace him. Is that right, sir?" Mattox could see the exit to the Pentagon just ahead on the left.

"That's about it, Bert. I just wanted you to have some insight into his background. I'll call right now and get you in to see him. Best of luck."

"Thanks, sir. I'll be in touch soon."

*****

Nelson Thompson's secretary showed Bert Mattox and Maggy Mosele into the Secretary's large second floor office. Thompson rose from his desk as they entered and extended his hand to both, then offered them seats on a burgundy leather sofa nearby, while he chose a comfortable matching lounge chair. He seemed especially surprised to see Maggy, but he offered her his sympathies over the death of Weissman and attempted to make her comfortable.

"I appreciate your seeing me on such short notice, Mr. Secretary. I know you are very busy." Mattox unbuttoned his suit coat and attempted to relax. Maggy sat very erect next to Mattox. "I hope you don't mind if Miss Mosele joins us. As you know, there have been three attempts on her life, and I guess I figured she was safer with me than anyplace else." Mattox was apologetic in his tone, but down deep he was happy for Maggy's company and knew her presence would evoke a sense of sympathy from Thompson and others they might meet.

"I must admit, Mr. Mattox, that I was surprised when the Attorney General called and indicated you needed to talk to me."

"I'm here, Mr. Secretary, about the investigation."

"Agent Mattox, I would love to help you, but I really don't see how I can. President Hansen was a very dear friend of mine. We were roommates in law school back in Michigan. My wife is at the White House now with Mrs. Hansen. I have a meeting in less than an hour with President Staton," he glanced at his wristwatch, " so I hate to rush you."

"We'll try to be brief, sir. I suppose you have heard about John Chamberlain?"

"Yes, I received word this morning from the White House, just before the story broke in the local media. Terrible. I've known John for years. We played golf a couple of months back, out at Burning Tree. How tragic for him to have been killed by a burglar."

"He was not killed by a burglar, Mr. Secretary. He was murdered by someone who knew him quite well."

"But according to the White House, robbery was the motive."

"No, sir. We believe that John Chamberlain was involved in the conspiracy to kill the President and the others."

Thompson looked surprised. "I can't believe a man like Chamberlain would have been involved in a plot to kill the President. My god, I was Seth's campaign treasurer. Chamberlain was one of our largest contributors through PACs his companies controlled. It makes no sense."

"That may be, sir, but we cannot ignore the facts. There is the possibility he was being blackmailed. There's also the possibility that he became disillusioned with the President. I believe many of Mr. Chamberlain's holdings were connected with the Defense Department, were they not?"

"Why, yes, but surely that wouldn't be reason."

"And haven't you and the President been cutting back on defense spending the past two years."

"Yes, but still, John Chamberlain? It really is hard to believe."

"Mr. Thompson, let me ask you about another man. His name is John Stewart, a Lieutenant Colonel in the Marines who was assigned to your office some time ago. Do you recall him?"

"John Stewart? Why, yes—Colonel Stewart. I didn't know him very well. He was on our staff here, but I think you'll find that the Secretary's staff is quite large. But I remember John. Good looking young man. We had assigned him as a congressional liaison. I believe he worked with Senator Lewellan's Intelligence Committee. I can check to be sure."

"I'd appreciate that, sir."

Thompson stood and walked over to his desk, picked up his telephone receiver, and pushed a button. "Anne, would you pull up Colonel John Stewart's file. Make a copy and bring it in here, will you? Thanks." He returned to his seat.

"Now what does Colonel Stewart have to do with all this?"

"Mr. Secretary, John Stewart killed Abdul, the assassin. He also killed a CIA agent named Martin, killed two of my men who were protecting Miss Mosele, and three times tried to kill her."

"John Stewart?" The Secretary sat forward with a look of complete incredulity spread across his face. "Colonel Stewart? I can't believe that. He had national security clearance, had to have it to work in my office."

Mattox leaned forward until his face was no more than inches from Thompson's. "John Stewart worked for one of John Chamberlain's companies."

"My god!" Thompson continued to focus on Mattox. "So you believe Chamberlain was the mastermind of the conspiracy to kill the President?"

"Possibly, but there were others involved, and we have to find them, Mr. Secretary."

"Others?" Thompson was about to pursue his question when his secretary knocked on his door and entered holding a computer printout.

"You wanted Colonel Stewart's file, Mr. Secretary?"

"Yes, Anne, would you please bring it over here?"

The middle-aged, diminutive secretary crossed the room and handed the three pages to the Defense Secretary, then withdrew.

Thompson was clearly disturbed. He suddenly realized that he might be under suspicion. He thumbed through the report. "Agent Mattox, it's not normal procedure, but I'll let you take this printout with you when you leave. I was right, however; Stewart was assigned to our legislative liaison staff, specifically the Senate Armed Services and Senate Intelligence Committees." He handed the printout to Mattox.

"I'm curious why you believe the conspiracy involves more than John Chamberlain. Are you at liberty to explain?"

Mattox continued to review the small print on the computer paper. "Mr. Secretary, do you play poker?" He glanced toward Thompson to gauge his reaction.

"No, Mr. Mattox, I don't. Bridge is my game, though I don't get a chance to play too often. What, may I ask, is the significance of that question?"

Mattox handed the printout to Maggy, who dutifully folded the papers and placed them in her purse. "Sir, you wouldn't know the term deadman's hand, then?"

"No, I'm afraid not. I assume there is a significance to the phrase since you brought it up."

"Yes, sir. Wild Bill Hickok was shot in the back in a saloon in Deadwood, South Dakota, while he was playing poker. The hand he held when he was shot contained two aces and two eights, all black."

"Interesting history, but I fail to see its significance."

"Bear with me, Mr. Secretary. Chamberlain had scribbled the word 'Deadwood' on a note pad he kept by the phone in his study. Add to that, a playing card, specifically the eight of clubs, was found in his wallet."

"Could be coincidence."

"No, sir. The CIA agent, William Manchester, also had a playing card in his wallet. His was the ace of spades."

Thompson sat silently for several moments. "So, you believe that there are at least two other people involved in the conspiracy and that one has an eight, the other an ace. Is that what you are suggesting, Mr. Mattox?"

"Yes, sir, I am." Mattox expected the Defense Secretary to explode, but he remained calm.

"I never asked you why you thought Chamberlain was murdered. Could you elaborate?"

Mattox laid out the details of his investigation and assumptions as Thompson held his fingers pressed tightly together in front of his chest.

"Then you must believe the person who killed Chamberlain is involved in this plot?"

"Yes, sir."

"What time was he killed, Agent Mattox?"

"Between 1:00 and 1:20 this morning."

Thompson hesitated. "May I call you Bert?" Mattox nodded. "You've been very good about not accusing me, but let me put your mind at ease. At 1:00 this morning, I was just leaving my office to go home. Two members of the Secret Service accompanied me. One was my driver."

Mattox smiled slightly. "Mr. Secretary, I apologize if I offended you in any way."

"No, Bert, I'm not offended. In some ways I'm relieved. You're not afraid to chase down some of the most important people in this city. In some circles I am considered a very powerful man." Thompson was not smiling.

"Those circles include me, Mr. Secretary."

Thompson stood and walked over to his desk and picked up a yellow legal pad, then returned to his chair. "You'll excuse me if I make some notes. I'm afraid it's part of my legal training. I can't think unless I can see everything in front of me."

"I know the feeling, Mr. Secretary." Mattox leaned to his right and squeezed Maggy's hand while Thompson wrote.

After several minutes Thompson spoke. "Good. Bert, let me pose some questions. Let's assume that Chamberlain and others wanted Seth out of the Presidency for reasons of policy. If they kill Seth, then they still have the Vice-President, who is married to Seth's policies. So they have to kill the Vice-President. But they took out the Speaker of the House and the President Pro Tem of the Senate, so, obviously, they wanted all four out of the way."

Mattox and Maggy sat silently as Secretary Thompson continued his soliloquy.

"The only reason they could want all four out is so Crawford Staton could become President. There have been no reported attempts on Staton's life have there?" He looked at Mattox. Mattox shook his head.

"Then they wanted Crawford in office. They may or may not have known about the problem with the 1947 Succession Act. If they did, then they have somebody in the Congress whom they want to move up."

Mattox and Maggy exchanged puzzled looks before Mattox asked, "Excuse me, Mr. Secretary, I don't follow you on the succession thing. What do you mean?"

Thompson laid his pad down on the arm of his large chair. "The

1947 Succession Act serves as the legal basis by which Crawford Staton became President. Prior to 1947, the law provided that if both the offices of President and Vice-President became vacant, the office then would fall to the Cabinet in order of seniority. As an example, there has been historical speculation that one of my predecessors, Edwin Stanton, the Secretary of War, was involved in the John Wilkes Booth conspiracy to kill Lincoln.

Maggy spoke for the first time. "I don't remember that."

"You might recall that the same night Lincoln was shot, one of Booth's cohorts was supposed to kill Vice-President Andrew Johnson, but the man got drunk and failed in his effort. An attempt also was made to kill the Secretary of State that night. A man with a knife entered William Seward's home and actually stabbed him. Had the conspiracy been completely successful, the Presidency would have fallen to the Secretary of the Treasury, a relatively obscure man named Hugh McCulloch. Stanton was next in line after McCulloch. Stanton was a Radical Republican and disagreed with Lincoln and Johnson over their plans for reconstruction."

"That's pretty flimsy evidence, if you don't mind my saying, Mr. Secretary," Mattox offered.

"Yes, but it was Stanton who suggested to General Grant that he not attend the play at Ford's Theater that evening with the Lincolns. And it was the War Department that was responsible for the security of Washington. Conveniently, one exit from the city was left unattended that evening in 1865, and Booth made his escape through that one exit. Finally, Booth was supposedly surrounded in a barn later, and it was the military who killed him before he could be questioned."

"Suspicious, I must admit." Mattox shook his head.

"Well, I don't know whether Stanton was involved or not. It's just speculation at any rate, but it illustrates the point about succession. When Harry Truman became President in 1945, he and Sam Rayburn, the House Speaker, were close friends. The two of them agreed that the Presidency should always be held by an elected official, not an appointed one. They were the ones behind the 1947 Succession Act which inserted the Speaker and the President Pro Tem of the Senate ahead of the Cabinet."

"So that's why four people had to be eliminated, in order to get to the Cabinet?" Maggy was becoming absorbed in the logic.

"Very possibly, Miss Mosele. But the problem is that the framers of the law intended for a Cabinet member to hold the office of Acting President only until a new Speaker or Pro Tem could be properly selected; then the Cabinet member would step down, and the new congressional leader would take over. At least that is what some experts claim the legislative history of the act suggests."

Mattox interjected. "But, Mr. Secretary, the news reports said the Attorney General and the Chief Justice recommended to Mr. Staton that he take the oath of office as President."

"That's correct, and therein lies our problem. Did our conspirators anticipate that Crawford would automatically defer to someone selected by the Congress, or did they want Crawford to become the President?"

There was a long moment of silence as the three collected their thoughts. Finally, it was Thompson who spoke first. "Frankly, I have trouble believing they would want Crawford in the office. After all, he was a part of Seth's team. The two thought exactly alike on national security policy."

Mattox studied the eyes of the Secretary. "Excuse me, sir, but what about Senator Lewellan? John Chamberlain held a fund raiser for him last year. We know that Lewellan's chief-of-staff accompanied Manchester to the Middle East, ostensibly, we believe, to make contact with Abdul. Now, Lewellan has been named Vice-President by President Staton."

"Interesting speculation, Bert, but Lewellan isn't Vice-President, yet. He must be confirmed by both houses of Congress, and I know for a fact he's not the fair-haired boy of most of the members of Congress." Thompson paused. "But still, Crawford is extremely popular right now, and I haven't heard a peep from Congress. Maybe he can pull it off."

"Mr. Secretary, why would President Staton have selected a man like Lewellan?" Maggy posed the question.

Thompson answered very slowly. "I really don't know, Miss Mosele. I just don't know. I've asked myself that question a thousand times the past few hours. The man has no depth. All he knows is bashing the Communists or anybody he believes still has Communist leanings." The Secretary glanced at his watch. "As a matter of fact, I have to meet with Lewellan, the President, and the Security Council in about half an hour. I'm afraid I'm going to have to take my leave." He stood and extended his hand to Mattox. "I wish you luck, Bert."

Mattox thanked him. He and Maggy started for the door before he remembered something. "Mr. Secretary, is it possible to get a copy of Stewart's complete service record? We have to find a common denominator between Manchester, Lampworth, Lewellan, Chamberlain, Abdul, and Stewart. Something has to tie them together."

"I'll have Anne find that information for you. It will take her a little while. You're welcome to wait, or I can have a courier bring it to you over at the bureau."

"Send it over, if you will, sir. I'm on my way over there now."

Thompson watched the handsome couple close the door behind them. The Secretary was very troubled, more so than he had let on to the Special Agent. He prayed that his worst apprehensions were groundless. Could it be that Crawford Staton was one of the conspirators?

Chapter 21

Dr. Tollefson finished his update on the Armenian situation to the National Security Council in the Cabinet Room. He was followed by the CIA director who reported the Russian fleet still at anchor in the Straits of Bosporous.

Secretary Thompson leaned forward to ask a question. "George, do you have any information on the composition of those divisions? Are they Border Troops? Do you know?"

"Yes, sir, as far as we can determine, they are the Russians' top units. And if I might anticipate your next question, Nelson, we believe there are no Muslim units involved in the buildup."

The President looked around the long table. "Any other questions?" There were no hands. "Thank you, George." The President hesitated as he referred to several papers stacked in front of him. "I received a cable from Secretary Engledow less than thirty minutes ago. It is 9:00 p.m. in Moscow. Bill reports he was met at the plane by the Foreign Minister, but all of his attempts to secure a meeting with Chenkov have been stymied. For the past two hours, he has been unable even to reach the Foreign Minister. He believes the Cabinet is meeting in the Kremlin."

Senator Jake Lewellan, who was seated opposite the President in a chair designated for the Vice-President of the United States, muttered, "More like they're getting their marching orders from the MOD."

Nearly everyone present had been surprised to see Lewellan enter the meeting, though they knew Staton had tapped him for the number two position in the government. It was unusual for a designee to move right in prior to confirmation, however. Thompson had asked the Attorney General about Lewellan's security clearance and had been told that the senator had gone through clearance prior to being named to the Intelligence Committee.

Thompson asked, "Where is Gorbachev, anyway? As the last Communist chief of state in the old Soviet Union, surely he would have a role to play if the old line Communists are still in control."

Heffelfinger raised a finger indicating he had an answer to the question. The President nodded in his direction.

"Secretary Thompson, as you know, after Gorbachev resigned in '92, he was given a dacha at a conclave outside Moscow built to house the old Communist elite. Under Yeltsin he ran a foundation he funded with his speaking fees garnered in the West. Since Chenkov came to power, the new leadership has held him on a short leash. You'll recall that old hard-liners tried to get rid of him just before the demise of the Soviet Union. The generals still blame his liberal social policies for the decline of Russia's international position. We understand he has been under a form of house arrest since last year. He has been at liberty to travel to Moscow, attend ballets, visit the university—things like that, but he is always accompanied by KGB guards. We are assuming his public remarks—and there have been damn few—and his movements are closely monitored. The new leaders apparently decided to treat him with velvet gloves, hoping he would not make waves."

Thompson followed up, "So you believe he is still housed in the dacha?"

Heffelfinger hesitated. "Yes, but. . ." The director hesitated.

Thompson smiled toward his friend, "There's always a but, isn't there, George?"

Heffelfinger acknowledged the jibe with a slight smile. "Yes, there is always a but, Mr. Secretary. I was about to say, but our contacts in Russia have not seen him for nearly twenty-four hours. We know he left his dacha on Wednesday, the day the President was killed. As a matter of fact, we understand there has been an increase in activity by the KGB near the compound. At this point, we are assuming the activity is in concert with the problems the leadership is having in Armenia."

The President turned to Admiral Birchfield, "Admiral, what progress can you report on *Thunderburst?*"

Birchfield referred to a two-page memorandum prepared by his staff which was lying in front of him. "Generally, the Chiefs are pleased, sir. Step II of *Thunderburst* was accomplished with 90 percent efficiency. A squadron of transports from Texas had to make an emergency landing in the Antilles because of mechanical problems, but the repairs were completed within six hours, and the squadron landed in Crete with minimal delay. As for Step III, as of ten hundred hours this morning, Washington time, approximately one third of our troops had taken positions on the ground in Turkey. The Iranian landings are due to commence at this very hour, sir. As you know, we anticipated multiple runs by our transports in order to deliver all 36,400 troops. We believe this can be accomplished within the next forty-eight hours."

Lewellan interjected. "Admiral, what are the troops doing after they land?"

Birchfield repositioned himself in his chair. "Senator, they are taking up defensive positions near the airport. They will probably maintain those positions until the remainder of the forces are on the ground, including ground transportation support."

"Admiral, if I might raise a question. Is it wise to keep all our forces bottled up together for the next several hours? The Russians have to know what we're doing. Isn't it possible for them to launch a pre-emptive attack against those forces and catch them all together, much like the Japanese caught all our planes at Pearl Harbor?"

Birchfield seemed nonplused by the question of military tactics. "Senator, the Chiefs share your concern, but Secretary Thompson issued instructions to us that the troops were not to move beyond a five-mile radius of their landing targets."

Everyone around the table turned his attention to the Defense Secretary. He leaned forward to respond. "The Admiral is correct, Senator. We are up against possibly as many as one million Russian troops. Our hope within this Council has been that the introduction of American troops within the territories of Turkey and Iran would serve as a bluff, to intimidate the Kremlin leaders into not crossing the borders. I don't believe even Admiral Birchfield believes that our forces in the area could withstand a major assault by the Russian troops. My orders were in concert with what I perceived to be the intentions of the President and this Council."

Lewellan continued his argument. "With all due respect, Mr. Secretary, I think you are placing our troops in very serious jeopardy. They need to move away from the landing zone so that the Russians have less of a concentrated target. I might add, based on what I know of *Thunderburst* and from Admiral Birchfield's briefing earlier today, any delays in deploying our troops toward the borders will lessen dramatically our chances of securing defensive positions on the high ground in that region. As I understand, it is a fairly mountainous area."

Thompson continued his defense. "That's correct, Senator. One of our immediate problems is the need for helicopter transport to deliver men to those high points. Approximately 200 choppers are committed to *Thunderburst*, but they won't begin arriving for another four to twelve hours, depending on the weather over there."

"Don't the Turks and Iranians have ground transports?" Lewellan continued.

"I suppose they do, though I have not been briefed on the numbers. *Thunderburst* was not designed to use nonfamiliar material and equipment. It is a self-contained operation. Given the circumstances, I believe the Chiefs are to be commended on their planning and the efficiency of this particular operation."

Birchfield looked surprised at the Secretary's compliment.

Lewellan persisted. "Mr. President, I would urge you to move those troops out by whatever means they have at their disposal—by Turkish transport, by choppers when they are available, by foot if necessary. Get them spread out and moving toward the borders. We can't afford to waste time."

Thompson interjected. "Mr. President, I believe Senator Lewellan is not fully conversant with your overall strategy and your three-prong approach to this problem. To move those troops so precipitately would be bad tactics and, worse, it would escalate the military prong of your approach. We still have Secretary Engledow in Moscow. Eventually, Chenkov will have to see him. You've already made your announcement of a Vice-President, and, quite frankly," Thompson smiled toward the Vice-President designee, "I think you probably scare the hell out of them."

Lewellan did not smile. "Mr. President, I know something about tactics. I spent three years in Vietnam combat and witnessed how these same damn political plans and considerations cost the lives of my friends and thousands of other soldiers. Damnit, Mr. President, we can't fight another war like we did in Nam." The senator crashed his fist down on the table.

President Staton, who had been absorbing the main points of the debate, appeared startled by Lewellan's outburst. "Well, Jake, I think you made your point in spades."

Thompson shot a quick look at the President at the mention of spades.

The President turned toward his left. "Admiral Birchfield, how do the Chiefs feel about all this?"

Birchfield straightened his dark blue tunic. "Mr. President, I believe that they would support Senator Lewellan's position. It is no secret to you or the rest of the people in this room that the more we can use our military knowledge without being hampered by political interference, the greater our chances of success. I see the senator's point. I would hate for our troops to get caught by surprise by the Russians. I think the sooner we move them out, the better for them."

Lewellan spoke again without gaining the President's attention. "Good, Admiral, I agree. But at this point let me add something else. The Russian leadership is obviously in a high-level meeting and incommunicado. That can mean only one thing. They don't want to talk to us. Mr. President, they still haven't gotten your message. We should put all our European forces on alert. Our troops stationed at our bases in Germany should be sent to the eastern border. If the Communists come after us, they'll do it with all their claws showing. They may have withdrawn their troops from Eastern Europe, but they still have nearly two million men within a day's transport to central Europe."

Thompson was incredulous. "I don't believe what I'm hearing. Communists! Hell, we're talking about Russia. My god, Senator, you're asking us to prepare for a full-scale war with the second most powerful nation on this planet. Do you have any idea what the consequences are of that action? If all-out war breaks out, the Russians outnumber us ten or twenty to one near Armenia. We'll be fighting in their backyard, not ours. Our NATO allies have indicated their lack of support for military action. This isn't Panama or Granada or some two-bit banana republic we're talking about. We're talking about one of the two most powerful nations in the world. We are not prepared for a conventional war with them."

Lewellan remained adamant. "And, Mr. Secretary, whose fault is that? Who has been trimming our forces for the past two and one-half years? I agree with you that we'll be at a disadvantage, but I also agree with the Council's first assumption, that the Russians will buckle before they'll commit. I am just suggesting prudent action. The more force we can demonstrate initially, the more likely they are to capitulate."

"Capitulate? What the hell are you talking about, Lewellan? Capitulate? That suggests we're already at war. They haven't done anything illegal, yet. So far, all of their actions have been defensive." For the first time in his two years as a member of the National Security Council, Nelson Thompson was losing his temper.

The President tapped his pen on the conference table as a gavel. "Gentlemen, bickering like this is going to get us nowhere. I've been listening to this discourse with great interest. I could put several suggested courses of action to a vote, but as you all know in the final analysis the decision has to be mine. I am persuaded that it is absolutely essential that the Russians believe that we have every intention of defending the territorial integrity of Turkey and Iran. What we have done so far appears not to have been sufficient. Therefore, I am going to follow Senator Lewellan's advice." He turned toward Birchfield. "Admiral, consider this a direct order. I want our troops to begin immediately to find defensive positions along the Armenian border. They are to use any means at their disposal for transport. I will deal with the Turkish leadership later if they complain about our use of their citizens' property."

He turned back toward the Secretary of Defense whose face was slowly turning red. "Nelson, I want you to issue orders to all our installations here and abroad to be on alert. I want our NATO forces to take up positions on the Polish border immediately."

Thompson could not restrain himself. "Crawford, are you out of your mind?"

The President's eyes narrowed. "Mr. Secretary, please get hold of yourself."

"No, Crawford, you get hold of yourself. What in the hell are you doing? You're going to push Chenkov right into the lap of the militants in the MOD. You'll be throwing the gauntlet in their face. You're giving them no room to maneuver."

"Mr. Secretary, I have given you a direct order. I expect you to carry it out."

Everyone around the table was silent. The tension between the Defense Secretary and the President was so intense, several became conscious of their own breathing.

"No, Mr. President, I will not issue that order. You are asking me to initiate a chain of events that can only have one outcome, war. And since we can't possibly win a conventional war with Russia, you will have to resort either to nuclear missiles, surrender, or withdrawal."

The President's red face betrayed his anger. He rose from his chair and glared down at his Defense Secretary, seated to his left. "Mr. Secretary, I am not asking you to do anything. I have given you a direct order."

Thompson responded by rising to attention. He was only two inches shorter than the President. "I repeat, Mr. President, I will not issue such an order."

"Then you are dismissed, Mr. Secretary. I am removing you from your position."

The President started to turn to his right when Thompson grabbed his arm and turned him back around. "No, you aren't, Staton. You don't have the authority. By rights you should not even be President."

The Attorney General covered his eyes with his hand. "Oh, no!" he muttered to himself.

The President jerked his arm back from the Secretary's hold. "Have you lost your mind, Thompson?"

"No, but I think there is reason to believe you have. Why haven't you shared with this Council or your Cabinet the problem with the Succession Act?"

The President looked stunned. "What do you mean?"

"You know exactly what I mean. Congressmen Schumacher and O'Bannon were in to see you earlier this morning. They told you that the law will require you to relinquish the Presidency as soon as a new Speaker or Pro Tem is elected. And if you think they'll ever approve that maniac," he pointed toward Lewellan, "you're crazier than even I think you are."

"What are you talking about, Secretary Thompson?" It was Dr. Tollefson, the National Security Advisor.

"It seems that Mr. Staton acted a bit hastily in taking the oath of office. According to experts on the Succession Act, it was the intent of the 1947 law that the Presidency would always devolve to an elected official, not an appointed office. Mr. Staton jumped the gun in taking the oath of office."

The Secretary of the Treasury turned toward the Attorney General. "Jacob, aren't you the one who advised Crawford to take the oath?"

The Attorney General was slow in responding. "Yes, I did, as did the Chief Justice. But I must add that we made that recommendation without adequate research in the midst of a crisis. I think the Congress might have a point. If you read the history of the act, there is little question of what Congress intended when they wrote the law."

Staton appeared dumbstruck. He collapsed in his chair. "But, Jacob, I depended upon you for advice."

The Attorney General leaned forward and threw his arms on the table. "Crawford, I'm sorry. At the time, I was honestly giving you my best advice. I must admit I was influenced by the need to put someone in charge of the government. We might have faced anarchy unless you had stepped forward."

Thompson sat down, his anger spent. "Crawford, I am sorry, but you can't follow through on those orders."

Staton stared over at Thompson, his body drained, his eyes unfocused.

From the end of the table, Birchfield exploded. "Well, what the hell difference does it make. Until Congress acts, we still have a commander-in-chief in Mr. Staton. I don't believe even the Attorney General would dispute that point."

The Attorney General nodded slowly.

"Then, until the courts can settle who by right should be President, I say Crawford Staton is President of the United States, and he has every right and responsibility to act as commander-in-chief. And I might add, Mr. Thompson, I consider your actions as nothing short of treason."

"Why, you old bloodthirsty bastard. You can't wait to get into a war, can you?" Thompson's voice was evenly modulated. "You don't want to wait and find out what the Russian Cabinet is doing? You don't want to wait on Engledow because it might ruin your little war, your chance for glory? How pitiful, Ogden, how pitiful."

An explosion of voices erupted around the table as everyone tried to speak. The President rose slowly from his seat, but everyone else stayed seated. "Gentlemen, I need time to think. This meeting is adjourned. I'll let you know when we'll reconvene."

Slowly the President, his shoulders hunched, shuffled from the room, followed by the faithful Lowenstein, who carefully directed a hateful stare in the direction of the Defense Secretary. Everyone around the table sat silent for several moments. Finally, Birchfield stood up.

"As far as I am concerned, the President of the United States has issued a direct order to me, and I intend to carry it out. I will notify our commander in Turkey immediately to move out."

"You do that, Ogden, and I'll relieve you of command and have you placed under arrest." Thompson also felt drained of energy, but Birchfield's defiance rekindled his resolve.

"You can't do that, Thompson. We all just heard the President relieve you of office. You have no authority."

The Attorney General interrupted. "I believe, Admiral, that just about everyone in this room will admit that the President lost his temper, that he spoke in haste. The President said he needed time to think, and I believe we owe him that. Until a written letter of dismissal signed by the President is delivered to Secretary Thompson, he is still legally able to discharge the duties of his office."

"But we heard the President. We all did. He fired Thompson."

The Attorney General again responded. "We heard a tired and troubled man admit he wanted time to think over what was said in this Council. Ogden, the man is under tremendous pressure. He needs support. As his oldest friend, surely you can see that."

Birchfield grabbed his gold braided cap and jammed it under his arm. He glared down the table at Thompson. "I am returning to my office. I will wait for the President's call." He turned and marched out the door.

Senator Lewellan sat slumped in his chair. "I for one believe deeply that the advice I have given the President is sound. I just can't believe the government is in such a shambles. What is to become of us?"

Thompson looked across the table at the Vice-Presidential

designee. A smile creased his lips. "Cheer up, Jake. It ain't over until the fat lady sings."

Lewellan looked puzzled. He failed to see the humor in the remark.

Chapter 22

Mattox sat in a chair at the end of the long conference table in the command center. The remnants of a tuna salad sandwich and a half cup of lukewarm coffee rested to his side. Maggy had ordered a chef's salad and was finishing the last few shreds of lettuce as the special agent moved around pieces of paper on the table in front of him.

"What are you doing, Bert?"

"It's all a big puzzle, Maggy, nothing more. All we need are a few more pieces, and the entire picture will materialize."

Both looked up as Agent Carl Peters entered the room carrying a computer printout at least three inches thick.

"Here's what you wanted, Agent Mattox—all the names of Chamberlain's employees in all his companies dating back five years. We also have the names of all members of the four clubs to which Chamberlain belonged in the Washington area." He laid the red binder on the table, being careful not to disturb the Mattox's puzzle.

"Good work, Carl. Do we have Stewart's military history from Secretary Thompson?"

"Yes, sir, it arrived about fifteen minutes ago by courier. Mary Alice has it."

"I want you to take all three lists to the computer and use the high speed scanner to input all the data. Then I want it all cross-checked by name. We're looking for common denominators. I want you to add the names of everyone in the government from the President down to office, bureau, and agency heads. Include every member of Congress. Our computers should already have that information. I want them cross-referenced against the other lists."

Peters was writing his instructions in his notebook. "This will take at least an hour."

"Then you had better get moving, Carl."

"Yes, sir. "I'll be back as soon as we have the results." Peters picked up the large volume and left.

Maggy stood and carried her plastic bowl over to the wastebasket. She came back to gather Mattox's lunch remnants. "What pieces are you missing, Bert, if I might ask?"

Mattox tilted his head and smiled faintly. "I'm looking for more linkage. I am assuming whoever killed Chamberlain knew him. I'm assuming that whoever is involved in this conspiracy was motivated to take over the government. That means we're dealing with powerful people, very powerful. I need to narrow the list of those who had a link with Chamberlain, who might also be in a position in government to influence the succession process."

"You told Peters to include everyone from the President down. Surely, you don't suspect President Staton?"

"I can't afford to dismiss him. But I pray to God he's not involved. A revelation of that kind would be devastating to the nation."

"I like him." Maggy had cleaned the table where Mattox had spilled his coffee and crumbs. "But, on the other hand, I like you, so what kind of judge am I?" She smiled broadly as she resumed her chair to his left.

Mattox leaned back in his chair and cracked his knuckles, causing Maggy to wince. "I'd say, Miss Mosele, that you have good instincts." A twitch of pain near the back of his head caused

him to reach for his bandage. "Almost as good as your right arm."
He gritted his teeth in mock pain as Maggy kicked his ankle under
the table.

*****

President Staton glared at the man sitting across from him in
the Oval Office. He had expected this confrontation. In some
ways he welcomed it. Tension had ceased to be alien to him. The
past forty-eight hours had provided him nothing but one crisis
after another, one move followed by a countermove. In the end, he
felt like a man sinking in quicksand. The harder he tried to
extricate himself, the deeper he sank. He did not know how much
longer he could keep fighting.

"Just what the hell was that scene all about in the Cabinet
Room, Mr. President?" The words Mr. President were spit out with
a clear flavor of scorn wrapped around each syllable.

"You heard Thompson. What was I supposed to do? Tell him he
was full of shit, that the Congress was full of shit. Hell, even the
Attorney General was backpedaling."

"Cut the excuses, Mr. President. You and I both knew that this
kind of challenge might be made. We discussed it two days ago.
You are the President of the United States. You took the oath of
office as President. Accept that the Attorney General screwed up.
That wasn't your fault. Actually, we anticipated his reaction."

Staton's eyes narrowed. "What do you mean you anticipated
what he would do? Are you saying you knew the President, the
Vice-President, the Speaker of the House, and the President Pro
Tem of the Senate were all going to be killed? Are you saying
that?"

The man in the chair across from the President stood. "That is
irrelevant. We know who killed the President and the others, and
he's dead. The man who hired him is dead. They're all dead. The
man who paid the assassin is dead. Perhaps we had some
advanced knowledge of the planning, but that is not to say we
approved or that we participated. There is no question that Seth
Hansen's policies were taking this nation to ruin. The recession

shows no signs of improvement. Our allies think that we're increasingly becoming a toothless lion, incapable of retaliating against our enemies."

The man stepped back two or three steps. "This Russian blunder could not have come at a more propitious time. We have within our grasp the opportunity to reestablish America's reputation as the premier military power in the world. We have the opportunity to rekindle our decaying economy by giving a rebirth to the defense industries. Face it, within six months you're going to be a national hero. Your popularity is going to be so high that Congress will not dare challenge your right to this office. And they'll accept your recommendation for Vice-President, even if they don't like it. They won't have any choice."

Staton continued to stare as he digested every word.

"One thing we have learned during the past three decades is that when a President is popular, the Congress buckles to his will. They have no guts. All those prissy bastards will know that in their own states and in their own congressional districts, you— Crawford Staton—are far more popular than they. They won't challenge you because it will cost them votes and possibly their precious little jobs, with their $150,000 annual salaries, their plush offices, free junkets around the world, their free mailing, and their fat pensions. You faced down two of the more powerful leaders this morning. If O'Bannon and Schumacher don't challenge you, none of the rest will."

Staton, weary of being talked down to, stood and faced his guest eye to eye. "Aren't you forgetting one very important item?"

"What could that be?"

"What happens if you miscalculate on Chenkov and the Russians? What if they don't back down? What if they force me into a corner, crush our army in Turkey and Iran, and leave me no alternative but to launch a nuclear attack? I assume you would recommend such a course of action as opposed to capitulation."

The man suddenly felt uncomfortable with the large President's presence. He turned away toward the fireplace. "Of course, we would never capitulate. They know that. That's why they won't force you into that corner. You still haven't learned, have you, even after all these years and all those miles of travel and talk with the Russians and the Chinese? They will never risk nuclear war with the United States because they know they can't win. That's the bottom line—winning. All generals think alike, Crawford. As MacArthur put it so aptly, there's no substitute for victory. If you can't win, you find a way to avoid losing."

Staton shook his head. "I wish sometimes that I had your self-confidence, but, in reflection, I guess you always had that, didn't you?"

"Call it what you will, Crawford, but the fact remains we hold the trump cards. Now get off your ass and reconvene the NSC. I still can't believe you let that son-of-a-bitch Thompson browbeat you. You looked like a whipped puppy in there."

Staton tossed his head back in seeming defiance. "And what if I don't? What if I call a press conference and resign? Where will you be then? Do you think you could control the Secretary of the Treasury?"

"Quit sounding like a spoiled baby. We both know you won't do that. I assume that exposure of your relationship with Lieutenant Thomas Bradley would still not be well-received by Gwen, or Natalie for that matter. And I imagine the rest of the nation's current popular flirtation with you would dry up like a sun-starved grape if they found out. In short, your career, your reputation, would be in the ash can."

The name Bradley sent spears of shock and fear through Staton's veins—his most secret demon let loose, overshadowing the good accomplished in forty years of public service, leaving his reputation, his family, his place in history all piled together on a junk heap of ridicule and condemnation. "You and I both know that was forty years ago. It lasted less than a week. We were young, on a seven-day pass in Tokyo. Hell, we were drunk the entire time. It's when we finally sobered up, we realized how foolish it all had been. I thought no one else knew about it. I can't believe after all these years, my best friend would be so cruel to use one simple mistake like that as a means of extortion. I can't believe it. Have you no conscience, Ogden?"

The Admiral resumed his seat. "Yes, Crawford, I have a conscience, and I have a duty. I swore an oath to defend this nation. That oath is far more important than what happens to people like you and me. The United States has been retreating too long. It's time to put an end to all this liberal pie-in-the-sky foolishness. As long as we are the most powerful nation on the earth, there will always be those who will want to topple us or kick us in the shin like those pissants Hussein in Iraq or Gadhafi in Lybia." Birchfield stopped. He felt more secure now, more in control. "Anyway, Crawford, I thought we covered all this two nights ago on the chopper from Andrews."

Staton walked over to his desk and slumped into his swivel chair. "And you think men like Jake Lewellan sitting here at the seat of power will preserve your precious American way and achieve your Pax Americana throughout the world."

Birchfield rose and walked over to the front of the desk. "Lewellan has the courage of a patriot. He has not been tainted by the embassy row crowd or thirty years of deal making in the Congress. If he is called upon, I feel certain he could sit here in this office and make this nation proud of him."

Staton shook his head. "God, I wish I was stronger. America deserves better than me at this terribly important time in its history. I'm nothing more than a puppet being manipulated by the industrial military complex that runs this nation."

Birchfield glanced at his watch. "We're wasting time, Mr. President. Are you going to reconvene the NSC or not?"

Staton looked up at his longtime friend, then turned away, his chin falling to his chest. He reached for his phone console and pushed a button. "Dr. Tollefson, please notify the members of the NSC that we will reconvene at 4:00 this afternoon in the Cabinet Room."

Birchfield again looked at his watch. "That gives you nearly three hours to pull yourself together. I want you to prepare Thompson's letter of dismissal and present it to him at that meeting. Be prepared, Mr. President, to accept Senator Lewellan's suggestions at the meeting. And for god's sake, don't ever cave in like that again." Birchfield straightened his tunic. "It's so out of character for you." He turned and walked out the door.

Staton picked up the gold letter opener on his desk and began tapping the desktop. He turned and gazed out the windows at the Rose Garden behind the White House. His depression ran deep, but so did his pride. Perhaps Birchfield was right about the Russians. If so, he could roll along and, in the end, perhaps fill out the next few months and be remembered as a strong chief executive. For the first time, he could understand why Gwen had turned to drink. He picked up the phone. "This is the President. Would you have the chief porter step into my office, please. I'm thirsty."

Chapter 23

The Pentagon
2:00 P.M

Secretary Thompson rested the receiver to the telephone on his shoulder, nudged against his ear. He had asked his secretary to get the Attorney General for him. As he waited for his Cabinet colleague to come on line, he ran his pen down the two or three sheets of notes he had sitting in front of him.

"Thank you, Jacob, for taking my call."

"Don't be ridiculous, Nelson. What can I do for you?"

"Jacob, I may not have much time left in this job. If Crawford gets his second wind, I may be fired prior to our 4:00 meeting this afternoon. By the way, did you get your notice from Tollefson?"

"Yes, just a few minutes ago. The President must be close to making up his mind."

"Obviously, that worries the hell out of me. Do you think I was out of line this morning?"

There was no hesitation. "No, Nels, I don't. I must admit you had more guts than I think I would have had. But I can't believe there wasn't a person in that room who didn't generally agree with you, excepting Birchfield and Lewellan, of course."

"Jacob, that's why I'm calling. I met with your Bert Mattox this morning. Are you aware of John Chamberlain's involvement in the conspiracy to kill the President?"

"I know that Mattox and the director believe that Chamberlain is the key to the investigation. I haven't heard from either of them in several hours. Did you learn anything new?"

"Enough to make me believe the conspiracy goes beyond Chamberlain. The only reason that all four of those in line of succession were killed was so whoever was behind the conspiracy could change the direction of policy in this country. In short, they would have to believe they could control the government."

There was silence on the line for several seconds. "Don't you mean, Nels, so they could control the Presidency?"

"I suppose so, Jacob. That's a terrible thought, but I can't escape it."

"Surely, you don't believe Crawford Staton was involved in a conspiracy to kill Seth Hansen and the others? Even with his unusual behavior the last couple of days, I can't bring myself to believe he was involved in any way."

"You may be right, Jacob. I hope you are. However, we can't escape the President's behavior pattern. He picks that maniac, Lewellan, as his Vice-President. Crawford has always had the ability to see the big picture. He's never been a man to favor short-term solutions to long-range problems. All his reactions to this Armenian mess are out of sync with his normal behavior."

"I agree with your conclusion, but assuming, for sake of argument, that he is involved, why would he draw suspicion to himself by making such a selection?"

"I don't have that answer, unless. . ." there was a long pause, "unless he is being blackmailed."

"Blackmailed? By whom?"

"I haven't figured that out, yet. Do you have any suggestions?"

Again, there was a long pause. "Nelson, let's take this in steps. First, Crawford had to undergo an exhaustive security check by the NSC and the FBI prior to his confirmation as Secretary of State. We both know what those checks involve. They reviewed his finances and his personal life since he's been in Congress. They checked on the stability of his marriage and the possibility of any family problems that could compromise him. Except for his wife's drinking problem, which we all have known about, he was as clean as porcelain. With his wife's inheritance and his own, the man is worth nearly two million dollars. All his investments are in treasury notes. He's never invested in the market, so there's no chance of insider trading problems."

"Jacob, what you're saying is that there is nothing outside of Gwen's drinking that makes him vulnerable, is that right?"

"Nelson, I said there is nothing during his public life. That goes back thirty years?"

"Are you suggesting there might have been something before that?"

"Nelson, let me ask you something." There was a long moment of silence. "Who is recognized as Crawford's oldest friend in this town?"

"I suppose it would be Birchfield. Weren't they in the Navy together back in the fifties?"

"That's right. Now let me ask you, have you noticed anything different in the way the two men have been acting toward each other the past two days?"

Thompson stopped to reflect. "No. I don't know what you mean?"

"Nelson, what has Crawford always called Birchfield, either in private or in our meetings?"

"I guess it's always been Oggy."

"That's right. He has always referred and deferred to him as Oggy. Now have you noticed that he hasn't used the name Oggy once during the past two days. It has always been by his title."

Thompson reflected back to their meetings together. "I suppose you may be right. I hadn't stopped to think about it. Everyone uses titles around this place so much, I guess I'm programmed for them."

"Well, think about it. I haven't seen any of the chummy comradery that used to go on between those two. No laughs, no jokes, no getting into the corner and sharing a story. I realize these have been serious times these last two days, but still, from my vantage point there has been a 180 degree turnaround in their behavior toward each other. You saw Birchfield in the NSC meeting when he exploded. He displayed no sense of empathy or sympathy for Crawford. Does that mesh with a man who is supposed to be the President's best friend?"

Thompson absorbed the observation fully. "If you're right, Jacob, how do we prove it?"

"I really don't have any idea. I haven't discussed this with Mattox, yet, but I feel I must before long. He's coming over here in about an hour for a briefing.

"Jacob, I have an idea. Are you familiar with Mattox's Deadwood theory?"

"What kind of theory?"

"Deadwood. Manchester had an ace of spades in his wallet. Chamberlain had an eight of clubs in his wallet. Mattox found a scribbled note on Chamberlain's desk with the word Deadwood printed on it."

"I still don't see the connection."

"Do you play poker, Jacob?"

"Haven't since I was in the army some thirty-five years ago, but I wasn't very good, even then."

The Secretary of Defense explained the story of Wild Bill Hickok and Mattox's theory.

The Attorney General paused after Thompson finished. "Sounds far-fetched to me, Nels, but I do know Birchfield is a hell of a poker player."

"How do you know that?"

"George Heffelfinger told me. They both belong to the Chevy Chase Country Club, and apparently George got goaded into sitting in on a standing poker game that's played there on Thursday nights. George said Birchfield plays every week, and that about two months ago the admiral took our esteemed CIA director for about fifty dollars. Can you imagine a man as wealthy as Heffelfinger complaining about losing fifty dollars?"

"That's very interesting, Jacob. Birchfield and Heffelfinger?"

"What are you going to do, Nelson?"

The Defense Secretary was drawing interconnecting boxes on his pad as he talked and thought. "Jacob, I think I'm going to try to make peace with the Admiral. Talk to you later."

Thompson did not wait for the Attorney General to say goodbye before he cut him off by hitting another button on his telephone console. "Anne, get me Admiral Birchfield."

*****

The thick, bellowing steam made vision beyond one or two feet impossible. Admiral Ogden Birchfield stretched his arms out in front of him as he walked slowly across the tile floor of the steam room located off the gymnasium in the Pentagon.

"I'm over here, Ogden, to your left." The Secretary of Defense reached out with his hand to grasp the admiral's outstretched arm. "Come on over and sit. After all we've been through the last few days, we're entitled to relax for a change."

Birchfield found a seat on the second tier of the white-tiled benches. Both he and the Secretary were wrapped in oversized white cotton towels.

"Quite frankly, Mr. Secretary, I was surprised to get your call. I thought after this morning, we had little to say to each other."

"I admit that I lost my temper. I don't like doing that. In fact, I can't remember blowing up like that since I was a kid back in Kalamazoo. I want to apologize. I said some things I wish I hadn't said."

The admiral grunted. "Apology accepted, Mr. Secretary. However, I think we're still miles apart on *Thunderburst* and our response to the Russians."

"I admit that I've never been enthusiastic about *Thunderburst*, Ogden, but I've been having second thoughts about your overall strategy toward the Russians. The fact they haven't yet moved into Turkey suggests they aren't willing to take the chance, just as you predicted."

Thompson could not see the admiral's face clearly enough to tell whether he believed him.

"Might I ask, Mr. Secretary, what prompted this change of heart?"

Thompson detected a tone of suspicion in the question. "Certainly. I tried placing myself in Chenkov's shoes. What would

I do? Would I be able to separate national pride from reality. In the end, I came to the conclusion that, faced with impossible alternatives, I would choose reality.'"

"Well, Mr. Secretary, like the good parson said, 'We're always happy to welcome converts to the rail."

Both men noticed the light from outside the room grow brighter as someone opened the door. The voice of the military attendant cut through the mist. "Secretary Thompson, your secretary says she has an important message for you."

Thompson feigned disgust. "Damnit, just as I was beginning to unwind. You hold on, Ogden, I'll find out what she wants and be right back." Thompson stepped on the lower tier, then onto the floor as he found his way toward the light.

After closing the door, the corporal on duty pointed to his left. "The phone is over here, sir."

"Tell my secretary I'll call her right back. She'll understand." Thompson knew that Anne was following the instructions he had given her prior to his leaving the office for the gym.

The corporal hesitated, momentarily confused, then braced himself. "Yes, sir." He turned and walked toward the wall phone.

Thompson turned and wound his way through ranks of tall, blue lockers to find a row bolted to the side wall of the dressing room. At mid-afternoon, the locker room was vacant. Thompson had arrived early enough to get the attendant to open Birchfield's locker combination on the pretext that he was leaving a friendly surprise for the admiral. The attendant had made no attempt to argue with the Secretary of Defense. After he had left, Thompson took a small piece of tablet paper and folded it several times and placed it inside the locker door at the bottom, which would effectively prevent the door from locking by blocking the vertical rod from falling through to the floor of the locker.

Now, he quietly lifted the latch to the locker and opened the door. Hanging inside was the admiral's dark blue tunic and trousers on hooks. He felt the pockets of the jacket. Nothing in the left. A set of keys in the right. He then lifted the trousers out. He felt for the billfold in the hip pocket and pulled it out, then began shuffling through the pictures, credit cards, and identification the admiral carried. No playing card. He tried again, this time more slowly, but still no eight or ace. "Damn!" he whispered. He continued searching through the pants. He found the admiral's money clip with about $200 in large denominations, but no playing card. He again searched each pocket of the coat. Nothing.

Thompson stood on his tiptoes to see the shelf at the top of the locker. Only the admiral's dark blue shaving kit rested on the shelf. He could not see the back of the shelf because of the height, so he reached up with his hand, around the kit. He felt every square inch of the metal shelf, but, again, nothing. The sound of the attendant slamming another locker in the far corner of the tiled locker room startled Thompson, and he jerked his hand back, in the process knocking the admiral's kit onto the floor and spilling its contents. Thompson leaned over to retrieve the shaving cream, toothbrush, toothpaste, and razor, when he spied a small package from the corner of his eye. He reached over and picked up an opened carton of Bicycle playing cards. They must have fallen out of the kit.

He sat down straddling one of the wood benches between the rows of lockers, placing the admiral's kit next to him. He opened the package of cards and began sorting through the deck. He made four piles, one for each suit. Just as he finished the last card, a warm damp hand grasped his shoulder. He nearly jumped as he turned around to see a red-faced Admiral Ogden Birchfield staring at the bench in front of him.

"What's all this about, Thompson? Besides being a liar and a traitor, should we add theft to your list of crimes?" He reached over Thompson, attempting to grab the cards, but Thompson stood quickly, blocking him.

"Listen, Birchfield, I don't apologize for anything. Not for duping you into coming down here. Not for my comments in the meeting today. Not for rifling your locker. I just made a quick check. There are four cards missing from your deck. Coincidentally, they happen to be the ace of clubs, the ace of spades, the eight of clubs, and the eight of spades."

"So what, Thompson? That doesn't prove anything except I have a bad deck."

"I don't think so, Admiral. It so happens the FBI has in its possession the ace of clubs taken from William Manchester's wallet. They also have the eight of clubs taken from Chamberlain's wall safe. It should be no problem for the bureau to make a check of this deck against those two cards in their possession. If there is no match, then I'd say you have no problem, and I will apologize for this illegal entry into your locker, but," Thompson took a step toward Birchfield who was about ten years older and two inches shorter than himself, "if they are a match, and you were involved in the conspiracy to kill Seth Hansen, I'll not only expose you, I'll rip your heart out with my bare hands."

The Secretary of Defense reached down and grabbed all the cards and replaced them in the deck. He then pushed the Chairman of the Joint Chiefs of Staff out of his way and spirited past him toward the other side of the room.

"You won't get away with this, Thompson. You're through. The President fired you. You'll have your precious letter of dismissal in less than an hour. You're through, Thompson. Do you hear me?"

Thompson's anger continued to boil as Birchfield's shouts faded into the back of his consciousness. As he dressed, the beaming smile of Seth Hansen ran through his mind. How young, how promising, how unfair. Killed by a cabal of power-seeking, self-righteous lunatics. How will Staton react? Will he try to protect his old friend and possible blackmailer? He would face that dilemma before the day was out. First of all, he had to get the deck of cards to the Attorney General.

Chapter 24

The Attorney General welcomed his guests to his spacious office, although he appeared surprised to see Margaret Mosele accompanying Mattox. Director Jameson, Carl Peters, Bert, and Maggy each took a comfortable chair in a corner of the panelled room. The AG sat at one end of a long sofa. He had just finished talking to Secretary Thompson, who had detailed his recent encounter with Admiral Birchfield.

"Well, Bert, you've made tremendous progress. I understand there is no doubt in your mind about the involvement of John Chamberlain in this conspiracy."

Mattox was relaxed. He liked the Attorney General, and he trusted him. In fact, the four people seated around the cherry coffee table were about the only people he completely trusted in the city. "Sir, there is no doubt. In addition to what we knew earlier, we can add the following.

"First, we have a copy of a cancelled check for $7,500 from one of Chamberlain's subsidiaries made out to William Manchester and dated January 5, which is approximately the time Manchester booked two first-class tickets to North Africa for himself and Lampworth."

"Secondly, a preliminary review of Chamberlain's corporate annual reports for the past two years shows a decline of over 35 percent in defense contracts and an overall decline of 70 percent in profits from three years ago for all JFC Industries. We have no reason to believe that Chamberlain was insolvent, but there's little doubt his companies' incomes have suffered greatly in recent years."

"We also heard from our New York office that Mrs. Chamberlain claimed her husband complained about every White House dinner they attended together. She made reference to her husband's assertion that Hansen was biting the hand that feeds him."

Mattox looked up from his legal pad. "One final piece of evidence we'd like to have is a direct link between the money paid to Abdul and Chamberlain's accounts. Tom Ashburn at the CIA is running that down for us."

The Attorney General leaned forward. "Are you suggesting that the conspiracy ends with Chamberlain?"

Mattox tossed his pad onto the table. "No, sir. I feel confident it goes much deeper."

The Attorney General locked onto the Special Agent's eyes. "Deeper? Are you suggesting someone in the government was involved?"

"Yes, sir. I feel there are at least two other conspirators. Their only motivation could have been to take over the government, at least to change President Hansen's policies."

"But why kill the Vice-President, Speaker, and Senator Howard?"

Mattox crossed his legs. "Obviously, the Vice-President was committed to Hansen's policies. The Speaker had championed the same policies in the House and had worked to pass many of the

President's most controversial bills. Senator Howard was an old New Dealer. This cabal was made up of right wingers, at least if Chamberlain is any indication of their thinking.

"Do you have any more evidence or speculation, Bert?"

Mattox nodded toward Peters, who reached into his briefcase and pulled out several sheets of computer paper and handed them to Mattox. "We ran a cross-reference on all present government officers above the rank of agency or bureau heads and members of Congress against a list of Chamberlain's employees for the past five years. We also cross checked the same lists against the membership rosters of clubs in the Washington area to which he belonged. Finally, we reviewed John Stewart's military record."

The AG interrupted. "I thought Stewart worked for Chamberlain."

"That's correct, sir. But a year ago he worked in the office of Secretary Thompson in the Pentagon. And before that he held several command positions dating back to 1982."

"Makes sense. Keep going." The Attorney General glanced at Director Jameson, who nodded, indicating he was very satisfied with Mattox's work.

Mattox continued. "There are nearly 600 people who hold policy-making positions in the government from the agency level upward and 535 members of Congress. We checked those names against Chamberlain's employee roster. Chamberlain owned thirteen separate companies. Two of them were very large—Fortune 500, but several were much smaller. We have the names of at least twelve people now in government who worked for him at one time or another." He handed the list to the Attorney General.

"Secondly, we checked Chamberlain's social friends—members of his clubs—against the list. He belonged to Chevy Chase Country Club, the Cosmos Club, the Capitol Hill Club, and Burning Tree Country Club. We found four names from the list you have, sir, who were members of one or more of those clubs. In addition, we found one hundred and twenty-seven names of administrative appointees and members of Congress who belong to those clubs, who did not work for Chamberlain." He handed a second list to the Attorney General.

"Then we checked the fifty or so names in Chamberlain's private telephone directory which he kept at home. We found twenty-five of those names on the membership rosters of the clubs and five names which were on the government lists." He handed another page to the AG. "We then checked Stewart's record against all lists. We found him associated with Senator Lewellan, with Secretary Thompson, and with Admiral Birchfield."

The Attorney General looked surprised. "Admiral Birchfield? What was the connection?"

Mattox handed the AG another sheet of paper. "You'll note that in 1988 through 1990, when Admiral Birchfield was commander of the Pacific fleet, CINCPAC, Major Stewart was assigned to his headquarters staff at Pearl Harbor. Technically, his assignment was deputy to the vice commander of CINCPAC, but we checked, and there was no vice commander during the time Stewart served at Pearl. That means he served Birchfield. This was before Birchfield moved up to Chief of Naval Operations, his present assignment."

Mattox noted the Attorney General did not appear surprised. "Also, sir, we found that Admiral Birchfield belonged to the Chevy Chase Country Club and that his wife contributed $1,000 last year to Lewellan's campaign."

The Attorney General surveyed the group with his eyes, then turned back toward Mattox. "So you have narrowed your list to Admiral Birchfield and Senator Lewellan. Is that it?"

Mattox leaned back in his chair. "No, sir, I am afraid not. There are three other major contributors to Lewellan's campaign and social acquaintances of Chamberlain."

The Attorney General did not like guessing games, and his irritation showed on his face. "Who?"

"President Staton for one. He belonged to Burning Tree and gave Lewellan $500 last year. Also, we discovered that in 1992, Mr. Staton's last full year in the Senate, he and Mrs. Staton were

Chamberlain's guests for one week at Chamberlain's home in Key West, Florida. Chamberlain was not there, but Staton claimed the vacation on his financial report to the Senate. The value of the vacation was placed at $3,000, including a free flight to and from Key West on a jet owned by JFC Industries."

The Attorney General placed the computer printouts on the coffee table. "Bert, this is extremely sensitive. You're naming the President of the United States as a suspect in a conspiracy to assassinate his predecessor."

Mattox did not flinch, but the charge made by the Attorney General frightened Maggy. She reached over and squeezed Mattox's hand. Mattox continued looking directly at the AG. "Sir, I think you worded it quite well—a suspect. I am not charging him."

The AG squirmed in his chair. "Let's move on. You said three people."

"Yes, sir. The second is George Heffelfinger of the CIA. He received financial contributions from Chamberlain, and they both belonged to Chevy Chase Country Club. He knows Senator Lewellan quite well, since Lewellan chairs the committee that oversees his agency."

The AG was not convinced. "I think you're stretching it on that one, Bert. I know for a fact that George thinks Lewellan is a nut. As far as the country club, hell, George is a millionaire. In fact, you might find that his family is worth more than Chamberlain. As for the contributions, Chamberlain contributed to the campaigns of anyone in power in Washington. He hedged all his bets."

Mattox smiled. "Yes, sir, I agree. I might add that the director volunteered to me that Chamberlain contributed to his campaign and that they were old friends. "

"Who's the third one?" The Attorney General leaned back.

"Alan Brownell."

The Attorney General leaned forward slowly. "This is really important, Bert. Brownell may well be in line to become President."

"Yes, sir, I figured that out after talking to Secretary Thompson. Brownell belongs to both Burning Tree and Chevy Chase. Back in the eighties, he received over $95,000 in PAC monies from companies controlled by Chamberlain."

Director Jameson interjected. "Frankly, Jacob, I've already told Bert I don't believe Brownell could be involved."

Mattox turned toward his ailing friend. "Yes, you did, sir, but you didn't tell me why."

"Quite simple really. If Staton is involved, then it is in his best interest to keep the Presidency. Therefore, both Lewellan and Brownell become bothersome. Both represent a threat to him. Now, if Staton isn't involved, and one of the other two is involved, it can't be both. They in effect are rivals for replacing Staton. It might be one or the other, but it can't be both. Because of other linkage that Bert has made with Lewellan, I'm inclined to accept him as the more logical suspect. Besides, I can't believe Brownell would risk being so close to the explosion if he had any idea of how devastating it was going to be."

The AG smiled at the director seated to his right. "Judge, I see you haven't lost your touch."

There was a knock on the door. A secretary entered. "Sir, there are four officers from the Pentagon here in my office who say they have a package for you."

The Attorney General stood. "Yes, have them come in."

The AG's guests seated in the corner of the room were surprised to see four uniformed officers enter the room. Mattox noted two with sidearms were corporals, one a lieutenant colonel, and one a full colonel. The senior officer had a briefcase handcuffed to his right hand.

"Mr. Attorney General, Secretary Thompson has instructed us to deliver this package personally to you. We will need your signature." The colonel took a chair to his left and lifted the case onto his knees. Using a key handed to him by the other officer, he opened the four separate locks to the case. He reached in and pulled out a sheet of paper. "Would you sign this, sir?"

The Attorney General scribbled his name and handed the page back to the colonel, who checked the signature against another document contained in the case. He appeared satisfied. He then pulled out a small cream colored envelope with the seal of the Department of Defense emblazoned on the front. He handed the package to the Attorney General. After politely excusing themselves, the four soldiers left.

The AG returned to his seat, carrying the envelope. "Sorry for the theatrics, but I have something here that may be very important." He then reviewed his earlier conversations with Nelson Thompson, detailing Thompson's speculation and his plan to search Birchfield's locker. When he came to the part about the search, he stopped and tore open the envelope. He reached into his pocket and took out a handkerchief. With the handkerchief he picked up the deck of cards and handed both over to Mattox.

"Check this for prints, Bert. Be sure Birchfield's are on there. I suspect that only Thompson's and the admiral's will be found. According to Nelson, you'll find four cards missing from that deck—two aces and two eights."

Mattox stared at the deck with a combination of glee and confusion. As he looked back at the AG, he saw a frown, which puzzled him. Mattox wrapped the deck in the AG's handkerchief and gave it to Peters, who placed it in his briefcase.

"Sir, I appreciate this evidence. If what Secretary Thompson reports is accurate, we may have moved a long way toward exposing this entire conspiracy."

The AG stood and began pacing. He said nothing. The FBI director signaled the others to sit and wait. After a few moments the Attorney General stopped and looked down at the others. "Gentlemen, Miss Mosele, one part of me hopes that Nelson is right and that we do have Birchfield, but another side is scared to death. The Chairman of the Joint Chiefs of Staff involved in a conspiracy to kill the President of the United States—can you imagine the confusion that such an announcement will bring, not only among the citizens of this country, but among the governments of the world?"

He continued to pace, this time speaking as he walked. "Only Director Jameson, here, is aware of how severe this crisis with Russia is becoming. If we release information about Admiral Birchfield's involvement, it could devastate our efforts to solve this Armenian problem peacefully. It might be just enough to tip the Kremlin leadership toward actions that would force the United States into war."

Mattox, Peters, and Maggy exchanged expressions of confusion. What was the AG suggesting? Mattox finally asked. "Sir, are you telling us that we can't arrest Admiral Birchfield; that if we have proof of his involvement in the murder of the four highest elected officials of the American government, we can't touch the man; that the highest ranking military officer in this country can commit treason and get away with it?" With each question Mattox's voice became stronger as his anger increased, and he found himself rising from his chair. Maggy stared up at Mattox with deep concern in her eyes. She understood what everyone was saying, but the tone and tension were overwhelming.

The AG appeared unaffected by Mattox's outburst. He walked back to his chair and sat down. "No, Bert, I'm not telling you that. What I'm saying is that we must for the good of the nation use discretion for a while. Birchfield's days are numbered. I promise you that. He will not be able to continue in his position, but how he goes and what penalty he pays and how much information is released to the public, those are questions we must ponder."

Mattox was about to explode again when the AG waved his hand, indicating Mattox should sit. "I know what you're going to say. Nobody is above the law. This amounts to a cover-up. As a matter of fact, I agree with you. If I could strangle Ogden Birchfield with my bare hands, I would do it. If I could expose this entire conspiracy to the American people today, I would do it, but, unfortunately, things aren't all that simple. I can't bring Seth back.

I'm not going to murder Birchfield, and if I have to choose between sacrificing public disclosure for a few hours, a few days, a few years, or forever in order to prevent a nuclear war, I will do that. Do you understand me?" He leaned forward as his light blue eyes narrowed and faced Bert Mattox a few feet away.

Mattox turned to the director, who nodded agreement. Both Peters and Maggy appeared bewildered. He took a deep breath. "Well, what the hell are we supposed to do?"

The AG leaned back. "Leave Birchfield to me. Get confirmation on that deck of cards, and I'll handle the admiral. In the meantime, we have at least one more conspirator to find. I think there's one name on your lists that might be our leading contender." He picked up one of the computer printouts and circled a name halfway down the page. He handed the list back to Mattox. "Check this man out." He glanced at his watch, then stood. "In the meantime, I need to get down to the White House. We have an NSC meeting at 4:00." He turned to the director. "Judge, I want you to go with me." Jameson nodded agreement.

The others stood also, ready to take their leave. Mattox clearly was not pleased. He was being asked to contribute to a possible cover-up of the most serious criminal conspiracy in the history of the United States. He understood the Attorney General's logic, but sacrificing principle for practical goals was repugnant to him. It smacked of too much politics. He started to leave without any further word when the AG put his arm around his shoulder.

"Bert, I know you have serious reservations with what I'm doing. All I can ask you to do is trust me and trust that the stakes are so high, higher than you can ever imagine, that to proceed full tilt as if this were an ordinary investigation, might mean the end of civilization." Mattox shot a quizzical look at the Attorney General. "I'm not kidding, Bert. If I'm right about the man I circled on that list, I want you ready to come to the White House this evening. One thing I promise you is that you will be the one to ferret him out and to make the final decision on what course we pursue. Fair enough?"

Mattox stopped at the door as the Attorney General removed his arm and offered his hand. Mattox stared at the hand, then at the AG's eyes. He saw an honest and deeply troubled man, not a self-serving politician. "Fair enough, sir." He shook the AG's hand, then made his exit. Maggy and Peters followed. The AG closed the door behind them and returned to the sofa to face Alec Jameson.

"Well, old friend, let's figure out how we're going to handle this."

Chapter 25

Admiral Birchfield left a meeting of the Joint Chiefs in their conference room to take a call he had been expecting for nearly half an hour.

"This is the ace of clubs. I just got your message."

"First of all, you can forget using our code. The FBI is on to it."

"My god, how?"

"That's not as important as the fact that about an hour ago Secretary Thompson rifled my locker in the gym and found the deck that I used for the four cards at Chamberlain's home last month. By now I'm sure the FBI is checking it against the cards they found on Manchester and in Chamberlain's safe."

There was heavy breathing on the other end of the line. "Then we're finished."

"Not so fast. They may think they have me over a barrel, but right now all they have is circumstantial evidence. They can't move against me with what they have, especially given my position. However, as far as I know, there is nothing to directly link you to our plan."

"Are you sure?"

"Hell, no, I'm not sure, but so far you haven't had to do anything directly, so there can't be any evidence. Use your head." Birchfield's impatience was evident in his tone.

"So what should I do?"

"Right now, do nothing. However, if by chance I am removed, or if anything happens to me, you'll have to be the one to step in."

"What can I do?"

"Keep on Staton. If they get rid of me, he's going to think the heat is off of him."

"But I don't even know what you have on the President. All you ever told the rest of us was that it's personal and that Staton would do anything not to let it out."

"That's right, but the fact is I don't have any hard evidence. So far it's been all bluff, but it's worked. He thinks I have evidence— photographs, I imagine. I've never let on what I have, and he hasn't pressed me."

"So what can I do without evidence?"

"Just use the name Bradley—Thomas Bradley. That will be enough. Indicate that you know everything I know. He'll be too scared to push you."

"But what should I do?"

"Goddamnit! Do what we all planned from the beginning. Keep him in office. Get Lewellan confirmed. We can't afford to let the Presidency slip back into the hands of a bunch of appeasers and self-serving politicians."

There was a long hesitation on the line. "Okay. I can handle it, but only if you are removed. Are you attending the NSC meeting at four?"

"Yes. Hopefully, the President will stick to his guns at least until we have *Thunderburst* fully deployed and Thompson fired. We're right on the threshold of forcing those Russian bastards into breaking. We can't let Staton crumble. Do you understand?"

"Yes, sir. You can depend on me."

"Good. I'll see you at 4:00."

*****

At 3:50 Admiral Birchfield's Chrysler Imperial pulled through the iron gates on Executive Drive. His driver pulled into a parking slot on the east side of the drive, opposite the Executive Office Building. Two cars away, the Attorney General of the United States and Alec Jameson of the Federal Bureau of Investigation waited quietly in the back seat of the director's Lincoln Town Car.

"He's here, Jacob. Are you ready?" The director's right hand was resting on his knee, but the AG could recognize the twitching even though the director consciously tried to control it.

"Are you sure you're up to this, Judge?"

"I'll be fine." The director paused. "You know, Jacob, I don't use profanity as a rule. I have always felt that it was an inadequate form of expression. However, I want to nail that son-of-a-bitch. He's a traitor. He's a murderer. The sight of him just turns my stomach."

The AG watched the face of his friend. There was a stern determination frozen in the aging flesh. It was good to see the director so stirred, even if the driving force was hatred. Preparations had already been made. He had called the Secretary of the Treasury to enlist his help with the Secret Service, which was technically under his supervision. The head of the Service, Don Schroeder, had been instructed to follow the Attorney General's instructions. The AG had asked Schroeder to meet him in the White House several minutes before the convening of the NSC meeting. The Secret Service and the Marine guards were the only people allowed to carry firearms in the White House, and the AG had indicated he might need Schroeder's cooperation in interrogating a member of the NSC who was under suspicion. No other information was given to the man charged with protecting the life of the President.

The nation's two chief law enforcement officers opened their doors and joined Admiral Birchfield as he passed in front of their car on his way to the meeting. They exchanged greetings and continued on to the west door of the White House. Inside, the three made their way down the hall toward the Cabinet Room, but just before turning down the corridor, the Attorney General grasped the admiral's arm.

"Admiral, the Judge and I need a few minutes with you before the meeting."

Birchfield pulled his arm away. "I have nothing to say to you two. We're due for a National Security Council meeting, and I do not intend to be late." He turned to walk the fifteen feet to the Cabinet Room when the door opened, and Secret Service Director Don Schroeder stepped out. He closed the door and crossed his arms in front of him.

The Attorney General stepped forward. "As you can see, Admiral, you're not going to that meeting until after you have talked to us. We can use Ed Collins's old office down this other corridor." The AG pointed in the opposite direction.

Birchfield stared at Schroeder, then back at the Attorney General, then at the director. Finally, he shrugged. "Why not? I have nothing to hide." He walked ahead of the two toward the large office located down the short hall from the Oval Office.

The director closed the door after the three had entered. The admiral placed his hat on the late chief-of-staff's desk, then plumped himself down in one of the deep leather chairs next to the window overlooking the north lawn. "Now, what's so urgent?"

The Attorney General and Director Jameson took chairs across from Birchfield. The two had already decided on their approach, including the use of facts, conjecture, speculation, and, if necessary, bluff. Neither man had experience at poker, but both knew enough about human nature to anticipate the admiral's reactions.

The Attorney General opened. "Admiral Birchfield, I am the only person alive separating you from spending the rest of your natural life in a federal penitentiary." It was a hard opening, but the admiral did not flinch.

"What in the world are you talking about? You don't expect me to believe a crock of bullshit like that, do you?"

Alec Jameson moved forward in his chair, his eyes riveted on the self-assured admiral. "Birchfield, I don't know what you think about me, personally, or my bureau, but surely you don't believe that given our resources, we are incapable of gathering enough physical evidence to convict you of first degree murder, of conspiracy to commit murder, of extortion, and of treason." The director, who by his nature was not a dramatic person, mustered all his skill to be as believable as possible.

Birchfield shuffled in his chair. Clearly, the specific charges levied by the director made him nervous. "Those are unbelievable accusations, Jameson, and without proof I consider them the most slanderous attack ever made on a man in my position."

The director leaned back in his chair. "You want proof, Admiral? Item One: the deck of cards taken by Secretary Thompson earlier today has been positively matched to the cards held by both Agent Manchester and John Chamberlain. Item Two: Lieutenant Colonel Stewart, the man who killed the paid assassin of President Hansen, as well as a CIA agent and two FBI agents, served on your headquarters staff in Honolulu. We have further proof that his promotions and even his appointment to the Secretary's staff were accompanied by your recommendation."

Birchfield's eyes narrowed. "Circumstantial. That's all you've got."

"I'm not finished, Admiral. Item Three: we have obtained a search warrant from a federal court here in the District to conduct a thorough search of your personal quarters and of your office in the Pentagon. We will be looking for clothing that contains certain fibers that we took from a chair in John Chamberlain's study the night he was murdered. We'll be looking for shoes that have residue from the very unusual Belgium crushed stone that Chamberlain had imported for his driveway. We will be examining the tires to your cars to find the same residue."

The admiral sat silently with his lips pursed tightly as the director continued. "Item Four: we are examining your telephone records and those of John Chamberlain to see how many times you two conversed on the phone in the past week, specifically last night just prior to his murder. Item Five: we will be examining all weapons owned by you or issued to you by the Navy. We will be searching for the missing bullet taken from Chamberlain's study. If the bullet and the weapon match the wound in Chamberlain's head, and if the bullet shows fragments of DNA matched to Chamberlain, and if it shows residue from the book where the bullet lodged, then Admiral, there's not a jury in this country that won't convict you."

The Attorney General took over. "Let me add to the Judge's litany, Admiral. We have absolute proof at this time that John Chamberlain's personal funds were paid to hire the assassin of President Hansen. We have incontrovertible evidence that Chamberlain, Manchester, Lampworth, and Abdul were all connected. We now know that you were a part of that same conspiracy, that because Chamberlain was about to be discovered, you murdered him. So in anticipation of your next question, we now have motive, opportunity, and physical evidence to indict you for both murder and conspiracy to commit murder."

The director continued the scenario. "And finally, Admiral, we come to extortion—extortion of the President of the United States. You have been blackmailing Crawford Staton since the day he assumed office in order to control national policy."

"Proof?" The admiral sputtered in a whisper.

The Attorney General responded. "Proof? All I have to do is confront the President with our evidence. When he discovers that you are to be arrested, indicted, and tried on the charges we have already enumerated, he will have no choice but to expose your efforts to extort him." The Attorney General paused as he stared at the nation's highest military officer. "I just can't believe that you thought you could get away with it, Birchfield. Did you think the rest of us were so naive that we wouldn't notice the change in the President's behavior. His actions the past three days have been completely out of character. And I cannot believe that a man who was entrusted with this nation's most powerful military position could be a traitor to that same nation."

Birchfield's eyes narrowed with anger as he sat with a fixed stare at the Attorney General. "Treason? What the hell do you know about treason? You two sit there in your smug positions of judgment. Where have you been for the past forty years as this nation gradually slipped into a second-rate status, as its power continued to be eroded, not so much from the outside, but from men like you—men who have never seen friends' faces torn apart by artillery shells, men who have spent their lives in the safe, cozy comfort of plush offices, men who have been engrossed in academic and theoretic rules of life? You call me a traitor. If it weren't for patriots like me, this nation would have become a colony of the dictators of the world long before now."

The Attorney General shook his head in disbelief. "Admiral Birchfield, I have no reason to question your heroism nor your military record, but it's men like you who put their own beliefs above the law, who believe they have some higher calling to the nation, rather than to the Constitution, who believe their insights are some kind of gift from God—yes, it's men like you from whom the framers of our Constitution wanted to protect us. You call yourself a patriot. I see nothing but another Adolph Hitler, a Hideki Tojo, a Saddam Hussein. They justified their actions on the basis of nationalism. Like you, they employed the most severe Machiavellian principles to achieve their ends. Like you, they were discovered and stopped." The Attorney General sank into his chair. "No, Admiral Birchfield, you are not a patriot. You are a traitor."

The three men sat silently for several seconds. Finally, Birchfield stood. "Am I under arrest? If so, let's get on with it. If not, I have a meeting of the National Security Council to attend."

Both men still seated nodded at each other before the Attorney General rose and stepped toward the four-star admiral. "Look, Birchfield, you are right about one thing. At this very minute all we have is a long list of circumstantial evidence. However, after our agents complete their search this afternoon, I feel certain we will have enough for my Criminal Division to secure an arrest warrant for you. I'd say you have approximately two hours left. In the meantime, you are not going to the National Security Council meeting. As Attorney General I am declaring you a national security risk. If you so much as open the Cabinet Room door, I will instruct Director Schroeder to remove you from the White House as a threat to the President's life."

Birchfield stood toe-to-toe in front of the Attorney General. He prided himself on his ability to read people's minds through their eyes—an ability that had made him a successful poker player through the years. The Attorney General did not budge. Finally, Birchfield picked up his gold braided cap from the desk, turned, and walked toward the door. As he was leaving, he turned slightly. "I will be in my office in the Pentagon." He opened the door and left.

The director stood next to the Attorney General. "Do you think he bought it, Jacob?"

"Yes, I do. Do you know why, my friend?"

"No."

"He blinked."

Chapter 26

When the Attorney General entered the Cabinet Room nearly ten minutes late, he expected to see the National Security Council in session. Instead, he found the room full of NSC members milling around in small groups. He approached the Secretary of Defense. "Nelson, could I have a word with you?"

The two men moved off into a corner where the Attorney General explained what had happened a few minutes earlier, omitting reference to the extortion of the President and the failure of the admiral to deny the accusation. The Secretary shook his head. "Jacob, this nation owes you a great debt. I'm glad it was you who faced him down and not me. I'm afraid I might have killed the bastard."

"It was tempting, Nelson, but we may still have to deal with him later. If our boys from the bureau strike out on their search of his home and office, we could have a serious problem indicting him."

Just then, the door connecting the Cabinet Room to a short hall leading to the Oval Office opened. The President, Dr. Tollefson, and Jim Lowenstein entered the room. All moved directly to their chairs. Others in the room did likewise. From the smile on the

President's face, many assumed something important was about to be announced.

"Gentlemen, I apologize for my delay. I just received a call from Bill Engledow in Moscow. It's after midnight over there. He has spent the past hour at the Kremlin talking to President Gorbachev."

There was a stir in the room, and members of the Council looked at one another, confused.

"That's right, gentlemen. Sometime during the past several hours, the Cabinet and MOD removed Chenkov from the Presidency and reinstated Gorbachev. We also understand that several military commanders are now under arrest. We don't have all the details at this time, but Bill believes Chenkov cracked from the pressure, and several of the more level-headed members of the MOD decided that Chenkov and his most militant advisors had to go. At present, Gorbachev is an interim appointment. He told Bill that he will convene the federal parliament in one month's time and let them select the President. Bill believes Gorbachev will stand for election, however, especially since it won't be a popular election."

Secretary Thompson leaned toward President Staton. "How does this all affect us in Turkey, Mr. President?"

Staton turned to his left and smiled. "Are you still here, Nelson?"

A nervous tension pervaded the room. No one knew whether to laugh or smile. Most decided discretion dictated silence. The President turned toward the other end of the table. "Where's Admiral Birchfield, anyway?"

The Attorney General answered. "Mr. President, the admiral asked me to extend his apologies. He was called back to his office in the Pentagon on some kind of personal matter."

The President hesitated, then turned back toward the Secretary of Defense. "Well, Nelson, I guess you still have a job for a while. Now, to answer your question, Secretary Engledow indicated that President Gorbachev promised him that no Russian troops would cross the Turkish or Iranian borders. He did ask that I use my influence with the leaders of those two countries in attempting to get them to control the sanctuaries being used by Muslim terrorists. I intend to do that immediately. I have instructed Secretary Engledow to proceed to Ankara from Moscow to meet with the Turkish premier. We will await Bill's report of that meeting before making a decision on Iran."

Thompson continued his questioning. "What about *Thunderburst?* Are we to assume that you are going to cancel Step III?"

The President shuffled his papers. "I've been pondering that question. Dr. Tollefson and I discussed our options just before we came to this meeting. In view of the events in Moscow, I think withdrawing our troops would be prudent. I have to believe Mr. Gorbachev's return bodes well for the situation, and, quite frankly, I think we need to do all we can to shore him up. We've learned the hard way over the past several months how volatile the political situation in Russia can be. So, Secretary Thompson, you may cancel Step III and order the troops back to their staging areas. We'll make a decision about withdrawing from Step II after we see what events unfold during the next few days."

Jake Lewellan, sitting across from the President, while reticent after the day's earlier meeting, still felt compelled to complain. "Mr. President, what makes you think you can trust Gorbachev? There must be a reason he was brought back. Possibly it is an attempt by the old Communist leaders to catch us off guard, to lull us into a false sense of security, to persuade you to issue the very type of order you just gave Secretary Thompson. Mr. President, I urge you to reconsider. What if you are wrong about their intentions?"

The President leaned forward and folded his hands together on the table as he stared directly at his designated Vice-President. "Because, Jake, President Gorbachev is coming to Washington tomorrow to attend the funeral services for the President and Vice-President. We have scheduled a meeting for 6:00 tomorrow evening, following his arrival. Engledow even offered him use of Blair House."

Lewellan was again about to protest the Russian President's use of America's official guest house located across Pennsylvania

Avenue from the White House, when the President cut him off. "Don't worry, Jake. He turned Bill down. He prefers the accommodations at the Russian Embassy."

The President turned his attention toward the Attorney General. "Well, Jacob, anything new on the investigation into the assassinations?"

The AG sat back in his chair and hesitated before answering. "Yes, sir. The FBI believes that the assassin was hired by John F. Chamberlain. They have accumulated enough evidence to tie him to Abdul's hiring and to a CIA agent named Manchester, and . . ." the Attorney General turned toward Senator Lewellan, "Jake, I'm sorry, but to your chief-of-staff, Roland Lampworth."

Lewellan looked horror stricken. "Roland Lampworth? I don't believe it. What does he have to do with all this?"

The AG rested his hands on the table. "Lampworth was an associate of William Manchester. Both knew Chamberlain, and we assume that in some way they worked for him. Chamberlain paid their first class air fare to North Africa in January in order to contact Abdul. Both men were killed by Abdul—we assume at the direction of Chamberlain."

The western senator slumped in his chair. "I just don't believe it. Roland Lampworth. You say he's dead?"

The Attorney General responded, "The FBI and local Florida sheriff's department have not released notification of his death, pending a conclusion of their investigation."

The President interrupted. "But why John Chamberlain? He was a friend of Seth Hansen's."

The Attorney General turned his head toward the President, who sat across the table. "No, sir, he wasn't. John Chamberlain was a friend to his class and to his business interests, which I might add have suffered greatly over the past two years due to defense cutbacks. We have it on unimpeachable authority that he was privately critical of President Hansen and his policies. We are assuming that he was motivated to change government policy."

The Secretary of the Treasury interjected. "That's unbelievable. But how did he think Seth's death would change policy? Assuming that his plan included the assassination of the Vice-President, Speaker Harley, and Jordan Howard, why did he think he could control the government through Crawford? It makes no sense."

All eyes turned toward the Attorney General. He looked across the table at President Staton, who immediately turned away. The President offered no attempt to respond.

The AG decided to answer. "Quite frankly, I don't know the answer to that question, Mr. Secretary. Perhaps he felt the chaos created by such a tragedy would be sufficient to drive any new administration and Congress back into a spending binge. Perhaps he felt the use of an Arab to carry out the assassination would give future administrations pause to re-evaluate American defense policies and defense spending. All I can do is speculate. At this point in time, we have no hard answers."

Secretary Thompson continued to watch the AG after he finished his explanation. He made no attempt to ask about Birchfield. Nor did the President.

The door leading to the Oval Office opened, and a Presidential aide entered, carrying a message. He walked around the table and handed the note to the President. Staton unfolded the paper and read. Everyone present watched his expression. Was it news from Turkey? Had Gorbachev been ousted again?

The President's expression changed little. If anything, there was a wry expression of confusion on his face. When he looked up, all the faces around the table were trained on him. He folded the note. "Gentlemen, I have just received word that Admiral Birchfield was killed in a traffic accident a few minutes ago."

The Attorney General's head dropped to his chest. The Secretary of Defense leaned back in his chair and sighed softly.

Dr. Tollefson asked, "What happened, Mr. President?"

The President slipped the note into his inside coat pocket. "Apparently, he dismissed his driver here at the White House, indicating he wanted to drive himself back to the Pentagon. As his car entered the Arlington Memorial Bridge, it speeded up uncontrollably and hit one of the large concrete support structures. He was thrown from his car. That's all the information I have."

Jake Lewellan appeared emotionally crushed. "Oh, my god!"

The President stood. "I think we had better adjourn, gentlemen. I want a full Cabinet meeting at 8:00 in the morning. We will discuss the Turkish situation and prepare for all the international guests who will be coming into the city beginning tomorrow. The caskets containing President Hansen, the Vice-President, and the Speaker of the House will be taken to the Capitol at noon to lie in state. We should all plan to attend."

Everyone else in the room stood as the President began to leave. The Attorney General walked around the table hurriedly to intercept the President before his exit. "Mr. President, Secretary Thompson and I need to talk to you privately for just a few minutes."

The President nodded his head knowingly. "Sure, Jacob, come on in. I rather expected you wanted to see me."

The Attorney General signaled the Secretary of Defense to follow them. Thompson stared quizzically at his Cabinet colleague. His mind was still focused on Birchfield. News of his death had not brought the emotional high that he had expected; rather, he felt empty, as if a great quest had ended. Birchfield was dead, and from what he had heard from the Attorney General, the public would never know what a traitor the late admiral had been. The feeling of emptiness would not go away. Perhaps it was time for him to resign and go back to Michigan.

*****

The President walked into his office and collapsed into the chair behind his desk. His two Cabinet members took chairs across from him. The President's face was difficult to read. The Attorney General sensed a complexity of emotions was running through his mind. His friend was dead, but his extortionist was also gone.

"Mr. President, thank you for seeing us. We need to talk to you about Admiral Birchfield and about your Presidency."

"I know, Jacob." He leaned forward and folded his hands together on his desk. "I suppose you know about Ogden and me? Isn't that why you wanted to talk?"

"Yes, sir, in part. Secretary Thompson and I, with the help of the FBI, figured out what was going on between you two. I assume he was using a form of extortion."

The President appeared both weary and contrite. "You assume correctly, Jacob. You know, fellas, I didn't know how to get out of this one. He had me by the short hairs." The President looked up at Thompson. "Nelson, I was depending on you to find him out. I tried to help. I guess a part of me wanted to be discovered, and a part didn't. You don't get to this great house without some ego. I couldn't shake my concern about how I'd be remembered in history. But I knew, if I could change my behavior enough, somebody would eventually figure out what was happening. That's why I deliberately stopped being chummy with Ogden and why I took such a ridiculous stand on *Thunderburst*. Nelson, you know that's not like me."

The Secretary of Defense nodded. "I must admit, Mr. President, it took me too long. You can't believe how intimidating this office can be, even when you know the man in it is acting like a lunatic."

"I suppose you're right, Nelson." The President turned back toward the AG. "Jacob, I gather you were not surprised by Ogden's accident."

The Attorney General frowned. "No, sir, I am not. Prior to the NSC meeting, Alec Jameson and I had a talk with the admiral. I'm afraid we didn't quite play fair. He knew his time was up and that we knew of his involvement in the conspiracy, but with regard to you, we could only speculate. I have to give the Judge a good deal of the credit. We certainly spooked him."

The AG looked at his Cabinet colleague on his left, then back at the President. "In many ways it is simpler this way. I think it best that Birchfield's involvement be buried here in this office. It would do no good for our foreign relations at this point and not with the future of this office still unclear."

The President leaned back in his chair. "I suppose you refer to the Succession Act? As much as I would like to keep this chair, I think you're right, Jacob. As soon as the House can elect a Speaker, I will relinquish the job. By the way, I had a call from Buddy

Schumacher. He indicates Alan Brownell has recovered nearly all of his memory. He feels that Alan will be able to stand for Speaker next week. That gives me a chance to get everybody up to speed over the next couple of days. At least I might be able to help Alan that much."

The two Cabinet members exchanged glances. This was the old Crawford Staton—the man of reason. Both felt much relieved. The Attorney General, however, had another concern.

"Mr. President, I'm afraid we still have a serious problem."

Both Thompson and the President offered puzzled expressions.

"There is one more conspirator to be found, and I'm afraid it is a member of your administration."

Staton looked totally defeated. "Oh, my god, no. You mean I have to go through all of this again? Someone else knows what Birchfield was holding over my head?"

"I don't know the answer to that, Mr. President, but it would not surprise me. We have a pretty good idea who it is, but we don't have enough hard evidence now to accuse him."

Thompson moved forward in his chair. "Who is it, Jacob? Tell me who it is. I'll drag a confession from him with my bare hands."

"Sorry, Nelson, that might spoil our case. No, what we have to do is smoke out this culprit. Mr. President, with your help, I think we can accomplish that this evening." The Attorney General opened his briefcase and pulled out a single sheet of paper. "This is a list of people, Mr. President, whom we would like you to invite to your office this evening, say at 7:00. I will be bringing both Director Jameson and Bert Mattox with me. I promised Mattox that he could make the final arrest and that he would be able to make the final decision on Birchfield. After all, Mr. President, Bert Mattox is the one who cracked this case and risked his life in the process."

The President scanned the list handed to him by the AG. "Nelson, your name is on this list." He smiled at the Defense Secretary, who in turn cast a questioning glance at the AG.

"Don't worry, Nelson. I just thought you'd want to be around at the end."

A relieved Secretary of Defense leaned back in his chair. "Thanks one hell of a lot."

The President lay the list down. "I'll have my secretary contact each of these people. I'll use a dinner in the Cabinet Room as an excuse. I don't want to use the facilities in the mansion as long as Mrs. Hansen is there. Sound okay to you, Jacob?"

"Fine, Mr. President." The AG stood to take his leave. "And, Mr. President?"

"Yes, Jacob."

"Put on your best acting clothes this evening. We may need you."

Both Staton and Thompson stood, and the three men shook hands. The President had the last word. "Well, gentlemen, today the world stepped back a few inches from the brink of nuclear war. Perhaps tonight, we can do a little something for our own peace of mind and for good old-fashioned American justice."

Chapter 27

When the Attorney General's party arrived in the Cabinet
Room, the others on the AG's list were already present, hovering
around the large table in small groups. The President was holding
court with a group that included Dr. Tollefson, Jim Lowenstein,
George Heffelfinger, and Nelson Thompson. To nearly everyone's
surprise, Congressman Alan Brownell, the House Majority Leader,
was seated in a chair next to the far wall, talking quietly to Buddy
Schumacher who was in his electric wheelchair. Mattox observed
that Brownell had even less hair than himself. Ed O'Bannon stood
protectively over both of them. A solitary Senator Jake Lewellan
stood by a window looking out onto the dusk-laden south lawn, lost
in thought. Finally, the director of the Secret Service, Donald
Schroeder, stood by the door leading to the President's office, his
eyes crisscrossing the room.

The Attorney General was satisfied. He nudged Mattox.
"They're all here. Wait until I give you a lead before you begin. We
may as well enjoy the dinner."

Mattox noticed the twinkle in the Attorney General's eye before
he winked, then he excused himself to greet the President. Several

of the men in the room cast a suspicious eye toward Margaret Mosele who, despite her very comely appearance, gave everyone pause to question her presence. Mattox had insisted that both Maggy and Carl Peters accompany them.

After several more minutes, the President moved to the center of the curved Cabinet table. The normal high back, swivel chairs had been replaced with regular wood-framed dining room chairs. "Miss Mosele and gentlemen, why don't we take our seats?" He held out his hand toward Maggy. "Miss Mosele, I would be greatly honored if you would sit by me during dinner." The physical presence of Crawford Staton and his grandfatherly smile were compelling, and after a quick glance at Mattox, who nodded, she walked around the table and sat in the chair being offered by the President. Everyone else found his name card on the table and took his seat.

Instantly, the door to the long corridor opened, and four porters, all erect and trim and wearing their starched white jackets, entered the room carrying large silver trays. Bowls of soup were placed in front of everyone, but no one picked up a spoon. All eyes turned to the President for their cue. Secretary Thompson detected a mischievous expression on the President's face.

The President turned to his right and smiled at Maggy. "Miss Mosele, as our special guest this evening, we will leave it to you to decide. Shall we eat this wonderful lobster bisque American style or European style?"

Maggy looked up at the smiling President, confused about the question. She paused, exchanged glances with Mattox, then turned back to the President. "Well, Mr. President, I would suggest everyone eat in the manner with which he is most comfortable."

There was a general low pitch of laughter throughout the room—all except Jake Lewellan. The President reached down and lifted Maggy's hand to his lips. "Maggy, if I can be excused for taking such a liberty, that was a perfect answer. The first time my wife and I attended a state dinner in this wonderful house, we were separated, and she was the only woman seated at a table of several academics—two Nobel laureates, I believe. We were both relatively young and not quite in tune to the social etiquette of civilization, yet. One of the Nobel winners, a man with a thick European accent, asked my wife the same question I just put to you." The President broke into an even wider smile. "Her answer was the same as yours. I take my hat off to the ladies."

The President released Maggy's hand as he reached for his spoon. "Actually, all it means is do you dip your spoon away and scrape it on the outside edge of the bowl, or do you dip it toward yourself and scrape it on the inside of the bowl, the latter being American, the former European?" Again, there was light-hearted laughter around the table. Even Senator Lewellan tried to fake a knowing chuckle.

During the next ninety minutes, the starched porters entered and left four more times. The soup was followed by a melon and fruit salad mixed with a special cognac dressing. The main entree was Yankee pot roast—at the President's request—served with small buttered red potatoes and asparagus with hollandaise sauce. Finally, with all the dishes cleared, each guest was served with a goblet of peppermint ice cream and a cup of specially blended coffee.

After the dessert dishes had been cleared and a second cup of coffee poured, the President nodded to the head porter, who directed his crew to withdraw. Everyone seemed satisfied with the ample, if not eloquent meal. The President leaned back in his chair and patted his stomach. "Many of you may not be big fans of Yankee pot roast or peppermint ice cream, but for an ole country boy from the hills of New England, it was grand fair. I figured that, with my days in this office numbered, I may as well enjoy its culinary delights before I leave."

Mattox watched everyone's expression around the table. The members of Congress looked down at their hands, afraid to show either delight or distress. Secretary Thompson sat impassively, his eyes focused on the President. Schroeder, Tollefson, Lowenstein, and Lewellan all looked confused and startled.

Lewellan, who was seated near the end of the table objected. "Mr. President, I don't believe we follow you. You still have another twenty months to serve out President Hansen's term, and then you will be a cinch for renomination and re-election, especially after today's events in Russia."

The President turned toward the man he had designated as Vice-President. "I can't believe you'd say that, Jake. I called back the troops. We never moved our NATO forces in Central Europe. Are you saying restraint defeated the Russians, not military action?"

Lewellan replied with self-assurance. "To the contrary, Mr. President, I am convinced that had you not taken steps to initiate *Thunderburst*—all three stages—and had you not let out very discreetly your determination to use whatever means were necessary to protect our men in Turkey and Iran, the Russian military warlords would have swept to the south in an instant. It was your decisive reaction to their build-up that caused their house to buckle. These generals and admirals in the MOD who actually know something about military strategy and tactics—not the ones whose positions are tied to their party affiliation—those professional soldiers are the ones who knew they could never defeat the United States in a full, all-out war. They are the ones who dumped Chenkov and brought back Gorbachev." Lewellan sat back satisfied. "All in all, Mr. President, I believe Admiral Birchfield was correct in his assessment."

The name of Birchfield was enough to trigger a change in the President's light mood. His large brown eyes narrowed as he stared at the Western senator. "For your information, Senator Lewellan, Bill Engledow called me from his plane on the way to Ankara just before dinner. He had not trusted the communications links from Moscow. He had it on authority of no less than Gorbachev himself, that it was the career generals who wanted to push ahead with the invasion of Turkey. It was the political generals—not all of them, mind you, but the more moderate ones—who feared the conse-quences domestically if Russia had been forced to gear up industrially and economically for a war. They are the ones who brought Gorbachev back. As for Chenkov, he was on the verge of launching a pre-emptive nuclear attack against the United States in retaliation for our build-up. In other words, *Thunderburst* came within a hair's breath of causing World War III, not averting it."

The President calmed. "So, as for your theory of a weak Russian Bear kowtowing to the muscle-bound American Eagle, that's just hogwash, Senator, hogwash."

The tension in the room picked up noticeably. The President seemed to sense the uneasiness. Perhaps it was just as well. Better to have everyone a little on edge than relaxed. He directed his attention to his left, across the table at the Attorney General. "Jacob, I think it's time that we let all our guests know why they have been invited here this evening for this small dinner party."

All eyes in the room shifted to the Attorney General. Nearly everyone had questioned this particular mixture of personalities. Why have this dinner on the night before the mourning services for President Hansen were to begin?

The Attorney General nodded toward the President. "Thank you, Mr. President." He looked around the table, stopping at each set of eyes to establish contact. "As you all know, Special Agent Bert Mattox of the FBI has been in charge of the investigation into the assassinations of three days ago. It is he who chased down the assassin, an Arab named Abdul and who uncovered the conspiracy to hire Abdul and carry out the mass assassinations. With your permission, Mr. President, I would like to defer to Mr. Mattox."

The President nodded. "Of course, Jacob." He turned to face the special agent.

Mattox tried his best not to show the nervousness that had gripped his insides. His stomach was aflutter, and his hands had begun to perspire. He wiped them with his large white napkin. He felt suffocated, sitting at the table. He needed air and freedom of movement. He backed his chair from the table and stood. "With your permission, Mr. President, I'll review briefly what we know and why the Attorney General requested this dinner this evening."

"Certainly, Bert. Take your time." The President leaned back, a knowing half smile on his lips.

Mattox began walking around the table, placing his hand on the top of each chair as he passed. "As everyone in this room knows, we have incontrovertible evidence that John Fairchild Chamberlain was the man who financed the hiring of the assassin who killed President Hansen, the Vice-President, the Speaker of the House, and Senator Howard. We also know that he did not act alone, that he was a part of a conspiracy involving three other persons. Their aim was to change American foreign policy and, if possible, control the government."

Several people around the table looked at one another, but none interrupted. Mattox continued as he paced, his eyes always fixed on the faces seated across from him. "The first conspirator was William J. Manchester, a career agent of the CIA. Director Heffelfinger had his suspicions of Manchester's relationship with the assassin. Manchester had been under surveillance by the Agency for several months."

Mattox stopped behind Senator Lewellan's chair. "We know that Roland Lampworth, Senator Lewellan's chief of staff, was an acquaintance of Manchester and that the two travelled to Algiers last January on a trip financed by Chamberlain to find and hire Abdul for the assassination. What these two men did not know was that their names were included in the instructions given to Abdul. After we informed the Algerian authorities of Abdul's death, they felt little need to protect him anymore, and they turned over to the CIA station chief in our embassy in Algiers, all of Abdul's possessions which they confiscated from his lodgings."

"Deputy Director Ashburn called my office late this afternoon with the information. Included was a computer-generated set of instructions detailing the ceremony at the FDR Memorial and listing as targets the four men who stood to succeed to the office of President of the United States. The names of Manchester and Lampworth were included, though they were to be killed after April 5 and away from Washington. Both men were murdered in Florida prior to the assassinations."

No one seated at the table moved. All eyes were glued on the special agent as he circled around them slowly. "We also recovered a series of numbered bank accounts, which the CIA feels it can trace to Switzerland or Grand Cayman. In either case, it is just a matter of time before we connect the money paid to Abdul to Chamberlain."

Director Heffelfinger interjected. "But, Mr. Mattox, why do you believe there were four people involved in the conspiracy? You have Lampworth, Manchester, and Chamberlain."

"Correction, sir. We have Manchester and Chamberlain. Lampworth was a bit player. Manchester couldn't afford to make direct contact with Abdul in Algiers. He knew it would compromise his position in the Agency. He needed someone he could guide and control to make that contact. Lampworth was a willing accomplice. He probably never knew he was in over his head."

Heffelfinger continued. "Then that means you believe there are still two more conspirators. Why?"

Mattox stopped behind Alan Brownell's chair. The Majority Leader had recovered all of his memory, but not his energy. His face was pale. He had insisted, however, on being present when he received the President's personal call. Mattox looked down at the shining head of the congressman. "How many in here play poker, may I ask?"

The hands of Brownell, O'Bannon, Heffelfinger, Peters, the President, and Schroeder went up.

"Does anyone know what deadman's hand refers to?"

Schroeder, of the Secret Service, volunteered. "It's two aces and two eights."

Mattox smiled for the first time. "That's right. Two aces and two eights, all black. It's the hand that Wild Bill Hickok was holding when he was shot in the back in a saloon in Deadwood, South Dakota. One or more of our conspirators played poker. One of them decided he needed some kind of code in order for the conspirators to communicate with one another, so each member of the conspiracy was given one of those four cards. We found one—

the ace of spades—in the wallet of Manchester. We found a second—the eight of clubs—in a wallet, locked in the safe at the home of John Chamberlain."

Mattox continued his pace, but stopped above the chair of Dr. Tollefson. "And we found the deck from which the cards came in the locker of Admiral Ogden Birchfield."

Tollefson nearly jumped from his chair, turning around to face the special agent. "Birchfield? Are you crazy? For god's sake, he was Chairman of the Joint Chiefs of Staff."

Mattox continued. "That's right, Dr. Tollefson. One of the most powerful men in the nation. A member of the National Security Council. The oldest friend of the new President of the United States, Crawford Staton. A man whose influence on American policy carried with it the endorsement of the entire military establishment of this nation."

Heffelfinger again interrupted. "Then you believe Admiral Birchfield was one of the four conspirators?"

"Not only that, Director, but we now have proof that he shot and killed John Chamberlain early this morning. In a search of his home conducted late this afternoon, we found a blue blazer hanging in his closet that contained a five millimeter bullet in one of the pockets. DNA tests on the bullet indicate a match with tissue taken from Chamberlain's brain. We also found a gun and silencer in Birchfield's office safe. We believe ballistics tests will confirm that it was the gun that fired the shot that killed Chamberlain."

Several of the men at the table shook their heads in disbelief. Congressman Schumacher finally posed a question. "So, Agent Mattox, you believe you have three of the conspirators, but you claim there were four. Is that correct?"

"Yes, sir. It makes no sense that they would use the deadman's hand with just three people involved."

Alan Brownell spoke for the first time, his voice soft. "If you are right, Mr. Mattox, then this fourth person has to be someone who could have an influence on the government. Manchester was the vehicle for hiring the assassin. Chamberlain was the man to finance the operation. Birchfield was the inside man on the Security Council. But I fail to see how this fourth person could benefit from the assassination of the four men killed Wednesday. By your line of reason, Crawford Staton would be the most likely candidate."

Mattox stopped behind the President's chair. "We considered that, Congressman." A detectable gasp could be heard around the table. "Mr. Staton knew Chamberlain. He accepted a free vacation from him when he was a senator. Chamberlain contributed to his campaigns. He was Birchfield's oldest friend." Mattox hesitated, deciding not to bring up the blackmail plot. "But, his policies are so closely tuned to those of President Hansen, it would make no sense for him to plot to take the Presidency, unless he was an egomaniac." He paused again. Everyone was afraid to speak. "But, I don't believe he is a maniac."

Heffelfinger leaned forward in his chair. "If not the President, then who?"

Mattox walked around to the CIA director's chair. "We considered you, Director Heffelfinger. You also knew Chamberlain. You also had political campaigns in part financed by Chamberlain. You belonged to the same social circles as Chamberlain and several of the same clubs. You knew Birchfield and were on record as having agreed with him on several of his positions on military policy."

"I don't deny any of that. I gave you most of that information, yesterday." Heffelfinger seemed nonplused.

"I agree, Director. I don't believe you are our conspirator."

Dr. Tollefson was becoming irritable. "You're playing games with us, Mr. Mattox. I don't appreciate such games."

Mattox walked toward the National Security Advisor. "But, Dr. Tollefson, you do like games. That's what world politics is all about, is it not? Games? Playing one pawn against another. Trying to keep the other side in check?"

Tollefson answered with a smug smile. "That's chess, Agent Mattox, not poker."

"True, Doctor, but bluff is another big part of world politics. Knowing when to hold and when to fold. You worked for a time with the Potomac Institute, Dr. Tollefson, prior to your appointment. Isn't it true that the Potomac Institute was created by a grant from JFC Industries Foundation and that John Chamberlain was chairman of the Institute's board of directors?"

"Yes, that's true, but I was on the academic side. I never met with the board."

Mattox passed by the security advisor. "Don't worry, Dr. Tollefson, I believe you. You're not our conspirator." Mattox continued pacing until he faced Senator Lewellan, who sat tightly in his seat, his hands in his lap, his pensive face drawn tight. "Now, Senator Lewellan is a great candidate for our fourth traitor."

Lewellan shot a sharp look at Mattox. He started to protest.

"Senator, just stop and think about it. You have a strong record in opposition to President Hansen's cuts in defense spending. Your re-election campaign last fall was heavily financed through the generosity of Chamberlain and his rich friends. Your own chief-of-staff was involved in the hiring of the assassin. A memorandum over your signature initiated the ceremony at the Roosevelt Memorial where the assassinations occurred. And now you have been designated Vice-President of the United States—just one heartbeat away from the Presidency, itself. I'd say that could make you our prime suspect, Senator, except for one thing."

Alan Brownell looked up. "And what's that, Mr. Mattox?"

"Senator Lewellan will never become Vice-President of the United States. You know that, Congressman." Mattox approached the ailing Majority Leader. "You, better than anyone else, know that he needs a majority vote in the House of Representatives and that, if you oppose him, he will never get such a confirmation. Your good friend, Congressman O'Bannon, controls the House Judiciary Committee, and his committee must approve Senator Lewellan's confirmation before it goes to the full floor. So between the two of you, you could block Lewellan's confirmation."

Congressman O'Bannon offered a curious smile. "To what end, Agent Mattox? Crawford could always pick someone else."

"Yes, sir, but you know that won't happen. You know that once Mr. Brownell is elected Speaker of the House, he becomes next in line to become President, and indeed, you have already suggested to President Staton that he resign. Is that not correct?"

"That is true, but he has already told us that he will not resign."

The President, who was enjoying the theatrics about him, leaned forward with all the dramatic bravado he could muster. "Ed, that's one reason I asked you, Buddy, and Alan to come here this evening. I wanted you to know that next Tuesday, when the Congress reconvenes and Alan is elected Speaker, I will resign my office in favor of him."

"You can't do that!" It was Jim Lowenstein shouting from the far end of the table. "You can't resign, Mr. President!" He rose and rushed around the table and leaned over to whisper in the President's ear.

The expression of the President did not change. "I never heard of him, Jim. Bradley? I've known a number of Bradleys. One of my Senate colleagues was named Bradley."

Lowenstein's face was flushed. Mattox noticed his hands trembling. "This upsets your grand design, doesn't it, Mr. Lowenstein?"

Lowenstein took a step back. "I don't know what you're talking about, Mr. Mattox."

Mattox walked slowly toward the executive assistant. "All your plans depended upon Mr. Staton's becoming President and holding the seat until Lewellan was confirmed. Isn't that right?"

Lowenstein continued to back up slowly as Mattox approached him. "I still don't know what you're talking about."

Mattox continued his patient pursuit. "All your plans, Lowenstein, those of your friends. Most of the people here probably don't know that you worked for the Potomac Institute prior to Secretary Staton's hiring you two years ago. They probably don't know that William Manchester was your roommate at

Vanderbilt in the late seventies. They probably don't know that you and Roland Lampworth worked together on a research project for Senator Lewellan's committee three years ago when you were a consultant to the CIA. You knew all of them, Lowenstein, every last one of the conspirators, yet you didn't tell anybody. You didn't tell the President. You didn't tell the Attorney General or the FBI. Why, Lowenstein? What were you hiding?"

Beads of perspiration popped from Lowenstein's brow as he continued his retreat toward the door leading to the President's office. He could not see Don Schroeder discreetly move to block the door. "There wasn't any reason to tell anybody. Almost everybody in this room knew those people. I wasn't any different. All you have is circumstantial evidence, Mattox. That's all. You have no proof."

Mattox continued to approach Lowenstein. "And what was all that about Bradley? Who was Bradley? What difference would that have on the President's decision? Did you think you had something on the President, Lowenstein? Is that it? Were you trying to pick up where Birchfield left off?"

Lowenstein turned to rush for the door, but collided with Schroeder. Mattox placed his hand on the young aide's shoulder and turned him around. He spoke softly. "It's all over, Lowenstein. They're all dead. There's nothing you can do now except make it easier on yourself. I must inform you, however, of your rights. You have the right to remain silent. You have the right to an attorney. You have the right to have an attorney with you during questioning. If you can't afford an attorney, the government will provide one for you. Do you understand these rights, Lowenstein?"

Lowenstein buried his head in his chest. His eyes welled up with tears. Schroeder could feel the man's body go limp. The head of the Secret Service glanced at Mattox, who nodded, then lifted Lowenstein under his right arm and opened the door. The two men disappeared. Mattox returned to his seat across from the President.

President Staton shook his head in disbelief. "Jim Lowenstein? I would never have believed it. I depended upon him. I never had any idea."

Mattox said nothing. The Attorney General leaned toward the President. "Sir, it's all over now. We must get on with the government."

Staton locked onto his Attorney General's eyes and understood. He turned toward the three congressmen. "Alan, I suppose this is somewhat of a shock to you, but I meant what I said a few minutes ago. I am prepared to resign once you are elected to the Speakership."

Buddy Schumacher interjected. "What if the Senate picks a Pro Tem, first?"

Staton smiled. "You forget, my friend, I am an alumnus of that fine club. The Senate has that small archaic rule called the filibuster. I think we can depend on our party's senators to forestall the opposition's attempt to elect a Pro Tem until after we have a Democratic Speaker." Staton leaned toward the Majority Leader. "How about it, Alan. Are you up to it? Can you handle this office?"

Alan Brownell looked at his two colleagues seated next to him, then at the President. "I have to tell you, Crawford, I don't relish your job. I know I can handle it, but I don't look forward to it. Most Americans will think you should stay in this office. They have confidence in you. Most don't know me. I will be a big surprise. On top of everything else that has happened, I'm not sure they can handle another quick change."

Staton leaned back. "Nonsense, Alan. The American people are the most resilient people in the world. They adapt to change. It's that adaptability that has made our nation great. Don't underestimate the public, Alan. They'll back you. Gwen and I will slip away to our little farm in Vermont. You won't have my shadow looming over you."

Alan stood hesitantly. "No, you don't, Crawford Staton. You don't hand off the football, then run off the field. You stay. I need you. We're going to need a new Vice-President. I can't think of anyone who could receive confirmation faster than you. If the public knows you're still in the inner councils of government, they're going to feel a lot better about what's going on. I think our allies and adversaries will feel there is greater continuity in our government, also." Brownell straightened himself fully. "I will not serve unless you agree to be my Vice-President."

Staton's eyes scanned around the table. There was a bobbing of heads from everybody but Jake Lewellan, who appeared dumbfounded. The President stood. "My friend, since you put it that way, I agree. I would suggest we move into the Oval Office and prepare a statement and also prepare how we're going to handle all those heads of state and government leaders due in town tomorrow. I'm afraid, Alan, there's no rest for the wicked."

The President walked around the table and placed his hand on the Majority Leader's elbow. "This way. Let me be the first to show you to your new office."

Everyone in the room stood as the nation's two highest leaders left the room. Mattox looked back across the table at Maggy. There were tears in her eyes. He nodded at her. "It's time to go home."

Epilogue

South Padre Island, Texas
May 1

The fresh, warm blush of wind brushed over the browning bodies of the two sunbathers lying on a large beach blanket stretched across the sandy shore on the Gulf of Mexico. Bert Mattox lay face up, white cream visible on the tip and bridge of his nose, a Washington Redskins cap protecting the top of his head. The scab caused by Maggy's frying pan had almost healed.

The special agent rolled over on his side to face the long sleek body of Maggy Mosele who was sporting a white bikini. The bronzed travel agent was propped up on her elbows reading a newspaper. He reached over and placed his hand on her back. She did not flinch.

"What's so damn interesting in the *Houston Chronicle?*"

Maggy continued reading. "Maybe you can take for granted meeting all those important people in the Cabinet Room, but I'll never get over it. Every time I read about them in the paper, I feel like they're family. There's a story here about your boss, Director Jameson, entering the Medical Center at the University of Pennsylvania for a routine procedure."

Mattox smiled but said nothing. The Attorney General had finally won his point with the judge.

"There's also a picture of President Brownell meeting with the new congressional leadership in the Cabinet Room ."

"Recognize anybody?" Mattox caressed Maggy's back, the sun tan oil oozing between his fingers.

"Speaker Schumacher is seated next to him. I don't know the others."

"What about the Vice-President?"

"He's seated across from the President. The caption reads "President Alan Brownell meets with his new congressional team following the record-setting pace of Vice-President Staton's confirmation." Maggy turned her head toward Mattox. "What about the blackmail, Bert? How come that hasn't come up?"

"Apparently, whatever evidence Birchfield possessed died with him. During interrogation Lowenstein admitted he didn't know anything about this Bradley character."

Maggy pushed the paper away and moved closer to Mattox. "I was surprised that Admiral Birchfield's involvement was made public. How'd you work that one?"

Mattox removed his hand and tried to wipe it dry on the blanket. "The Attorney General, the director, and I had a long talk. In the end, we decided that we couldn't put Lowenstein on trial without divulging Birchfield's involvement. I think they both finally agreed that the public could handle the news. In the end, Lowenstein pleaded guilty, so much of the more sordid part of the conspiracy never had to come out. Mr. Staton was right. Americans are pretty resilient."

Maggie continued as she rested her cheek on her folded hands. "I still can't believe that these men, supposedly among the brightest in the country, would use something as silly as a poker hand in their scheme."

Mattox chuckled. "In a way I am surprised, too; but the fact is that, except for Manchester and Abdul, these men were amateurs when it came to international intrigue. Lowenstein confessed that it was he who pushed for some kind of code system that would protect, Manchester, Chamberlain, Birchfield, or him if any of them thought he was being followed or eavesdropped upon. It was Birchfield, the consummate poker player, who apparently placated his young colleague with the four cards from deadman's hand."

"What about the bullet from Birchfield's gun?" Maggie asked.

"Again, Birchfield never thought he'd be caught. Apparently, he believed that Chamberlain's death would end our search. He was smart enough not to leave the bullet in Chamberlain's library, but gave no thought to discarding it. My guess is that, when he got home, he put that blue blazer of his in the closet and never gave it another consideration. That's where our agents found the bullet, by the way."

Maggy closed her eyes and rolled onto her back. The sharp rays of the sun beat down on her face. "How come you picked this place for your vacation, anyway?"

Mattox rolled onto his back. "Remember how John Martin talked about South Padre Island and how wonderful it had been for him to see his first large body of water. I guess I thought John would have liked us to come here."

Maggy said nothing. With her eyes closed, the exuberant face of the young Hawkeye flashed through her mind. Bert was right. He would have appreciated being remembered.

Both sunbathers continued to bask in the ninety degree sun.

"You're a good man, Bert Mattox."

"I know."